1·49 *

D0539918

of pure reading ple...

100 Reasons to Celebrate

We invite you to join us in celebrating
Mills & Boon's centenary. Gerald Mills and
Charles Boon founded Mills & Boon Limited
in 1908 and opened offices in London's Covent
Garden. Since then, Mills & Boon has become
a hallmark for romantic fiction, recognised
around the world.

We're proud of our 100 years of publishing
excellence, which wouldn't have been achieved
without the loyalty and enthusiasm of our
authors and readers.

Thank you!

Each month throughout the year there will
be something new and exciting to mark the
centenary, so watch for your favourite authors,
captivating new stories, special limited
edition collections...and more!

Dear Reader

After the manuscript that became *The Mysterious Miss M* was rejected over and over again as 'too risky', I despaired of ever seeing it in print, but I loved it enough to enter it in the 2003 Romance Writers of America® Golden Heart® contest. Before it even won the Golden Heart I received a magical call. The Mills & Boon® editor who had judged the contest wanted to publish it.

That is how I became a Mills & Boon author! Me, an author for the *grande dame* of Romance publishers, the ones who started it all!

Two Mills & Boon books later my *A Reputable Rake* won the coveted RITA® award for 2006, one of Romance's highest honours.

The Mysterious Miss M started me on a journey of connected Mills & Boon books, one leading to the other. When I finished one book, there was always another character who begged for the next book. When I wrote *Innocence and Impropriety*, Tanner insisted upon being next and I could hardly wait to accommodate him. So here is Tanner's story in *The Vanishing Viscountess*, teamed with my debut novel, and I'm proud to present them for the Mills & Boon Centenary.

Best wishes

Diane

THE VANISHING VISCOUNTESS

AND

THE MYSTERIOUS MISS M

Diane Gaston

MILLS & BOON®

Pure reading pleasure

All the characters in this book have no existence outside the imagination of the author, and have no relation whatsoever to anyone bearing the same name or names. They are not even distantly inspired by any individual known or unknown to the author, and all the incidents are pure invention.

First published in Great Britain 2008
Harlequin Mills & Boon Limited,
Eton House, 18-24 Paradise Road, Richmond, Surrey TW9 1SR

© Harlequin Books S.A. 2008

The publisher acknowledges the copyright holder of the individual works as follows:

THE VANISHING VISCOUNTESS © Diane Perkins 2007
THE MYSTERIOUS MISS M © Diane Perkins 2004

ISBN: 978 0 263 86236 2

Set in Times Roman 10½ on 12 pt.
04-0108-168862

Printed and bound in Spain
by Litografia Rosés S.A., Barcelona

CONTENTS

As a psychiatric social worker, **Diane Gaston** spent years helping others create real-life happy endings. Now Diane crafts fictional ones, writing the kind of historical romance she's always loved to read.

The youngest of three daughters of a U.S. Army Colonel, Diane moved frequently during her childhood, even living for a year in Japan. It continues to amaze her that her own son and daughter grew up in one house in Northern Virginia. Diane still lives in that house with her husband and three very ordinary housecats. *Innocence and Impropriety* features characters you will have met in *A Reputable Rake*.

Visit Diane's website at http://dianegaston.com or email her at diane@dianegaston.com

Previous novels by the same author

THE MYSTERIOUS MISS M
THE WAGERING WIDOW
A REPUTABLE RAKE
INNOCENCE AND IMPROPRIETY
A TWELFTH NIGHT TALE
  (in *A Regency Christmas*)

THE VANISHING
VISCOUNTESS

To Mallory Pickerloy,
a lovely reader whose name is worthy of a heroine

Chapter One

$\backsim\!\!\diamond\!\!\sim$

October, 1818

The gale roared like a wild beast. Under its savage attack, the ship creaked and moaned and begged for mercy. Shouts of the crew echoed the ship's distress as men struggled to work the pumps and save the rigging.

Adam Vickery, the Marquess of Tannerton, or Tanner, as he was known to his friends, sat with the other passengers in the packet ship's cuddy, awaiting his demise. He remained still, arms crossed over his chest, eyes closed, reviewing his life.

He found it wanting. He'd left no mark on the world, no son to inherit his title and lands, no child to carry on his bloodline. All he had done was maintain what his father, grandfather, great-grandfather, and all the Marquesses of Tannerton had built. If he were truly honest with himself, he would say he'd not even done the maintaining. Other men did that work for him: his estate managers, men of business and secretaries. They toiled while Tanner enjoyed his gaming, his sport, his women.

A loud crack sounded and a thud on the deck shook the

whole ship. A woman wailed. Tanner opened his eyes to see the woman clutching an infant and a small boy to her breast. The cabin was filled with many women like her, shaking in fear, and men, like Tanner himself, cursing their helplessness. There was no way to stop the storm, no way to calm the sea, no way to hold the timbers of the ship together.

His gaze fell on one woman who neither wailed nor cowered from the storm. With an expression of defiance rather than fear, she stood next to a Bow Street Runner, leather shackles on her wrists, obviously his prisoner. Only a few hours ago, at the beginning of this voyage from Dublin to Holyhead, Tanner's gaze had been drawn to her, so dignified in her plight. What crime had she committed to warrant her escort from Ireland? He'd been too blue-devilled to bother inquiring about her, however. Now he wished he'd spoken to her, or at least smiled at her. She seemed every bit as alone as he.

When the winds began their fierce assault, the first mate had gathered all the passengers into this cabin. He'd told them they were close to the Anglesey coast. Of course, the Anglesey coast could be rocky and treacherous, although the man neglected to mention that part.

What could be worse? Tanner wondered. Plunging into the cold depths of the Irish Sea? Or being dashed upon some craggy rocks?

Either would mean death.

The first mate popped in a second time when the storm intensified. "All will be well," he reassured them. None of the passengers believed him. Tanner could see it in their eyes. He felt it in his own soul. Tanner watched a man remove a miniature from his pocket and stare at it, a portrait of a loved one he would never see again, of someone who would soon be grieving.

Who would grieve for the Marquess of Tannerton? His

friend Pomroy would likely drink a toast to his memory now and then. A mistress or two might consider him a fond memory. Perhaps the Duke of Clarence or even the Regent himself might recall him after the space of a year or two, but more likely not. Algernon, his fribble of a cousin, would be terrified at the prospect of inheriting the lofty title and its responsibilities. Tanner rubbed his face, regretting he'd never taken Algernon in tow and taught him how easy it all was. Algernon could busy himself with purchasing new coats or the latest fashion in boots or all the watch fobs and stick pins he fancied.

The Bow Street Runner began pacing, Tanner noticed, and the prisoner flashed the man an undisguised look of contempt.

Would she have anyone to mourn her?

She stood with her chin high and her startling blue eyes vigilant. He disliked thinking of what the sea would do to her, turning her body all bloated and white.

He glanced away, shaking that horrible image from his mind, but no matter where he looked, his eyes were drawn back to her.

She was tall and slender, with the same dark hair and piercing blue eyes of the woman who'd briefly captivated him a year ago. That was where the resemblance ended, however. Rose O'Keefe had made the right choice when she'd chosen Tanner's former secretary, Jameson Flynn, over Tanner himself. Flynn had offered the Vauxhall singer marriage, something Tanner would never have done. Flynn had also loved her.

Tanner laughed inwardly at the irony of it all. The secretary preferred over the marquess. He could not muster any resentment, however. Rose had picked the better man.

He frowned and bowed his head. Tanner's zeal had not

been to love Rose, but to outwit another rival for her favours. Three people had died as a result. Three lives on his conscience because of his heedless selfishness.

Purchasing the Dublin theatre for Flynn and Rose did not make amends for the destruction Tanner had set in motion, but it did give the married couple the means to a new life. That was the very least Tanner could do. He'd travelled to Dublin for their opening performance, and now he was crossing the Irish Sea again, heading back to England on this Holyhead packet.

The ship had been scheduled to land hours ago, but the storm stalled them and now the day was late. He pulled his timepiece from his pocket. It was near nine p.m.

Another shuddering crash came from above. Tanner stuffed his watch back into his pocket and glanced at the prisoner. Her eyes flashed with alarm. Tanner could not blame her. Her life— and his own empty one—appeared to be edging towards the end.

The cabin door sprang open and the first mate, drenched and dripping on to the wooden floor, yelled, "Everyone on deck! To the boats. Women and children first."

The death knell. The captain no longer expected the ship to remain intact. It was time to risk the lives of the women and children in the small boats.

There were quick anguished embraces as goodbyes were tearfully said. Panicked men tried to push in front of mothers clasping the hands of terrified children. Tanner rushed forward and pulled the men back. He used his stature and strength to keep the way clear. The prisoner was the last woman out of the door, her Bow Street Runner pushing her on, his hand firmly clamped around her arm. The man could have at least untied her shackles. What could it matter now? At least allow her to die free.

Tanner was the last person to come up on deck. As he stepped out into the air, the rain sliced him like knife blades, the wind whipping in all directions. The ship's masts no longer stood tall and proud, but lay like snapped twigs on the deck.

The sails, now in tatters, resembled nothing more than rags flapping haphazardly in the tempest. Tanner stepped over pieces of wood, remnants of sails and other debris. A loose barrel rolled towards him. He jumped aside, nearly losing his footing on the slick surface of the deck. More than once he had to grab hold of whatever was near to keep from falling.

Tanner pushed his way through to where the women and children were being loaded into boats. Although he feared the effort futile, Tanner pitched in, helping lift women and children over the side of the ship to crewmen waiting in the boats. Lightning flashed, illuminating the shadow of the shore, so distant when the sea churned like a cauldron, violently pitching the ship. The boat's fragile passengers would have a treacherous ride.

Let these people survive, he prayed.

He lifted a child into waiting arms and her mother after her. This was the last boat, and the crewmen manning it were already starting to lower it to the sea. Tanner reached for the woman prisoner, who, outwardly calm and patient, had held back so the others could go before her. Tanner scooped her into his arms to lift her over the side, but, at that same moment, the Bow Street Runner shoved them both, knocking them to the deck, jumping into the boat in her place. Tanner scrambled to his feet, but it was too late. The boat had hit the water, the crewmen rowing fast to get it away.

"Bastard!" Tanner cried. In the howling wind, he could barely hear his own words.

The prisoner's eyes blazed with fury and fear. She struggled to stand. Tanner grabbed her arm and pulled her to her feet.

"The ship's going to break apart!" the first mate cried, running by them.

Tanner glanced wildly around. Some of the crew were lashing themselves to pieces of mast.

"Come on," he shouted to the woman, pulling her along with him.

Tanner grabbed rope from the rigging and tied her to a piece of broken mast. He would be damned if that scoundrel Bow Street Runner survived and she did not. He lashed himself next to her, wrapping one arm around her and the other around the mast. The ship slammed into rocks, sending them, mast and all, skittering across the deck.

The vessel groaned, then broke apart in a cacophony of cracks and crashes and splintering wood. Their piece of mast flew into the air like a shuttlecock, the wind suspending them for several moments before plunging them into the churning water.

The impact stunned Tanner, but the shock of the needle-sharp cold roused him again. The howling of the wind, the hissing of the rain, the screams of their shipmates suddenly dulled to a muffled growl. The water was inky black and Tanner had no idea which way was up, but his arm was still around the woman. He had not lost her.

Their wooden mast began rising as if it, too, fought to reach the surface. Tanner kicked with all his strength, his lungs burning with the urge to take a breath.

When they broke the surface of the water, it was almost as great a shock as plunging into its depths. Tanner gulped for air. To his relief, he heard the woman do the same. She had survived.

Then a wave crashed over them and drove them forward.

Tanner sucked in a quick gulp of air before they went under. Again they resurfaced and were pushed forward and under once more.

When they popped to the surface, Tanner had time to yell, "Are you hurt?"

"No," she cried.

He tightened his grip on her as another wave hit. If the sea did not swallow them, the cold would surely kill them.

Or the rocks.

This wave thrust them further. Through the sheen of rain and sea, Tanner glimpsed the coast, but jagged rocks lay between, jutting up from the water like pointed teeth. Another wave pelted them, then another. The ropes loosened and were washed away. The woman's grip slipped from the mast. Tanner could hold on to the mast or the woman. He held on to the woman.

Her skirts were dragging them down and her bound wrists made it hard for her to swim. Tanner kicked hard to keep them above the water, only to see the rocks coming closer. He swivelled around to see if other survivors were near them, but not a soul was visible. No one to help them. No one to see. Perhaps no one to survive.

The next wave drove them into one of the rocks. She cried out as they hit. Another wave dashed them into another rock. Tanner tried to take the blows instead of her, but the water stirred them too fast. He lost feeling in his arms and legs and he feared he would lose his grip on her.

Not another death on his conscience. Tanner could not bear it. *God, help me save her,* he prayed. *Help me do something worthwhile. One last bloody something worthwhile.*

He slammed into a jagged rock and everything went black.

When Tanner opened his eyes, he felt cold wet sand against his cheek. He could see the water lapping the shoreline inches from his face. Its waves sounded in his ears, and whitecaps seemed to wink at him. There was hard ground beneath him, however. Hard solid ground.

The woman! He'd lost her. Let go of her, damn him. Despair engulfed him as surely as had the Irish Sea. His limbs felt heavy as iron and his soul ached with guilt. He'd let go of her.

A light glowed around him, bobbing, then coming to a stop. Suddenly someone's hands were upon him, rough hands digging into his clothes, searching his pockets.

He seized one of the groping hands, and his attacker pulled him upright, trying to break free. Tanner's grip slipped and he fell back onto the sand. The man advanced on him, kicking him in the ribs. Tanner rolled away, trying to escape the blows, but the man kicked him again.

"Your money," the man snarled as he kicked him once more. "I want your money."

Every English coast abounded with wreckers, people who flocked to the shore eager to see a ship founder, so they could seize whatever bounty that washed ashore. Tanner had never thought to meet one.

He curled himself against the onslaught of the man's boot, as he struck again and again. A loud thwack sounded and the man collapsed on top of him. Tanner shoved him off and sat up.

The woman stood above them, a long piece of wood, part of the ship, no doubt, in her trembling, still-shackled hands.

Marlena Parronley stared at the prone figure, the brute who had so violently attacked her rescuer, the Marquess of Tannerton. She'd hit the villain with all her remaining strength.

Perhaps this time she really *had* killed a man.

Tannerton struggled painfully to his knees, staring at her, holding his sides, breathing hard.

Marlena had recognised Tannerton immediately when she'd first seen him on board ship, but he'd shown no signs of remembering her.

Thank goodness.

That first Season in London—her only Season—he'd attended many of the entertainments, but he was already a marquess and she was a mere baron's daughter, a Scottish baron at that. He'd provided her and Eliza with some excitement in those heady days, however. They'd called him Tanner, as if they had been admitted to that close circle of friends he always had around him. They'd peeked at the handsome marquess from behind their fans, he so tall, his brown hair always tousled. And his eyes! They'd been in raptures about his mossy green eyes. She and Eliza had devised all manner of ways they might meet him, none of which they'd dared to carry out.

Too bad they had not thought of being caught in a gale on a ship that broke apart and tossed them in the sea.

We forgot that one, Eliza, Marlena silently said.

"Have I killed him, do you think?" she asked the marquess.

Tanner reached down to place his fingers on the man's neck. "He's alive."

Marlena released a breath she'd not realised she'd been holding.

Tanner rose to his feet.

"Are you injured?" he asked, his breathing ragged.

She shook her head, sending a shiver down her body. He still showed no signs of recognising her. He pulled off his wet gloves and reached for her hands to work on the leather bindings. When she'd been on the ship they had chafed her wrists, but she was too numb to feel them now. Her teeth chattered and she started trembling all over, making his task even more difficult. He leaned down to loosen them with his teeth.

Finally the bindings fell to the sand and she was free. Marlena rubbed her wrists, but she could not feel her hands.

"We need to find shelter. Dry clothing." He glanced around.

They were in a small cove, dotted with jutting rocks and a small patch of sand. Steep black cliffs imprisoned them as certainly as the walls of Newgate Prison.

Tanner touched her arm. "If that fellow managed to get in here, we can get out."

She nodded, but suddenly any strength she'd possessed seemed to ebb. It was difficult to think. The cold had seeped into her very bones.

He rubbed her arms, then pressed a hand on his ribs and winced. "Come now. We'll be warm and dry very soon."

He picked up the man's lantern and circled their prison walls. She could do nothing but watch. A huge wave tumbled ashore, soaking her feet again, but she could only stare at it swirling around her ankles. He crossed over and took her arm, pulling her away from the water.

He'd once danced with her, she remembered, although he never knew it. Lady Erstine had held a masquerade ball, a respectable one, and she and Eliza attended, having spent many agonising hours deciding what costume to wear. Tanner had danced one dance with Marlena without knowing who she was. Eliza had been green with envy.

"Stay with me," he said, holding her firmly.

What looked like one massive black rock was really two, with a narrow corridor between them. He held her hand and pulled her through. They climbed up smaller rocks that formed a natural stone staircase. When they finally reached the top, they found flat and grassy farmland. The storm had passed at last, but in its wake blew a cool wind that made Marlena's clothes feel like ice.

In the distance they spied one light. "A farmhouse," he said. "Make haste."

Marlena had difficulty making sense of his words. She liked his arm wrapped around her, but disliked him making her walk, especially so briskly. He made sounds with each breath, as if every step brought pain. Pain would be preferable to feeling nothing, Marlena thought. She was no longer aware of her arms or her legs.

The light grew nearer, but Marlena forgot what it signified. Her mind felt full of wool and all she wanted was to sleep.

She tried to pull away from him. "Rest," she managed to say. "Sleep."

"No." He lifted her over his shoulder and carried her.

They came to a cottage with a lone candle burning in the window. Tanner pounded on the door. "Help us! Open the door."

Soon a grizzled man in a white nightcap and gown opened the door a crack.

"Quick. I must get her warm," Tanner told him.

"Dod i mewn," the man said. "Come in, come in."

Tanner carried her inside and made her stand in front of a fireplace. The dying embers on the hearth gave heat, but the heat felt painful after the numbing cold.

"Bring some blankets," Tanner ordered. "I must warm her."

The man tottered into another room, and Tanner began stripping her of her clothing, which seemed a very odd thing for him to do, but nice, because her wet clothes were so very heavy, and she wanted to feel light again.

Suddenly dry cloth covered her shoulders and Tanner made her sit in a chair close to the fire.

The old man threw more lumps of coal into the fireplace,

and poked at it with the poker, which only made it hotter and more painful.

"M'wifc and son are at the wreck," the man explained.

Oh, yes, Marlena dimly remembered, as shivers seized her. She had been on a ship that had broken apart. She remembered the shock of the cold water.

A cat ambled by, rubbing its fur against her legs. "Cat," she said to no one in particular, as her eyelids grew very heavy.

Marlena woke to find herself nestled in a nice warm bed with heavy bedcovers over her. She did not seem to have on any clothing at all, not even a shift. Next to her, also naked and holding her close, lay the Marquess of Tannerton.

Chapter Two

The woman felt warm against him, warm at last, when Tanner had thought never to be warm again. He slipped his hand down her smooth back, savouring the feel of her silky skin under his fingertips. He could still smell the sea on her, but they were both blessedly dry. And warm. He had saved her from the sea, thank God.

Thank God.

A shuffle sounded in the room and a murmur, and the woman pushed away from him with a cry.

He sat up like a shot.

The woman slid away to a corner of the bed, clutching the blanket up to her chin. Morning light shone through the small window and three pairs of eyes stared at them both, the wrinkled old man who had opened the door to them the night before, a wrinkled old woman and a younger, thick-chested man.

"What the devil?" Tanner growled.

The spectators jumped back. The old man gave a servile smile. "M'wife and son are back."

Tanner glared at them. "You disturb our privacy."

In actuality, he and the woman were the intruders. Tanner had given the old man little choice but to relinquish what was surely the bed he shared with the old woman. The night before all Tanner could think of was to cover the woman in blankets and warm her with his own body—and be warmed by hers. He'd left their clothing in a pile in the front room and carried her to the little bedchamber behind the fireplace, ordering the poor man to bring as many blankets as he owned.

The younger man—the farmer's son, obviously—rubbed his head and winced, and the hairs on the back of Tanner's neck stood on end. The son, he would swear, had been his seaside attacker. Tanner frowned. Their place of refuge suddenly seemed more like a lion's den.

He quickly regained his composure. "What are you doing in this room?" he demanded again, checking his finger for his gold signet ring and feeling under the bedcovers for the purse he'd had sense enough to remove from his coat. He held it up. "Were you looking for the purse?"

The younger man backed away to where clothing hung by pegs on the plastered walls above two wooden chests.

"We merely came to see if you required anything, that is all." The old woman simpered.

Tanner scoffed. "All three of you at once?"

The young man gave a chagrined expression and inclined his head.

Tanner glanced at his companion, still huddled under the blanket. He turned to the others. "Leave us," he commanded.

The old man and woman scurried towards the door. Their son moved more slowly, his hand returning to his head.

"We require our clothing." Tanner added.

The woman paused in the doorway. "Your things are still damp, m'lord." She tipped her head in a servile pose. "I've hung them out in the sun and the wind. 'Twill take no time at all to dry."

"Good." Tanner's tone turned a shade more conciliatory. "Treat us well and you will be rewarded." He lifted the purse.

The son smiled. "What else do you require, m'lord?"

"Some nourishment, if you please."

The man bowed and closed the door behind him.

"They thought they could nick my purse," Tanner muttered, rubbing the stubble on his chin. He did not have the heart to worry her with his suspicions about the farmer's son. "How do you fare, miss? Are you all right?"

She moved beneath the blanket as if testing to see if all parts of her still worked. "A little bruised, but unharmed, I think."

Her eyes flicked over him and quickly glanced away. Tanner realised he was quite bare from the waist up. From the waist down, as well, but the covers concealed that part of him. He reached for a blanket and winced, pressing a hand to his ribs.

"You are bruised," she cried, reaching towards him, but immediately withdrawing her hand.

He looked down at himself, purple bruises staining his torso like spilled ink. "Nothing to signify," he said, although his breath caught on another pang of pain.

He glanced at her again and the humour of the situation struck him. It was not every day he woke up in a naked embrace with a woman whose name he did not know.

He gave her a wry smile. "I do not believe we have been introduced."

Her eyelids fluttered, reminding him of shy misses one encountered at Almack's. "No, we have not."

He made a formal bow, or a semblance of one there in the bed only half-covered by a blanket. "I am Tannerton. The

Marquess of Tannerton. Tanner to my friends, which, I dare say—" he grinned "—I had best include you among."

The blue of her eyes sparkled in the morning light. "Marquess—" She quickly cast her eyes downward. "My lord."

"Tanner," he corrected in a friendly voice. "And you are…?"

He had the feeling her mind was crafting an answer.

"I am Miss Brown, sir."

It was a common name, and not her real one, he'd wager.

"Miss Brown," he repeated.

She fussed with the blanket, as if making sure it still covered her. "Do you know of the others from the ship? Did anyone else survive?"

He gave her a steady look. "The Bow Street Runner, do you mean?"

She glanced away and nodded.

He made a derisive sound. "I hope he went to the devil."

She glanced back at him. "Did any survive?"

"I know nothing of any of them," he went on, trying not to think of those poor women, those helpless little children, the raging sea. "We were alone on the beach, except for the man who tried to rob me." The man who had just left this room, he suspected. "We made it to this cottage, and all I could think was to get you warm. I took over the farmer's bed and must have fallen asleep."

She was silent for a moment, but Tanner could see her breath quicken. He suspected she remembered the terror of it all.

"I believe I owe you my life, sir," she whispered.

Her blue eyes met his and seemed to pierce into him, touching off something tender and vulnerable. He glanced away and tugged on the covers, pulling off a faded brown blanket. He wrapped it around his waist and rose from the bed. "Let me see about getting you some clothes. And food." He turned towards the door.

"A moment, sir," she said, her voice breathless. "Do—do you know where we are? Who these people are?"

"Only that we are in a farmer's cottage," he replied, not entirely truthfully. "There was a lamp in the window. I walked towards its light."

She nodded, considering this. "What do they know of us?"

His gaze was steady. "I did not tell them you were a prisoner, if that is your concern."

She released a relieved breath. "Did you tell them who you are?"

He tried to make light of it all. "Last night I only saw the old man. I fear I failed to introduce myself. My manners have gone begging."

"Good," she said.

"Good?" His brows rose.

"Do not tell them who you are."

He cocked his head.

"A marquess is a valuable commodity. They might wish to ransom you."

She was sharp, he must admit. Her mistrust gave even more credence to his suspicions. He had thought to bully these people with his title, but he now saw the wisdom of withholding who he was—as well as who she might be.

He twisted his signet ring to the inside of his palm and put his hand on the door latch. "I will not say a word." Her lovely face relaxed. "Let me see about our clothing and some food and a way out of here."

She smiled and he walked out of the room, still holding the blanket around his waist.

It took Marlena a moment to adjust when he left the room. The marquess's essence seemed to linger, as well as the image of him naked. She and Eliza had been too naïve to speculate on how the Marquess of Tannerton would look without clothing, but she could now attest that he looked spectacular. Wide shoulders, sculpted chest peppered with dark hair that formed a line directing the eye to his manly parts. She'd only glimpsed them upon first awakening, but now she could not forget the sight. He was like a Greek statue come to life, but warm, friendly and flirtatious.

He might not recognise her as the notorious Vanishing Viscountess, subject of countless Rowlandson prints and sensational newspaper stories, but he did know she'd been a prisoner. He would, of course, have no memory of the very naïve and forgettable Miss Parronley from Almack's.

She hugged her knees. As long as he did not recognise her, she was free. And she intended to keep it that way.

She had no idea what piece of shore they'd washed up on, but it must be closer to Scotland than she'd ever dared hope to be again. She longed to be in Scotland, to lose herself there and never be discovered. A city, perhaps, with so many people, no one would take note of a newcomer. She would go to Edinburgh, a place of poetry and learning. Who would look for the Vanishing Viscountess in Edinburgh? They would think her dead at the bottom of the sea.

She'd once believed she'd be safe in Ireland, in the ruse she and Eliza devised, governess to Eliza's children. Not even Eliza's husband had suspected. Marlena had been safe for three years, until Eliza's brother came to visit. Debtors nipping at his heels, Geoffrey had come to beg his sister for money.

Marlena would have hidden from him, or fled entirely, but Eliza and the children had been gravely ill from the fever and she could not bear to leave. Geoffrey discovered her tending to them. He'd recognised her instantly and suddenly realised he could raise his needed funds by selling the whereabouts of the Vanishing Viscountess.

Geoffrey had long returned to London the day Marlena stood over Eliza's newly dug grave in the parish churchyard, the day the magistrate's men and the Bow Street Runner came to arrest her.

She swiped at her eyes. *At least we nursed the children back to health, Eliza.*

She rose from the bed and wrapped the blanket around her like a toga. The room was tiny and sparse, but clean. There was no mirror, so she tried to look at herself in the window glass, but the sun was too bright. She felt her hair, all tangles and smelling of sea water. It was still damp underneath. She sat back on the bed.

She must look a fright, she thought, working at her tangled locks with her fingers, still vain enough to wish she appeared pretty for the handsome Marquess of Tannerton.

Except for the bruises on his chest, he had looked wonderful after their ordeal—his unshaven face only enhancing his appearance, making him look rakish. She inhaled, her fingers stilling for a moment with the memory of how his naked skin had felt, warm and hard with muscle.

Her whole body filled with heat. It had been a long time since she'd seen a naked man and a long time since a man had held her. She tried to remember if she had ever woken naked in her husband's arms. Perhaps she never had. He usually had fled her bed when he finished with her.

So long ago.

The door opened and the old woman entered, the scent of boiling oats wafting in behind her.

"Your gentleman says to find you some clothes, ma'am. Yours are ripped and would take too long to mend." She handed Marlena her stockings, which had somehow remained intact. "I told your gentleman I've just the thing for you in here." The woman rummaged through one of the wooden chests. "I've put the kettle on as well, and there is some nice porridge boiling."

Marlena slipped on her stockings. Porridge sounded as heavenly as ambrosia at the moment. Until she'd smelled it, she'd not known she was ravenous.

"That is very kind," she said to the woman. "What is your name?"

"I'm Mrs Davies, ma'am." The woman leaned over the chest, still looking through it.

Marlena made her voice sound friendly. "Thank you, Mrs Davies. Where are we, might I ask?"

"At our farm, ma'am." The woman looked at her as if she were daft. Her mouth opened, then, and she finally understood the question. "About a mile or so from Llanfairynghornwy."

Marlena blinked. She had no idea where that was, nor did she think she could repeat its name. "Is there a coaching inn there?"

"There is a coaching inn at Cemaes."

"How far is that?" Marlena asked.

"About five miles, ma'am."

Marlena could walk five miles.

The old woman twisted around, leaning on the edge of the chest. "But if I think of it, you'll want to reach Holyhead, not Cemaes."

Holyhead was the port where the ship had been bound. "How far is Holyhead?"

"Ten miles or so the opposite way, to reach the ferry, that is. You'll need a ferry to take you to Holyhead, ma'am."

Marlena nodded. Holyhead would likely be where other survivors would be bound, making it the last place she'd wish to be.

The woman turned back to her rummaging, finally pulling

out a shift and tossing it to Marlena, who quickly slipped it on. Next the woman pulled out a faded blue dress.

"Perhaps this will do." She handed it to Marlena.

The dress was made of wool in a fine, soft weave that seemed nothing like a farm wife's dress. Marlena stood up and held it against herself. The dress was long enough for her, although she was taller than most women and certainly a good foot taller than Mrs Davies. The dress would totally engulf the farm woman and would be big on Marlena as well.

Some other woman from some other shipwreck had once worn this dress. Marlena whispered a prayer for that woman's poor soul.

"It will do very nicely," she said.

The woman straightened and thrust something else at Marlena. "Here's a corset for you."

"Thank you." Marlena smiled. "I am so very grateful to you."

The woman started towards the door.

Marlena stopped her with another request. "I would like very much to wash. Would it be too much trouble to bring me some water?"

The woman looked heavenwards, as if she'd been asked for the moon, but she nodded and hurried out of the door.

Marlena inspected the corset. Its laces looked as if they could be tightened to fit her. She lifted the dress to her nose and was grateful that it smelled clean. She was eager to be clean herself, eager to wash the salt from her skin. What she would not give for a nice long soak in warm bathwater, but she would content herself with a quick wash from a basin. She paced the room, thinking, planning. She could easily walk to Cemaes this very day, but what would she do then? She had no money.

She must beg money from Tanner, she decided. It was her only choice. She was uncertain of him, although it was a good sign he'd not betrayed her to this farm family. If he discovered she was the Vanishing Viscountess, however, he would certainly want to turn her over to the local magistrate. It was best to slip away as soon as she could do so.

A knock sounded, and Tanner walked in with her basin of water, a towel over his arm like a valet. She grabbed the blanket and wrapped it around the shift. He was dressed in what looked like his own shirt and trousers. His hair was damp. Marlena touched her still-tangled hair, envious that he had been able to wash out the salt and the memory of the sea.

"Your clothes are dry?" she asked.

"Dry enough." He placed the basin on a small table in the corner of the room. "I thought you might like this." He pulled a comb from the band of his trousers. "I've washed it, although these people seem clean enough."

She took it from him. "Oh, thank you!" She immediately sat back on the bed and attacked her locks. "Have they told you anything of the shipwreck?"

He shook his head. "These people are a close-mouthed lot. The son left, but I hope it was merely to return to the beach. I gather these people are wreckers."

Like the man who attacked Tanner. The man she hit on the head. She remembered that suddenly, but it was like a murky dream.

"The mother and son were out there during the storm last night." He walked towards the door. "Is there anything else you need?"

"My shoes," she replied. "But do not leave yet."

He waited.

She took a breath. "I need to ask you—to beg you—to let me go."

His brows rose.

She went on quickly, "Mrs Davies—the wife—says there

is a town five miles from here with a coaching inn. You may go on to Holyhead, but let them all think me dead. Please. I want only to go home. That is all I desire." Not all she desired. She needed money, but she'd make that request only if he gave his permission to flee.

He leaned against the door. "Where is home?"

"Scotland," she said truthfully and an image of her Scottish home jumped into her mind. *Parronley,* home of her ancestors and her carefree childhood.

He peered at her. "You do not sound Scottish."

"I was sent to school in England." This was true, as well. At lovely Belvedere House in Bath, where she'd met Eliza. She'd been very keen to rid herself of any traces of a Scottish burr in those days, so eager for the other girls to like her.

He pressed a hand against his ribs. "Tell me why the Bow Street Runner was bringing you back to England."

Marlena flinched, feeling his pain. Her mind raced to think of a story he would believe. She borrowed one from a Minerva Press novel she and Eliza once read. "I was a lady's companion to a very nice elderly lady. I was accused of stealing her jewellery."

His mouth twitched. "And you did not do it."

"I did not!" She was not guilty of stealing jewellery or any other crime. "I was wrongly accused, but there was no way to prove it. Her son placed the jewels in my room."

How she wished she had been accused of the theft of jewels. Far better that than standing over the bloody body of her husband and being accused of his murder.

She made herself face him with a steady gaze. "I ran away to Ireland, but they sent the Bow Street Runner after me."

His eyes probed her. They were still that lovely shade of mossy green she remembered from those giddy assemblies at Almack's. "They went to a great deal of trouble to capture you."

She gave a wan smile, but her mind was racing to recall the details of the novel. "Not all the jewellery was recovered. My lady's son sold the rest. He made it look as if he was trying to recover it all, going so far as having me tracked down in Ireland for it." She glanced away from Tanner, and her voice came from deep in her throat. "He placed the blame on me."

In truth, it had been her own cousin who contrived to have her blamed for Corland's murder, and her cousin Wexin had once been a member of the Marquess of Tannerton's set. That had been seven years ago, when Marlena and Eliza had had their first Season, but for all Marlena knew Tanner could still count Wexin among his friends.

In that lovely Season, when she and Eliza had been so full of hope, she'd begged Wexin to present them to the handsome marquess. Wexin refused, although she and Eliza had been undaunted.

"Who were these people who employed you?" he asked.

"I cannot tell you," she replied truthfully again. "For all I know, the son may be one of your close companions." Like Wexin had been. "You would believe them and not me." She fixed her gaze on him again. "Let me go, I implore you. Let me disappear. Let them think I am dead."

He stared back at her, not speaking, not moving. Panic spread inside her like a wild weed.

"You have no money. How will you get on?" he asked.

She took a breath. "I would beg a little money from you."

He gave her a long look before speaking. "First wash and dress and eat. We shall both leave this place, then we will decide what to do next." He opened the door and walked out.

Her nerves still jangled. He had not precisely agreed to help her, but he had not sounded as if he would turn her in, either. She had no choice but to wait to see what he would do.

Marlena washed and dressed and managed to get her hair into a plait down her back. When she walked out of the bed-chamber in her stockinged feet, the smell of the porridge drove all other thought and emotion away. She sat in a plain wooden chair across from Tanner at a small table. The old woman set a bowl of porridge in front of her. Marlena's hand shook when she dipped her spoon into the steaming bowl. The first mouthful was too hot. She blew on the next spoonful and the next and ate as quickly as she could. Tanner ate as hungrily as she.

The old farmer and his wife watched their every move.

When they finished, Tanner turned to them. "Bring the rest of my clothing, my boots and the lady's shoes. The lady also needs a cloak. You will undoubtedly have a cart. I should like you to take us to the nearest town."

"Holyhead?" the farmer asked. "You'll need a ferry to reach it."

Tanner reached into the sleeve of his shirt where he had tucked his purse. He opened it and took out a sovereign. "Very well."

The farmer's eyes grew wide at the sight of the coin. Both he and his wife sprang into action, leaving Tanner and Marlena alone.

Marlena gave him an anxious look. "I will not go to Holyhead. Just leave me, I beg you. I will not even ask you for money."

He shook his head. "I'll not leave you." He leaned closer to her. "But I have no intention of going to Holyhead either. Let them think that is where we are bound."

Warmth spread through her, and she did not think it was from the porridge. She wanted to throw her arms around him in gratitude. Instead she composed her emotions. "Mrs Davies told me Cemaes is five miles from here in the opposite direction from Holyhead."

"Then we shall go to Cemaes." He smiled.

Mrs Davies brought Tanner's coat, waistcoat, boots and Marlena's half-boots. She rose and took her shoes from the woman's hands. They were still damp and the leather tight, but she did not care. Tanner was going to help her to get to Cemaes.

Arlan Rapp sat in front of the fire in the inn at Llanfwrog, sipping hot cider, waiting for his clothes to dry through and through. He puzzled what he should do next.

All he really wanted was to return to London and get paid for his work, but he'd better not do that until he discovered if the Viscountess Corland had been lost with most of the other passengers and crew, or if she had by some miracle survived.

The Vanishing Viscountess had vanished again. That would make a good story for the newspapers, he'd wager, but he'd rather it not be widely known he'd been the one to lose her.

He stared into the fire and pondered the choices he'd made. He refused to feel guilty about taking her place in the last boat. She'd been as good as dead from the moment he first put her in shackles. He would have taken her back to a hangman's noose, nothing less. The Vanishing Viscountess had killed her husband in a jealous rage. Everybody knew her husband rutted with any female he could find. The Viscountess had been caught red-handed. Her cousin had discovered her standing over Viscount Corland's dead body, bloody scissors in hand. There was no doubt that she'd committed the murder.

She had escaped, however. The guilty always ran away if you gave them half a chance.

She'd escaped again, Rapp thought, rubbing his face. He hoped drowning was an easier death than hanging by the neck.

He took another gulp of cider. A log sizzled in the fireplace. He glanced around for the serving girl, who seemed to have disappeared. Rapp's stomach growled, ravenous for breakfast. He was also bone weary from being up all night, pulled out of the sea by local folk and sent to this inn in a wagon with the handful of other survivors.

Rapp bowed his head, thinking of the women and children in his boat. They had not been strong enough to hang on when the wave washed over them.

Rapp suddenly wanted to hurry home to his wife and children. He wanted to kiss his wife, hug his two sons, hold his baby girl. It was only right that he'd seized the chance to survive. His wife and children needed him.

Only eight passengers survived, as far as he knew, and a few more crewmen. The Vanishing Viscountess was not among them. If her body lay at the bottom of the sea, it might never wash up on shore. Rapp cursed the storm. Wexin would not pay him without proof that the Viscountess had perished.

He'd have to investigate, make absolutely certain she was among the dead. He was a Bow Street Runner. It should be a simple matter for him to discover who survived the shipwreck.

The serving girl finally set down a plate with bread and butter and thick pieces of ham.

He nodded his thanks. "Bring me paper, pen and ink," he asked her.

He'd pen a letter to Wexin, reporting the shipwreck, and one to his wife, as well, telling her he loved her, but that he must delay his return to London until he had searched up and down the Anglesey coast.

Chapter Three

By the time Mr Davies's old horse pulled the cart to the front of the cottage, Tanner was more than ready to leave this place. He had no wish to tarry until the son returned.

Tanner pressed a hand to his still-aching ribs, remembering the strength of the man's boot. He had no wish to meet young Davies again.

He stepped aside for Miss Brown to walk out ahead of him. The red cloak the old lady had found for her was threadbare, but Tanner supposed it would keep her warm enough. His lack of a top coat did not worry him overmuch. The temperature was not that harsh and would keep him alert.

Mrs Davies trailed behind him. "You promised us payment, sir."

He turned to her. "I will pay when your husband delivers us where we wish to go." He strode on.

She skipped after him. "How do we know you will pay? Your lady is walking away wearing my clothes. We can't afford to give our possessions away. Times are hard."

He stopped again and the old woman nearly ran into him. "You will have to trust my word as a gentleman, will you not?" He walked over to where Miss Brown waited next to the cart.

He did not know how much of her story to believe, but he'd be damned if he'd turn her over to a magistrate. No matter what she had done, she'd paid for it by what that deuced Bow Street Runner made her endure, leaving her to die while he saved himself. As far as Tanner was concerned, that alone should give her freedom.

Saving her life absolved him, in part, for the other deaths that weighed on his conscience. He would see her safe to help repay that debt.

He touched her arm. "I will climb up first, then assist you."

His ribs only hurt mildly as he got up next to the old man. He reached for Miss Brown's hand and pulled her up. As she settled next to him, he wanted to put his arm around her. He wanted to touch her, to keep fresh the memory of their naked embrace. He remembered the feel of her in his arms as he lay between sleep and waking. Her skin, soft and smooth and warm. Her curves, fitting against him as if tailored to him.

"Let us go," he told the farmer.

Mr Davies snapped the ribbons and the old horse started moving.

"You make him pay, husband!" Mrs Davies shouted after them.

The old horse pulled the cart past the vegetable garden, colourful with cabbages and kale. Wheat was already planted for the winter crop and a rook swept down and disappeared into the field of swaying stalks. The cart rolled at a slow speed finally reaching a road, leaving the cottage some distance behind.

At the road, Tanner turned to Mr Davies. "Take us to Cemaes."

The old man's head jerked in surprise. "Cemaes is north. You'll be wanting to go south to the ferry to Holyhead."

"We wish to go north. To Cemaes," Tanner said.

Mr Davies shook his head. "You want to go to Holyhead, I tell you."

Tanner felt a shiver crawl up his back. He'd wager the old man had some mishap planned on the road to the ferry. He held up the sovereign, which glittered in the sunlight. "If you wish to earn this coin, you will take us to Cemaes." He returned the coin to his pocket. "If not, we will walk from here." Tanner began to stand.

The farmer gestured for him to sit. "I'll take you to Cemaes," he grumbled and turned the horse and cart north.

The road, still muddy from the rains, wound past more farmland and other small cottages like the Davies's. Sometimes Tanner could glimpse the sea, looking calm this day, like a slumbering monster that had devoured its fill. The old man kept the frown on his face and did not speak. Miss Brown gripped the seat to steady herself as the cart rumbled along, but she, too, was silent. The cart jostled her against him, from time to time, keeping Tanner physically aware of her.

Her face was obscured by the hood of the cloak, and Tanner missed watching the play of emotions on her face. He'd seen her angry, earnest, frightened and relieved. He would enjoy hearing her laugh, or seeing passion light her face.

He also wished to discover her real name and the names of the people from whom she had supposedly stolen jewels. If she confided in him, he could help her. Even if she was guilty of the theft, he could make her troubles disappear. Money, power and influence overcame justice most of the time. If he repaid the son for the jewels, he'd wager the theft would be totally forgiven.

Tanner could not gaze at her without being obvious, so he

settled for the warmth of the sun on his face, the scent of the fresh sea air and fragrant fields, and the sight of the peaceful countryside. It was not precisely an Arcadian paradise, not with men toiling in the fields and cottages too small for comfort, but it was solid and timeless and vastly preferable to the cold, fickle sea.

As the sun grew higher in the sky, they passed a windmill spinning in the breeze, and a standing stone placed there by Celtic people long erased from history. Tanner guessed the time to be about noon. He dug his fingers into his pocket for his timepiece. It was no longer there.

His head whipped around to the old farmer driving the cart. The old man had gone through his pockets, he'd wager. "I wonder what time it is," he said.

The old man's jaw flexed.

Tanner coughed and winced as the pain in his ribs kicked at him again. Miss Brown looked over at him with concern in her eyes. He returned a reassuring smile, before glancing back to the old farmer.

He ought to deprive the man of the sovereign he'd promised, glad he'd had the presence of mind to hang on to his purse after he'd peeled every piece of wet clothing off his body, making a sopping pile on the cottage floor. Miss Brown had been shivering so violently, Tanner had been desperate to make her warm.

Mr Davies flicked the ribbons and glanced at Tanner nervously, fearful, no doubt, that Tanner would challenge him on the theft of his timepiece.

Tanner glanced back to the road. Let the man keep the watch, he said to himself. As payment for his bed. Tanner would have given the man anything for that warm bed. For *her.* To save her from the killing cold as he had saved her from the killing sea.

* * *

Two slow hours passed and Tanner suspected they could have walked faster than the old horse moved on the muddy road. Finally rooftops and a church bell tower came into view.

"Cemaes," said the old man, lifting his chin towards the town.

Miss Brown leaned forward. What was she thinking? Tanner wondered. What plan was she making for herself?

They came to the first houses, gleaming white, edged with chrysanthemums and marigolds. Up ahead the buildings became thicker and Tanner could see people walking about.

Miss Brown put her hand on Tanner's arm. "May we stop here?" She gave him that earnest look again.

He drank it in for a moment, then turned to the old man. "Mr Davies, you may leave us off here."

The old man's bushy brows shot up. "It is no distance to the inn."

"Good!" Tanner responded in a jovial voice. "Then it shall be only a short walk for us. Stop, if you please."

The farmer shrugged and pulled on the ribbons, halting his horse. Tanner climbed down and reached up for Miss Brown. Putting his hands on her waist, he lifted her down to the road and was reluctant to let go of her. He fished in his pocket for the sovereign and handed it up to Mr Davies, who grabbed it quickly, as if fearing Tanner would change his mind. Without a word of farewell, the man flicked the ribbons again, and the old horse clopped its way into town, to the inn and some refreshment for them both, Tanner suspected.

"You gave him a sovereign." Miss Brown said in a disapproving tone.

Tanner kicked a pebble into the street. "Yes."

She rolled her eyes.

"Too much?"

"I dare say," she responded. "Half that amount would have been generous."

He tilted his head, somewhat chagrined. "Especially since the man also stole my watch and I highly suspect his son was the man you hit over the head."

Her jaw dropped. "Tell me it is not so." Outrage filled her face. "How shabby of them to take such advantage."

This was an odd reaction for a supposed thief, Tanner thought. "Well, it is done…" He glanced around him, at the cobblestones in the street, at the tidy houses. "Why did you wish to be let off here?"

The sun illuminated her features and made her eyes sparkle like sapphires. He felt momentarily deprived of breath.

"I wanted a chance to talk with you." She gazed at him intently. "To prepare."

It took a moment for him to respond. "Prepare for what?"

She frowned in concentration. "I cannot enter that inn saying I am Miss Brown off the shipwrecked packet from Dublin, the prisoner escorted by a Bow Street Runner. I must think of some fiction to tell them."

Tanner nodded. He'd not thought much beyond being rid of Mr Davies and finding an inn with good food and a comfortable bed, but, then, he was not much accustomed to thinking ahead while travelling. The next meal, the next bed and the final destination were all he considered, and half the time they were arranged by his valet or his secretary.

She went on. "And I cannot walk in as the companion of the Marquess of Tannerton."

He felt a bit like a rejected suitor. "Would that be too scandalous?"

"It would be too foolish." Her expression turned patient,

as if speaking to a dull child. "The Marquess of Tannerton is sure to create a great deal of interest, especially if the marquess almost drowned. If I am seen with you, I will become an object of curiosity as well, and that I cannot have. I must slip away without anyone noticing me."

This woman must never look at herself in a mirror, Tanner thought. Surely she could not go anywhere and not be noticed.

"I see." He nodded, trying not to be distracted by his vision of her. "What do you propose?"

Her expression gave the impression of a mind turning like the intricate gears of his stolen watch. The road forked a few paces away and led to a stone bridge over a stream. She gestured for him to walk with her. They strolled to the bridge, where they stood side by side, leaning on the wall, gazing into the stream, swollen and brown from the previous day's storm.

She turned to him. "I—I must be on my way. The sooner I leave Anglesey, the sooner I will be forgotten. I want it thought that I drowned in the shipwreck. If they think me dead, no one will search for me."

Tanner disliked hearing her speak of being "on her way."

"Where will you go?" he asked. "Scotland is a big place."

She searched his face for a moment before turning her gaze away. "It is best for me not to say."

He frowned, unused to anyone refusing an answer to his question. Her mistrust wounded him when she so clearly needed a friend.

She turned back to him, her voice low and desperate. "I need some of your money."

He stared at her.

Nothing would be easier for him than to hand over the entire contents of his purse. He could get more money for himself later, on the mere strength of his name. Even in this remote place someone would extend the Marquess of Tannerton credit, enough to arrange for a post-chaise to carry him back to London. He could return to his townhouse in a matter of days.

He usually solved his difficulties by handing over money and letting someone else take care of it. Ironically, one of the rare times he'd taken it upon himself to solve a problem, three people died.

Perhaps he ought to leave her here in Cemaes.

Suddenly some of the colour drained from her face and her breathing accelerated. "Forgive my foolish request," she whispered. "You have done more than enough for me. I do not need your money."

She spun away from him and started to walk away.

He seized her arm. "Wait."

His conscience could not let her go, even with his purse in her hand. He knew he could help her. His name and influence—and his money as well—could save her from the hangman's noose or transportation or whatever fate might befall her if she was caught again.

"I have another proposal." He spoke in a low voice. "Come to London with me. Let me use my influence to help you. Whoever has caused you this trouble is not likely to have friends as highly connected as my friends, nor as much money as I possess. I am certain I can settle this matter for you. My power and influence are considerable."

She stepped away from him. "No!" She took a deep breath. "No," she said more quietly. "I thank you, but—but—you are mistaken. My trouble is—" She clamped her mouth shut on whatever it was she had been about to say.

He kept his gaze steady. "No matter what your trouble is, I assure you, I can help."

She shook her head. "You cannot know " Again she

stopped herself from speaking. "It is safer for me to run. No one will look for me, because they will think me dead. They will forget me, and I may start my life anew."

She gazed at him with such intensity Tanner felt the impact resonate deep inside him. He moved towards her. What made her think *he* could forget her? What made her think he could let her be dead to him now when he'd refused to let her die in the sea?

"Surely you cannot travel alone," he tried.

"Of course I can." She glanced away, and he could sense her mind at work again. "I might be a governess travelling to a new place of employment. Who would question that?"

He did not like this idea. Some men would consider an unescorted governess fair game. "Someone would ask who employed you, for one thing. They would ask where you were bound."

"Then I would fashion answers."

She was slipping away. He remembered that horrible moment when he'd woken up on shore and thought she had slipped from his grasp. He did not want to let go of her now any more than he had wanted to then. True, he might easily return to his comforts, the diversions of London, the hunting parties he and Pomroy planned to attend, but how could he be content now if he thought her adrift, alone?

He glanced away, his mind whirling, as he'd fancied hers had done. All he could think to do was delay.

He gripped her arm, holding on to her like he had done in the sea. "I'll give you the money." He made her look into his face. "There is no obligation to pay it back. It is a trifling amount to me, I assure you, but listen to me. I am afraid our taciturn Mr Davies is at the inn this very moment loosening his tongue with a large tankard of ale." He glanced in the direction of the inn. "He will tell everyone we are husband and wife—that is what he and his wife concluded about us and I did not correct their impression. Did you?"

She shook her head. "I did not."

He went on, "Davies will tell them we are from the shipwreck, a husband and wife from the shipwreck. If we act as strangers now, we will increase suspicion about you, not reduce it."

She considered this. "Yes, that would be true."

His spirits rose. He held on to her still. He took a breath. "In this town we must also be husband and wife."

"Husband and wife?" She stared at him, a worry line forming between her brows.

Acting as husband and wife meant sharing a room. Tanner longed to hold her again, longed to again wake with her in his arms, to know he had kept her safe.

He looked into her face, suffused with reluctance, and realised she might not be as thrilled at the prospect of sharing a bed with him as he was with her.

"I will not take advantage of you," he said in as earnest a tone as he could muster, although his body pulsed with desire for her.

She glanced away, and again turned her eyes back to him, eyes as blue as the sky behind her. "Very well. Tonight we are husband and wife."

He heard the unspoken end to her sentence. Tomorrow they would part. Still, his spirits soared. He would have this brief time with her and maybe wherever they were bound on the morrow would reassure him she'd be safe.

He offered her his arm. "Shall we prepare? We must concoct a story for ourselves, must we not? Names. We need to have names, and, to own the truth, I do not think Brown is a good choice."

"Why?" she asked.

"It is the sort of name a gentleman gives to an innkeeper when he does not wish his identity known." He winked.

She gave a light laugh. "Is that so?

"It is." He smiled. "Select another name."

"Smith?" A corner of her mouth lifted.

He rolled his eyes, playing along with her jest. "You are not good at this, are you?" He put his mind to the task, but the only names he could think of were ones too connected to him. Adam. Vick. Tanner. "I am hopeless as well."

"I have an idea," she said. "How about the name *Lir? Lir* is the god of the sea in Irish mythology."

He peered at her. "You know Irish mythology?"

"I lived in Ireland." She cast her eyes down. "I read about it in a book there."

"How do you spell it? Like Shakespeare's King Lear?" he asked. "Because I know how to spell that Lear. The Irish always use—well—Irish spellings."

She gave him a look that mocked the one he'd given her. "You know Shakespeare?"

He laughed.

Her eyes twinkled. "We can spell it like King Lear."

He smiled back at her, his heart gladdened at her mirth. Their first night together had been full of terror. This one ought to be peaceful and happy. He vowed he would make it so.

"I shall be Adam Lear, then. Adam is my given name." He waited for her to tell him her given name—hoped she would say it, so he might have that small piece of her to keep for himself.

She said nothing.

He took a deep, disappointed breath. "I believe I need an occupation as well."

Marlena enjoyed their short walk to the inn, and their creation of a story to tell about themselves. The Marquess of

Tannerton became Mr Adam Lear, stable manager for Viscount Cavanley, Adrian Pomroy's father, although they agreed it would be best to avoid mentioning Pomroy if at all possible.

Pomroy was another name from Marlena's past, from that one London Season. She had not thought of Pomroy in her four years of exile in Ireland or really even three years before that, not since her Season. She remembered him as a most ramshackle young man. She and Eliza thought Pomroy was a relentless flirt, devoid of even one serious bone in his body. They'd laughed at his antics behind their fans, but neither she nor Eliza mooned over him the way they mooned over his good friend, Tanner. Even though they had been very green girls then, they knew an attachment to Pomroy would be a foolish one.

It was unfortunate that Marlena's judgement of character had not been that astute when it came to Corland, but then, her husband had disguised his true nature. Pomroy had been as clear as glass.

As Marlena walked at Tanner's side, she almost again felt like that carefree girl who'd enjoyed every moment of her Season. Tanner made her laugh again, something she'd not done since Eliza took ill. Marlena feared she was much too glad she would be spending another night with Tanner.

Imagine it, Eliza! she said silently. *I will be married to the Marquess of Tannerton. Very briefly, however. In name only, and a false name at that.*

She remembered then how warm his skin had felt, how firm his hand on her body. Her skin flushed with the memory.

She spied Mr Davies's horse drinking water from a trough at the inn, and the truth of her situation hit her once more. She was the Vanishing Viscountess, trying desperately to vanish once more. She was not the wife of the Marquess of Tannerton nor plain Mrs Lear. She was not even Miss Brown. She was a fugitive, and if Tanner was caught aiding her, he would face the same punishment as she faced, the hangman's noose.

She and Eliza had not known that fact when Marlena had fled to Ireland with her friend and became her children's governess. Once in Ireland, they had read a newspaper that described the penalty for aiding the Vanishing Viscountess, but Eliza had refused to allow Marlena to leave.

Tanner squeezed her hand as they walked in the door of the inn. "How are you faring, Mrs Lear?"

"A bit nervous, Mr Lear," she replied. At the moment, more nervous for him than for her. She stood to earn life from this masquerade. He risked death.

"We shall do very nicely," he said.

She pulled him back, "Tanner," she whispered.

He gave her a warning look. "It is Adam."

She bit her lip. She must not make such a mistake again. "Do not act like the marquess."

He gave her a puzzled look.

"Do not order people about," she explained.

He tilted his head, appearing very boyish. "Do I order people about?"

She nodded.

The innkeeper approached them. "Good day to you! Are you the lady and gentleman from the shipwreck?"

Mr Davies had indeed been talking of them.

"We are," said Tanner, his affability a bit strained. "And we are in need of a room for the night."

"If we may," added Marlena.

"If we may," repeated Tanner.

The innkeeper smiled. "We will make you comfortable, never fear. If you are hungry, we are serving dinner in the taproom. We have some nice pollack frying. You must let it be our gift to you for your ordeal."

Marlena was touched by this kindness.

"We thank you," said Tanner. He laughed. "I confess, a tall tankard of ale would be very welcome."

The innkeeper walked over and clapped him on the shoulder. "Ale it is. For you, m'lady—?"

"Lear." She cleared her throat. "Mrs Lear. I should like a glass of cider, if you have it."

"We do indeed," said the innkeeper.

Soon they were seated, drinks set in front of them. Marlena glimpsed Mr Davies, who gave them a sidelong look before slipping off his chair and walking to the door.

A woman wearing a bright white apron and cap walked over. "I am Mrs Gwynne. Welcome to our inn. My husband said you had arrived. From the shipwreck, are you?"

"We are." Tanner extended his hand. "It is a pleasure to meet you, Mrs. Gwynne."

"You poor lambs." She clasped his hand.

"Have you heard of any other survivors?" Marlena asked.

The woman clasped Marlena's hand next. "Not a one, but if you made it, others may have as well, God willing. Now, what can we do for you? Besides giving you a nice room and some food, that is. What do you need?"

Tanner rubbed his chin, even darker with beard than it had been that morning. Marlena suppressed a sudden urge to touch it.

"All we have is what you see," he told Mrs Gwynne. "Is there a shop where we might purchase necessities?"

She patted his arm. "There certainly is a shop; if you tell me what you want, I will purchase it for you."

"That will not be necessary. I will visit the shop." Tanner glanced at Marlena and back to Mrs Gwynne. "I have thought of something else you might do, however."

"Say what it is, Mr Lear. I'll see it done."

His gaze rested softly on Marlena. "A bath for my wife."

Marlena's mouth parted. There was nothing she could more desire.

Mrs Gwynne smiled again. "I will tell the maids to start heating the water."

She bustled away and soon they were brought a generous and tasty dinner of fish, potatoes and peas. After they ate, Mrs Gwynne showed them to their room, a chamber dominated by a large, comfortable-looking bed. There was also a fire in the fireplace and a nice window looking out at the back of the inn. The best part, however, was the large copper tub half-filled with water.

"There are towels next to the tub, and a cake of soap. The maids are still bringing the water, and one will assist you if you like." Mrs Gwynne folded her arms over her considerable chest.

"Thank you," Marlena rasped, her gaze slipping to Tanner.

"I'll leave you now," the older woman said. "Mr Lear, when you wish to go to the shop, either my husband or I can direct you."

"I will be down very soon," he said.

After the innkeeper's wife left, Marlena walked over to the tub and dipped her fingers into the warm water.

"Am I sounding like a marquess?" Tanner asked.

She smiled at him. "You are doing very well."

He blew out a breath and walked towards her. "That is good. I confess, I am uncertain how not to sound like a marquess, but if I am accomplishing it, I am content." His eyes rested on her. "I should leave, so you can have your bath."

She lifted her hand and touched him lightly on the arm. "Thank you for this, Lord Tannerton."

"Adam," he reminded her, his name sounding like a caress.

"Adam," she whispered.

His eyes darkened and he seemed to breathe more deeply. He glanced away from her. "What ought I to purchase for you?"

She thought the bath more than enough. "A comb, perhaps? A brush? Hairpins?"

He smiled. "I shall pretend I am an old married man who often is sent to the shop for hairpins. Anything else?"

She ought not to ask him for another thing. "Gloves?"

"Gloves." He nodded.

There was a knock on the door and he crossed the room to open it. It was the maid bringing more water.

She poured it into the tub. "I'll bring more." She curtsied and left.

"I will leave now, as well." Tanner opened the door and turned back to her. "Save me the water."

Marlena crossed the room to him. "Forgive me. I did not think. You must have the water first. I will wait."

He reached up and touched her cheek. "You first, Mrs Lear."

By the time she could breathe again, he was gone.

Arlan Rapp trudged down the Llanfwrog road to the blacksmith shop. A huge barrel-chested man, twice the Bow Street Runner's size and weight, hammered an ingot against his anvil. The clang of the hammer only added to the pain throbbing in Rapp's ears. He'd walked from one side of Llanfwrog to the other, but few villagers were even willing to admit to knowing of the shipwreck. He'd recognised plenty of them from when what was left of his boat washed up to shore. The villagers had grabbed crates and barrels. A few had been good enough to aid the survivors. He'd been whisked off to the inn, he and the others who had washed up with him.

He waited to speak until the smithy plunged the piece of metal into water. "Good day to you, smithy," Rapp said.

The man looked up. "Do you require something?"

Rapp smiled, although his fatigue made him feel anything but cordial. "Only a bit of information."

The blacksmith just stared at him.

Rapp cleared his throat. "I am from the packet ship that was wrecked last night."

No understanding showed on the smithy's face, but Rapp doubted anyone in Llanfwrog was ignorant of the previous night's bounty.

He went on. "I am searching for survivors, specifically a woman who had been my companion."

"I know nothing of it," the man said.

"Perhaps you have heard talk," he persisted. "Perhaps someone told you of survivors. I am most eager to learn her fate."

The blacksmith shook his head. He took another piece of glowing metal from the fire.

"I would pay for information," Rapp added, although he much preferred not to part with his still-damp money.

The smith placed the hot metal on the anvil and picked up his hammer. "Bodies wash ashore sometimes."

That was a grisly thought, but if the Viscountess's body washed up on shore, he could cease his search and go home to his wife.

"Where would bodies be taken?" Rapp asked, but the smithy's hammer started again and its din drowned out his words. He gave up.

No sooner had he walked out of the blacksmith shop than a smudged-face boy tugged on his coat. "I can show you bodies, if you want to see 'em."

Rapp squatted down to eye level with the little eavesdropper. "Can you now?"

The boy nodded energetically. "About ten or so."

Rapp took a breath and stood, squaring his shoulders. "Excellent, my good fellow. Take me there now." A few minutes of unpleasantness might mean he could be in London within a few days and still receive his reward.

"It'll cost you tuppence," the boy said.

Smart little cur, Rapp thought sourly. He fished the coin from his pocket and showed it to the boy. "Take me to the bodies and a tuppence you shall have."

Chapter Four

Tanner's shopping expedition proved to be a novel experience. He'd never shopped for ladies' hairpins before, nor any of his own necessities, for that matter. He typically sent his valet to procure things like razors and shaving brushes and polish for shoes and combs and toothbrushes. He dawdled in the shop for as long as he could to give Miss Brown time for her bath. The shopkeepers and two other customers were full of questions about the shipwreck, unknown to this village before Davies brought news of it. He practised being Mr Lear, although he could answer few questions about how much salvage had washed ashore.

When he left the shop and stopped for another tankard of ale in the taproom, the patrons there had more questions. The extra alcohol made him mellow and, while he talked, a part of his mind wandered to how Miss Brown might appear in the bath, how slick her skin would be, how scented with soap.

Because he had little information about the shipwreck, interest in him waned quickly. He drank more ale in solitude, if not peace. There was nothing peaceful about imagining Miss Brown in the bath. When he eventually carried the packages up the flight of stairs to the room he would share with her, his eagerness to see her made it difficult for him to keep from taking the steps two at a time. He walked down the hall to the door and, balancing the packages in one arm, knocked.

"Come in," she said.

He paused, took a breath, and opened the door.

She was dressed and seated in a chair by the fireplace, pressing a white towel to her long mahogany brown hair. He inhaled the scent of soap and wanted nothing more than to embrace her, soft and warm and clean.

"You are back," she said in a breathless voice.

He felt equally as robbed of air. "I tried to give you ample time."

She twisted the towel around her hair. "I fear you have waited too long. The water has gone quite cold."

He smiled at her. "It cannot be as cold as what we've already experienced."

She shuddered. "No, it cannot." Her eyes lifted to his and held him there.

He mentally shook himself loose from her. It was either do that or do something foolish. "The packages," he said, carrying them over to the table in the corner. He unwrapped one and brought it to her. "I suspect you would like these now." He handed her the brush and comb he had purchased.

They were crafted from simple tortoiseshell. Tanner thought of how many sets of silver brushes and combs he'd had his former secretary, Flynn, purchase for his mistresses. There was nothing so fine in the Cemacs shop, but Miss Brown's eyes glowed with excitement when she took the items from his hands.

"Oh, how wonderful," she cried. "I can comb out the tangles and brush my hair dry."

No gift he ever gave a mistress had been so gratefully

received. He grinned, pleased he had pleased her. She was too busy working the comb through her hair to see.

Tanner strolled over to the tub and felt the water, now on the very cold side of tepid. At home, his valet would be hovering with pots of hot water to add, making certain his bath remained warm from start to finish.

She rose from her chair, still holding the comb. "I could ask Mrs Gwynne for more hot water."

They faced each other over the tub and it took Tanner a moment to remember to speak. "You cannot go out with your hair wet."

"I shall put it in a quick plait," she assured him. "I will need to go out anyway so that you can bathe."

He could not help gazing at her. It took time for him to compose another thought, that thought being he did not wish her to leave. "Will not the Gwynnes think it odd that Mrs Lear walks to the public rooms with wet hair?" He reached over and fingered a lock, marvelling at how it already shaped itself in a curl. "They would not expect you to leave your husband merely because he bathes."

She held his gaze, and he fancied her mind working again, mulling over this latest puzzle.

"I believe you are correct." Her eyes were large and round. "I shall position my chair so that my back is to you, and I will comb my hair with the lovely comb you have purchased for me."

With resolution, she marched back to her chair and set it to face the fireplace. Tanner watched her pull the comb through her hair, wishing it was his fingers doing the task.

He shrugged out of his coat and waistcoat and laid them on the bed. Sitting next to them, he removed his boots and stockings. As he pulled his shirt from his trousers, he watched Miss Brown totally absorbed in combing her hair.

He laughed.

Her comb stilled. "What amuses you?"

He had not realised he'd laughed aloud. "Oh, I was merely thinking that when I'm in the company of a woman, undressing is usually a quite different prospect."

She paused for a moment and then began combing again. "Have you been in the company of so many women, Tanner?"

He faced her, naked and aroused and wishing she would turn and see the evidence of his desire for her. He wished she would come to him and let him make love to her right at this moment, to the devil with bathing.

Such thoughts were dangerous. He'd promised her he would not touch her. "I have known enough women, I suppose," he mumbled instead, padding over to the tub, cringing as he tested the water again.

Again she hesitated before speaking. "I suppose you have lots of mistresses."

He frowned at her assumption of him. "I assure you I am quite a success." His attempt at a joke fell flat to his ears. Truth was, he tended to be involved with only one woman at a time, and none but the briefest of encounters in this last year. At the moment he was wondering what the appeal had been in any of them.

She cleared her throat. "Are there towels folded nearby? And the soap?"

He walked around the tub to see them. "I've found them."

Bracing himself, he put one leg in the water, which was as cold as he expected. He forced himself to put the other leg in and began lowering the rest of him, making the water splash loudly in the room.

"Ye gods!" He shot up again when the water hit the part of him most sensitive to temperature. "Ah!" he cried again as he lowered himself a second time, but now it was because his ribs hurt from jumping up so fast.

"It is too cold," Miss Brown said. "I knew I ought to have sought hot water."

"It is tolerable," he managed through the pain and the chill.

He picked up the soap and lathered himself as quickly as he could, grateful for having had the foresight to do a fairly decent job of washing his hair that morning. In his rush, the soap slipped out of his hand and fell into the water. He fished around for it, making a lot of noise doing so. When he finally caught it and lifted it out of the water, it slipped from his hand again, this time clattering to the floor and sliding too far away to reach.

"Deuce," he muttered.

"You've dropped the soap?" she asked from her seat facing the fireplace.

"Yes." This was a damned odd conversation to have when naked with a woman. "It is of no consequence. I believe I am clean enough."

She stood. "I will fetch it for you."

"It is not necessary, I assure you." he told her.

"I do not mind."

Before he could stop her, she turned to face him. Their gazes caught, but she lowered her lashes and searched for the soap, picking it up and bringing it to him. He quickly glanced down to see how much of himself he was revealing at this moment. The water was too cloudy to see anything.

"There you are." She placed the bar of soap in his hand as calmly as if she'd been handing him his hat and gloves. After wiping her hand on a nearby towel, she returned to her chair and resumed combing her hair.

Tanner guessed he was as claret-faced as she'd been unflappable. "You are not missish, are you, Miss Brown?"

"Mrs Lear," she corrected. "And you are correct. I am too old to be missish."

"Old," he repeated. "How old are you exactly?"

She chose another lock of hair to work the comb through. "Now that is a question no woman wishes to answer."

He shot back. "As old as all that, then?"

She turned her head to him and smiled. "I am twenty-five."

"Good God," he cried in an exaggerated voice. "You are in your dotage!"

She laughed. "And you, sir, are teasing."

He liked the sound of her laughter. He also liked that she was not prone to blushes and foolishness like that. He never could abide the young misses who flocked to London during the Season, looking for husbands when they'd barely been let off leading strings. Miss Brown was ever so much more interesting.

He turned back to his bathing, frowning at what it might mean that she was not missish. What was her experience of men, then?

He realised he was merely sitting in the water, which was turning him into gooseflesh.

"I warn you, I am about to rise from this bath and stand up in all my glory." He started to rise, but stopped. "You may wish to look, seeing as you are not missish."

He tried to make it sound like a jest, although he wanted her to look at him with a desire matching his own of her.

Because of the cold water, however, a part of him was not showing to its greatest advantage. In fact, it had no glory at all.

"I'll look away," She kept her back to him while he dried himself and donned his shirt and trousers.

"It feels glorious to be clean, does it not?" she said.

"Indeed," he agreed, pressing his hand to his ribs. "But I would be happier if I had a clean shirt." He picked up one of the packages and walked over to the bureau upon which sat a mirror, a pitcher and a bowl.

She switched to the hairbrush and turned around again. "It must be wretched wearing the same shirt."

He smiled at her. "It is not that bad. It merely smells like the devil." He rubbed his chin. "I suppose I shall have to shave myself. Now that is a wretched prospect."

He unwrapped the package and took out a shaving cup, brush and razor. She picked up the soap and brought it to him, her long dark hair falling about her shoulders in soft waves. He wanted to touch it again. In fact, he wanted to grab a fistful of it.

Their gazes caught for a second when she handed him the soap. She lowered her eyes and walked back to her chair.

He took a deep breath and started to lather his face. "It is a fortunate thing my valet developed a toothache on the day we were to leave for Dublin."

"I meant to ask you if anyone accompanied you," she said in a sober voice.

"No one." Thank God, because he did not wish to have more lives on his conscience. Chin and cheeks lathered, he turned away from the mirror to look at her.

"I am glad of it," she murmured.

"I am as well," he responded.

He turned back to the mirror and scraped at his beard. "Pomroy and I once went two weeks without shaving." He made another stroke with the razor. "We went to one of my hunting lodges, but it rained like the devil. There was nothing to do so we drank great quantities of brandy and grew beards."

She giggled. "I wonder you had the energy for it."

"We wagered to see who could grow the longest beard in two weeks." He smiled. "I won it."

"Who was charged with measuring?"

"Our poor valets." He laughed. "We made them switch."

He twirled his finger for emphasis. "Pomroy's valet measured my beard and my valet measured Pomroy's. It made the two men very nervous."

He scraped at his cheek some more until his face was nearly clean of soap, except for tiny lines here and there. He rinsed off with the clean water and dried his face.

He presented himself to her. "How did I do?"

To his surprise, she reached up to stroke his face. "You did well," she murmured.

The part of him that had retreated during his bath retreated no more. He leaned closer to her, so close he saw the lines of light and dark blue in her eyes. Her hand stilled, but her fingers still touched his cheek.

He wanted to breathe her name into the decreasing space between them, if only he knew it.

There was a loud knock on the door.

"Deuce," he murmured instead.

He walked to the door. "Who is it?"

"It is Mrs Gwynne, lamb. If you are finished with your bathing, we've come to fetch the tub."

He glanced over to Miss Brown. She nodded.

"You may fetch the tub." He opened the door.

Removing the bath was almost as laborious as filling it had been. The maids had to make several trips. The towels were gathered up for laundering and, when all this was accomplished, Mr Gwynne appeared to carry the copper tub out of the room. Mrs Gwynne remained the whole time, chatting in her friendly way, pleased, Tanner suspected, that she had made her guests so happy.

"Now," the innkeeper's wife went on. "If you would care to come to the taproom, we have a nice supper. We also could give you a private parlour for dining. Or, if you prefer, we'll bring the food to you here."

"It shall be as my wife desires." He turned to Miss Brown.

As his wife desires, Marlena repeated to herself, her heart pounding at the way his voice dipped low when he spoke the word *wife.* He spoke the word softly, intimately, as if he had indeed kissed her as he had been about to do. Her whole body tingled with excitement.

"I should like to stay here," Marlena responded.

She did not want to break this spell, this camaraderie between them, this atmosphere that had almost led to a kiss.

"We are commanded, Mrs Gwynne." Tanner smiled at the woman.

Marlena enjoyed Tanner's teasing manner. She and Eliza had not known of his good humour all those years ago, something that would undoubtedly have given them more to sigh over. Now his light-heartedness made her forget she was running for her life.

Mrs Gwynne said, "We shall be back directly."

After she left, Marlena asked, "Did you truly agree, Tanner? With having supper here in the room?"

He walked back to her, and lowered himself in the chair adjacent to the one she had been sitting in. He winced as he stretched out his long legs. "I wanted to do what you wanted."

She did not miss that his sides still pained him.

"It is just that my hair is not yet dry," she rattled on. "And I do not wish to put it up yet." And also that she liked being alone with him in this temporary haven.

"You do not have to convince me. Your desire of it is sufficient." His eyes rested softly upon her.

Her desires had never been sufficient for her husband to do what she asked. Early in her marriage she'd learned that Corland's desires took precedence and that she must do what he wanted or he would be in a foul mood. Later in their three-year marriage, she had not cared enough to attempt to please him.

It occurred to her that she had been on the run for as long as she had been married. In a way, Corland still directed her life. It was a mystery to her why Wexin had killed Corland, but because of it, she was on the run.

Marlena fiddled with the brush in her hands, disliking the intrusion of Corland and Wexin in her time with Tanner.

How would it have felt if Tanner had, indeed, kissed her?

It had been so long since a man had kissed her. Corland's ardour for her, mild at best, had cooled after the first year of their marriage, after her money had dwindled and his debts increased. After she discovered his many peccadilloes. Actresses, ballet dancers, their housemaid.

Her last sight of her husband flashed into her mind, lying face up on the bed, eyes gaping sightlessly, naked body covered in blood.

She shuddered and glanced at Tanner, so gloriously alive, so masculine even as he slouched in his chair.

His expression had sobered. "What is it?"

She blinked. "I do not understand what you mean."

He gestured towards her. "You were thinking of something. Something disturbing, I'd wager."

She averted her gaze. "Nothing, I assure you."

When she glanced back at him, he frowned, and the peaceful, intimate feelings she'd had a moment before fled.

All she need do was think of Corland and clouds thickened.

There had been a time when she blamed all her woes on her husband. He was to blame for many things—his gambling, his debts, his affairs—but he would never have done to her what her own cousin had done. Who could have guessed Wexin was capable of such treachery?

Was Wexin still among Tanner's friends? she wondered. If she had so difficult a time believing what her cousin had done, surely Tanner would not believe it.

"Do not be angry with me, Tanner," she murmured.

His brows rose in surprise. "I am not angry." He gave her a very intent look. "I merely wish you would tell me what cloud came over you. Tell me your secrets. Trust me. I know I will be able to fix whatever is wrong."

She shook her head.

"Then at least tell me your name," he persisted, putting that teasing tone back into his voice, but still looking at her with serious eyes. "Tell me your given name. I gave you mine. Adam. When we are private together, let me address you with one name that belongs to you."

She stared back at him.

Would he know the Vanishing Viscountess by her given name? Would her name be enough to identify her as Wexin's cousin, Corland's widow, the young girl who'd had such a *tendre* for him at age eighteen that she blushed whenever he walked past her?

Marlena had been named for a distant French relative who'd died on the guillotine in the year of her birth. She had been Miss Parronley to everyone, save childhood friends and family and Eliza. And Wexin, of course. Even the newspapers after Corland's death and her flight had never printed her given name. She could not think of a single instance when Tanner would have heard of the name Marlena and, if he had, would never associate it with the Vanishing Viscountess. She opened her mouth to speak.

Tanner stood, blowing out a frustrated breath. "Never mind." He ambled over to the window. "Forgive me for pressing you."

The moment to tell him had passed. Her body relaxed, but she grieved the loss of the easy banter between them.

"I asked Mr Gwynne about coaches," he said, still looking out of the window. "I told him we were travelling north." He turned to her.

"Yes, I wish to travel north," she said.

"To Scotland, correct?"

She nodded.

"Well, Mr Gwynne's recommendation was to take a packet to Liverpool." He looked at her intently. "Where in Scotland?"

She bit her lip.

He made a frustrated sound and turned away.

"Edinburgh," she said quickly. "I wish to go to Edinburgh."

He turned back, lifting a brow. "Is Edinburgh your home?"

She hesitated again.

He waved a dismissive hand. "I ought to have known not to ask."

She turned away, her muscles tensing. "A ship."

"Could you bear it?" His voice turned soft.

She faced him again and saw sympathy in his eyes. "If I must."

"It sails in the morning."

"I will be ready." She would get on the packet, in any event, no matter if her courage accompanied her or not. She stood, but was hesitant to approach him. "What will you do?"

His brows rose. "Why, accompany you, of course. It would look odd otherwise."

She released her breath. The ship would be a little less terrifying with Tanner at her side.

Liverpool would certainly be big enough a town for her to pass through unnoticed. From there she could catch a coach, perhaps to Glasgow first, then on to Edinburgh.

So close to Parronley. Her estate. Her people. One place for which she yearned, but dared not go.

She was Baroness Parronley, a baroness in her own right.

The Parronley barony was one of the few that included daughters in the line of succession, but Marlena would have preferred not to inherit. It meant losing her dear brother Niall and his two little sons. Her brother and nephews perished of typhoid fever. So unexpected. So tragic.

Marlena had been with Eliza in Ireland when they read the account in a London newspaper that Eliza's husband had had sent to him. Marlena could not even mourn them, her closest family. She could not wear black for them, could not lay flowers on their graves.

With the shipwreck she would eventually be pronounced dead, the end of a baroness who had never had the chance to claim her title, the end of the Parronleys. Wexin would inherit. Her people, the people of Parronley, would be in the hands of a murderer.

Another knock on the door sounded, and Mrs Gwynne herself brought in their supper on a big tray. Two steaming meat pies, a pot of tea, and a tall tankard of ale.

Tanner took the tray from the woman's hands and set it on the table. "Ah, thank you, Mrs Gwynne. You even remembered ale."

She beamed and rubbed her hands on her apron. "After all these years, I ought to know what a man wants."

He smiled at her. "You knew what this man wants." He lifted the tankard to his lips and took a long swallow.

After the woman left, Marlena picked at her food. The camaraderie she'd shared with Tanner had disappeared. They ate in silence.

As she watched him finish the last of the crumbs of the meat pie's crust, she blurted out, "You do not have to travel to Liverpool with me, if you do not wish it."

He looked up at her with a mild expression. "I do not mind the trip."

She sipped her cup of tea. "If it were not for me, you would probably be headed for London tomorrow."

"Probably," he responded.

She regarded him. "I do not even know if there is someone in London awaiting your return."

His eyes clouded. "The usual people, I suppose."

She flushed, embarrassed that she had not considered what his life might be like now. He had been the marquess of her memory, dashing and carefree and unmarried. "Forgive me, but I do not know if you are married. If you are—"

"I am not married," he replied, his voice catching as he pressed his hand to his side. "A delay in my return should not inconvenience anyone overmuch. My affairs are well managed and rarely require my attention."

She felt a disquieting sense of sadness from him. Still, that once innocent, hopeful débutante brightened.

He was not married.

Their meal struggled on with even fewer words spoken until Mrs Gwynne again knocked. Tanner rose stiffly.

"I've come for your dishes, lamb," she said as he opened the door. "But first I have something for you." She placed folded white garments into his hands. "Nightclothes for you."

"Thank you," Marlena exclaimed, surprised again at the woman's kindness. She placed their dishes on the tray.

"That is good of you, Mrs Gwynne." Tanner took the garments and placed them on the bed. "Might we purchase them from you?"

The woman waved a hand at him. "Oh, I hate to ask you for money after all you have been through."

"I insist," he said.

Mrs Gwynne gave him a motherly pat on the cheek. "Then we will settle up tomorrow, Mr Lear. Is there anything else you might require?"

"I can think of nothing." He turned to Marlena.

She shook her head and handed Mrs Gwynne the tray full of dishes. She walked over to open the door for the woman.

Marlena stopped her before she crossed the threshold. "Wait." She glanced over to Tanner. "Would it be possible for someone to launder my—my husband's shirt? He would so like it to be clean."

Mrs. Gwynne brightened. "It would indeed be possible. I'll see to it myself and dry it in front of the fire." She stepped over to Tanner again. "Give it over, lamb."

Tanner glanced at Marlena before pulling the shirt over his head and draping it over Mrs Gwynne's arm. "Thank you again."

The innkeeper's wife smiled and bustled out of the room.

Tanner turned to Marlena. "That was thoughtful of you."

His skin glowed gold in the light from the oil lamp and the fireplace, but he was no less magnificent than he'd appeared that morning or as he bathed. Just as one is tempted to touch a statue, Marlena was tempted to run her fingers down his chest, to feel his sculpted muscles for herself.

She resisted. "No more thoughtful than you asking for my bath. I would say we are even now, except for the matter of you saving my life."

His mouth curved into a half-smile. "We are even on that score, as well. Do you not recall hitting Mr Davies-the-Younger over the head?"

"I am appalled at that family, the lot of them." She shook her head.

He smiled. "You'll get no argument from me on that score."

He picked up one of the garments Mrs Gwynne had brought them and put it on, covering his spectacular chest. "I'll walk down with you to the necessary, before we go to bed."

Go to bed repeated itself in her mind.

The sky was dark when they stepped outside to the area behind the inn where the necessary was located. Marlena was glad Tanner was with her. The darkness disquieted her, as if it harboured danger in its shadows.

When they returned to the room, he said, "Spare me a blanket and pillow and I will sleep on the floor."

"No, you will not," she retorted, her voice firm. There was no way she would allow the man who had rescued her to suffer through such discomfort. "Not with those sore ribs of yours. You must sleep in the bed."

He seized her arm and made her look at him. "I'll not allow you to sleep on the floor."

Her heart pounded as she looked directly into his eyes. "Then we must share the bed."

Chapter Five

Marlena's heart pounded as Tanner stared at her. He said nothing.

She must have made a terrible mistake, must have mistaken the meaning of his almost-kiss. Surely he would give her some sign of wanting to make love to her after her brazen invitation. Not this silence.

She felt the rebuff as keenly as she'd once felt those of her husband. Corland, however, had voiced his disgust at her wantonness. She'd believed him, too, thinking herself some unnatural sort of wife to desire the lovemaking, until she discovered that Corland had no such disgust of other women bedding him.

Tanner's reaction confused her all the more.

Perhaps she was not a temptation to any man. She'd not really had the opportunity to find out while playing governess to Eliza's children.

"I—I ought to speak more plainly," she prevaricated. "I meant we ought to share the bed, which is big enough. I was not suggesting more."

He swung away from her, so she could not tell how this idea—outrageous all on its own—had struck him.

He finally turned back to her. "You wish only to share the bed."

She nodded, wishing she had merely insisted upon sleeping on the floor and been done with it.

"I will turn my back while you undress, then." He faced the chest where the water and bowl were.

Marlena undressed as quickly as she could, although her fingers fumbled with the laces of her corset. She slipped the nightdress over her head and noticed the comforting smell of lavender lingering in the fabric. She laid her clothing over one of the chairs so that it would not wrinkle.

She crawled beneath the covers. "I am done."

He'd been so still as she undressed, adding to her discomfort, but he moved now, removing his boots and the coat he'd donned over his nightshirt when they'd gone below stairs. She peeked through her lashes at him, watching him unfasten the fall of his trousers and step out of them, the nightshirt preserving his modesty.

He walked towards the bed and climbed in beside her. The bed shifted with his weight. When he faced away from her, she wished it could have been as it had been that morning, his arms around her, bare skin touching bare skin. She was certain she would never sleep a wink the whole night, but soon after his breathing became even and rhythmic, she drifted off.

The dream came. She'd not had the dream in ever so long, but now, with all the fear and danger, she dreamt it like it was happening all over again.

She'd been restless, unable to sleep that terrible night. Corland and Wexin made plenty of noise when they returned from their night of debauchery. Wexin often slept off the effects of their entertainment in one of the bedchambers, so it did not surprise her that he stayed the night.

When she finally dozed, a woman's cry woke her. Earlier in the day the housekeeper had warned her that her husband had his eye on Fia Small, the new maid, a girl Marlena had hired mostly because she came from near Parronley and was so very young and desperate for employment. A light shone from beneath the door connecting her husband's bedchamber to hers.

Again in her dream, Marlena rose from her bed and walked to the door. She turned the key and opened it.

A man who looked as if he were dressed in women's clothes grappled with someone, something in his hand, trying to strike with it. Marlena ran and grabbed his arm. The weapon was a large pair of scissors and the person with whom he struggled was the new maid. He swung around to Marlena, slashing the weapon towards her.

"No!" the girl cried, trying to pull him off Marlena.

He flung the girl away.

Marlena fought him, both her hands grasping his arm, holding off the lethal scissors. She finally saw the man's face.

In her dream the face loomed very large and menacing.

It was Wexin. *Her cousin.*

"Wexin, my God," she cried. The dream turned him into the image of a demon. He drove her towards the bed and she fell against it, losing her grip on his arm. He brought the scissors down, but Marlena twisted away.

She collided with her husband, her face almost ramming into his. Corland's eyes were open and lifeless, blood spattered his face, pooling at the wound in his neck.

Before she could scream, Wexin called out, "Help! Someone, help!" He tore off the woman's robe and threw it at Marlena. He thrust the scissors into her hand.

Footsteps sounded in the hallway.

Wexin swung around to the maid. "I'll see you dead, girl,

if you speak a word of this. There will be nowhere you can hide. Your lady here has killed her husband. Do you understand?"

Marlena threw aside the robe—her robe, she realised. The scissors in her hand was sticky with blood. Her nightdress was stained with it. Wexin pulled off his gloves and stuffed them in a pocket. He was clean while she was bloody.

The maid glanced from Marlena to Wexin and back again. With a cry, she ran, scampering through the hidden door that led from Corland's room to the servants' staircase.

Wexin laughed at the girl's escape. "There goes your witness, cousin," he sneered. "You have killed Corland and there is no one to say you have not."

Marlena jolted awake, her heart pounding.

The nightmare had not ended, however. A man leaned over the bed and slammed his hand over her mouth.

Tanner woke with a start.

A man, no more than a black figure, had his hands on Miss Brown. Tanner grabbed for the man's coat, knocking him off balance.

The man released Miss Brown and pulled out of Tanner's grip. Tanner sprang from the bed and lunged at him before he could reach her again. They both fell to the floor, rolling and grappling, until slamming against the mantel, the coals on the hearth hot on Tanner's back. They illuminated the man's face.

Davies, the son come back to finish what he'd started on the beach.

"No!" Miss Brown ran towards them, pulling the back of Davies's collar.

"Stay back!" Tanner yelled, although he was perilously close to having his nightshirt catch fire.

Davies released him and scrambled to his feet. Miss Brown backed away from him, but he came at her, clamping one big beefy hand around her neck. Tanner stood and advanced on him.

"Keep away or I'll kill her," Davies warned, squeezing her throat for emphasis, and dragging her towards the door.

"Leave her," Tanner commanded. "The purse you want is in the bed."

The man glanced to the bed, but shook his head, squeezing Miss Brown's neck tighter. "She'll be worth more, I'll wager." The man swallowed. "I saw your ring. Only a rich man wears a ring with pictures on it. You'll pay me more than what's in that purse for her."

Tanner suddenly felt the weight of the signet ring on his finger, the ring that was so much a part of him. He'd tried to disguise it, but Davis had obviously seen it for what it was.

"I'll have you arrested and hanged," Tanner growled.

"I'll kill her first," the man replied.

A choking sound came from Miss Brown's lips. Tanner had no doubt Davies would make good his threat.

"I'll not pay for her if she is dead," Tanner said, playing for time.

Tanner kept his distance as Davies neared the door. He could barely see in the darkness, but he knew one thing. He would never let that man take her out of the inn.

The intruder reached the door, and Tanner could hear him fumbling with the key to unlock it. "Do not raise a din," Davies warned, "or I'll snap her neck and run for it."

He lifted the latch and swung the door open. At that same moment, Miss Brown brought her heel down hard on his foot.

Smart girl!

Davies cried out in pain and she twisted away from him.

Tanner came at him, landing his fist square on Davies's jaw and spinning him around into the hall towards the stairway. The man's hand groped for the banister, but slipped, and he tumbled down the stairs.

Tanner rushed after him. By the time he reached the stairs, Davies was back on his feet and out of the building. Heedless of his bare feet, Tanner ran down the stairway and into the inn's yard, the nightshirt tangling between his legs and hampering his progress. Davies disappeared into the darkness.

"Hell," he yelled, stamping his foot and lodging a stone painfully between his toes.

Breathing hard, Tanner limped back to the inn where Miss Brown stood framed in the doorway.

He hurried to her, touching his hand to her neck. "Did he hurt you?"

She placed her palms on his ribs. "No, but what of you? Has he injured you more?"

He had forgotten that his ribs still pained him. He put his hand over hers and pressed his side. "Nothing of consequence."

He wrapped his arms around her, holding her close with only the thin fabric of their nightclothes between them.

A commotion sounded behind them. The innkeeper and his wife appeared, along with several curious lodgers.

"What is this?" asked Mr Gwynne, in his nightshirt, robe, and cap.

Tanner reluctantly released Miss Brown. "A man broke into our room and tried to rob us."

"Oh, dear!" Mrs Gwynne's hand went to her mouth. "Who would do such a thing? And you with so little. Did he take anything of value?"

Tanner put his arm around his pretend wife. "My purse almost, but we stopped him." He glanced towards the yard. "He ran off."

"Shall I alert the magistrate?" the innkeeper asked.

"No!" cried Miss Brown.

Tanner tightened his arm around her to let her know he understood she would not wish to speak to a magistrate. "It is no use. The man is gone, and it was dark. I'd not know him in the light."

"You poor lambs!" Mrs Gwynne ushered them inside and closed the door. "What can we do for you?"

"We need only to return to sleep. I am certain he will not come back." Tanner blew out a breath and reconsidered her offer. "I might appreciate a glass of port, come to think of it."

"I'll fetch you a whole bottle," said Mr Gwynne.

The other lodgers crowded around them with questions, sympathy and speculation. Tanner suppressed his natural inclination to merely order them away. He was not precisely sure how Mr Lear the stable manager might act in such a situation, so he merely answered what he could and thanked them for their concern.

Acting as a husband came easier. Tanner kept a protective arm around Miss Brown and walked her through the entrance hall to the staircase. He only released her when Mr Gwynne handed him a bottle of port and two glasses. She hurried up the stairs and Tanner followed.

When they reached their room, the door was ajar and a breeze blew through from the open window, undoubtedly how Davies had gained entry.

As soon as Tanner closed the door behind them, he faced her. "Are you certain he did not hurt you?"

She gazed up at him. "Very certain."

He wanted to touch her, to examine her all over, to reassure himself she was unharmed, but his hands were full and he was fairly certain his touch would not be welcome.

For a fleeting moment earlier that night he'd believed

she'd invited him to do more than share the bed. Thank God he had not acted on that belief. A second later he realised he'd presumed too much.

"Would you like some port?" He placed the glasses on the table and pulled out the bottle's cork. "I am in great need of it."

"Yes." She put her hand over his, and his desire for her flared anew. "But I will pour for you."

She took the bottle, and Tanner paced. The encounter with Davies had set his blood to boiling and he had not yet calmed down. He still burned to pummel his fists into the bastard's fleshy face and beat it to a pulp.

All that unspent energy was in grave danger of being misdirected. Not in violence, but in passion. He surged with desire for this woman who again had been in danger. Tanner felt the need to have her. Now.

He shuddered. He must force himself to remain civilised.

He walked over to the window, closing it and taking a taper from the fireplace to light the lamp on the table. Anything to keep his hands off her.

"The money!" he cried, nearly dropping the taper.

She looked up, holding a glass in midair.

Tanner rushed over to the bed and groped under the pillow. The door of the room had been open for several minutes. Anyone might have walked in. He exhaled in relief as he pulled out the purse.

Her arm relaxed. "Thank goodness." She held out the glass to him. "Was it the money he was after—or—or me?"

He returned the purse to its place under the pillow and took the drink from her. "I would not have let him take you," he murmured, brushing a lock of hair off her forehead.

She looked up into his eyes, and he felt the surge of passion return.

She poured port into the other glass. "Do you think Davies knows who I am?"

Tanner took a sip, the sweet, woody wine warming his throat, but not cooling his ardour. "*I* do not know who you are."

She averted her face. "I mean, he still seemed to think me your wife, did he not?"

"My wife," he murmured.

He took a gulp of the port. The light of the fireplace behind her revealed the outline of her body beneath the thin white fabric of her nightdress. A vision of her naked filled his mind, full high breasts, narrow waist, flat stomach, long silken legs.

Lust surged through him. Curse him, she'd already made it clear that sharing a bed meant only sharing a bed.

He glanced away from her, but looked back again to see her lips touching the glass, her pink tongue darting out to lick off a stray droplet of port. He downed the contents of his own glass and walked over to the table to pour another one.

With his back to her, it was easier to speak. "Davies saw my ring when we were at the farmhouse, evidently. I doubt he could identify the crest, although someone more knowledgeable might do so. I've since turned it around on my finger."

"So he thought me your wife?" she asked again.

"I believe he did." It fitted with what Davies had said about wanting Tanner to pay for her.

She finished her port. "What time does the packet ship sail?"

He turned around to answer her, but a sharp pain pierced his ribs. He leaned on the table until the worst of it had passed. "Mid-morning," he answered in a tight voice. "And another one later in the day. Mr Gwynne said we should be at the docks by ten o'clock for the morning departure."

She put down her glass, and crossed over to him. "You are hurt." She gently touched his ribs. "Is it where he kicked you? You must go back to bed."

She put his arm over her shoulder to help him over to the bed. Instead, he turned and wrapped his arms around her, taking pleasure in merely holding her.

"Let us both go back to bed."

She looked up at him, a question in her eyes.

He garnered more strength than he'd used to battle Davies. "To sleep?"

She stared at him. "To sleep."

She doused the lamp, and helped him to the bed, sweeping the covers back and waiting for him to climb in. She moved to the other side and climbed in next to him, covering them both with the blankets.

This time, rather than turn away, Tanner faced her. He put his arm around her and drew her close. The pain protected him from doing more and finally exhaustion brought him sleep.

Lew Davies stumbled into the cottage as dawn peeked over the horizon. He did not trouble himself to be quiet, still too angry at this latest failure. The other wreckers had found all sorts of treasure. Crates of cargo and bits of jewellery, coin, clothing from the dead. Why did he have to find a fellow who was alive? The only thing his family had to show for the best shipwreck in years was a bloody timepiece with that same picture on it that had been on the man's ring. Davies did not even know where they might sell such a thing.

He shrugged out of his coat and let it fall to the floor. His foot pained him like the very dickens from where the woman had stomped on it, his jaw ached from the man's fist, and his muscles were sore from the tumble down the stairs. He'd been lucky to escape.

He was sick of being foiled by these two fancy people. First on the shore, then on the road to the ferry when his father's cart never showed up for him to ambush, and finally in Cemaes. He flopped down into a chair and pulled off his boots, tossing them into a corner.

He'd been stupid to decide to take the woman instead of the purse. The idea just came to him suddenly when he'd grabbed her. He should have left as soon as the man saw his face. If he was lucky the gentleman wouldn't go to the magistrate about him.

From now on, he'd stick to wrecking and hope for another storm off shore very soon.

The bedchamber door opened and his mother tottered out. "Well, did you nab the purse?"

He rubbed his jaw. "No, they woke up. I was lucky to get away in one piece."

She clucked her tongue. "We need that money."

"I know, Mam." He dragged a hand though his hair.

She crossed the room and picked up his coat, hanging it on the peg on the wall. "Well, I want you to try again, but this time take the woman."

He gaped at her. "Take the woman?"

"You heard me." She stood with her fists on her hips. "A man came asking questions after you'd gone. Looking for the woman, he was." She pumped some water into the kettle and placed it on the fire. "He bought her clothes from me, if you can imagine it. More like rags they were, but I'd not have got a half-crown for 'em elsewhere."

He sat up. "He gave you half a crown for them?"

"Well, yes, he did." She opened the tin box where she kept the chicory and took out a piece of the root.

"Half a crown." Davies still could not believe it.

"That fellow told me she was running from the law and that he is supposed to bring her to London. I'll wager there is a big reward or else this fellow would not pay half a crown for her rags."

"A reward?" Davies's foot started paining him and he lifted it on to his knee to rub it. "What about the gentleman she was with?"

"I told the fellow about the gentleman, but he didn't have anything to say about him." His mother shrugged as she plopped the chicory into a tea pot. "I did not tell we had the man's timepiece."

Davies put his foot back down and sank his head into his hands. He could have earned a big reward if only he had not let go of her.

"So this is what you have to do," his mother went on. "You go back to Cemaes and get the woman. If she's gone, follow her until you find her and bring her back. We will take her to London for the reward."

He looked up at her. "You'll have to give me money."

She checked the kettle, which was starting to hiss. "I'll give you the sovereign the gentleman gave us, but you must find her before that man does."

"Did you tell him they went to Cemaes?"

She glared at him. "I'd not do anything so daft, but I reckon he'll find out before the day is through."

Young Davies reached for his boots. "I'll do it, Mam. I'm going back to Cemaes right now."

His mother waved a dampening hand at him. "First you have some chicory tea and some bread and cheese. I'll not send you out again without something in your stomach."

He leaned back in the chair. "Yes, Mam."

He'd obey his mother, but as soon as he'd eaten, he'd walk back to Cemaes and wait for the perfect time to nab the woman. He did not think he could get in her room again, but he could follow her and the gentleman wherever they went. He didn't care how long or how far it might be.

With a big reward at stake, he'd nab her, all right.

Chapter Six

Marlena gripped the ship's railing as land came into view, a welcome sight indeed. She'd felt the whole trip as if she had been running, rather than merely scanning the sky for storm clouds and the sea for surging waves. Tanner remained next to her the entire time, unwavering and as solid as land beneath her feet.

She supposed it was good to board a ship so soon after another one broke to pieces around them, like remounting a horse after being thrown off its back. When she'd first seen the ship, her fear had tasted like bitter metal in her mouth, but she'd forced one foot in front of the other, gripping Tanner's arm all the way, and she'd made it onboard.

"We should be close to landing," he said, gazing out at the land, still just a line of green and grey on the horizon. For the last hour they had seen more and more sails in the distance, other ships traversing to and from the busy port of Liverpool.

"Yes," she responded. Words had not come easily to her during the voyage, but he did not seem to mind, making comments here and there that demanded no more of her than monosyllables in return.

She felt him flinch and knew another pain had seized him. It was no use for her to beg him to go below and sit; he would not leave her side, and she could not leave the deck where she would at least not be surprised if danger descended upon them again.

He remained beside her while the day waned and the land came closer and closer. The nearer they came to the port, the easier it became to breathe, but, at the same time, Marlena felt like weeping. Setting foot on the solid ground that was Liverpool also meant parting from Tanner and continuing her journey alone.

She glanced at him. The plain felt hat Mr Gwynne had given him looked incongruous with his expertly tailored coat and trousers.

He must be cold, she thought. Why did he not leave her and go below?

He turned his head and caught her watching him. He smiled. "What is it? Do I have a smudge on my nose?"

She looked away. "No." She decided against asking him one more time to leave her and seek somewhere warm. "I was merely thinking that the hats you have in London must be so much finer than this one."

He cocked his head. "Perhaps, but, I tell you, this hat is quite comfortable. I may not give it up."

"The Gwynnes were dear people," she said.

Both Mr and Mrs Gwynne insisted they keep their money and send payment for the room when they reached their destination. "You'll have many expenses," the innkeeper had said. "We can wait for payment." The Gwynnes had also insisted they take the nightclothes with them and a small satchel in which to carry their meagre belongings. And the hat.

Tannerton's eyes, now the colour of the sea, turned soft.

"Never fear. I shall see the Gwynnes are well rewarded for their kindness."

If things had happened differently, she could have done the same. Baroness Parronley ought to have been a wealthy woman. The last she knew, her brother had well managed the family's estate and fortune.

There was no use repining what could never be.

"I wish I could repay them," she murmured.

How would Parronley fare under Wexin? Would he gamble its fortune away as he seemed bent to do when he and Corland went out together night after night? Wexin had never liked Parronley. He used to tease Marlena and her brother Niall that they lived in a savage land.

Who was the savage in the end? Wexin's face flashed before her once more, and Corland's bloody body.

"You've gone off once more."

Tanner's voice startled her. She glanced back at him, feeling as if she'd just awoken from the dream.

One corner of his mouth lifted. "I surmise you will not tell me what you were thinking."

She turned back to stare out at the land, very close now, the mouth of the Mersey River in plain view. "I was thinking of nothing at all."

She felt his position shift and his arm brushed against hers. "I dare say it was not nothing." He paused. "Do not fear. I will not press you." He tilted his head, looking boyish in the floppy hat. "I do wish you would tell me your name. I dislike calling you Miss Brown."

She made herself smile and tried to make the topic into a joke. "You ought to be calling me Mrs Lear, at least for a little while longer."

The expression he gave her was impossible to decipher, something resembling disappointment or, perhaps, wounding.

She turned away from him again. Soon she would part from him and she would not see his face again. She blinked away tears. It was for the best. Perhaps he would never discover he had aided and abetted the Vanishing Viscountess.

A shout went up from the first mate and soon the deck was teeming with crewmen, all busy at their stations as the ship sailed into the mouth of the Mersey River towards the docks. It suddenly seemed as if a multitude of ships dotted the water, like a swarm of insects all flying towards a lamp.

The activity freed her from having to talk with him further as they sailed up the river. Liverpool's buildings came into sight, a town swollen with brick warehouses and a sprawl of lodgings for the people whose lives depended on this busy port.

"Oh, my!" She swivelled around in alarm as a large ship loomed up on the opposite side of the packet, dwarfing their vessel and looking as if it would collide with them.

"Do not fear." Tanner touched her arm. "I am certain these captains have navigated this port many times without mishap."

She found it hard to breathe again, nonetheless. Even so, there was so much to see, so much going on, that time passed more swiftly than it had on the open sea. Soon the packet ship reached its dock and soon after that, they were among the first of the passengers to disembark.

The docks were bustling with activity, even as the daylight waned. Cargo was unloaded and carried into the warehouses. Raucous shouts came from nearby taverns, where seamen tottered from the doorways, swaying on their feet. Marlena was one of but a handful of women on the dock, and it seemed to her that all the men stared at her. Some of them looked like the pirates of storybooks, dark and dangerous and, above all, dirty.

She felt a *frisson* of fear travel up her back at the prospect of facing men such as these without Tanner at her side, but soon they must come to more civilised streets. At least she felt quite anonymous in this motley crowd. If Tanner left her at this moment, no one would notice.

Tanner stopped and looked around. "We need to discover where to go."

Marlena tried to breathe, but not enough air reached her lungs. "Perhaps we should part here. Say goodbye."

He scowled at her. "The devil we should. I should feel as if I am leaving a lamb to be slaughtered."

As if to prove his point, a huge sailor stumbled towards them, but Tanner was quick enough to step out of the man's way.

"See?" He pulled her to safety. "I'm not abandoning you to the mercy of such miscreants."

The man paused a moment, glancing back at them before weaving his way in the direction of another one of the passengers on the packet.

A pickpocket, she realised. "Take care for your purse," she warned Tanner.

"I have it well concealed," he reassured her. 'Come." He increased their pace.

Leaving the warehouses behind, they found the road where a line of hackney coaches waited.

Tanner approached one of the jarveys, who was leaning against his vehicle. "Take us to an inn, man. A respectable one for the lady."

The jarvey gave Marlena an assessing look. "A respectable inn, eh?" he said lazily.

Marlena knew she must present an odd picture in her ill-fitting dress and shabby cloak. Tanner was not much better for all his once-elegant coat and trousers had endured.

"Looks more like Paradise Street, if you ask me." The man chuckled.

Marlena guessed this Paradise Street housed less-than-respectable ladies. She pulled at the hood of her cloak to disguise her face.

"A respectable inn, sir," Tanner repeated in a firm voice.

"Aye." The man roused himself to open the door of the coach.

Tanner helped Marlena inside and climbed in beside her. She straightened her skirts and glanced out of the window of the coach as it started to move. "When we arrive at the inn, perhaps you can wait a bit and we will walk inside at different times."

"I think not," Tanner said.

Marlena's head jerked back to look at him. "Very well. We can say we merely shared the coach."

He gave her a level stare. "We will remain together."

Her heart beat faster, although she did not know if his words were the cause or the intensity of his eyes. "I do not understand."

He shifted his gaze to look around him. "After last night, do you think that I would allow you to make your journey alone?"

"But that was merely the Davies's son. I daresay such a thing could not happen again." She tried to make her voice sound nonchalant.

"The Davies's son is not the only man who might endanger you." He caught her in his gaze again. "Did you not see how the sailors looked at you on the docks?"

She blinked. "But we are not at the docks."

He gestured to the front of the coach. "Neither is the jarvey who is driving us. You recall his impertinence, do you not?"

She indeed recalled it. Her fingers fiddled with her skirt. "I shall be all right. I can look after myself. I did so with Davies, did I not?"

He shook his head. "I'll brook no argument. I am staying with you until you reach a place where I might safely let you go. I could not look myself in the mirror if I did not."

She clutched his sleeve and pleaded with her eyes. "You do not understand. If I am caught again and you have been found to have assisted me, you could suffer the same punishment." She shook his arm. "Think of it. What would be my punishment for stealing a wealth of jewellery? Never mind that I really did not do it."

He turned to her, placing his hands on her shoulders. "I have no fear of that. My position and my money will be enough protection. Let me take you back to London. I have told you, I can make the whole matter disappear."

She turned away. Perhaps a marquess could make a theft disappear by paying back the amount lost, but there was no way to pay back the murder of a peer.

Three years before, the newspapers that reached her and Eliza in Ireland had for weeks detailed everything about the murder. The bloody robe, the scissors from her sewing basket, her bloody hands. Wexin's eyewitness account. No one would believe anything except that she was the murderer.

Even if she could find Fia Small, the maid who'd shared her husband's bed that night, who would believe a maid over an earl?

Fia had run that night, the same as Marlena, and Marlena could not blame her. She hoped the girl had escaped, because, if not, Wexin had probably killed her, too.

She turned back to Tanner. "Do not risk yourself for me, Tanner, I beg you."

He reached up to caress her cheek. "I will finish what began on the ship from Dublin, Mrs Lear," he murmured. "How could I do any less?"

Fia Small hoisted four tankards of ale at once in her two hands and carried them to the table where men she'd known her whole life sat for a bit of rest after a hard day's work.

"We thank you, Fia," said Lyall, giving her a long and significant look.

"Ay, we thank you," echoed his twin, Erroll.

She knew who was who only because Erroll had a scar across his forehead, but as a child it had taken her years to remember which name went with which boy.

"Well, aren't you two talking like honey's pouring from your lips?" Mr Wood, one of the nearby crofters, shoved Lyall and laughed.

The Reverend Bell grinned from his seat on the other side of the table.

"You know they are merely being polite," Fia retorted. "You might take a lesson or two from them, Mr Wood."

Errol and Lyall laughed, and Lyall shoved Mr Wood in return.

It was plain as a pikestaff that both Lyall and Erroll were sweet on her. Fia did not take their interest seriously. They were merely at an age when they wanted to be married. Almost any passably handsome and biddable girl would do. She'd turned down proposals of marriage from other men in the village these past three years and those men always found another girl to marry. True love did not last a long time.

At least that was what the songs said, old Scottish songs of love sung sometimes in the taproom, unhappy love that usually ended with somebody dying. Sometimes when Mr. McKenzie, a tutor to some of the local boys, had too much whiskey in him he recited the poems of Robert Burns:

O my Luve's like a red, red rose,
That's newly sprung in June.

Ha! She much preferred it when he recited "To A Louse On Seeing One On A Lady's Bonnet at Church." That poem made her laugh and had more truth in it.

There was no such thing as love, Fia knew. Men mistook lust for love, but it really was merely lust.

"Fia!" one of the men on the other side of the room called to her. "We're thirsty over here."

"I'm coming over." She walked towards the man, knowing Lyall and Erroll's eyes were on her back.

Once Fia had pined for the excitement of the city, travelling all the way to London and begging for work from Miss Parronley—Lady Corland—the Baroness, she meant. If only Fia had been content with her little part of Scotland.

She liked working in her uncle's tavern. It was hard work, and it kept her very busy most of the time. No time left over to think.

She trusted the twins would soon tire of making moon eyes at her and they'd turn their two heads towards some girls who might believe in true love. Or in the need to have a husband.

Fia next served some strangers staying at the inn. There were never many travellers passing through Kilrosa, but sometimes the laird had people come to see him. Most people travelling in this area stopped at Peebles where the coaches came through. Even Parronley, five miles down the road, received more visitors than Kilrosa. She eyed the strangers carefully, but they did not seem to take any special notice of her.

A part of her would always fear that *he* would find her and silence her for good. Lord Wexin, an equal to the devil in her mind.

She scooped up empty tankards and walked into the kitchen, greeting her aunt, who was busy stirring the stew that would feed anyone asking for a meal.

She carried the tankards into the scullery, pausing when she saw the huge man standing there with his arms elbow-deep in water, his shirtsleeves rolled up so that she could see his muscles bunch as he scrubbed a pot.

She gritted her teeth and entered the room. "More for you."

Bram Gunn swung around and wiped his arms on his apron. He smiled at her. "I'd say thank you, but I would not mean it."

He took the tankards from her, and she gave an awkward nod of her head as she turned to leave.

"How is it out there this evening?" he asked her. "From the dishes that have come back to me, it is a busy one."

He always tried to engage her in talk, ever since he had come back from the Army. He'd come home from France only a week ago, leaving the 17th Regiment behind him, so he said. He planned to stay in Kilrosa and help with the inn now that her cousin Torrie was in Edinburgh becoming educated.

It shouldn't be so hard to talk to him. She'd grown up with Bram, after all, like he was her own kin. He was her uncle's son, born to her uncle's first wife who died birthing him. Fia's aunt, her mother's sister, raised him. It seemed to Fia that Bram had always been around when she was a wee one, until he left to be a soldier.

"'Tis busy enough," she said.

He grabbed a large tray. "Shall I clear tables for you?"

Bram was always trying to do nice things like that. Fia told herself he was being a good worker for his father, not being nice to her.

"If y'like," she said.

She started to leave again, but this time he stopped her with his huge hand upon her arm. "Wait, Fia. Have I done something to anger you?"

She stepped back. "Nay."

He shook his head. "Then did I do something to frighten you, because you always seem in a hurry to be away when I'm near?"

"Don't be foolish," she retorted.

But there was too much truth in what he'd noticed. She felt

both afraid of him and angry, though she could not explain it, not even to herself. He did not look on her with that same sort of wanting that Lyall and Erroll had on their faces, but those lads did not make her think about being a woman like Bram did. She could feel her breasts when Bram was near. She felt her hips sway when she walked. And she ached sometimes, down *there,* and the remembering would come. Lord Corland. And Lord Wexin.

Bram walked close behind her through the kitchen. Even with the scent of the stew cooking, she fancied she could smell him, the fine scent of a man.

"If something troubles you about me—or anything else— you can tell me, y'know." His voice was low pitched, rumbling so deep Fia felt it as well as heard it.

"Nothin' troubles me but getting the work done," she told him, entering the taproom and walking to the bar. "Nothin' troubles me at all."

The hackney coach pulled into a coaching inn whose sign depicted a black man in exotic garb.

"It is not too late for us to enter separately," Miss Brown said.

"Say it no more." Tanner placed the strap of the satchel over his shoulder. "I will stay with you until you have reached safety in Scotland, if that is the only help you will allow me to give you. We can hide behind being Mr and Mrs Lear or any fiction you wish to create. It matters not to me, but I'm not leaving your side."

The intensity of her frown dismayed him, but he was determined. If he parted from her, he would always fear harm had come to her. He refused to have her life on his conscience adding to the tally.

He climbed out of the coach first and turned to assist her. The coach driver called down from the box, "This is the

Moor's Head, a place respectable enough, with all the coaches coming and going."

Tanner handed the man some coins. The inn looked adequate. He took Miss Brown by the elbow and escorted her inside.

They registered as Mr and Mrs Lear again, but this time the innkeeper had little interest in them, except to ask for payment in advance. He called a maid to show them to the room.

When the maid left and shut the door behind her, Tanner put their satchel down on a chair. Miss Brown, a frown still on her face, removed her cloak and hung it on a peg.

He'd hoped for gratitude from her, at least.

A lie. He hoped for more than gratitude.

He wanted her. She fired his blood in a way totally new to him.

His interest in women typically burned very hot upon the first encounter, at which time he would do anything to make the conquest. Flynn had been excellent at assisting him at this stage, purchasing the correct gift, finding the correct housing if matters went that far, arranging perfect liaisons. Tanner's love life had not been quite the same since Flynn left, but, then, Tanner had not found a woman to interest him until now.

Tanner could not deny he burned hot for Miss Brown, whoever she really was, but the difference was, he cared more for saving her than winning her.

Typically, hesitancy on the woman's part served to increase his resolve to win her. Miss Brown's hesitancy merely brought back the loneliness he'd been wallowing in shortly before the shipwreck.

Tanner gave himself a mental shake. No matter that she affected him differently, the important thing was to preserve her life, the life he'd saved in the storm.

He glanced at her. "Are you not hungry? I'm famished.

Shall I have the innkeeper secure us a dining parlour and some food?"

She swivelled to face him, elbows akimbo, looking the tiniest bit resigned, but not liking it at all. "If you insist on making this journey with me, no matter how unnecessary— no, *foolish*—it is, then we ought to consider how much money you possess before eating in dining parlours."

Tanner almost smiled. That tirade seemed better than an I-wish-never-to-see-your-face-again one. In fact, it seemed quite sensible.

He fished out his purse and dumped the coins on the bed. She walked over to stand next to him to count the money.

"Thirty-one pounds!" she cried.

He frowned. "It is not much, is it?"

"It is a great deal to some people." She recounted it. "But we'd best save where we can."

That would be a novel experience. Tanner was unused to saving. In any event, he was made quite happy by her use of the word *we*. "What do you suggest?"

"For one thing, no private dining room. We should eat in the taproom."

"Very well." He scooped up the coins and returned them to his purse.

The taproom was crowded and noisy, which did not bother Tanner overmuch, except for it being unpleasant for her. It was not much different from White's on a crowded night, except the smells were different. Neither better nor worse, necessarily, merely different.

They could talk little during their meal, at least about how they were to go on, because they risked being overheard— if, that is, they could even hear each other above the din. Tanner bought a bottle of port to take with them above stairs. When they returned to their room, he lit the lamp, removed his boots and settled in a chair by the fire with the port. Miss Brown sat in a chair next to him.

He poured her a glass. "We should create a plan."

She took the glass. "If you insist on coming with me, perhaps you have considered how it may be done."

He had not, really, but he could be roused to do so. He took a sip of his port. "I believe I can discover a way to travel to Edinburgh."

Chapter Seven

It should be astonishingly simple to reach Edinburgh, Tanner thought. The only limitation would be the amount of money remaining in his purse, but he had no doubt he had enough to get her safely to Edinburgh.

He wished Miss Brown would be as pleased to extend their acquaintance as he was. The look she gave him before crawling between the covers made it clear she was still peeved with him for not leaving her.

He ought to be amused by the irony. Women usually had their hysterics because he *did* leave them. Those women were easily consoled when money was offered to them. This woman refused the help his wealth could offer.

It made for a fitful night's sleep. During the hours that he lay awake, acutely aware of her warm body so close to his, he puzzled over the best way to get her to Edinburgh, to a place where she could be forever buried in the identity of someone she wasn't. Forever Miss Brown, perhaps.

He could not even toss and turn for fear of waking her, so he slipped out of bed and walked to the window, which faced the street, quiet now in the dead of night.

They ought to sail to Glasgow, that was what they ought to do. It would be fast. They'd be in Edinburgh in under a week if travelling first by ship to Glasgow, then by coach.

He had not yet suggested sailing to Glasgow, however. She'd been terrified enough on the ship to Liverpool. He'd been afraid as well, if truth be told. If he never sailed again, it would not trouble him in the least.

He took a deep breath and set off a spasm of pain that encircled his chest. He stood still, waiting for the spasm to pass. Davies's boot had done proper damage to his ribs. Tanner did not know what disgusted him more, Davies kicking a man who'd barely survived a shipwreck or Davies putting his hand around Miss Brown's throat.

Yes, he did know. His blood still boiled whenever he thought about Davies touching her, hurting her. Tanner's own hand curled into a fist with the memory.

The tensing of his muscles set off another spasm. He groaned and pressed both hands to his ribs and held them there until it subsided.

She stirred in the bed and he feared he'd wakened her. She murmured something and rolled on to her back. Dreaming, he realised.

"No," she cried suddenly. "No. Do not do it. Do not." She thrashed her head to and fro. "No!" she cried louder, her hands grasping at the air.

He rushed to her side and clasped her hands in his own, folding them against her chest. "Wake up, now," he said, trying to sound calm. "Wake up, now. It is a dream."

Her eyes flew open and she gasped, staring at him for a moment, still in the dream. Then she sat up and threw her arms around his neck. "This time he was going to kill you," she cried, burying her face into his neck.

He let his arms encircle her and he held her close, holding

her as if she were a small child. "See, I'm all in one piece. It was only a dream."

Curse Davies, he thought. Frightening her into nightmares like that.

"It always seems so real," she said, clinging to him.

The notion she was like a small child vanished like smoke through an open flue. She felt all woman to him, all soft, warm woman. How the devil was he to control his response to her trusting embrace?

"Just a dream." He carefully pulled away from her. "Lie down now and try to go back to sleep."

She grabbed his hand. "You will not leave me?"

He smiled at the irony of her speaking the same words they'd argued over half the evening. "I'll not leave you."

Thinking it would be wiser to go in search of some frigid bath water, he nonetheless crawled into bed beside her.

She moved over to him, lying like a nesting spoon against him. "Hold me, Tanner. Do not leave."

He took a bracing breath at the exquisite pleasure of it and made his ribs hurt all the more. It was not only his ribs that tortured him, however, but another much sweeter torture.

Her body trembled in his arms, and, among other needs, the need to protect her surged through him. He waited to hear her fall asleep before he placed his lips on her smooth, soft cheek.

"Mmm," she said, snuggling closer.

His last waking thought was a renewal of his vow to get her safe to her destination, to make certain the life he'd saved remained saved.

Marlena had a vague memory of waking during the night and asking Tanner to hold her, but she was not certain of it and dared not ask him if she'd done so. Instead she slipped from the bed and dressed and was pinning up her hair when he woke, stretching and giving her that lazy smile of his.

"Good morning." His voice was rough with sleep.

He rubbed his face, shaded again with his dark beard, and she wished she could rub it, too, to feel it scratch her fingertips.

He sat up and winced.

She frowned. "You are still in pain."

The corner of his mouth turned up again. "Only when it hurts." His eyes glittered with amusement at his joke. He stood. "I merely have to start moving again."

He walked over to the satchel and removed his shaving things, carrying them to the bureau upon which sat the water pitcher and bowl. She could not help but watch him. He glanced in the mirror after soaping his face, catching her at it.

She quickly turned away and busied herself with straightening the bed covers.

After he was dressed they went below stairs for breakfast. Tanner told the serving girl their belongings had been stolen rather than lost in a shipwreck. He asked where they might purchase clothing.

"You are fortunate," the girl responded. "It is not far." She gave them the direction.

The taproom was nearly empty at this hour, so after the serving girl walked off to fetch their food they were free to talk as they wished.

"I have been thinking about the trip to Edinburgh," Tanner said. "I dare say the fastest way would be by ship to Glasgow."

Marlena's heart seemed to rise into her throat. "Indeed." She swallowed. "How long on board?"

He tilted his head. "More than one day, for certain."

"Oh, my," she whispered. She picked up her teacup, but held it in two hands because she was shaking. She mentally scolded herself for her cowardice.

Setting her chin, she gave him a direct look. "If we must go by ship, we must."

His eyes seemed to shine in the low light of the taproom. "We do not have to travel by ship. Perhaps public coaches would not be more than a day or two longer."

She glanced away. "It must be your pleasure, since you insist upon being my escort." And, of course, his money would pay for the trip.

He took another sip of tea. "If you are not in too great a hurry, public coaches will do."

Two more days with him would be heavenly.

She glanced around, but no one seemed within earshot. "You must need to return to London as soon as possible. They will think you dead."

His brows knitted. "I have thought on this. Flynn, the man I visited in Dublin, was the only one to know I was on that ship. I dare say he won't learn of the wreck for two days or more, and then it will take a few days for a letter from him to reach London. I suspect no one will worry overmuch even then. I should have more than a week before I need to send word of my survival. My presence is not required. I may stay away as long as I wish." A bleakness flashed through his eyes, but so fleetingly she thought she must have imagined it. "We may travel by coach."

Marlena's muscles relaxed. No sea journey and two extra days with him. She ought to chastise herself for being selfish.

She met his gaze again. "Thank you, Tanner," she whispered.

His expression softened. "We are decided, then."

They finished their meal and left the inn in search of the clothes market where the serving girl had directed them.

"I need only a shirt or two and other underclothes," Tanner said. "And a top coat."

She glanced over at him. "You need a coat and trousers as well, if you wish to look the part of a stable manager."

He paused on the pavement to look down at himself. "Is my coat too shabby now?"

She examined him as well. "On the contrary, your clothes are too fine. Your coat fits you as perfectly as if it was made by Weston, and your trousers by Meyer."

He grinned. "They were."

After walking several minutes they found the street with its clothing traders, one stall after another, all calling to passers-by to come to examine their wares. Marlena found two dresses almost right away, and she picked through a box until she found two shifts that would fit her that looked tolerably clean. At another stall, she discovered corsets of all shapes and sizes and selected one that she could put on without assistance.

He walked away briefly, but soon returned to her side carrying a portmanteau. "I purchased this. We can pack as we go along."

She placed her purchases inside.

At other stalls Marlena picked up small items: a proper hat to shield her face from the sun, a sturdier pair of gloves, a spencer so she would not always have to wear the cloak. When they turned their attention to men's clothing, Tanner took the task in his stride, though he must never in his life have worn clothing that had once belonged to another. They found him a good brown coat and a pair of wool trousers, as well as a caped top coat, all that had seen better days. When he slipped on the coat to check its fit, she realised that it was the man who made the clothes, in his case, not the reverse. He looked every bit as handsome in a plain brown wool coat as he did in the one that came from Bond Street.

It was afternoon by the time their battered portmanteau was filled with clothes. Marlena could not remember when she had so enjoyed a shopping expedition, even though neither of them could have ever imagined making such purchases a short time ago. They dropped the portmanteau off at their room in the Moor's Head and ate dinner in the taproom before venturing out again to discover the schedule of public coaches.

Lew Davies left his dark corner of the taproom and hurried through to the outside door. He'd not yet found the right opportunity to snatch the woman. This time he'd be smarter and catch her alone and unawares, rather than break into their room at night.

In Cemaes, he'd followed them to the docks and boarded the same ship to Liverpool as they'd boarded. On the ship he'd watched them as best he could without them seeing him. He'd followed them off the ship in Liverpool and caught a hackney coach to follow behind the one they had got in. He even took a room at this same inn and had been following them all day, but everywhere they went, too many people were around, especially at that clothing market.

Davies watched the man drop some coins on the table as he and the woman rose to leave the taproom. Davies waited a moment before following them into the street, but he'd waited too long. They were no longer in sight. Not to worry. They would return to the inn eventually, and he'd already scouted out a good place to catch her unawares.

He returned to the taproom to have one more tankard of ale.

By the time he and Miss Brown had returned to their room in the inn, Tanner felt a pleasant sort of weariness. He lounged in a chair, the pain in his ribs settling into a tolerable ache.

He'd enjoyed this afternoon's adventure. Haggling with vendors had been much more enjoyable than he could have imagined, and he did not know when he had been required to figure out the best coaching route to anywhere.

Tanner watched her unfold their nightclothes and other thoughts filled his mind, infinitely more carnal. He'd have a few more days with her, a few more days to burn with wanting her. It occurred to him to merely ask her for what he craved from her with his body and his soul, but how was she, so indebted to him, to refuse him?

She stood in front of the mirror and removed the pins from her hair. Tanner watched her dark, touchable curls tumble down to her shoulders. If that were not enough, she drew her fingers through her locks and shook her head so that her curls bobbed a quick dance before settling again.

Dear God.

He blew out a breath. "Let me know when you wish to walk down to the necessary."

She turned around, now brushing her hair.

He shifted in the chair.

"In a little while." Her voice was soft. Caressing. "Unless you wish to go now."

At least the topic of the conversation was sufficiently dampening. He did note, however, that she gave the decision back to him. Even in this matter she would acquiesce to his wishes. It would be no different if he asked for a kiss. Or more.

"No need for haste on my part," he said.

A few minutes later he followed her down the stairs, through the corridor to the back of the inn and through the door to the yard where the necessary was located. Adjacent to the stables, it was convenient for those whose carriages and coaches merely stopped for a quick change of horses, as well

as those staying at the inn. She'd donned her newly purchased spencer against the crisp chill of the night. The horses
in the stables nickered as a door slammed in the distance.

She entered first and, as he waited for her, he kicked at
pebbles in the cobbled yard and listened to the muffled voices
coming from the taproom. He laughed to himself that this was
yet another example of the intimacy he shared with the sec-
retive Miss Brown. Except for the obvious ultimate intimacy
about which he could not stop thinking, he'd never been closer
to a woman. And he did not even know her blasted name.

She came out and he smiled at her. "I'll be only a minute."

When he finished, he heard muffled sounds from outside
and rushed out.

She was gone.

Another sound came from a dark, narrow passageway next
to the building. He hurried in that direction and, in the
darkness, could barely make out a man walking at a fast clip,
carrying a bundle over his shoulder.

Tanner charged after the man, who broke into a run,
reaching the alley behind the buildings. Tanner caught up
with him and seized him from behind. The bundle slipped
from the man's shoulder, a blanket wrapped haphazardly with
rope. The bundle's contents were struggling to get free.

Tanner swung the man around. There was just enough
light to see it was Davies.

"You!" Tanner growled, pushing him back against a wall.
"If you have hurt her—"

Davies seized a wooden box stacked up next to him and
slammed it into Tanner's already injured ribs. The jolt of
pain loosened Tanner's grip, and Davies squirmed out of his
grasp and ran down the alley.

Tanner turned to the bundle. "It is me," he reassured her,
pulling at the ropes.

They loosened easily and she threw off the blanket and pulled out the cloth Davies had jammed in her mouth.

"Ah," she cried, taking deep breaths. "Who was it? Who was it?"

He pulled her to her feet. "Davies." He felt her neck, her arms. "Are you hurt?"

She shook her head, still breathing hard, eyes flashing in alarm.

He clutched her to him. "I thought I'd lost you." But this was not the time to panic. "Come. We must leave here."

He retraced his steps back to the inn and they hurried inside and up the stairs to the room.

"Pack up everything. We are leaving now," he said.

"Now?" she cried.

He scooped up his razor, soap and shaving cup and shoved them into the portmanteau. "Now."

She picked up her hairpins while he rolled up their night-clothes. They stuffed everything into the portmanteau and hurried down the stairs. They crossed the empty entrance and went out into the street.

"We'll go to another inn. I noticed one on the way to the clothes market." He held her arm, and they walked along at a brisk pace, trying at the same time not to call attention to themselves.

Tanner watched for Davies, but it was impossible to tell if he was following them or not. There were too many dark places for a man to hide.

They finally reached the inn and entered the taproom to ask for the innkeeper. His brows rose in surprise at the request for a room at such a late hour, but he took their money and showed them a room two flights up.

It had little more than a bed and a table and two wooden chairs, but Tanner did not care as long as it kept her safe. He dropped the portmanteau on the floor and waited while the innkeeper laboured at lighting a fire. When the innkeeper left and closed the door, Tanner brought one of the chairs to it and wedged the back of the chair under the door latch. Then he crossed over to the window and looked out. A man would need a ladder to climb up to it.

Tanner turned back to her. "I think this is safe."

"Tanner…" Her voice cracked and she stared at him with pleading eyes.

He stepped towards her and took her in his arms. "You are safe now, I promise you. I promise you." He held her as close as he could and she moulded herself to him, clinging as if they were one person.

God forgive him, he'd lose his battle with his carnal desires if she did not break away from him.

When she did pull away, he threw his head back in frustration and relief, his breath ragged. He closed his eyes, trying to compose himself.

Her hands, fingertips soft and warm, closed on the back of his neck and pulled him down to her, down to her waiting lips.

The floodgates of his desire were nearly unleashed with the touch of her mouth against his. He forced himself to kiss lightly, trying with all his strength not to take more than she offered. Perhaps all she wanted to give was a mere kiss of thanks for thwarting Davies again.

They separated, and into the breach she breathed his name again. "Tanner." She closed the distance between them and this time pressed her mouth against his, opening her lips, taking his breath inside her.

He groaned and spread his legs, his hands reaching around her to press her against him. Her tongue touched his teeth, like a tapping on a door. He flung the door wide and invited her inside, letting her tongue dance with his. Her fingers dug into his hair, massaging his scalp, sending shafts of need to his loins already so on fire he might torch them both.

She made small noises as she kissed him, the sound rousing him even more.

"Make love to me," she murmured against his lips.

He broke away to stare at her, uncertain if he had heard her correctly or if his own desire merely rang in his ears.

She grabbed fistfuls of his hair and found his lips again. "Make love to me," she repeated.

He tilted his head, trying to see into her eyes. "Do you mean this?"

"Yes. Yes," she said, pulling him by his hands to the bed. "Now, Tanner. I want you to."

"You are certain?" he asked again.

She laughed. "Yes."

Now that the invitation was clear, he could barely move. Irony, again. "Have—have you done this before, Miss Brown?"

She backed into the bed and still pulled him towards her. "Yes, I have done it before."

His mind started whirling. She'd said she was a lady's companion. Since when was a lady's companion experienced in lovemaking?

"Oh, very well," she cried, suddenly pushing him away. "I did not mean to offend you."

"Offend me?" He was totally confused now.

"By throwing myself at you." She looked as if she would cry. "Forgive me."

"Forgive you?"

"Stop repeating what I say!" She whirled around and pressed her forehead against the window frame.

"Repeating—" he started, but caught himself.

He had mucked up something, but he was uncertain what. All he knew was, he'd been on fire for her—was still on fire for her—and he had somehow sent her skittering across the room.

"What the devil is going on?" His voice came out harsher than he intended.

Her fingers fiddled with the curtain. "I forgot myself." She took a shuddering breath and turned, hiding half her face with the curtain. "It has been a long time."

"A long ti—" He shook his head. "Talk plain, Miss Brown, or I may be echoing you into the next decade."

A small giggle escaped her lips.

Now he was really confused.

"I am sorry, Tanner." She gave him a wan smile. "I—I was so upset about Davies and having to run here. I did not mean to be so forward. I know you do not…think of me in that carnal way. I think I must have just needed—"

"Not think of you in that carnal way?" he repeated, then shook his head again. "What makes you think I do not think of you in a—carnal way?" Good Lord, he could hardly think any other way when he was with her.

"You looked at me so."

"Looked at you so?" He lifted his hand when he realised he'd repeated again.

She laughed.

He smiled. "I seem to have some affliction."

She waved a dismissive hand and walked back to the bed. "Perhaps we ought to go to sleep. It has been a long day."

When she passed close to him, he grasped her arm. "Let me clarify one thing," he murmured. "I think of you in a carnal way, Miss Brown." He made her face him and he rubbed his hands down her arms. "And I would very much like to know you in a carnal way, if you would wish it."

"If I would wish it," she repeated. She smiled. "I would wish it very much."

Chapter Eight

Marlena waited, her heart pounding, hoping. She longed to let her fingers explore where her eyes once wandered, to feel the muscles of his chest, the ripples of his abdomen, the roughness of his cheek, shadowed now with beard. She dared not act the hoyden again. He might change his mind; if he did, she might shatter like glass.

His eyes looked dark and soft in the dim light of the room. He gently lifted her chin with his fingertips and lowered his face to hers. With soft, gentle lips, he brushed her mouth, and, though her heart pounded, she remained still while he sampled, wishing he would instead take more of what she yearned to give.

The emotions of the night still stormed inside her: Terror at being captured, rage at being bound, frenzy at their impulsive flight. Marlena burned with the need to release all the passion her emotions ignited. If she stayed quiet and still much longer, she would surely combust.

Tanner broke off the kiss. She drew in a breath and held it. If she pulled him back to her, she feared he would withdraw altogether. To her great delight and relief, he, instead, slid his hands to her shoulders and gently turned her around. He untied the laces of her ill-fitting dress and pulled it over her head, tossing it aside. Next his fingers lightly brushed her as he loosened the laces of her corset. When freed, she grasped his hands and held them against her ribs, relishing the warmth of them, the strength of his fingers. She longed to move his hands to her breasts, but she feared showing so much wantonness.

She turned back to face him. "Shall I help you now?" she asked. She could not resist placing her hands upon his broad shoulders, sliding them down to his chest and underneath his coat.

One corner of his mouth lifted in a half-smile, but his words were breathless. "Recall, my coat fits well. You must peel it off."

She looked into his eyes. "I shall be delighted to do so."

She slid the coat off his shoulders and then pulled on first one sleeve, then the other. Reluctant to stop touching him for even an instant, she flung the coat over a chair. Tanner's half-smile was replaced by eyes that seared her with smouldering fire. She could not look away as she unbuttoned his waistcoat.

He stood very still while she removed it, and again she feared appearing too eager for him, wanting just to rip it off.

"Do you make your valet do all this work?" she asked, trying to slow herself.

He looked down at her with his half-smile. "My man would be shocked if I did not. A marquess must not undress himself, after all."

She undid the Dorset buttons at his neck and pulled his shirt from the waistband of his trousers. As she lifted it, the white cloth of the shirt billowed out to form a canopy that enclosed them both.

From inside the canopy, while the blood was racing through her veins, she laughed softly. "You are Mr Adam Lear now, are you not?"

His half-smile fled. "But who are you?"

It seemed as if the blood in her veins turned to ice. She continued to pull his shirt over his head, but she turned away to place it on the chair with his coat, and to retrieve his waistcoat from the floor.

She heard him move away, the ropes of the bed creaking as he sat upon it.

She turned back towards him and saw him pulling off his boot.

"I will do it." She crossed over to him and tugged at the heel of his right boot. It reluctantly parted from his foot. The left boot did the same.

"They are in sad need of polish, are they not?" he remarked, but the warmth had gone out of his voice.

Marlena suddenly felt as if thousands of tiny doors had quietly closed on all the impassioned emotions of a few moments before. She'd heard the doors latch the second he asked, *But who are you?*

With her head bowed, she turned and set the boots next to the chair. She dearly wished she could tell him who she was, laugh with him about her silly infatuation with him when she and Eliza first spied him at Almack's, describe to him how she and Eliza had decided he'd become much more handsome after they discovered he was a marquess. He'd enjoy a folly like that.

She could never be that girl again, however. She'd become the Vanishing Viscountess, the woman who, hiding in Ireland, had been hunted all through England, the woman who still had a price on her head, a reward her cousin Wexin offered for anyone who could prove she was dead or else bring her back to face her fate.

She walked to the portmanteau and took out their night-clothes, draping them over her arm.

"Will you not come back?" he asked, his voice low.

She glanced at him in surprise. "Come back?"

The corner of his mouth turned up again. "You've caught the affliction."

Her brows knitted. "Affliction?"

He grinned. "The Repeating Blight."

She smiled.

He offered his hand.

She raced forward to take it, dropping the nightclothes on the floor. His fingers closed around her hand and drew her back to where he sat.

"Now where did we leave off?" he whispered, his voice warm again. He brought his gaze to hers.

"I removed your boots," she said in a tone a little too clipped, a little too loud.

"Ah, yes." He placed his hands at her waist.

She stood between his legs. His fingers pressed into her flesh and suddenly those thousand doors blew open in a brisk, hot breeze. She closed her eyes, relishing the sensation again.

He gathered the fabric of her shift in his fingers, inching it up her legs before pulling it off altogether. A moan escaped his lips. She opened her eyes, suddenly nervous.

Corland said she was too tall, too thin, and she feared she would see disappointment on Tanner's face. Instead, his eyes caressed her. He touched her neck and his hand slid down to her collarbone, to her breast. He stroked her as lightly as he had kissed her. Sweet, sweet torture.

He moved over on the bed to make room for her, and she climbed up next to him, reaching for the buttons of his trousers, but he stopped her, holding up a finger that he twirled around and pointed to her legs.

He smiled at her. "Your stockings."

She reached down to remove them, but he held his finger up again. With more sweet torture, he pushed her stockings down her legs, his hands touching her bare skin. She gripped the bed covers to keep from writhing under his touch. When her stockings, too, were tossed aside, his gaze seemed to feast on her.

"You are lovely, Miss—" He started to use the name she'd given him, but cut himself off, and his expression hardened for a moment.

Not wishing to again lose what was building between them, she shifted positions, getting up on her knees. "Now you recline and I will roll your stockings off."

He lay back, but his eyes remained on her. Never before had she been so aware of her nakedness, and never before so relished it.

She removed his stockings and began to unbutton his trousers. His arousal pressed against the fabric. A thrill flashed through her and she daringly let her hand brush against it, wondering if she'd be brazen enough to touch it without the barrier of clothing. His muscles tensed and his breath was ragged.

Marlena had never removed a man's stockings before, certainly not a man's trousers. Corland came to her already undressed, covering himself in only a banyan. Sometimes he had not even troubled himself to remove her nightdress. In those first months of their marriage, though, when she'd been in love with being married, she had not known any better. The belief that Corland loved her had been sufficient to make lovemaking a thrill. She'd relished being touched, being kissed, feeling close to another person. Her body had responded.

Later Corland had used her eager response like a weapon against her, saying it gave him a disgust of her. Of course, he had no such disgust for the many other women he coupled with. She'd refused him her bed after that discovery, but it mattered little to him.

At this moment, however, she no longer cared if she acted unnaturally wanton. She was consumed with wanting the pleasure a man could give, and she wanted it with Tanner. Perhaps she had always wanted that pleasure from Tanner. Perhaps that had been what her once-girlish infatuation had been all about.

Do you think so, Eliza? she asked silently.

With a surge of energy, she pulled off his trousers.

As she moved from him, he grabbed her arm. "If you leave this bed to fold that garment neatly on to the chair, I vow I will start repeating everything you say."

She glanced back at him, the bubble of laughter tickling her chest. "I was about to do so."

With a flourish, she tossed his trousers into the air, letting them fall to the floor wherever they might.

He smiled. "Come."

She slid closer to him, and in a swift movement he was above her. His legs, rough with hair, pressed against hers. The male part of him also pressed against her. She was seized with an urge to look at it, like he had looked upon her, but he covered her with his body, and she soon forgot anything but the contour of the muscles that rippled beneath his skin, the weight of him, the heat of him.

Tanner raised himself up on his arms, enough for her to breathe and for him to kiss her. There was no gentleness in this kiss, no restraint.

She could not hold back now either, not even if he required it of her. She abandoned herself to kissing him back, taking his tongue inside her mouth, wanting more of him inside her.

She writhed beneath him, and he broke off the kiss. She burned with impatience. He must take her now! *Now.*

He did not. Instead he engaged in the exquisite torture of nibbling on her neck and sliding his lips to her breast. He took her nipple into his mouth, warm and wet and sending shafts of aching need throughout her.

She moaned, arching her back for more. He obliged her, tasting her other breast, tracing her nipple with his tongue, sliding his hand down her body to touch her in her most intimate place.

She gasped with surprise that he would touch like this. Corland had never done so—but soon she moaned at the delicious sensations Tanner's touch created. Suddenly, he slipped a finger inside her, another shock. Another delight. Her release came, rocking her with pleasure, and she clutched at him until the sensations eased.

She'd finished before they'd even started. Disappointment mingled with her satisfaction. "Oh, Tanner," she cried.

He removed his fingers and again held himself over her. "I wish I knew your—" He cut himself off, shaking his head.

He lowered his lips to hers instead, and, to her surprise, her body flared to life again. She ran her hands over his shoulders, his back, his buttocks, as firm as the rest of him. With his knee he urged her legs apart and she trembled with anticipation. In a moment he would enter her. In a moment they would be joined. They would become one.

She held him back, splaying her hands on his chest. He gazed down at her with puzzled eyes.

"Marlena," she rasped, barely able to make the word leave her lips. "My given name is Marlena."

He flashed a smile and kissed her again. "Marlena," he whispered low and deep.

He entered her, and Marlena abandoned thought and

embraced sensation. The air was filled with the scent of him and of their lovemaking. The only sound was their breathing and the caress of their skin as they moved in rhythm. His skin was hot and damp with sweat, and inside her he created feelings more intense than anything she could ever have imagined.

She did not want this to end and yet she rushed with him to its climax, building, building, until from beneath her closed eyes she saw flashes of dancing light. As her pleasure exploded within her with even more intensity than before, she felt him spill his seed inside her, his muscles bunching underneath her fingers.

She felt his muscles relax, felt the weight of him envelop her before he slid off and lay at her side.

"Marlena," he repeated, wrapping his arms around her, clasping her against him.

She melted into him like candle wax under a flame, warm from the passion they shared and from the heat of his body. Tomorrow she would think of how glorious it had been to make love with him, but now she was content to think of nothing but the comforting rhythm of his heartbeat.

When Tanner opened his eyes, she was still asleep next to him, his arm encircling her. He could feel her breath on the skin of his chest: warm, then cool, warm then cool. She felt soft and sweet. Her hair tickled his hand. He grasped a strand between his fingers and toyed with it.

Light shone through the window. They should rise and leave Liverpool as soon as possible. Once Davies realised they were no longer at the Moor's Head where he had last seen them, he would begin to check other inns nearby. They needed to be gone before he reached this one.

It seemed damned odd of Davies to pursue them this far.

For a farmer's son to travel to a city like Liverpool seemed nonsensical all on its own, but it seemed clear his intent was not to steal money, but to abduct Marlena.

Marlena.

She'd given him her name at last, while they made love, a gift that made his emotions surge when he joined with her. It must be her real name, as well, because the name was too unusual to be invented. Something else unique about her.

His ribs began to ache. A change of position would alleviate the discomfort, but he was loathe to wake her, so peaceful in sleep.

He distracted himself from the pain by setting his mind on the problem of Davies's pursuit. It would be foolish to assume Davies would give up now if he had not yet done so and it would be an easy matter for him to discover their direction if they travelled by coach. He could easily catch up to them by hiring a horse—

Tanner almost sat up, but stopped himself lest he woke her.

Hiring a horse.

A horse might travel all manner of routes, but a public coach had a predictable schedule. If he and Marlena—he enjoyed even thinking her name—*rode* on horseback to Edinburgh, they could stray from the coaching roads. It would be nearly impossible to find them. They could change identities whenever they wished, stay at inns in smaller villages.

He grew more excited the more he thought of this. If they owned rather than hired horses, they would be even more difficult to discover.

Tanner frowned. Purchasing a horse cost more money than he could afford. There must be a way...

His arm fell asleep beneath her and his ribs felt like someone was drumming on them from the inside. He tried very gingerly to shift her body, just a mite.

She stirred. "Mmm." Her eyes fluttered open and she looked into his face. And smiled.

He smiled back and suddenly his aches and pains vanished.

She stretched and propped herself up on one arm, glancing towards the window. "It is morning."

"Well into morning," he responded.

"I suppose we should get up." She made no move to do so, however.

He gazed at her, her creamy skin, the swell of her breasts, the deep pink of her nipple. He caressed her neck. "In a moment."

Her eyes darkened. He leaned down and touched his lips to hers. This time she did not restrain herself as she had initially the night before. This time she kissed him back, twining her arms around his neck, pulling him down to her.

His blood raced again and he was instantly hard for her. "Marlena," he murmured against her lips.

She laughed from deep inside her, and found his lips again. He relished this eagerness of hers, a match to his own. She'd surprised him the night before, and pleased him. He was more than ready to be pleased by her again.

Davies waited in a dark corner of the taproom of the Moor's Head, waiting to see the man and woman who called themselves Mr and Mrs Lear come down to breakfast as they'd done the previous morning. The hour was growing later and later and he was beginning to worry.

He'd bungled another attempt to capture her. It was that gentleman's fault. The gentleman always interfered. Davies vowed he would not stop him the next time he had a chance to grab her.

He rose and strolled to the entrance hall where he found

the innkeeper talking with a man Davies had not seen at the inn before. The man was dressed in what Davies would call city clothes and he spoke like a city man, too.

"I have a message for Mr Lear," the man told the innkeeper. "Very important. Where can I find him?"

Davies's ears pricked up at the name Lear.

"I have not seen Mr Lear come below stairs this morning, sir." The innkeeper held out his hand. "I will see he gets the message, if you like."

The man shook his head. "I have to give Mr Lear the message myself. It is not written down. Just tell me what room he is in."

The innkeeper seemed to consider this. With a shrug, he said, "One flight up, three doors on your left."

The man bowed and quickly took the stairs. Davies waited only a moment and then followed him. As Davies reached the top of the stairs, he saw the man trying the doorknob. He had not knocked.

The man opened the door and entered the room. Davies quickened his step. If this man had come for the woman, Davies figured he knew who the man was—the man who had bought the woman's clothes from his mother.

Davies reached the room, and the man came out, almost colliding with him. He appeared furious.

Davies peeked inside the room. It was empty. "They are gone?"

The man looked at him in surprise. "Who are you?"

"Lew Davies."

"Davies…" Recognition dawned on his face. He gave Davies an assessing gaze. "What do you know of them?"

Davies frowned, unsure how much he should say. "I've been watching them. I followed them here from the ship and I know this is their room." Davies decided not to tell the man about his failed attempt to capture the woman. Or that he'd failed twice. "They were here last night."

"Well, they are not here now." The man peered at him. "Why do you follow them?"

"My mam figures there is a reward or you would not pay money for the woman's rags." Davies shrugged.

In a swift movement, the man grabbed his collar and pulled him down so that their faces were an inch apart. "Now you listen here, Davies. I'll brook no interference in this matter. If you value your health, you will stop this and go home to Anglesey to your miserable little farm."

Davies tried to pull away, but this man's grip was too strong. "I'll not go home empty-handed."

The man released him. "I dislike competition. I'm a reasonable man, however. If you give me any useful information to assist me, I'll pay you ten pounds. You must agree to give up this chase, however, or I promise you, if I see you again, you will never return to that farm of yours."

Davies considered this. Ten pounds was pretty good money and he was heartily sick of this chase. "The gentleman with her wore a gold ring with pictures on it."

"What pictures?" the man asked.

Davies rubbed his face. "A stag and an eagle." He thrust out his hand. "Now give me the ten pounds and you'll see no more of me."

The man reached inside his coat and withdrew his purse.

Marlena donned one of her new dresses. Her newly purchased dress, she should say. Although not even as fashionable as the clothing she wore as a governess, the dress was a pleasure to put on after the ill-fitting gown Mrs Davies had begrudgingly given her. And for which Tanner had paid.

She glanced at him standing by the mirror in a shirt not

nearly as fine as the one now packed in the portmanteau with his finely tailored coat. For her sake Tanner was willing to wear baggy trousers and an ill-fitting coat.

She watched him carefully draw the razor down his cheek. Marlena pressed her fingers to her own cheek, remembering how rough his beard had felt against her skin. She sighed, and the mere memory of their lovemaking brought all her senses to life again.

After all the dangers they had endured together, perhaps their lovemaking had been inevitable. Whatever the reason, she would treasure the memory when she reached Edinburgh and must say goodbye to him.

Tanner wiped his face with a towel and turned to her. "I am—unused to making love with ladies' companions." His expression was troubled. "Do—do you know how to care for yourself?"

She did not know what he meant. "Care for myself?"

He averted his eyes. "You know. Prevent a baby."

She had become accustomed to not thinking about this. She waved a dismissive hand. "Do not fear. I am unable to conceive."

She expected him to look relieved. Instead, he looked sympathetic.

Corland had not been sympathetic. After a year of frequent visits to her bedchamber, he'd forced her to have a painful and humiliating examination by a London physician. Afterwards the man put a hand on Corland's shoulder and solemnly pronounced Marlena unable to have children.

Corland had wheeled on her, eyes blazing. "And how am I supposed to beget an heir?" he'd shouted at her, as if the physician's horrible news had not broken her heart.

Tanner dropped the towel on the bureau and walked over to where she stood. He said nothing to her, but lightly touched her arm before crossing to the bed where she had laid out his new-but-old waistcoat and coat, both brown in colour. She took his place at the mirror to pin up her hair.

He was stomping his boots on when he said, "I'll go below and see if they can give me pen and ink and sealing wax." He crossed the room to her and placed a kiss on her neck. "If you can spare me a moment."

She turned and put her arms around him. "Perhaps not."

He leaned down and kissed her, pressing her against him, urging her mouth open with his tongue. She regretted all the clothing they wore, the late hour, the need to hurry out of that inn. All she wanted was to tumble into the bed with him once more.

She managed to release him and draw away. "I will survive your absence if you are not gone too long." He tried to steal another kiss, but she playfully pushed him away. "Go."

Flashing a grin, he walked to the door and removed the chair wedged against it. "Put the chair back." His tone was stern. "And do not answer the door to anyone but me."

She nodded and walked over to him. He gave her another swift kiss before leaving.

After they had made love that morning and she lay in his arms, he told her his new idea of how to safely reach Edinburgh.

On horseback.

They would continue to pretend to be a stable master and his wife, but say they were on a working holiday to discover what horses were bred in whatever part of the country they happened to be at any given moment. He explained that she would have to ride astride, as a stable manager's wife would do, not as a lady in a side saddle.

Marlena had ridden enough in Ireland with Eliza, but she had not ridden astride since a child, climbing on ponies in the paddock, trying hard to keep up with her brother, Niall, and Wexin. Tanner suggested they purchase a pair of trousers for her to wear under her skirts to protect her legs. That idea amused her. She'd often envied her brother and cousin their breeches, when she'd been confined by her skirts.

Tanner's plan to purchase the horses was even more amusing—and daring. He planned to write a note, signed and sealed by the Marquess of Tannerton's signet ring. The letter would authorise his stable manager, the bearer of the letter— Tanner himself— to purchase horses on the marquess's behalf. The money would be transferred from the Liverpool bank. Tanner wrote another letter of reference for "Mr Lear" to show, also signed and sealed by the marquess. With any luck, someone in the horse market of Liverpool would accept the documents. When the letters reached London, his men of business would certainly be puzzled, but they would honour them.

And it would be proof that Tanner had survived the shipwreck and had been in Liverpool. By that time, however, he would likely be on his way back to London.

Within an hour Tanner and Marlena were riding in a hackney coach on their way to a horse market, with no one in the inn wise to their destination. Within three hours, Tanner stood haggling with a horse trader, while Marlena stroked the snout of a sweet bay mare with whom she had fallen in love.

Even though their pace would be slower than if changing horses frequently, the horses needed to have stamina and strength for a cross-country ride. It meant adding more days to the trip than a coach would have taken, but Marlena could not help but look forward to more days—and nights with Tanner.

As if reading her thoughts, Tanner glanced over at her. She did not dare show how much her heart was set on this horse lest the dealer raise the price. The same dealer also had a strong brown gelding that suited Tanner.

Tanner winked, and she knew the horse would be hers to ride. He followed the man into a room off the stable and Marlena hugged the neck of the horse.

"Dulcea," she whispered the horse's name, "I do believe you will be mine. For a while at least."

A few minutes later Tanner joined her. "It is done." He smiled. "Though my guess is each horse is a good four years older than he told me. No matter, they should do us nicely." Dulcea nudged him with her nose and he patted her neck. "Two forgettable horses." He turned back to Marlena. "Now to the saddle maker. With any luck we should leave Liverpool and our pursuer this very day."

He offered her his hand and she grasped it. Marlena had given up on happiness when Mr Rapp, the Bow Street Runner, arrived at Eliza's graveside, but this trip, alone with Tanner, through the beautiful countryside, swelled her heart with joy.

Chapter Nine

Fia made slow work of gathering the wash from the lines behind the inn. The sun had bleached the bed linens a dazzling white and they flapped in the breeze like an army of flags. It was too fine a day to hurry at her task, a day that almost cheered her.

She pulled one of the bedsheets off the rope strung from one post to another and did battle with a wind determined to prevent her from folding it. The sheet blew over her face for the third time, its scent as fresh as the air around her.

"Would you like some help with that, lass?"

She knew who spoke without seeing him, would have probably sensed his presence even if he'd not spoken. She'd been all too aware of Bram Gunn since his return to Kilrosa.

He caught the end of the sheet and uncovered her face, starting to help her fold the cloth even before she'd answered.

"I can manage this if you have other chores to do." She tried not to look at him, the sun lighting his face and giving reddish glints to his dark hair.

He smiled at her. His two front teeth still overlapped a bit, she noticed. They'd been a distraction every time he'd spoken to her. "If you need help, I've nothin' else to do."

He took the corners of the sheet and walked them over to her, so she could hold them against the corners already in her hands. He was a large man and she felt dwarfed by his size when he came so close. She wondered if the French soldiers he'd fought in the war found him an awesome sight when he charged at them.

Fia shook her head and took the folded ends he offered her. They repeated the process until the sheet was too small for two people. She placed it in the basket and he took the next sheet off the line for her. Somehow the silence between them made Fia too aware of his thick-muscled arms and the lingering scent of the lye soap used to wash the dishes.

"This must seem tame work after the Army," she said.

He smiled, handing her the ends of the sheet. "I prefer it tame. I was fair sick of fighting."

"Uncle Gunn used to say you liked soldiering. He thought you would never come home." She took the ends.

A shadow crossed his face. "Och, I'd had my fill by Waterloo, but the Army took several years t'let me go."

Everyone knew the Scottish regiments saw very hard fighting at Waterloo. Several families around Kilrosa and Parronley lost sons and husbands and brothers to the great battle. It upset her to think Bram, too, might easily have been killed.

He smiled again as they brought the ends of the next sheet together. "And Da thought you would stay in London and marry some fancy footman or shopkeeper."

She glanced away. "London was not what I thought it would be."

They met again and his warm brown eyes were filled with sympathy. "Da also wrote about the business with Miss Parronley. Lady Corland, I mean. It must have been a nasty place for you to be, when she killed him."

She kept her eyes averted. "As they say."

When she looked his way again, his expression was puzzled. She placed the second piece of folded bed linen in the basket and he was ready with another one, the breeze giving him a struggle with it. She grabbed the flapping ends.

He went on, "I must admit, I was glad to hear you'd come home where you have family to look out for you. I thought one of the village boys would have married you by now, though."

She peered at him, thinking he might be fishing for an explanation. Or perhaps Uncle Gunn had already told him she had refused offers of marriage. "Well, I'm not married."

Of all people, she would not wish to tell him why she was not married, that she'd sinned so greatly, sharing Lord Corland's bed, even though it was for fear of being tossed out on the street. Or about how she'd stolen some coins from Lord Corland after he'd finished with her and had fallen asleep. How she'd been putting on her clothes when Lord Wexin came in, dressed so funny. From the dressing room she watched Lord Wexin stab Corland in the neck with a pair of scissors and she'd cried out. Lord Wexin had then tried to stab her with the scissors.

She'd be dead next to Corland if Lady Corland had not come in and fought Lord Wexin off so bravely. Fia had been a terrible coward. She had run away after Wexin threatened to kill her. She'd packed her things and used the coins she'd stolen to travel home to Kilrosa. When the news of the event reached Scotland, Fia learned that everybody thought Lady Corland had killed her husband and Lady Corland had also run away.

Fia had been glad that Lady Corland had escaped, because Fia was still afraid Lord Wexin would kill her if she told anybody what she had seen that night. She did not know if she would have had the courage to tell, even if Lady Corland had not escaped.

Fia did feel a terrible guilt that Lady Corland could not become Baroness Parronley, like she should be. They said that Lord Wexin would inherit Parronley if Lady Corland died. If Wexin came to Parronley, Fia would run away again, but this time she would have no place to go.

"Fia?" Bram stood waiting for her to take the ends of the sheet he held for her.

She snatched the sheet from his hands. "I don't have time for all this talking. I can fold faster on my own. Go to your own chores, Bram."

She expected him to look cross, but his eyes were only tinged with wounding. "Ah, lass," he murmured.

He helped her finish folding the sheet, but turned away when it was done and walked back towards the kitchen door.

Marlena woke in the Carter's Arms, an inn in the lovely Lancashire town they'd reached the previous afternoon. Her muscles felt a bit sore after the ten-mile ride through the countryside, but they did not hurt too badly. She rolled to her side and watched the man lying next to her.

They'd made love again the night before, to her great delight. It had been a languid, leisurely kind of lovemaking, bringing her a night's sleep uninterrupted by nightmares. She smiled, feeling truly rested for the first time since Eliza and the children had taken ill.

Marlena let her gaze fall on Tanner's face, so boyish in repose. She felt a swelling of emotion for this man, so good, so strong, so clever—clever enough to find a way to take her to Edinburgh that no one would think to follow.

He'd purchased a road book and set them on paths where coaches did not travel. The coach from Liverpool went to Ormskirk, so they journeyed on roads west of Ormskirk, ending up a little closer to Scotland, in this lovely little village of Kirkby, with its redbrick buildings and white stucco inn. They'd had a lovely afternoon of sunshine and crisp breezes, setting a comfortable pace for the horses, all of them becoming more acquainted. She smiled just to think of it.

"Thank you, Tanner," she whispered.

His eyes moved beneath his lids, and she examined the fine lines visible at their corners. The lines deepened when he smiled. He had a strong nose, she thought, but soft cheeks. The beard that shadowed his chin was a bit lighter in colour than his hair, his thick, curly hair, so wayward, its flecks of grey barely visible at his temples. His hair always looked as if someone had just run their fingers through it.

Marlena took a finger and lightly touched one of his curls. *If you could only see him now, Eliza,* she said to herself.

To her surprise, tears stung her eyes. She knew it was because she'd need to say goodbye to him in Edinburgh. He had been so good to her. Would he have been so willing to help her to make love to her—if he knew she was accused of murder?

He opened his eyes and smiled at her, the lines around his eyes creasing. "Good morning." The lines deepened. "What troubles you?"

She blinked and returned his smile. "Nothing troubles me."

He looked sceptical.

She took a breath. "I suppose I am finding it difficult to believe Davies will not charge into the room or ambush us on the road."

He took a strand of her hair and twirled it around his fingers. "How can he know where we are headed when I do not even know myself?"

She laughed. She loved how he made her laugh when she thought she would never laugh again.

He stretched his muscles, then winced and pressed his side.

She covered his hand with her own. "It still pains you?"

He reached across himself and put his other hand over hers. "Not so much when you touch me."

She slipped her hand from his and stroked his chest, letting her fingers explore the hair peppered there. She returned to the part of his ribcage where there remained a purplish bruise. "Does it hurt still?"

His eyes turned dark. "I would not care if it did."

He pulled her on top of him and kissed her, a long lazy kind of kiss. When it ended she stayed on top of him, liking how his skin felt against hers. She touched his face, tracing where his beard grew.

"Does it hurt to shave?" she asked.

He gave her his appealing half-smile. "Only when I cut myself."

"You could grow a beard like old men sometimes do." She rubbed her finger on his chin.

He pulled her face down to his, scraping his scratchy chin against her. "I could do that. Would you like me to grow a beard?"

She rested her elbows on the mattress next to his ears and fingered his curly hair. "I am certain I cannot tell a marquess what to do."

He laughed. "But you might tell Mr—" He stopped himself. "Who the devil am I today?"

"Adam Timon." She gave him a stern look. "You must remember it."

As they'd ridden through the peaceful countryside the previous day they had discussed using different names each place they went. Tanner suggested using names from Shakespeare. "So I'll have a chance of remembering them," he'd said. He'd made her laugh then, proposing names like Yorik and Coriolanus and Florizel. At least she'd heard of those names. She had never heard of Shakespeare's *Timon of Athens*.

"Adam Timon," he repeated, flashing a smile. He swiftly kissed her, scraping her face with his beard. "May I make love with Mrs Timon, do you suppose?"

"If you promise to remember her name," she retorted.

His lips caressed hers more gently. "I'll remember." He kissed her again and whispered against her mouth, "Marlena."

She felt a flutter inside, glad she'd given him her name, something of her true self. She started to slide off him, to share more of herself with him.

He stopped her. "Stay with me," he murmured.

Her brow wrinkled in confusion, but he soon showed her the purpose of his request, positioning her and entering her this new way. She gasped and quickly realised she must set the rhythm of their lovemaking. She would be responsible for their pleasure this time.

Feeling giddy with the power of it, she moved against him, watching his face.

He pressed his fingers into the flesh of her waist. "Marlena," he groaned.

She watched his passion grow in the changing expressions on his face and felt it in the pressure of his hands and the flexing of his muscles. She was giving him pleasure, giving him herself, as she so ardently wished to do. There was so much she could not share with him, but she could share this pleasure. She could totally share this part of herself.

The need built inside her, as well, and she moved faster and faster until their pleasure erupted in unison, rocking them both. Marlena abandoned herself to the pulsing release, crying aloud as it reached the peak of intensity.

After the sensation ebbed, she rested on top him, as if she were his blanket. His hand lazily stroked her back.

"We should get up," she murmured.

"We should," he agreed, but he continued to stroke her. "In a minute."

She fully savoured that minute of languor, hating the moment of parting when she finally slid off him. To her delight, he pulled her back, rising over her and delaying their departure a little while longer.

Two hours later they were on the road again, with extra food packed in case they became hungry and a plan to continue north, on any road except the way the public coach would travel. The coach from Liverpool passed through Preston and ended its day at Kendal. Tanner plotted an alternative route, choosing half that distance to see how the horses fared at the end of the day.

Leaving Kirkby, they passed carts and riders and people walking to and from the village. Tanner greeted those who looked at them with curiosity. He was doing quite well at not acting like a marquess. Even so, Marlena could not see how people could not take note of him and remember him, he rode with such confidence and made such an impressive sight.

Marlena feared one of the faces of the people they passed would be Davies, but he could not know where they were bound. He could not know she was the Vanishing Viscountess, although each day passing made it more possible that a newspaper would reach here, reporting that the Vanishing Viscountess had been in a shipwreck and was missing. She was reasonably certain Davies could not read, but he would certainly hear others talking about her being lost at sea.

How many others had died? she wondered. Had Rapp died? She almost dreaded to know.

As they followed a dirt path through the moors, she relaxed. Here it felt as if she and Tanner were the only people in a beautiful world of undulating fields, brown and green and purple from the heather. The air was fragrant with heather and peat and the day was as fine as God could have created.

"It is so lovely," she said, overcome by the beauty of the place.

He smiled at her. "Indeed."

His eyes reflected the green of the hills. She would remember that when their journey was done.

He glanced at her again and began to sing, "Oh the summer time is coming, and the trees are sweetly blooming..."

When he finished the stanza, she laughed. "How is it you know that song?"

He rolled his eyes. "It has been sung at many a *musicale* at which I've had the misfortune to be trapped." He grinned at her and sang the second verse.

A breeze swept through the fields, rippling the colours. Marlena joined him in the chorus. "...all around the blooming heather, Will ye go, Lassie, go..."

This is happiness, she thought. *Look at me, Eliza, I am happy.*

Howard Wexin sat in a comfortable chair in the library of his London townhouse, sipping an excellent brandy he'd managed to procure and gazing absently at the leather-bound volumes filling the mahogany bookshelves that lined the wall. He'd managed quite a nice collection of books, he thought.

The room was elegantly but comfortably furnished. The large black lacquered desk at one end of the room made the tedious business of sorting his papers and reading correspondence almost a pleasure. The comfortable chair in which he sat was upholstered in Chinese brocade, as was the nearby *chaise longue*. The very best of Chinese porcelain and the occasional marble bust of learned men completed the decoration.

Wexin smiled.

His lovely wife, Lydia, was a marvel at choosing the best in décor. Every room of this London townhouse, which her father had purchased for them as a wedding gift, bore the mark of Lydia's excellent taste.

Wexin was grateful, oh so grateful that the Earl of Strathfield had permitted his daughter to marry him. Wexin had possessed equal rank with Strathfield, but Wexin had had no fortune. His father and grandfather had nearly spent the family into ruin. He had not married Lydia three years ago for the extravagant dowry her father offered and he'd fight a duel with any man who said he had. He had married Lydia because he adored her. Nothing could have stopped him from marrying her.

Nothing except her father.

Wexin stared into his brandy glass, remembering how close he had come to incurring Lord Strathfield's disapproval, to losing his lovely Lydia.

He smiled.

The Earl of Strathfield had, in fact, been of great emotional support to Wexin in those difficult days searching for his cousin Marlena to bring her to justice. The earl had even put up some of the money for the reward of her capture—or proof of her death.

That whole sordid affair would soon be over and justice finally served. After three years Marlena had been found in Ireland. She ought to be on her way to London at this very moment. Ironically, when justice was finally served and dear cousin Marlena hanged, Wexin would become the prosperous new Baron Parronley. Wexin had never expected this good fortune. He'd been way too far down the line of succession.

When, several months ago, news arrived of Niall's death and the death of his sons, Wexin could not believe it. As soon as Marlena was disposed of, Wexin would have both his Lydia and wealth. Life was very, very good.

He took a generous sip of the brandy, relishing its fine taste and comforting warmth as he swallowed.

A knock sounded at the door, and one of the footmen entered. "The mail has come, sir."

Wexin waved his hand. "Place it on the desk, if you will."

The footman bowed and left the room.

Carrying his glass, Wexin rose from his chair and settled in the leather desk chair. He might as well sort the mail now and see if there was anything important, such as a letter from the Bow Street Runner confirming arrival at Holyhead.

On top were two letters for his wife, one from her mother, one from her sister. He smiled at those, knowing they would bring her pleasure. Next was marked Llanfwrog. Odd. He broke the seal and scanned to the signature, his excitement growing. *Arlan Rapp,* the Bow Street Runner.

As Wexin read, however, he shot to his feet. A shipwreck? It was only a bloody short voyage from Dublin. How could there be a shipwreck? She was missing. He looked for the date of the letter. Four days ago.

This was not good news, although, if the Vanishing Viscountess were at the bottom of the Irish Sea, it would save the nasty attention and expense of a trial. He would have to wait longer for the Parronley fortune, in that event, and he greatly needed the funds.

Wexin took a larger gulp of his brandy.

The door opened and his wife, the beautiful Lydia, Countess Wexin, swept in. Her blonde curls were a confection of artful disorder and her morning dress showed enough creamy décolletage for him to feel hungry for her.

"The mail has arrived?" She breezed over to him and planted a kiss on his head. "Is there anything for me, my darling?"

He lifted his face for a proper kiss and pulled her into his lap, pressing his hand against her belly. He hoped she was with child this time. She'd miscarried twice, but perhaps this time the baby would take. He deserved an heir.

He held up the two letters. "Would these be for you, I wonder?"

She snatched them from his hand. "My mother! And my sister!" She slipped off his lap and hurried to the *chaise*. "I must read them straight away."

Her sister remained in Wiltshire at the country home of her wealthy baronet husband. Her mother and father were in Venice, halfway on a Grand Tour.

Wexin gazed fondly at her. "What is the news?"

She waved a quelling hand at him. "Do let me finish, then I will tell you."

He refolded Rapp's letter and placed it in one of the drawers. There was one more letter. He glanced at it and saw that it, too, was from Llanfwrog in Anglesey. He broke the seal. This letter was dated three days ago. There must be news if Rapp wrote again after only one day.

Wexin took a deep breath and read.

"Dash it!" he exclaimed. She was alive. Worse, she had vanished once more.

"What is it, Howard?" Lydia asked.

He looked up. "Nothing. A business matter. Read your mail and do not heed me."

He read the letter again. Rapp had discovered her clothing. She was in the company of a man who'd worn a gold ring and who spoke like a gentleman, and it was known she was travelling north. Rapp said he would follow her and made assurances that he would find her, seize her, and return her to London, but Wexin could not merely sit still and wait. The man had lost her once—who was to say he would not do so again?

Curse her! Damned chit. Marlena had always been an annoyance, even when they were children. She always wanted to do whatever her brother, Niall, did. Niall, like as not, would indulge her and ruin their games.

This whole matter was Corland's fault anyway. The cursed man had not been able to win at cards even when luck stood at his shoulder. It had not been Wexin's fault that Corland resorted to moneylenders who'd been breathing down his neck. It had not been gentlemanly of Corland to call in his vowels, however, money he knew Wexin could not pay, then to threaten to tell the Earl of Strathfield and all the gentlemen of White's Club that Wexin refused to pay his gambling debts.

The Earl of Strathfield might have forgiven Wexin for being the cousin of a murderer, but he would never have forgiven him for not paying debts of honour. If Corland had made good his threat, Strathfield would have refused for his daughter to marry Wexin.

And nothing could have stopped him from marrying Lydia. Nothing.

He just wished he could finish mopping up the mess Corland had created for him. Hang Marlena and be done with the matter.

Wexin covered his mouth with his fist as he rested his elbows on the desk and pondered what to do about his dear cousin Marlena, the Vanishing Viscountess, who ought to vanish for good. He doubted she would go back to Ireland.

She was friendless there now. There was only one place he could think of where she would go.

To Parronley. Perhaps she would rally supporters to her cause, and prevent her return to justice here in England. Or perhaps she knew the whereabouts of the maid, the girl who nearly foiled his whole scheme and could foil it still. Unless Wexin found her first.

He glanced over at his wife, her lips moving slightly as she read, breaking into a smile or a frown at whatever the words said on the page. He would still do anything to keep her.

She put down the letter and glanced over at him. "Shall I read them aloud to you?"

He rose and walked over to her, joining her on the *chaise*. After she read her letters he would tell her that important business would take him away from her for a time, though he hated even a day not in her company. If he used a fast coach and changed horses often, it would take four days, five at the most, to reach Parronley. He could not fathom how long it would take to find Marlena.

When he returned to London and the matter was resolved, nothing would ever again threaten to destroy his happiness.

"Read to me, my dearest," he said. "I am all yours."

Chapter Ten

One eventuality for which Tanner had not prepared in his brilliantly conceived plan was for rain. A grave error.

The moors, so serene and beautiful, now were dismal, cold, and wet. The horses, real workers the last three days, were slogging through, but too many of the side roads were like bogs. They'd been forced to stay on the main route, the route the coaches took.

He swivelled around in the saddle to check on Marlena, who followed a little behind him, looking forlorn in her cloak, rain dripping from its hem.

"Let me give you my top coat," he called to her.

She shouted back, "I've said no."

True. She'd refused his top coat at least three times.

"It is as soaked through as my cloak, is it not?" she added. "It would not help."

That was the closest she came to complaining, admitting that help of some sort would be desirable.

They ought to have stopped at the inn in the village they'd just passed, at least longer than the time it took to give the horses some oats and a rest, and themselves something hot to drink next to a warm fire. It had been a coaching inn, however. Some coaches were still on the roads. Even though it was unlikely Davies would find them after so many days and so many miles, Tanner had not been willing to take the chance.

They came to a fork in the road with a signpost bearing the name Pooley Bridge.

Good God. Pooley Bridge.

He had no idea they were near Pooley Bridge.

He turned around to Marlena again. "We'll stop near here."

She followed him unquestioningly as he followed the sign to Pooley Bridge. They soon entered the town, its narrow streets and stone houses familiar. He'd visited only the year before. Then he'd travelled to the area from Northumbria, which was perhaps why he had not realised how near they were. A year ago, after Flynn left him to marry Rose O'Keefe, Tanner had dragged Pomroy along on a tour of all his properties. They'd been gone for weeks.

Had it been only a year? It seemed a lifetime ago that he and Pomroy rode through this town and drank whisky and ale with the farmers and fishermen at the local pub. It even seemed a lifetime ago that Tanner had visited Flynn and Rose in Dublin. A lifetime since he'd stood in the cuddy of the packet ship home, lamenting his useless existence, diverting himself only by watching the woman who now shared his bed.

Sometimes it seemed to Tanner that time began when he and Marlena plunged into the bone-chilling sea. He had been reborn in a manner of speaking, with a new identity and new names each time the sun rose in the sky. Dash it. What was his name today? He had totally forgotten. Lennox, perhaps.

It did not matter.

"That was an inn," Marlena called to him, her tone a tad irritable.

He turned to her. "I saw it. We'll not be stopping there."

She scowled from beneath the drooping hood of her cloak.

"Soon we'll stop," he assured her. "Soon."

The streets were nearly empty of people, and, as he hoped, those caught outside in the rain appeared not to notice that the marquess again rode through their town.

Tanner and Marlena crossed the bridge over River Eamont and were soon in a tree-lined lane. The bright reds, yellows and oranges of the autumn Lake District foliage were muted by the grey curtain of rain.

"Have you made a wrong turn, Tanner?" she called to him.

He brought his horse to a stop and waited for her to come alongside. "Losing faith in me, are you, Marlena?"

She frowned. "I have lost faith in everything these last few hours. Ever since the rain soaked through to my skin."

His brows knitted. "I told you. I will give you my top coat—"

She held up her hand. "Do not even say it. I might snap your head off for it."

He laughed. "Miserable, are we? Do not fret. I promise we shall be warm and dry before you know it."

"We are headed into wilderness, Tanner."

Soon, however, the wilderness opened up, revealing a great expanse of lawn at the end of which was a large stone house, three storeys high.

"Tanner?" Marlena said.

He trotted ahead.

"Tanner," she called again. "This is somebody's house."

He trotted all the way to the front entrance and dismounted.

She followed him. "Tanner, this is somebody's house."

"I know." He extended his hand to help her from her horse.

They climbed the stone steps, and Tanner sounded the knocker on the door, striking it as loudly as he could.

"I greatly dislike this idea," Marlena grumbled. "It was not in our plan to visit houses."

He pounded the knocker again. "Neither was rain."

The two horses drooped their heads and nuzzled the grass, not even bothering to nibble. Tanner knew precisely how they felt. Too weary of being wet and cold to even think of eating.

He sounded the knocker again.

"There is nobody at home." Marlena pulled at his arm. "Let us go back to the village."

"There must be someone home." He pointed towards the roof. "I saw smoke from a chimney."

Finally the door opened a crack.

"Kenney, is that you?" Tanner asked.

The man opened the door wider. "My lord?"

Tanner laughed. "It is indeed. Let us in, man, and have our poor horses tended to. They are as weather-worn as we are."

The man nodded and stepped aside so they could enter.

"Whose house is this?" Marlena whispered as Tanner put his hand on her back and escorted her inside.

He leaned down to her ear. "Mine."

"Oh, dear," said Kenney, looking down at his plain brown breeches and brushing off a coat patched at the sleeves. "Let me assist you. Or should I see to the horses?"

Poor man. This was the shock of his life, the marquess visiting without notice, catching him in his comfortable old clothes instead of livery. "Tell us which room has a fire burning and we shall tend to ourselves. I should like the horses cared for immediately."

Kenney's face creased with wrinkles. "The kitchen has a fire, but that is the only one, my lord."

Tanner took Marlena's arm. "Then we will head for the kitchen, if you will alert the stable. Have them bring the baggage we carried on our saddles as well."

Kenney bowed. "Very good, sir."

Tanner led Marlena through the hall, down a corridor and some stone steps to reach the kitchen. As they came near, he heard the sound of pots rattling.

"Mrs Kenney! Ho there. You have visitors," Tanner called a warning. He did not wish to give her too bad of a fright.

"Oh!" she exclaimed as she turned towards the doorway. "My stars, it is you, my lord. Such a surprise." She eyed Marlena with blatant curiosity. "Good gracious me."

Tanner brought Marlena forward. "Mrs Brown." He put strong emphasis on the *Mrs,* hoping both Mrs Kenney and Marlena would heed his saying of it. A married woman could be excused behaviour for which an unmarried woman would be condemned. "This is Mrs Kenney, wife to Mr Kenney whom you have already met. The Kenneys are the caretakers of the house."

Mrs Kenney curtsied. "Welcome to Dutwood House, Mrs Brown."

Mrs Kenney's curiosity about the unaccompanied woman her employer had brought to his Lake District house was almost palpable. Tanner had no doubt Mr and Mrs Kenney would gossip with the villagers about Marlena after they left, but he'd brook no ill treatment of her while she was here. He trusted the Kenneys were wise enough to realise that.

"Mrs Kenney," he went on. "Mrs Brown is chilled to the bone. May I depend upon you to keep her by the fire and find some dry clothes for her? I will run above stairs and change out of my wet things. I believe I left some clothing here."

Mrs Kenney sprang into action. "Oh, my poor dear. Come here at once."

Mrs Kenney was so genuinely sympathetic, Tanner decided he had nothing to worry about from her. She would treat Marlena well.

The older woman ushered Marlena to the hearth of the large kitchen fireplace and helped her remove her soaking wet cloak. Tanner shrugged out of his top coat and draped it over a chair near the fire. He gave a quick squeeze to Marlena's arm and hurried out, hoping his memory had not failed him and he'd left some clothing in the bedchamber there.

Fia had nothing to do but look out of the window of the inn and watch the rain pouring down. Visitors were few, scattered at tables, merely passing time until the rain stopped.

She did not much relish being idle. It was so much better to be busy. Being busy gave her no time to think.

Someone walked up behind her. She could feel who it was.

Bram.

"It is a nasty day." He stood next to her.

She had hardly spoken to Bram these last few days, ever since he'd helped her bring in the washing and made her think on things she'd rather not think on. Worse than that, he had hardly spoken to her.

"Yes," she managed to reply.

It was a puzzle to her why she could feel the heat of him, even though he merely stood next to her. She could feel his breathing and sometimes she even fancied she could hear the beating of his heart. Fia worked around numbers of men every day. The taproom was a favourite place for men to gather, but she never felt the presence of any of those men this acutely.

With everything so quiet, she was even more sensitive to Bram, whose presence seemed big enough to fill the whole room, rather than just the space by her side.

He rocked on his heels, holding his hands behind his back. "The only thing rain is good for is to give us a rest."

She turned to him. "Surely rain is good for crops."

He smiled. "That is true."

She wished he would not smile. His smile made things flutter inside her. She turned back to the window. "I'd rather be working than standing here doin' nothing."

"Bram!" her uncle called from across the room. He was sitting with his feet up on a chair, passing the rainy interlude in conversation with Reverend Bell. "If you've a mind, the glasses could use a bit of wiping."

"Enough restin', I gather." Bram nodded to his father and smiled at Fia. "Come help me, lass."

What could she say? She'd already told him she did not like to be idle.

Bram smiled down at her with his warm brown eyes. "It will give you something to do."

She lifted one shoulder and moved a chair aside so she could go to the bar without walking next to him.

He stepped behind the wooden counter over which his father served the drinks and handed her a cloth, then a glass. She wiped it and gave it back to him to put back on the shelf.

"I have been troubled by something." Bram handed her another glass.

He expected a response. Since he was not looking at her, it was easier for her to oblige. "By what?" She wiped another glass and gave it back to him.

He took it from her hand. "I must apologise to you. The other day when we were out of doors in the fine weather folding sheets, you might have thought I was prying into your troubles."

Her heart raced. "I have no troubles." She reached for a glass and made the mistake of looking into his eyes.

"As you say, lass." He gazed back at her, and she felt something melt inside her. "All the same, I am sorry. I did not mean to distress you."

She snatched the glass from his hand. "I was not distressed."

She wiped with extra vigour and thrust it back at him. He accepted it with annoying calmness. In silence they finished all the glasses on one shelf and started on those on the next.

He finally spoke again. "It is said Lyall and Erroll are vying for your hand."

She handed another wiped glass to him. "Losh, they are mere lads. I do not heed them."

"They are not much younger than you are, surely," he went on. "You are twenty-one, if I'm doing the sums correctly."

She did not miss that he remembered her age. "And they are eighteen. It is a big difference."

"So a man and a woman must be the same age? To marry, that is."

"I did not say that."

"Och, but I think you did say that. You said—"

She interrupted him. "I meant only that a lad of eighteen is too young, when the lass is three years older."

"What if the lass is younger than the man? Is that different to you?" He took a glass from her hand and gave her another one.

"It would be different, aye." She wiped.

He inclined his head towards the vicar. "So if Reverend Bell sought your hand, that would be all right, then?"

She handed the glass back to him. "I'll not be marrying Reverend Bell and he's not wanting me, anyway."

He winked at her. "I was talking about age. Making a point, you might say."

She turned away from him. "My marrying or not marrying is not a matter for you to concern yourself over."

He touched her shoulder. "Come," he said in a soft voice. "I was merely talkin'. I did not mean to poke at you."

"I was just talkin', as well," she mumbled. She took another glass from his hand.

They continued their work again, but this odd awareness of him was worse when they were silent. She smelled the soap of the scullery on him, as well as the smoke of the kitchen fire. She felt each shift of his feet, each move of his muscles. He did not seem a man to be inside a house, even on a rainy day. She could easily imagine him in shirtsleeves, striding through the fields, rain plastering the cloth to his chest, parting his hair into wet curls—

She frowned and wiped twice as hard. She hated being at leisure to think.

"You—you are so much talkin' of marrying," she said, her voice accusing, even though the problem was inside her own head. "Maybe you are thinking of marrying. Maybe you have your eye on some lass here in Kilrosa or in Parronley, now you are done with soldiering."

His expression sobered and his fingers brushed hers as she handed him the glass. "The time is not quite right. I must wait a wee bit more."

She blinked up at him in confusion, not catching any sense to his words. His expression unsettled her so much it felt like her insides had coiled into knots. She wanted to be at peace, not to feel, but just to work and forget.

Ever since Bram had returned home, her peace had fled and she'd started thinking again about Lady Corland and Lord Corland and that horrible night. She again felt that same sick fear she'd felt for months after she ran away from London. It was as if Bram somehow made her numbness go away and now she must feel everything inside her.

"What is it, Fia?" He stepped towards her and put a concerned hand upon her arm. "You look so distressed."

She pulled away. "It is nothing, Bram. Give me another

glass. Let us finish this task. I've—I've decided to mop the floor after this."

His eyes continued to gaze upon her with concern, but they continued through the shelves until all the glassware was clean.

At the coaching inn in Penrith, Arlan Rapp sat nursing his ale, talking across the table from a local man. He'd asked the man if he'd seen a gentleman and lady passing through.

The man rubbed his chin. "A well-looking woman?"

Rapp nodded.

"Saw a fellow in Clifton travelling on horseback with a well-looking woman." He took a gulp of ale. "The man was no gentleman, though. Tall fellow. Just a man and wife travelling, seemed like."

"On horseback, you say?" Rapp lifted his eyebrows.

"That is so."

Rapp drummed his fingers on the table.

Several towns before someone had spoken of a tall man and a pretty woman. No horses had been mentioned, however. Horses explained a great deal.

In Liverpool Rapp had discovered that the elusive Mr and Mrs Lear had fled the Moor's Head and stayed at a different inn. They had made enquiries about ships to Glasgow, but had not booked passage. Even though the Viscountess and her companion had purchased seats on the public coach to Kendal, they had not used them.

Rapp knew deep in his gut that the Viscountess was headed to Scotland. He had to follow that belief. Trust that he would find her.

He lifted his tankard to his lips.

They were on horseback.

He'd assumed they had hired a private coach. He'd been wrong, but now at least he was on their trail. If he did not find the Viscountess on the road, he would certainly locate her in Parronley. He would pen another letter to Wexin, appraising him of his progress. He'd sent a letter from Liverpool, but this time he could be even more confident he would apprehend her.

He gazed out of the window where the rain continued unabated. Wherever they were at the moment, they would not travel further this night. Suddenly the bed in the room he'd let at the inn sounded very appealing.

He stood and threw some coins on the table. "I thank you for your information and bid you goodnight. Have more refreshment on me."

Chapter Eleven

Mrs Kenney brought Marlena a nice linen shift and the very softest wool dress her fingers had ever touched. The kitchen fire had warmed her enough that she could step into the scullery for a good wash before donning the dry clothing. She simply went without her corset, which was still too wet, but that was not so awful a thing.

Tanner returned to the kitchen, dressed in plain, comfortable clothes that Marlena imagined were intended for hunting.

"What have you that we might eat, Mrs Kenney?" Tanner asked.

"Some soup is all, m'lord." Her forehead wrinkled in worry.

Tanner smiled at the woman. "Soup sounds splendid." He turned to Marlena. "Does soup not sound splendid to you, Mrs Brown?"

"I should like nothing better," Marlena responded truthfully.

During their meal he entertained her and Mrs Kenney with tales of his visit last year with Pomroy, including a more detailed telling of the beard-growing competition. Marlena was full of admiration for him. He eased Mrs Kenney's distress at being totally unprepared for the arrival of her employer, by showing her that everything she did pleased him. And he eased Marlena's own discomfort, for surely the Kenneys thought her to be Tanner's mistress.

Marlena and Tanner left the kitchen when Mr Kenney reported that fires were built in other rooms prepared for their use. Tanner showed Marlena to a wainscoted drawing room with furniture built for comfort rather than fashion.

She settled herself on a large sofa facing the fire and wrapped a blanket around her for added warmth. Mrs Kenney brought them tea.

Tanner gave her an uncertain look. "Do you mind if I leave you for a moment? There must be a bottle of brandy in this house somewhere that Pomroy and I overlooked."

"Go," she said. "I shall be very happy by this fire with my cup of tea."

While he was gone she sipped her tea and allowed herself the luxury of thinking of nothing at all but the glow of the peat fire, the hiss of moisture escaping it, and the lovely scent that hearkened her back to childhood.

He strode into the room. "Found a bottle!" He lifted it into the air.

"Do you plan to drink your way through this rainstorm the way you and Pomroy did the last time you were here?"

He sighed in mock dismay. "I fear not. There is just this one bottle of brandy and no more than three bottles of wine. I shall save those for our dinners."

He opened the bottle, poured a glass and lifted it to his lips. His eyes closed in satisfaction. "Ah. I have missed this."

He never requested brandy at the small village inns where they'd stayed. To even inquire about brandy would have signalled him a gentleman in disguise.

"Are you not enjoying our trip, Lord Tannerton?"

"Not enjoying it?" He rolled his eyes. "Sleeping at inns that have been the very essence of mediocrity, eating the blandest food England has to offer, being required to recall which blasted name I possess each day—not to mention getting soaked through to the skin—what was there not to enjoy?"

She laughed, but then sobered at the honesty in his words. "Do you regret your insistence on accompanying me?"

He strolled over to the sofa, brandy glass still in hand. Brushing a curl off her forehead, he murmured, "There have been some compensations."

The mere tips of his fingers aroused her senses. Until the rain, their days on the road had been filled with breathtaking vistas and picturesque little villages. Their nights had been filled with lovemaking even more remarkable, more than adequate compensation for the discomfort they endured.

She moved over on the sofa and patted its cushioned seat. "Sit with me."

He lowered himself into the seat and wrapped an arm around her shoulders. Marlena nestled against him, savouring the scent of him mingling with the scent of burning peat.

"You must have had a more enjoyable time with your friend Pomroy," she murmured. "Staying at the finest inns, drinking the best brandy, and eating fine food."

He kissed the top of her head. "Good God, no!" He shuddered. "Pomroy and I were heartily sick of each other by the time our stay was complete." He tapped her on the nose. "Some advice for you. Do not embark on a long journey in the sole company of another person, no matter how great a friend."

She sat up and stared at him. "Is that not what you and I are about?"

He gave a chagrined smile. "Forgive me. I must have sounded gravely insulting."

She settled back against his chest. "You may indeed become heartily sick of me by the time we part."

He did not respond for a while, but tightened his arm around her. "I think not."

She knew she could never tire of his company. He made the morning worth waking for and filled the nights with exquisite pleasure. When she was forced to part from him, her world would turn as grey and dismal as this relentless rain.

Marlena wanted him to think of her as she was now, although she supposed he would eventually read accounts of the Vanishing Viscountess, who drowned in the Irish Sea. He would learn her true identity then. Would he believe she was a murderess? She would never have the chance to know.

Edinburgh should be no more than two or three days' ride now. In two or three days Marlena would vanish for good. She nestled closer to him, wishing the rain would never stop and they would never have to leave this place.

"How many houses do you have?" she asked him, just wanting to hear him talk, to feel his voice rumble in his chest as her ear rested against it.

"Let me see." He took a sip of brandy and she heard him swallow. "Six, I believe. Seven if you count the townhouse in London. I have my properties written down somewhere."

"Seven houses," she whispered. "Did you live in one of them over the others?"

"At Tannerton Hall, almost exclusively."

She and Eliza had managed to get their hands on *The Berkshire Guide: An Account of Its Ancient and Present State* from the lending library and they had all but memorised the entry describing Tannerton Hall as one of the largest and most magnificent houses in the county, the house and gardens designed by William Kent. She was certain she could still recite the description of its ponds and cascades and its sham ruins.

"Until I was sent away to school," he added. "Where I met Pomroy."

Marlena remembered her brother Niall leaving for school at age nine, looking very brave and, at the same time, as if he might cry. Tanner might have even known Niall from Eton, but she could never ask.

"You and Pomroy are indeed friends of longstanding." Like she and Eliza had been.

"We are," he agreed, taking another sip of his brandy. "Pomroy and I are too much of a kind."

That was not how she remembered it. Pomroy had always been full of outrageous mischief, frivolous beyond measure. Tanner, she and Eliza realised even then, had been made of something more solid and dependable.

"Useless creatures, Pomroy and I." He finished the contents of his glass.

"Useless?" she asked.

He shrugged. "When you have an elevated title, the people you employ are the ones who have the knowledge and skill to do the work. Not me." The clock sounded the nine o'clock hour. He inclined his head towards it. "Like the clock. The hands are what you see, but it is all those tiny wheels and things inside that truly keep the time."

She felt sad for him, that he could so belittle himself. "So what do you do with your time?"

He stared at his glass. "Play cards, attend the races, show up at country-house parties." He looked over at her and smiled. "I've even been known to attend the opera." Even his smile seemed sad.

He gently eased her away and walked over to the table where he'd left the bottle. He carried it back to the sofa and poured himself another glass. Marlena reached for her tea and finished the last of it.

He lifted the bottle to her. "Do you desire a glass? I am quite willing to share."

She shook her head. The wine from their dinner had been enough to make her eyelids heavy. She did not desire to fall asleep when she could spend her time with him.

He sat down next to her and she snuggled beside him again, taking his free hand into her own. "I think your hands are very nice."

He gave a low laugh and squeezed her fingers. "When they are against your skin, they do seem to be of some use."

She sat up and faced him. "Do not speak of yourself as useless when you have done so much for me."

He drew her back against him. "My finest moment, perhaps. Dashing from the privy to rescue you. Devising a means of escape that neglects to take into account the likelihood of rain—"

She put her fingers on his lips. "Stop this. I will have no more of it."

He grasped her hand and placed a kiss on her palm. "Very well, if you do not wish to hear me enumerate my many faults, there is no recourse but to talk about you."

The very last topic of conversation she would have chosen.

He went on, "For a start, where did you live as a child?"

She leaned against him again, not answering him. Her heart wanted him to know her, wanted them both to share all their experiences, their hopes, their dreams. She'd once wanted the same with Corland, but he used her girlish confidences to mock her later. Tanner was Tanner—he was not Corland and could never be, but there was little Marlena could tell Tanner without divulging herself to be the Vanishing Viscountess, pursued by a man Tanner once called a friend.

"I grew up in Scotland," she finally said. "And I, too, went off to school."

"Where in Scotland?" he asked.

She hesitated. "The Lowlands."

He shook his head in seeming exasperation. "Where did you attend school, then?"

"England."

He edged her away, placing his hands on her shoulders so she faced him. "Tell me more, Marlena."

She could not look at him. "It is enough."

He blew out a breath. "Tell me something. Anything. How did you get to be a lady's companion? How did you wind up in Ireland?"

She glanced away, trying to recall the details in the novel she and Eliza had read. "I—I was orphaned and had to make my own way. The school found me the position."

His eyes continued to watch her with scepticism. "Why Ireland?"

For this answer, she could only think of the truth. "When—when I ran away, I went to a friend who took me to Ireland to hide."

His eyes grew dark. "What sort of friend?"

She was puzzled. "I do not understand."

A muscle flexed in his cheek. "A gentleman friend? The man who…introduced you to lovemaking, perhaps?"

"Oh!" She realised why he might suppose this. The fiction she had told him about herself had not included a way to explain her experience in lovemaking. "No, it was not a gentleman. A school friend."

He nestled her against him again. "Then who was the man who—"

She told the truth. "A man who thought women in his employ must serve him in all ways." That described Corland very well.

"The son?" Tanner's arm flexed. "The man accusing you of theft?"

She did not say a word to counter the conclusion to which he'd leapt.

"That bloody bounder."

Yes, he had been. She hated allowing Tanner to believe something untrue.

Tanner must have known her husband. Gentlemen gathered at the same clubs and gaming hells in London. Marlena suspected Corland would have been very charming to a wealthy marquess. Her husband had been quite a charming man when he chose to be, to all appearances a fine fellow, in the same way everyone had thought Wexin to be a fine fellow. Tanner cared about her, she knew. He might believe in her innocence.

She still could not tell him the truth, however. If she told him the truth and he believed her, he might insist on clearing her name. She feared he would only earn the noose for himself if he admitted helping her, an accused murderess.

He twisted around to face her again. "Tell me who this man is. I will avenge you for it. I will make certain you need never fear his despicable wrath another moment."

Yes, he would risk his life for her, she had no doubt.

She put her arms around his neck and snuggled into his lap. "There is no need to avenge me. Soon he shall think me dead and it will all be over."

He held her face in his palms. "It will not be over for me until I know this enemy."

"If I named names," she said truthfully, "no good would come of it."

He released her and rose to his feet. "Do you have so little faith in me?" He picked up his glass and finished his second brandy. "I do not care if you are a jewel thief or not. Let me help you. You do not need to go to Edinburgh—"

"No." She put her legs up on the sofa and hugged her knees. "No," she repeated.

Tanner rubbed a hand through his hair, staring at her. He turned and reached for the brandy bottle again. He could fix this for her. He longed to fix it for her. Pummel that bounder into a bloody pulp for what he'd done to her. That was a task he would perform with pleasure.

At least he could get rid of the charges against her. Why would she not allow him to do so?

He poured himself more of the brown liquid and took a gulp, hoping the brandy would burn some calmness into his chest.

It did not work.

He looked down at her. "Tell me enough for me to help you," he asked again. "Tell me the name of this man and I will make certain he is laid so low he'd dare not lift a finger against you. You would not need to hide. You could—" He cut himself short.

He'd been about to say that she could come back to London with him. She could marry him. He could see that she was protected and cosseted for ever.

It had not been clear to him until this moment. He wanted to marry her. *Her*, not one of the fine, unblemished girls at Almack's who circled him like vultures, waiting for the instant he decided to give up bachelorhood. This was the moment and this was the woman to whom he wanted to give his hand.

He lowered himself down in front of her, his hands on her knees. "Tell me all if it, Marlena. Do not keep secrets from me. Do not decide I cannot help you."

She turned her head away.

He stood again and reached for his brandy, resisting the impulse to smash the glass and the bottle into the fireplace, to flare into flames.

"It grows late." It wasn't long past nine. In London the entertainments would just be starting, but he was suddenly bone weary. "I believe I shall go to bed." He turned to her. "Do you wish me to escort you to your bedchamber, or do you stay here longer?" His voice, so devoid of expression, sounded as if it came from someone else's lips.

Her eyes were huge when she looked up at him. "I shall retire now."

She unfolded herself and stood in her stocking feet. He imagined her feet would be cold on the wooden floors until the riding boots he'd purchased for her and her own pair of half-boots dried. How long before their clothing dried and the rains stopped? How long before he must let her go?

Tanner imagined their clothing was laid out to dry somewhere in the house. He'd told Mr Kenney to open only the rooms they might use. He had readied the drawing room, a dining room and two bedchambers.

Tanner took a candle from the drawing room, its small flame lighting only a few feet around them. The dark wainscoting faded into black as they walked in silence up the stairway. At the top a sconce lit the hall leading to the bedchambers, set side by side. An ancestor and his wife must have slept in the rooms Kenney had chosen. There was a connecting doorway in between. Mr and Mrs Kenney had made the correct assumption about Tanner and his 'Mrs Brown.' They simply had chosen the wrong night.

He walked her to her door. "You have your own bed," he said, still in this voice that did not feel like his own.

"Yes." She went inside, closing the door behind her.

Tanner leaned his forehead against the doorjamb, his mind and stomach churning with emotion.

If she did not allow him to help her, he would have to let her go, to say goodbye, to lose her into whatever name and life she disappeared when he delivered her to Edinburgh. He might never be able to find her again.

He pushed himself away from the wall and walked to the next door, the bedchamber designated for the lord of the house. When he entered, he saw that a lamp burned on a table. Tanner blew out the candle he held in his hand and set it down, looking around the room. Mr and Mrs Kenney had done a fine job of making the house ready and comfortable for them. He'd see they were well rewarded.

He'd been keeping a tally of those people along the way who had helped them or even merely been kind. They'd all be rewarded.

His purse was on the bureau. He walked over to it and poured out the coins. Not too many remained.

Perhaps Mr Kenney would be willing to loan the marquess a little spending money.

Tanner dropped the purse, still damp from the rain. He removed his coat and waistcoat, and kicked off his shoes. After washing, he put on the silk banyon Kenney had unearthed from some trunk. The garment still smelled of cedar. He strode to the door connecting his room with Marlena's, the silk robe billowing as he moved.

She might turn him away, but that would be preferable to her feeling that he had turned her away. His time with her was too precious to squander on a selfish need to have matters his own way.

He opened the door.

She sat at the dressing table in a white nightdress, turning around at the sound of his entrance. As he walked slowly towards her, she turned back to the mirror and brushed her hair.

He took the brush from her hand and did the job himself. From the light of a lamp, her hair looked black as midnight, pouring over her shoulders like liquid night, falling in soft waves and feeling like silk beneath his fingers.

She stared at him in the mirror.

He gave a wan smile. "As a lady's maid, am I coming up to snuff?"

A ghost of a smile appeared on her lips. "I shall have to make do with you."

He leaned down and planted a kiss on the top of her head. "I perform other duties as well."

Her eyes darkened. "Such as?"

He squatted down, turning her chair towards him. "Such as apologising." He wrinkled his brow. "I am not precisely certain for what I am apologising. Not for wanting you to confide in me. Not for wanting to make things right for you." He stroked her neck with his thumb. "For making you think I did not want you, perhaps. That was dishonest of me."

She clasped his hand. "Tanner…" she began, her face pinched in distress.

He made her look into his eyes. "If you wish to sleep alone, I will return to my bed." He could not help but add, "My cold and lonely bed…"

She laughed and rose from the chair, pulling him up with her. "I am certain we both have had enough of being cold."

He lifted her into his arms, his banyan falling open as he did so. She slipped her hands up his bare chest to wrap around his neck. He placed her upon the bed linens and threw off the robe, letting it float to the carpeted floor.

She reached for him and he obliged her, climbing on the bed next to her and wrapping her in an embrace all at once. His kiss was hungry, needful, as if he'd already experienced what it would be like to lose her.

She pulled up her nightdress and he broke off the kiss only long enough to tug the garment over her head and toss it away. She was beneath him, warm and soft and already pressing against him, urging him to enter her, to take her fast.

He thrust himself into her as if he too felt the need to hurry. Gentleness was forgotten as he took her as fast as she demanded and as hard as he wanted. She met him with each stroke, nails digging into the flesh of his back, uttering sounds from deep in her throat. He, too, could not remain quiet, his growls melding with hers in a strange duet, a song they both seemed powerless to silence.

He drove her faster and faster—or was she driving him? He did not know. They were like one person, not separate, not alone, not lost to each other.

Sensation rose, higher and higher, more and more intense. Thought vanished and sheer need took over, and still he moved with her, feeling the same growing crescendo inside her.

He felt her release vibrate and pulse around him, her cry ringing in his ear as his own release came, his own cry, his own symphony of pleasure.

It took a while for the sensation to ebb enough for him to collapse beside her. Though no longer connected to her in the most intimate way, he still felt they were one.

He wanted to crow with masculine delight at it, this feeling of belonging to another person, being a part of her.

"Now that is better," he murmured into her ear, tasting it with his tongue.

"Better than what?" she asked, squirming under his lips, her hands exploring his flesh.

He rose on one elbow. "Than being a damned fool." He lowered his mouth to her lips and tasted them again with more leisure. She pressed herself against his leg. Her fingers played in his hair.

With some rationality restored, Tanner decided it was far preferable to enjoy the time they had together than to rage at its impending end. Besides, he still had a few days to change her mind. She would not be rid of him so easily.

If he accomplished nothing else in his life, he was determined to accomplish this: making Marlena his marchioness, his wife.

He settled next to her, holding her close. "Do you know what, Miss Brown?"

She wrapped a leg over his. "What, Lord Tannerton?"

"I am in a puzzle."

"A puzzle?" Her fingers were now twirling the hairs on his chest.

Dear God. It did not take much from her to arouse him again. He almost could not talk. "That bout of lovemaking was quite...pleasurable—"

"But?" Her hand was now splayed on his stomach.

"Mmm, uh, it has also been very nice to proceed at a leisurely pace." He rubbed his thumb on her arm, hardly parity with what she was doing to him.

"And?" Her hand slipped lower.

"I—mmm—was about to suggest we try it slowly and—ah—debate which we prefer later."

"Very well." She touched him, circled him with her hand.

Other women had touched him so, but the jolt of emotion that accompanied the sensations she created was totally unique.

He lay on his back and flung his arms over his head, savouring each daring touch.

Suddenly she stopped and rolled away from him. "You must think me terribly wanton."

He turned to her, touching her on the shoulder. She curled up in a ball.

"What is it, Marlena?" he whispered.

"I was being too—too bold, too dissolute, too trollopy."

A laugh escaped him. "Trollopy?"

She rolled over to face him. "Is that not a word?"

He pulled her into his arms, his face level with hers. "I like you trollopy," he murmured. "In fact, I did not think your wantonness terrible in the least."

She blinked. "You did not?"

He kissed her on the forehead. "I was rather enjoying how...trollopy you were behaving."

She laughed. "Are you ever serious? I do not know what to think."

He searched deep into her eyes. "I am entirely serious, Marlena. Your enjoyment, your boldness, is a delight."

She regarded him a long time. "Then I should like to delight you more."

It took Wexin two days before he had made all the arrangements to travel to Parronley. He hired three men to accompany him, men who could be trusted to do what he wanted if he paid them enough. He'd hired them before, when he'd first searched for Marlena and that maid. Even though the men had not found either of them, he'd paid them well and they were more than willing to work for him once more, even to perform his ultimate wish, if he desired them to. He had a fast post-chaise ready to transport him and a coachman who thought they could reach Parronley in four days.

Perhaps he would find the deed done already. Perhaps the Bow Street Runner had already recaptured Marlena. All the better. One thing he knew, Marlena would never escape again.

His valet made a final tug on his neckcloth, brushed the fabric of his fine coat and declared him ready to attend the opera. He and Lydia were to go in the company of friends, including two gentlemen who wanted his support in a bill they would present in the Lords.

Soon, he thought with a rush of excitement. *Very soon my worries will be over.*

He nodded to his valet and crossed the room to his wife's door.

He knocked and opened it. "Are you ready, my dear?"

Her maid was fastening a garnet necklace around her neck. "One moment, Howard."

The maid stepped back. "There, ma'am."

Lydia fussed with the jewels. "Thank you, Nancy." She stood and turned to her admiring husband. "I am quite ready now."

"You look ravishing," he said.

The maid held out her velvet cloak. Wexin took it and draped it over his arm. "Let us go then, my dear."

She held his arm down the marble staircase. "I do wish you would not go off on business tomorrow, Howard. I shall miss you so."

He patted her hand. "And I shall miss you."

They reached the hall where the butler bowed and said, "The carriage is waiting, sir."

Wexin took his hat and gloves from the man and put them on.

"Then allow me to accompany you," Lydia persisted. "I should like to go with you.

He turned to assist her into her cloak. "I would not dream of putting you through something so tedious." He smiled. "I assure you, I will return very soon."

Her beautiful eyes were tinged with unhappiness.

He patted her on the hand again. "Do not look so sad. I shall bring you a gift."

She frowned. "I do not want a gift. I want to be with you."

"Ah, but it shall be a great gift." He smiled. If only she knew how great a gift he planned to give her. He planned, after all, to secure their future together.

Chapter Twelve

Marlena woke to the sound of rain pattering against the window glass. For a moment she thought it was still night, it was so dark in the room, but she could spy a very grey morning through a gap in the curtains.

Tanner was not next to her. She sat up and combed her fingers through her tangled hair.

"Good morning." Tanner stood in the doorway connecting his bedchamber to hers. He rested against the doorframe, dressed in the coat and trousers he'd worn the night before.

"You are dressed already," she said.

He smiled and crossed the room to her, leaning down to give her a warm kiss.

He murmured against her lips, "I could easily undress again."

She was tempted and laughed. "What time is it?"

"Eleven."

"Eleven!" She grabbed her nightdress and put it on. "I had no idea it was so late! Why did you not wake me?"

He sat on the bed. "To what purpose? It was my pleasure to let you sleep as long as you wished."

She slipped off the bed and padded over to the water pitcher and bowl to splash water on her face. "I am not used to staying in bed so long."

Marlena had not slept this late since Corland had been alive and she'd had so little to do.

He walked over to her and hugged her from behind. "Shall I act the lady's maid this morning?"

She reached up and stroked his hair. "I do not know a lady's maid who acts as you do."

He stilled. "Did you once have a lady's maid, Marlena?"

She wished she had not spoken. It was becoming more and more difficult to lie to him about herself, especially when Tanner knew her more intimately than anyone else ever had.

"I did have a lady's maid." She averted her gaze.

The muscles of his arms flexed as if he were surprised that she answered him. They stilled again as if he were thinking of asking her another question about herself.

She turned to him. "Perhaps you can sit on the bed? You make a particularly distracting lady's maid. I will tell you when I need you."

He nuzzled her neck before complying.

It was erotic in its own way to have him watch her wash up and dress. True to his promise, he assisted her in tying the laces on her dress, brushed the tangles from her hair, and, when she was ready, he escorted her below stairs for a simple breakfast of fresh bread, cheese and coddled eggs.

"What did you do while I was sleeping?" she asked as they ate.

His brows came together. "I wrote a letter to London. News of my being aboard the wrecked ship should be reaching my people by now, as well as the documents for the horse purchase." He pierced a piece of egg with his fork and smiled. "My cousin Algernon will be delighted I did not drown. He would have apoplexy if he thought he must become the marquess."

Marlena could not recall ever meeting Tanner's cousin, but she could too easily imagine how those close to Tanner would grieve his loss. "Of course you must let them know you are alive."

He became serious again. "By the time the letter reaches my secretary, you shall be…settled. You need not fear. No one will question my decision to visit one of my properties."

His concern for her brought an ache to her heart. No man had ever cared so much for her. No man had ever put her needs above all else.

For all her initial protests that she could make this journey alone, she knew now she could not have done it without him. She not only owed him her life—she owed him her freedom. The thought of parting from him became ever more unbearable.

He took a sip of tea. "Kenney will carry the letter into the village as soon as the rain clears."

Marlena could imagine Mr and Mrs Kenney telling their friends in the village that the marquess had brought a woman with him. She was confident they would never realize her true identity. Even if they read of the shipwreck, Tanner had said nothing to them about being on the ship. They would never know enough to connect Tanner with the Vanishing Viscountess.

Tanner would know, however. Marlena's appetite fled.

He cleaned his plate and leaned in his chair, balancing it on its two back legs. "What shall we do today?"

She half-expected the chair to slip out from under him, but he seemed heedless of the possibility. "Whatever you wish. I confess it will feel odd to be inside instead of travelling." To be at leisure instead of running.

He smiled. "Let us go on a treasure hunt."

"A treasure hunt?"

He lowered the chair again, to her relief. "We'll explore the house. My grandfather was fond of this house. I can recall visiting him here. Let us see what treasures he and my grandmother left behind. We may discover something useful for our trip."

By mid-afternoon they were in the attic, digging through big wooden chests. Tanner had discovered a lovely wool shawl, now draped around Marlena's shoulders. He also unearthed a gentleman's white wig and coat of bright green silk.

He put both on. "These might have been my grandfather's, although I can well remember my father in wig and lace." He posed for her. "How do I look?"

She giggled. "Quite foppish, actually."

He grinned and knelt down to rummage through the cedar-lined trunk.

"How old were you when your father died?" she asked.

He looked up. "Nineteen."

"So young?" She tried to imagine him that young having such an important title thrust upon him.

He shrugged. "He was thrown from his horse."

"And your mother?"

He pulled the wig off his head and busied himself with the contents of the trunk. "I was about ten. She died in childbirth."

She knew he did not have any brothers or sisters so he had lost his whole family, just as she had.

He sat back and fixed his gaze on her. "And your parents?"

She stared at him for a moment, then told the truth. "My—my mother died of childbirth fever. My father died much later. He was struck by lightning."

"Struck by lightning?"

She nodded. "I confess to having a fear of storms ever since."

His eyes filled with sympathy and he reached across the trunk to stroke her cheek. "And have you any family left?"

Tears stung her eyes as an image of her brother and her sweet little nephews formed in her mind. She shook her head.

"Then we are alike, you and I. Alone," he murmured.

The ache in Marlena's heart returned as their gazes held.

Tanner withdrew his hand and returned to the chest. Marlena peeked inside at more bright-coloured brocades that Tanner folded over as he searched deeper.

"I do not think pink silk is the thing to wear while travelling, do you?" He glanced up at her, his usual good humour returning—except for a remaining hint of emotion in his eyes.

She smiled. "Perhaps not."

He felt along the sides and the bottom and pulled out a flat wooden box. "Here's something."

He opened the hinged lid. Inside were lovely ladies' handkerchiefs of white linen and lace.

"You must have these." He said this in the most casual of voices.

She lifted one and unfolded it. "They are beautiful."

He gazed at her, one corner of his mouth lifting into a wistful smile.

He looked down at the box again. "There is something else." He unfolded one of the handkerchiefs to reveal a lady's ring.

He placed it in Marlena's hand.

"Oh, my!" She held it up to the light of their lamp.

It was a delicate sapphire ring, its glittering blue stone encircled in tiny gold leaves and flowers. "It is so lovely."

She handed it back to him, but he would not take it. "Try it on."

She slipped it on the ring finger of her right hand and it

fitted her as if made for her. She held her hand so he could see how pretty it was.

He smiled. "It must have been my grandmother's."

Marlena admired it a moment more before she began pulling it off.

He stopped her with his hand. "Wear it. I want you to have it."

"But it is a family piece," she protested.

He waved a quelling hand. "I want you to have it."

She gazed down it again. "I shall treasure it always."

They turned their attention back to the trunk and then to the next trunk and the next, eventually selecting two old top coats that might prove useful on the journey, as well as the lace handkerchief and Tanner's grandmother's sapphire ring. When they were finished it was nearly time for dinner.

That evening when they sat in the drawing room, Tanner read *Timon of Athens* from a copy of the Shakespeare play he'd discovered in the library. Marlena relaxed by the fire, listening to his deep, expressive voice, the woollen shawl wrapped around her shoulders, the sapphire ring sparkling in the firelight. She wished the rain would never end. She wished she could stay right where she was, with Tanner, for ever.

As she did every Sunday, Fia accompanied her Uncle Gunn and Aunt Priss to the old stone church that had stood between Parronley and Kilrosa for over two hundred years. Bram, of course, was also one of the party, and it was only natural that he walked next to Fia. Even though the sun shone, the roads were still muddy, and Bram took hold of Fia's arm when the ruts in the road made walking difficult.

Fia followed her aunt and uncle to their usual pew, filing

in after them. Bram sat next to Fia, looming over her like he always did. She picked up the prayer book and opened it.

Soon the service began, and Reverend Bell recited the Ten Commandments, the congregation responding in unison. When the reverend came to *Thou shalt not commit adultery,* Fia closed her eyes.

"Lord, have mercy upon us, and incline our hearts to keep this law," she answered along with the others. She hoped God knew how fervently she meant what she said.

Sometimes Fia felt as if she did not belong in the church with all these good people. Still, the sound of their collective voices in prayer, the light filtering through the coloured glass of the windows, the smell of wood and stone and people, all gave her comfort.

Reverend Bell began his sermon, speaking on the virtue of moderation. Fia had to stifle a smile at his choice of topic, this man who spent so much time drinking immoderately in the taproom of the Black Agnes. She made the mistake of glancing at Bram, whose twinkling eyes reflected her amusement.

When the last amens were spoken, the congregation filed out of the church and back into the sunshine. Most lingered to greet Reverend Bell and the elders, as well as to pass time with their neighbours. Fia drifted off to the edge of the group to wait for Uncle Gunn and Aunt Priss, who were as busy chatting as were the others. Pretty Jean Skinner waylaid Bram and now held him captive with her flirting and her silly talk.

Fia glanced away and took another step back. Lyall and Erroll gave her a friendly nod as they walked by, but, as she had predicted, their affections had been transferred elsewhere, to the Brookston sisters, who giggled at every word they said. For once, though, Fia wished they would pay her such attentions, so that perhaps she could be distracted from this odd pain in her chest from watching Bram with Jean.

To her shock Fia felt tears stinging her eyes. She blinked several times, but the tears kept forming anyway. She was also finding it hard to breathe without shuddering. If anyone noticed, what would she ever say? How could she explain?

"Aunt Priss," she called out, hoping she was too far away for her aunt to see anything amiss. "I'm startin' for home."

Her aunt nodded and waved and Fia spun on her heels, trying her best not to look like she was in a big hurry.

As soon as she reached the top of the hill, she turned off the road. Her aunt and uncle would visit with their friends for at least half an hour. She could take the time to collect herself before she walked back to the inn and began working. She did not want to start bawling while she was working. That would be nearly as bad as bawling outside church. Somebody would ask her what was wrong, and she didn't know the answer to that question.

She took the path that led up another hill, climbing to the top where a castle once stood. It was naught but a pile of old stones now, but she liked the place. She climbed up on one of the stones, warmed by the sun, and sat cross-legged, gazing down at Parronley House in the distance.

Seeing the fine house made her think of the lady who ought to be living there now. Everybody knew Lady Corland was now Baroness Parronley, since her brother and his little boys died. It was Fia's fault that the Baroness could not return to her house. If Fia had not sinned with Lord Corland, maybe all the awful things would not have happened.

If only Fia had not left Kilrosa. If only she'd stayed and waited and heeded the scriptures and remained a virtuous girl, she might be worthy to marry a good man.

She did not try to stop the tears. She had not cried for over two years now and she had thought all her tears were gone. But then Bram came home and now she felt like spilling tears every day. Seeing him with Jean had done it this time.

Some day Jean or some other good, decent girl would marry Bram in that very church where Fia sat next to him this day. Maybe if Fia cried out all her tears now, she would have no more to shed when Bram married.

Fia rocked back and forth, arms wrapped around herself, keening with grief. That day Lord Corland died, it was like she had died, too, and Lady Corland—Baroness Parronley. She and Baroness Parronley might as well be dead.

"What is this, lass? Why are you weeping?"

She jumped and snapped her head up to see Bram walking towards her. She turned away from him, but he soon was standing in front of her.

"Are you ailing?" he asked.

She took a shuddering breath and shook her head.

His hand touched her arm. "Fia lass, tell me what is wrong."

She wiped her eyes with her fingers. "I came here to be alone, Bram."

His hand fell away. "I saw you leave the church and somethin' told me to follow. You don't do weeping like this without reason. If something is so wrong, let me aid you."

She lifted her face to him and stared into his eyes. "You cannot help me." She glanced away. "There's nothing to help me."

He climbed up on the stone and sat beside her. She moved away, but could not go far or she'd fall off.

He stared out on to the valley below. "You were just a wee lass when I left for war, Fia. Twelve years old, but already the bonniest lass I knew. Bright-eyed and lively and full of wanting to know everything. You were the daughter Mam

Priss prayed for." He shifted his position. "What happened in London to change you?"

She tried to shrug him off. "You were gone, Bram. You do not know that anything changed me but time."

He lifted his hand, but dropped it again. "Mam Priss said you came back different. And you came back after Miss Parronley killed her husband."

She twisted away from him. "She'd be Baroness Parronley."

"Baroness, then." He peered at her. "Does it have to do with the murder, then?"

She jumped off the rock. "You all talk a great deal."

She started running down the hill but he caught her from behind and spun her around. She tried to swing a fist at him and to pull away, but he held her fast.

"Let me go, Bram," she cried, struggling, but unable to dislodge his large hand around her arm.

He pulled her against him and wrapped his arms around her, engulfing her with his huge warm body. "I will hold you 'til you tell me, lass. I promise to tell no other, but let me know what disturbs you and I'll not bother you over it again."

"Are you forcing me, Bram Gunn?" she mumbled into his chest.

"Ay, I am indeed." He murmured, holding her closer. "Now commence with talking."

"First you have to let me go," she said.

"Say something that is not blather and I'll think on it."

She could never tell him how her heart seemed to cleave in two pieces when he smiled at Jean Skinner. That would be too shaming, but, in the shelter of his strong arms and warm body, she thought it might be safe to tell him about that terrible night. She wanted to tell Bram, who seemed so strong he could carry anything, including this burden she had carried alone for so long.

"I'll do it. I'll do it," she said. "Give me room to breathe."

He loosened his hold on her only a bit.

"Lady Corland did not kill her husband," she began.

His brows rose.

"I was there, Bram." She felt herself turn cold as she remembered it. "I saw it all."

He took her hand and walked her back to sit upon the rock, settling next to her. "Tell me of it, lass."

She took a breath. "I was in the room—in—in Lord Corland's bedchamber."

Fia glanced at Bram, expecting to see his lips purse in disapproval. Instead, he merely nodded for her to go on.

"A man entered the room. He did not see me, but I saw him. He—he was dressed oddly. In Lady Corland's robe. I knew it because it had a lace trim." She swallowed. "The—the man walked over to the bed and leaned over. At first I thought he was going to kiss Lord Corland, but instead—instead..." She faltered.

"Who was the fellow?" he asked mildly.

She turned to face him. "Lord Wexin."

"Lord Wexin?" His eyes widened.

She nodded. "Lady Corland's cousin. The man who inherits Parronley if she is dead." She glanced away again. "He—he—pulled out scissors and—and stabbed Lord Corland in the throat." Her fingers flexed and her hand jabbed as if it were she holding the weapon.

He covered her hand with his own.

Her voice rose higher in pitch and the words poured out. "I guess I screamed, because he came after me then, but Lady Corland ran into the room and stopped him from stabbing me and I thought he would kill her, too. Instead he cried out for help, like it wasn't him doing the stabbing. He—he put the scissors in Lady Corland's hand and the robe, too—it was all full of blood—and then he told me he would kill me if I told anyone what I saw."

Bram's arm tightened across her shoulder.

She pulled away and looked him in the eye. "I ran away then, Bram. I ran and didn't stop until I reached Kilrosa."

"No one can blame you for running, Fia." His expression remained open and accepting.

She felt waves of guilt, however. "You don't understand, Bram. I—I left Lady Corland with him blaming it all on her. It is said she ran away—but what if he found her and killed her, too?"

He took her hand between his two strong ones. "Now, lass. That did not happen. If it did, he would come claiming Parronley, now, wouldn't he?"

His hands felt warm and rough with calluses, but so gentle and calming.

He made her look him in the eye. "Now, y'see, you have nothing to worry over."

Her breathing slowed. Her muscles relaxed, as if she'd indeed passed the weight on to his shoulders and off hers.

His eyes were warm and comforting. "Nothin' will hurt you, Fia. Nothin'. I'll see to it." He paused a moment. "I will take care of you, Fia. For always."

"What are you saying, Bram?" she whispered, feeling the blood drain from her face.

He averted his gaze and his cheeks turned pink. "I'm asking to court you, Fia."

She pulled her hand away. "No!"

The baffled and wounded expression on his face nearly broke her heart.

"You do not understand, Bram." She shook her head. He tried to turn his face away, but she held his chin and looked into his eyes. "Do you not wonder why I was in Lord Corland's room?"

He seemed to look at her very deeply. "You were in Lord Corland's bed."

Her jaw dropped. He spoke the truth like it was nothing.

He smiled wanly. "You were out in the world alone, lass, in a gentleman's house. The world is a treacherous place, I've learned, a place full of temptation—"

"Temptation? It wasn't temptation, Bram." She blew out a breath.

He responded in a quiet voice. "I meant only that I'd not judge you for whatever happened."

She slipped off the rock and stood before him. "I went willingly enough, Bram. I did not want to lose my employment, which he said I would and that no one would hire me again. I did not have any money. I'd seen enough of London to know what happened to girls with no money, and I didn't want that to happen to me. So I bedded him and stole his money so I could get home." She backed away, adding, "Reverend Bell's sermons say I'm not fit to be married, and I'll not pretend I am."

She spun around and started walking down the hill, but she did not make it far before Bram fell in beside her. They walked in silence.

When they were halfway back to Kilrosa he spoke. "War makes a man do terrible things, Fia."

She darted a glance at him, not knowing why he was speaking.

He went on. "A soldier's job is killin'. The commandment says, 'Thou shalt not kill.'"

Fia frowned, puzzled as to why he was telling her this.

He stopped walking and gazed into the distance. "Some of those Frenchies were no more than lads, but I killed them. I can still see their faces, some of them—" He bowed his head and fell silent. When he lifted it again, he looked directly at her. "So I'll not judge what another person does to stay alive, in either body or soul."

He reached for her hands and she allowed him to take them. She lifted her face to his, her breath stolen by the tenderness in his expression. He glanced around, but they were alone on that stretch of road. Very slowly, he leaned down to her and placed his lips on hers.

Chapter Thirteen

Tanner and Marlena spent three wonderful days in Dutwood House. The rain had ceased after their first full day there, but it took time for the land to dry enough for them to venture back on their journey.

Tanner had been delighted to provide her with a chance to rest, to heal her horse-weary legs and his sore ribs. She was able to sleep as late as she wished each morning. All that was required of them was to decide what card game to play, what book to read aloud to each other.

Their time together at Dutwood gave Tanner a taste of what life with her would offer. He was a man easily bored, but all their forced leisure had not brought him even a moment of tedium. Everything they had done had delighted him, mind and body.

Because he'd shared the time with her.

They had ventured out of doors the previous day, donning old boots and trudging through the woods to the lake and back again. The fresh crisp air had put roses in Marlena's cheeks and her blue eyes glittered as brightly as the sapphire in the ring she wore beneath her glove.

Now the idyll was over, but Tanner was resolved that it would not be over for ever.

Mrs Kenney sent them off with a hearty breakfast, knapsacks full of bread and cheese, and laundered, dry clothing. The clean air and bright sun made for an exhilarating morning and the horses at least seemed to relish the return to their journey.

Rather than backtrack to Penrith and the Pooley Bridge, Tanner decided they should travel north through Greystoke, threading their way along minor roads to return to the coaching road near Calthwaite.

Still on his property, their horses climbed a hill below which was the Greystoke road. The valley was alive with colour, the trees even more vibrant with yellow and gold than before the rain.

Tanner glanced at Marlena. She made a lovely picture on the bay mare, with all the bearing of a marchioness, even if riding astride like a farmer's daughter.

"It is lovely here." She gazed out over the fields ahead, lying before them like square patches on a peasant's quilt. Marlena swung around to look behind her where Dutwood House still peeked through the trees.

She sighed. "I shall miss this place."

As would Tanner. Dutwood House was perhaps the most humble and rustic of his properties, but it very lately had become his favourite, because he'd shared it with her.

"By God," he exclaimed suddenly, inadvertently pulling on his horse's reins. "I have an idea." The horse danced in confusion until Tanner got him back under control. "Why not live at Dutwood? You need not go to Edinburgh. You could wait here. You would be Mrs Brown, whom I allowed to live in my house—"

"No, Tanner." Her expression turned stony. "I could not "

"But you could," he insisted, the plan rising fully formed into his head. He would leave her here and return to London. He'd set about discovering her identity and the identity of the man who was her enemy—her seducer. It should not be too difficult. How many lady's companions were accused of theft? Whose father had died of a lightning strike? When he'd cleared her name, he would travel back to Dutwood and return with her as his wife.

"What better place to hide away?" he persisted.

She brought her horse nose to tail with his. "No, Tanner. I've involved you in my troubles enough. You already take too much of a risk merely escorting me to Edinburgh."

He waved a dismissive hand. "You take the risk too seriously."

"I assure you I do not." She spoke quietly.

He signalled his horse to start down the hill, not looking back, but hearing her following him.

When he reached the bottom of the hill, she called to him. "Tanner?"

He turned and waited for her to catch up.

She brought her horse alongside his and reached over to grasp his arm. She made him look into her pain-filled eyes.

"Being with you has been the happiest time in my life." She lowered her head. "But I must leave you in Edinburgh."

He leaned towards her, and with a small, desperate sound in her throat, she closed the distance to put her lips on his. He kissed her back, pouring his emotions into the touch of his lips, trying to show her he would not give her up so easily.

When they finally broke apart, he managed to smile at her. "I shall endeavour to make our last days together as pleasant as possible."

"Yes." Her smile was as forced as his. "It is a lovely day and there is so much beauty to see."

He gazed at her. "So much beauty."

He vowed he would not distress her further, that he would do his best to make her laugh, anything to keep the pain from her eyes.

But he would not give her up so easily.

"Shall we avoid the main coaching route again?" he asked. "These roads seem dry enough."

"It will be safer, will it not?" she responded. "And it will make our trip longer."

He smiled.

They rode at a leisurely pace, stopping by crystalline streams to refresh the horses while they ate Mrs Kenney's bread and cheese and drank the one last bottle of wine from the Dutwood House cellar. As the afternoon wore on, they approached a little village, not far from Carlisle and near the border to Scotland.

Tanner halted his horse and looked down at the village. "If there is a half-decent inn here, I suggest we stay."

"It looks large enough for an inn," Marlena said. "And as sweet a place as Cumberland could offer."

The houses were grey stone and white stucco, in neat rows on the main street and fanning off to the side. An old stone church stood at one end of the town. Thin wisps of smoke came from the chimneys.

As they rode in, Tanner turned to her. "Who are we today, by the way?"

She laughed. "Mr and Mrs Antony."

"Antony," he repeated. "Antony... I have lost the habit of being someone else."

They found the inn, a small but cosy place. Tanner dismounted and held his hand out to help Marlena from her horse. They found the innkeeper inside and arranged for a room.

"Would you care for refreshment?" the innkeeper asked. "We are serving a mutton stew."

"Excellent," Tanner replied. "I need to see to the horses. Is there somewhere my wife could sit undisturbed until I return?"

"There is a private room off the taproom. She is welcome to wait for you there."

Tanner raised his brows to Marlena.

"I think that sounds lovely," she said. "Especially if I might have some tea."

"Indeed, ma'am." The innkeeper led her to the taproom and Tanner walked outside.

He gathered their baggage and placed it right inside the inn's doorway. Then he led the horses to stables kept by the village's smithy.

From the entrance, he could see the smithy talking to another man with a horse. Tanner waited at the door.

"I am looking for someone," Tanner heard the man say to the smithy. "A man and woman."

Tanner stilled.

"They were on horseback. Have they passed through here?"

"Not my stable. You can ask at the inn," the smithy said. "What is the name, in case they show up here?"

The man cleared his throat. "That is the thing. They are not travelling under their own names. The woman is a fugitive. There is a reward for her capture. If you assist me—"

Tanner did not wait to hear more. He backed up the horses, who whinnied in protest at not getting their expected bag of oats. He pulled them back to the inn and ran inside finding the innkeeper in the hall.

"Where is my wife?" Tanner demanded.

The innkeeper looked alarmed. "This way." He led Tanner through the taproom to a small private parlour.

Tanner wasted no time. "We leave now." He threw some coins on the table.

Marlena's eyes grew large with fright, but she followed him, running ahead to the horses while Tanner grabbed their luggage.

She was already seated on her horse. Tanner tossed her one of their bags.

"Go," he said, mounting at the same time.

From behind him, Tanner heard a shout. "That is them! Stop them!"

They took off at a gallop, too fast to be stopped. When they were clear of the town, they slowed the horses, but not to the leisurely pace of that morning. Tanner kept them moving north, keeping an eye on the position of the sun. When the road bent too far in another direction, he led them off the road and over the countryside. He pushed the horses as much as he dared, aware that the animals were tiring and the day advancing. Already the sun was low in the sky and the foliage leeched of vibrant colour. They must stop soon.

Over the crest of a hill, Tanner spied a river wending its way through the valley. Its banks were thick with trees and foliage.

"We'll stop by the river," he called to Marlena.

They descended the hill and followed the river along its banks until Tanner found a sheltered spot where it would be easy for the horses to drink. Tanner's gelding dipped his muzzle in the water even before Tanner dismounted. Tanner helped Marlena from the mare, and, while the horses drank, he fetched the road book and the satchel containing the leftover cheese, bread, and wine. He led Marlena to the shelter of a nearby tree.

"Eat something," he said.

She nodded and pulled out a piece of bread, handing the satchel back to him. "Are we in Scotland now?"

"I believe so." He opened the road book, straining his eyes in the waning daylight. "This must be the River Esk. I think I know about where we are." He closed the book again. "I had better tend to the horses."

Once the horses had enough water, Tanner led them to a patch of grass. They immediately gnawed at the green blades. Taking a cloth from one of the bags, Tanner wiped the sweat off his horse.

Marlena joined him. "Is there another cloth?"

He pulled one from the bag and handed it to her. She tended to her horse, eyeing Tanner cautiously as she worked.

They had barely spoken during the hard ride from the village, but she must realise he was consumed with questions, questions that invaded his mind as he rode, blocked only by the more pressing need to see her to safety.

"We will not reach an inn tonight." Tanner would ask his questions later, after they had settled themselves. "We must stay here. Build a fire."

She made no complaint about spending the night outdoors. She did not grumble that she would be cold or whine that she was hungry and thirsty.

"I'll collect firewood," she said instead.

Tanner removed the bags from the horse's saddles and loosened their girths. Marlena cleared an area for the fire while Tanner walked upstream to a place where the water flowed swiftly. He filled the water skins he'd had the presence of mind to toss in their bags before leaving Dutwood. In a still part of the river he spied some large fish nibbling at the underwater plants, mere shadows in the waning light.

He walked back to Marlena, who had gathered some rocks from the river's edge and was placing them in a circle.

"Give me a hairpin."

She reached under her bonnet and pulled a pin from her hair. "What is it for?"

He picked up a stone and sharpened one end. "To hook a fish. I just need something colourful for bait."

"I'll find something." She rummaged through one of the bags and pulled out a tiny piece of ribbon. "Will this do?"

"It will."

He hated the loss of ease between them and feared he might never find it again.

Tanner walked back to the fish-filled pool and uncoiled a length of string. He tied the improvised hook on one end and stuck the piece of ribbon on it before dropping it into the water.

He used to fish like this when a boy wandering around Tannerton, bothering the gameskeeper enough times that the man eventually took him under his wing and taught him all manner of useful things. Tanner had nearly forgotten them.

At the small pool he and a big fat fellow of a fish sparred until the fish finally took the bait in its mouth. Tanner jerked up on the string and his fish threshed noisily in the water until he pulled him out.

When he returned to Marlena, she had stacked thick pieces of wood with plenty of tinder underneath.

"You've built outdoor fires before," he commented.

"Yes," she admitted.

He opened his tinderbox and struck a flame.

He roasted the fish, which they ate with their fingers, remaining silent. It was obvious to Tanner that Marlena had hidden something from him about herself, something so important a reward was on her head and a Bow Street Runner was pursuing her.

After he ate, Tanner rose to check on the horses, safely tethered nearby. When he returned, the sun was no more than a glow on the horizon, but the fire burned brightly. Marlena still sat by the fire, hugging her knees and wrapped in his grandmother's woollen shawl.

He sat near her.

She spoke, breaking their long silence. "It was Rapp, wasn't it?"

Tanner nodded.

She stared into the fire. "I thought Davies was pursuing us, but it was Rapp. Rapp knows I am alive."

He fixed his gaze on her. "There is a reward on your head, as well. I heard him speak of it. Do not tell me it is due to the theft of a few jewels."

Marlena lowered her head to her knees, then turned to gaze at him. The flames of the campfire illuminated his handsome face, filled with anger and confusion and pain. She took a deep, ragged breath, aching with the knowledge that everything had changed.

Rapp knew she was alive.

"Answer me," Tanner demanded.

She swallowed and averted her gaze, not knowing how much to tell him. She quickly glanced back. "Did Rapp see you? Did he see your face?"

He looked puzzled. "I do not think so, but—"

"That's good," she whispered, more to herself than to him.

"You did not answer me," he accused, his voice turning deeper, rougher.

There was only one way to convince him that matters had changed. She must tell him the truth. "I am an accused murderer."

His brows rose.

She fought for courage to continue. "I tell you this much only to impress upon you how serious this is. There is no fixing this, Tanner. They mean to see me hanged—you, too, if you are discovered helping me." She searched his face to see if he comprehended. "It is not too late for you. Rapp still does not know who you are."

He waved his hand. "Never mind that. Who are you supposed to have murdered?"

Marlena gave him a direct gaze. "My husband."

He gaped. "Husband!"

She turned her face away. "Yes."

He laughed drily. "So your tale of being a lady's companion accused of theft—that was a lie?" It was more a statement than a question.

She nodded.

"And this man who supposedly seduced you…" He glared at her.

It seemed too difficult to explain that she had partially told him the truth. She had described Corland. "A lie, Tanner. It was all a lie." She bowed her head.

His hand closed into a fist. "You were *married?*" He put a biting emphasis on the word *married.* "You were not some lady's companion at the mercy of her employer's son—" He broke off as if he was too angry to form words. Tanner rose to his feet and paced next to her.

She looked up at him. "Tanner, you must see I did not know you at first. I could not tell you I was an accused murderer. You were a marquess and, as such, how could I know you would not turn me in? The shipwreck gave me a chance to be free. I could not allow anything to jeopardise that chance."

He was too tall for the glow of the campfire to reach his face. She could not see his expression, but she could feel his emotion. "I was not always a stranger, Marlena, not after we shared a bed."

She glanced away.

He persisted, his voice low and pained. "A husband, Marlena. How can you justify not telling me you had been married? Married."

His words were like a sharp sword. "Tanner, I regret—" She covered her face with her hands, before lifting her head to him again. "I ought to have informed you of the danger I placed you in."

"The danger?" He scoffed.

"It was wrong of me."

He pulled off his hat and swept a hand through his hair. "Do you think I care of that?" He paced again, then leaned down to her, grabbing her chin in his hand. "When we made love, Marlena—you should have told me a husband preceded me. Who was he? Am I to know that?"

She pulled away from his grasp. "No."

He straightened, his face in shadow again. "No?"

Marlena rose to her knees. "I will not tell you. Not now. Not when Rapp knows I am alive."

"I fail to see what that has to do with it." He placed his hands on his hips.

"We must separate. Rapp will pursue me, do you not see that? If he or anyone discovers you have been seen with me—" She broke off again, sitting back on her legs. "Your ignorance of me may offer some protection. You shall be able to protest that I duped you—which I did—and you had no idea whom you assisted."

He stared down at her. "Do *you* not see that I am not speaking of Rapp, but of you and me and what I thought was real between us?"

She wrapped her arms around her waist. Wounding him so much cut her up inside like a thousand knife blades.

He folded his arms across his chest, almost a mirror image of her. "We are close to Edinburgh. Two, three days at the most. I will take you to Edinburgh and that will be the end of it."

He was mistaken. The end had already come.

He turned from her and strode over to where they had placed their bags. He returned to toss one of them at her.

She caught it and clutched it to her breast.

"It will be cold tonight," he said in a flat voice. "Cover up as much as possible."

He turned and walked away, the darkness covering him. Marlena fingered the sapphire ring he had given her before opening the bag to do as he'd bid.

After he returned to the campfire, Marlena feigned being asleep. She watched him through slitted eyelids as he settled by the fire, making a pillow of one of the bags and covering himself with a top coat.

She watched him thrash around in search of a comfortable position. When he settled the campfire illuminated his face. When the furrows in his brow eased and the rigidity of his jaw slackened, his features took on a boyish vulnerability. She knew he had finally fallen asleep.

Marlena had watched him until the fire dwindled to embers and dawn glowed through the trees. She now rose carefully, trying not to make a sound.

She rolled the extra top coat they'd brought with them from Dutwood House and stuffed it in the bag. With one last long look at him, she mouthed, "Goodbye." Forcing herself to turn away, she carried the bag to Dulcea.

The horse nickered in greeting.

"Shhhhh," she whispered.

She slung the bag on the horse's back and tightened the girth. Tanner's horse became interested in this project and nudged her with his muzzle. She turned and stroked the gelding's neck.

"Take good care of him," she whispered, rubbing her cheek against the horse's coarse hair.

The animal snorted and nodded as if understanding her command.

She untied the reins of the mare and led her away on foot, mounting only when she was at some distance. She followed the river, which led her north as she needed to travel, pushing the horse to walk as fast as possible over the uneven ground.

When the sun rose in the sky and melted the mist, she stopped to remove Tanner's grandmother's shawl from under her cloak, holding it against her for a moment, as if embracing Tanner again. She folded it and put it in the bag. Dulcea put her nose in the clear water of the river and drank. Marlena then led the horse to a little glade where she nibbled some grass.

The land around Marlena looked like the hills of home. The Scottish air even smelled like home. What she would give to see Parronley again, to have the comfort of familiar old faces, to feel home once more. Likely no one would remember her there; thirteen years had passed, and she had changed so much. She doubted anyone could find the young carefree girl she'd been at age twelve in her face now. She did not even speak the same as she once did. She'd lost her Scottish burr like she had lost everything else of her life in Scotland.

Marlena turned around in her saddle to gaze back from where she'd come, from where she had left Tanner. Was he awake now? Perhaps when he found her gone, he would curse her so much he would turn south and make his way back into the safe life of the Marquess of Tannerton.

She remounted her horse and threaded her way upriver. The River Esk flowed near Parronley, she remembered. All she need do was follow the river, then watch for signs pointing to Edinburgh to the east. She stayed on the natural terrain, although it slowed her pace. Sometimes she'd glimpse the road and be tempted to use it. Then a carriage or a cart or a rider would pass by, and she'd shrink back to the river bank again.

Try as she might to think only of the land ahead of her, Tanner invaded her thoughts. She tried not to imagine how he must despise her, not only for lying to him, but also for sneaking away while he slept.

When the sun grew high in the sky, she selected a spot for her and the horse to drink from the river. After they were refreshed, she walked the mare up a hill to get her bearings. The horse nibbled on the grass, but Marlena had brought with her only one small piece of bread and two smaller chunks of cheese, leaving the remainder for Tanner. She nibbled on one piece of cheese, careful to eat only half.

At the crest of the hill, Marlena saw that the river led into a town. Within the town the river broke into two branches. Which branch was the River Esk? The sun was now directly overhead, so she could not tell which way was north. Worst of all, it appeared she had no choice but to ride down and cross the bridge. She could not avoid being seen.

She sank to the ground, resting while Dulcea ate her fill. The town bustled with activity. Perhaps the number of people would protect her. She could attempt to merge with them unnoticed as she passed through.

She led the horse back down the hill and continued to follow the river bank until she found a good place to join the road when no horse or vehicle was in sight. Soon, however, she was among several other riders, carts and pedestrians. A sign indicated the town's name was Langholm, a name that only dimly rang in her memory, a market town, perhaps. Its stone-and-stucco buildings reminded her of

Parronley, as did the hills rising around it like the frame around a painting.

As she entered the town the smell of roasting meat and baking bread wafted from the shops and inns. Her hunger increased, but she was determined to save her meagre stash of food for the night. One establishment she passed smelled of cooking fish, reminding her of Tanner's fish dinner the night before.

Trying to look as if she belonged with the flow of traffic, she rode closer and closer to the bridge. The sun seemed to hover over her left shoulder now, and the bridge seemed to lead her north. Her nerves calmed, even though seeing children dashing through the streets, shopworkers standing in doorways, farmers driving their carts, all made her feel very alone.

I'll become used to it, won't I, Eliza? she said to herself. *I'll become used to being alone.* Used to being without Tanner.

She passed the parish church and prayed God would keep her safe. And keep Tanner safe. It comforted her somewhat that Eliza would be looking down in heaven watching out for her. *Watch over Tanner, too, Eliza,* she begged.

The bridge was very near now and Marlena's heart beat faster. Her ordeal was almost over and it had been astonishingly easy. When she reached the bridge, she breathed a sigh of relief. She crossed, already searching for a place where she might leave the road again.

Out of the corner of her eye she saw a horse come from behind her. The horse rode so close she felt it brush Dulcea. When the horse's muzzle came level with Dulcea's shoulder, Marlena spied a man's arm reaching towards her.

She signalled Dulcea to take off at a gallop, hearing a voice behind her. "Halt, my lady."

She did not look back. She galloped past a farm cart and

some pedestrians who jumped to the side at her sudden approach. She could hear horse's hooves behind her in pursuit.

He caught up to her at an empty dip in the road, a place where no one could see a man accosting a lone woman, no chance someone would come to her aid. Rapp tried to grab her horse's bridle. She jerked the horse's head away from him and Dulcea reared and gnashed her teeth.

Rapp backed his horse away. "Give it up," he demanded. "I have you now."

"No!" she cried.

Dulcea reared again.

Suddenly there was the pounding hooves of another horse. A lone horseman bore down on them.

Tanner!

He reached them in an instant, looking more like a bandit than a rescuer. His face was covered by a cloth and he advanced on Rapp, not slowing his pace, and knocked Rapp from his saddle with one swing of his arm. Rapp's horse skittered away.

"I'll get you," Rapp cried, jumping to his feet, his fist in the air.

Tanner turned to Marlena. "Come on," he cried, as Rapp went for his horse.

Marlena set Dulcea into a gallop again, Tanner riding at her side. They galloped away from Langholm. When the road rose high they looked behind and saw that Rapp was following, although his form was a mere speck in the distance. When the road dipped again, Tanner turned them off through a break in the trees.

"This way," he called.

They rode to a place where the trees and brush cloaked them, slowing their tiring horses to a walk. Soon they reached the banks of a narrow stream, shallow enough that the rocks beneath the water were clearly visible.

"The horses must rest." Tanner dismounted and only then pulled off the cloth that masked his face. "Let them drink here."

He walked over to her and held out his hands to assist her from her horse. She put hers on his shoulders, and he grabbed her waist, holding her until her feet reached the ground. He still did not release her.

Looking into her eyes, he said, "Stay here. I am going to obscure our trail."

She nodded and he moved off, grabbing a small branch to carry with him. She held the reins of the horses by the riverbank, pulling their heads away when it seemed as if they were drinking too fast.

Her emotions were in turmoil. Her heart had leapt into her throat when she had seen him coming to her rescue. She wanted only to touch him, hold him, taste his lips. At the same time she felt as if she had doomed him to a terrible fate.

For if Rapp knew she was alive and correctly guessed that she had been headed towards Scotland, Wexin also knew this and Wexin was twice the danger Rapp was.

Marlena's heart beat faster when she heard Tanner return, leaves swishing as he approached. He walked with his head down. The dear, rumpled hat the innkeeper in Cemaes had given him obscured his face. As he came close he lifted his head, his expression thunderous as if he were holding back a maelstorm of anger. After glaring at her, he walked upstream a little way, disappearing around a bend.

When he came back he walked over to her. "How are the horses?"

"They seem to be settling," she replied, almost unable to breathe. "I did not let them drink too much all at once."

He nodded in approval.

"Tanner—" she began.

He held up a hand, and could scarcely look at her. "How did you intend to find your way to Edinburgh without even a map?" he snapped.

"I was going to follow the river. The River Esk flows near Edinburgh."

He shook his head. "That is a different River Esk."

Her eyes widened in surprise. She had no idea there could be two River Esks in Scotland. She might have been wandering the countryside for days without food or money.

"Enough of this foolishness." He gave her a level look. "I'll see you to Edinburgh. I'll see you there safely, but you stay with me. I'll not have your life on my conscience as well."

She opened her mouth to ask him what he meant, but he turned away from her, looking upstream.

"We ride in the water," he said. "Even if Rapp finds where we left the road, there is a chance we can still throw him off."

He helped her to remount and she rode her horse into the stream. He mounted and did the same, but rode his horse across to the other bank and then he made the horse back up into the water.

A clever ploy. The sort of trick Niall would have played on Wexin when they were gambolling over Parronley as boys.

They stayed in the stream for as long as they could, but the rocks underneath were slippery and difficult for the horses to walk upon. Tanner led them to the far bank of the stream and in a moment they were back to a landscape of rolling, grassy hills.

Tanner dismounted. "The horses need to feed."

She slipped off her horse before he could assist her.

He walked up to the crest of the hill, his very stride conveying an aura of command, of power. She watched him, as hungry for his smile, his laughter, as she was for food. Her stomach hurt and she pressed her hand to it.

When he returned he said. "There is nothing to be seen to give me any bearings. I think we should stay off the roads and ride north as best we can."

"Tanner—"

He fixed his gaze on her. "I am remaining with you."

She nodded, her throat tight. His words had an axe-hard edge.

She had assumed the pain she caused him would drive him away. Instead he had come after her, rescuing her once again, saving her life one more time.

He'd done more than save her life, however; he had made her want to live again.

After Corland was killed, Marlena's way of life died, too, then her family died—Niall and his dear little sons. Then Eliza. Everything Marlena thought worth living for had gone. Seeing Tanner again on the ship from Ireland rekindled those days when life had been full of dancing, and dreams and happiness. She'd briefly found happiness again at Tanner's side.

He glanced over at the horses. "We'll let them eat as much as they want, then we'll start off again."

He avoided sitting with Marlena, but rather paced to and fro, looking out on the valley, perhaps expecting Rapp to appear below. When Tanner and Marlena mounted their horses and rode again, their pace was slow over the hilly terrain.

In spite of her worries, Marlena was awed by the Scottish landscape, so unexpected and yet familiar at the same time. The hills retained a hint of the vibrant green they wore in summer, but had donned browns and oranges and purples as well.

She had forgotten how much she loved this land.

"Oh, hell," Tanner muttered.

She glanced towards him.

He pointed to the horizon where black clouds formed a line, like an army ready to attack.

"Rain," he said. "We had better find some shelter."

There was not much shelter to discover in the wilderness, however. When they came to the crest of yet another hill, the ruins of a castle came into view. They headed for it as the first of the raindrops started to fall and the roll of thunder sounded in the distance.

"If we are fortunate, it will have a roof," Tanner said as they approached the huge crumbling building, its brownish-grey stone walls whispering of days long gone.

"There is thunder, Tanner."

The stone was the same colour as Parronley, Marlena noticed, trying to distract herself from the approaching thunderstorm.

There was, indeed, a room large enough for the horses, sheltered on three sides with enough of a roof to keep the rain away. One tower of the castle remained intact, its stone staircase circling up to the battlements from which arrows once flew and vats of hot oil were poured on invaders.

They took the bags and saddles and blankets off the horses and carried them to the staircase of the tower.

"No fire tonight," Tanner said as he dropped the bag on the stairs.

"No fish, either," Marlena responded, trying to disguise her fear of the building storm.

He turned to her with concern. "You must be hungry."

She opened her bag. "I have some cheese and bread saved. We can share it." She broke it apart and gave the larger piece to Tanner. He took out a skin that he'd filled with water and handed it to her. With old stone walls surrounding them, they ate and drank in silence while the heavens opened up and lightning flashed, followed seconds later by a loud clap of thunder.

"Put on as many clothes as you can," Tanner told her. "I will check on the horses." He was no more than a silhouette against the tower's threshold.

"Tanner—" Marlena began, wanting to ask him not to leave her alone with the thunder and lightning crashing around them.

He turned away and began to walk out.

"Wait!" She felt like she could not breathe.

He looked over his shoulder.

"The storm…" She took a breath.

"I'll return. Stay here." His eyes bore into her. "No more leaving, Marlena."

"No more leaving," she repeated.

Fia looked up when the door of the taproom opened, and Lyall and Erroll Gibb entered, in mid-conversation, hair dripping from the rain.

"Och, no harm will come to them," Lyall said to his brother. "You are worried for naught."

"You know how these Englishmen can be, Lyall." Erroll nodded to Reverend Bell who sat over in a corner, his hand wrapped around a glass. "You cannot trust them with your women."

Erroll tripped on the leg of a chair, grabbing it before it fell and making it look as if he'd chosen it to sit upon.

Lyall flopped down in the chair opposite him. "There's naught we can do about it."

Fia walked over to them. "I hope you both wiped your boots before tracking mud in here."

Lyall smiled up at her. "That we did, Fia, so hold your scold."

He gave her that besotted stare, and she worried that

perhaps his affections had not been attached to one of the Brookston girls, after all.

"What will you be having?" she asked them both.

"Ale," replied a disquieted Erroll.

"Ale," agreed his brother.

"Ale it is." She nodded, but Erroll blocked her way with his arm before she could be off to the tap.

"Tell us, Fia." His brows knitted together so tightly they looked as if they were only one jagged line across his forehead. "You worked in London, in a fancy house—"

She felt a knot grow in her stomach. "It was long ago."

"Ay, but—" Erroll swallowed as if he had difficulty bringing out the right words to speak. "We were wonderin' what it was like. What the English laird of the place was like."

She felt blood drain from her face.

He went on. "I mean, could ye trust the man?"

Fia struggled to find her voice. "What reason do you have for asking me the question?"

Lyall reached over and whacked his brother on the shoulder. "You idiot! You know what happened where Fia was. Miss Parronley-that-was and all that." He looked at her in apology for his brother. "Don't mind him, Fia. He's daft."

Her knees shook.

Errol tossed his brother a scathing look. He turned back to Fia. "I was just askin' because Mary and Sara Brookston went to work at Parronley and I was worried because—"

She stopped him. "Why did they go to work at Parronley?" The house had been shut up with minimal staff ever since Baron Parronley and his two boys had died, and his poor, grieving wife went home to her parents. Lady Corland was the Baroness, but, of course, no one knew where to find her.

Lyall answered, "Lord Wexin showed up, wantin' to stay

there; seeing as he will be the laird there some day, they opened the house and needed girls to help with the cleaning."

Lord Wexin.

The room went dark and the sounds of people talking became like echoes.

Fia had feared this day. She'd hoped it would never come. Parronley House was an old and draughty place that had been neglected for years. Before they died, the young baron and his children only came for summers. With Lady Corland gone and no one in charge, things were in even more disarray. The crofters continued to farm the land, but not much else happened there. Fia hoped Wexin would stay on his own English estate and leave Parronley alone.

"I'll fetch your ale," she mumbled, walking through the maze of tables and chairs by memory.

The only reason for Wexin to come to Parronley would be if he inherited, and if he inherited it meant that Lady Corland was dead.

This likelihood loomed over Fia like a shroud. If Lady Corland were dead, it was Fia's fault. No matter how, no matter where. Her fault for not telling what she saw.

Fia managed to reach the bar where Bram was drawing ale while his father took a rest.

Her vision cleared enough to see Bram look upon her with concern. "What is it, lass?"

She forced her voice to sound unaffected. "Two ales for the Gibb brothers."

He reached over the bar to her. "No, I meant, what is it with you? Are you ill?"

Though her heart was beating a rapid tattoo, she made herself look him in the eye. "I'm not ill. I merely want you to give me two ales."

He paused, still examining her like her sleeve had caught

fire or something. He eventually drew two ales from the tap and handed them to her.

She carried them to Lyall and Erroll and did not tarry a moment in case they would start talking again. She went straight to the kitchen and kept walking through to the outside door.

Her aunt was stirring a pot of soup. "Are you ill, Fia? You look pale."

Fia pasted a smile on her face. "I'm in need of air," she said. "The taproom is quiet enough. I'll be only a moment."

She stood in the shelter of the doorway, trying to will herself to stay put and not run into the rain and as far away from Kilrosa and Parronley as she could get. To run like that would only be foolhardy. She needed to pack. She needed her money. She needed a place to go.

Because if Wexin found her here, he would kill her.

Chapter Fourteen

The night was over, the patrons gone, and Fia had somehow made it through. It helped that the rain thinned the numbers in the taproom, and that she became numb, acting like one of those automatons she'd seen in shops in London. Her aunt and uncle were abed, due to rise early and fix the breakfast. Bram was in the kitchen. Fia was alone, wiping the tables. In the solitude, she could think.

Wexin visited Parronley, not Kilrosa. It would be odd of him to come to Kilrosa when Parronley was the closer village. He could have no business here. Kilrosa had no one more important than Laird Hay, whose lands bordered the village and were not nearly as vast as the Parronley lands. She could easily keep out of Wexin's path. He could not possibly stay long.

If Wexin came to live in the area, though, she would have to leave. There would be no other choice to make. Perhaps Erroll and Lyall could find out from the Brookston sisters, if she could think of a way of asking them without raising their curiosity.

Fia wiped the last table and set the chairs up on top of it, so she could mop where the mud had inevitably been tracked in. She turned to go and fetch the mop and bucket and nearly ran into Bram, standing with his arms folded.

She must have numbed herself so well she had not sensed him, but now her heart pounded in her chest and her blood raced through her veins.

"You startled me," she said, her voice too breathless. "I thought you were cleaning the kitchen."

"The kitchen can wait." He merely watched her, his brown eyes looking black in the dim light. "What happened to you tonight?"

She shook her head and started to march past him. "I have no time for your silly questions, Bram. Nothing happened. It was a dull night."

He seized her arm and bent down to her. "Somethin' frightened the blood from your face, lass, and you near to fainted. Tell me."

She tried to pull away. "Do you not have work to do?"

He held fast and stared into her eyes. "Nothin' is more important than you, lass."

She felt as if her knees would give out from under her, but Bram's hands kept her upright.

He flipped a chair off the table and sat her down in it. Then he grabbed another and sat facing her. "Now tell me of it."

"Oh, Bram…" her voice cracked and tears of fear filled her eyes "…Lord Wexin is at Parronley."

His eyes grew wide. "Lord Wexin!"

"Aye." Her body trembled. "I am afraid. He will kill me, Bram. I know he will kill me."

He took her by the hand and gently settled her on his lap, wrapping his strong arms around her. "There now," he murmured in a soothing voice. "No harm will come to you. I will see to it."

She pulled away from him. "You must not go near him,

Bram. Do you hear me? Don't get any foolish ideas. I won't stand for it. I won't."

He held her tight against his chest. "Och, if you keep actin' this way, I'll be thinking you care about me."

"I do care about you, Bram. I couldn't bear it if something happened to you because of me." Her words were spoken into his chest.

He held her and rocked her and she almost felt safe. "I'm afraid his comin' here means something bad. Like he's killed Lady Corland or something. He's never come before." She shuddered.

"What does he know of you, Fia? Would he guess you are here?" he asked.

She shook her head, rubbing her cheek against his apron, which smelled of hops and ferment and comfort. "I do not think he knows my name or anything about me. He would have come for me before if he knew. I thought about this a long time and I figured out that he could not very well ask about me, not without causing people to have questions he would not want to answer."

"Ay," Bram said, the sound rumbling in his chest. "He'd be revealing you were in the room."

"You have no idea how many months it took me to realise that." She sighed. "Bram, I'm worried about why he's here. He's found Lady Corland, is all I can guess. She must be dead."

He brushed the hair from her brow and tucked it back under her cap. "That may not be, lass. I'll invent an errand in Parronley and find out what I can." He gave her an intent look. "But if anyone comes here who frightens you, tell Da you are sick and hide yourself until I come back."

Rain dripped through the roof of the castle ruins, making puddles on the stone floor. Tanner rubbed down the horses and checked their tethers. The two animals seemed content enough in their makeshift stable, munching on the blades of grass that grew up through the cracks in the floor as if they were feasting on troughs of hay. By the time Tanner finished, the scant light had waned and the storm intensified, lighting his way back to the stairwell with flashes of lightning.

When he reached the doorway, he could not see Marlena on the stairs and, for a fleeting moment, feared she had run off again.

"I did what you said." Her tremulous voice floated down from above and he could just make out her shape sitting several stair steps up from the open doorway.

"What I said?" he repeated, remembering how when he'd repeated things before it had led to lovemaking.

"I put on as many clothes as I could," she said. "And I took out some clothes for you, as well." She lifted some dark garment to show him.

Lightning flashed and she gasped, clutching the garment to her as the thunder followed.

He hurried up the steps. "The storm will pass soon."

She handed him the coat. "I know."

He removed his top coat and put the coat she'd given him on top of the one he already wore.

"I moved everything up here. It is not so damp and is more sheltered from the wind." The shaking of her voice was unmistakable.

He sat beside her and covered them both with his top coat. She had placed their bags on higher steps to act as pillows, and the horse blankets beneath them as the cushions for their stone settee.

Lightning flashed again and she flinched.

He put his arm around her. "We're safe enough here."

She laughed softly. "It is silly of me to be afraid."

He drew her closer, needing her as much as she needed his comfort.

His anger had fled, but a knot of fear still lingered. She'd come so close to being captured, and he no longer knew if his fortune and influence could save her.

Tanner closed his eyes and again saw Marlena battling the Bow Street Runner, who nearly had her in his grasp. His blood still burned with the thought of that man's hands upon her.

When Tanner woke that morning to find her gone, he'd been frantic with worry and enraged at himself for not anticipating her flight. With luck, guesswork and prayer he had followed her trail and finally caught a glimpse of her in the crowded streets of Langholm. He'd seen Rapp as well and he'd feared they were too far ahead for him to catch them up in time.

The storm quieted, the lightning faded, and the thunder seemed to roll away. Tanner felt Marlena relax and she seemed to melt against him.

When he'd embarked on this adventure, his intention had always been to save her, to give back a life, to atone for those lives that were lost because of him. He had not expected to fall in love with her.

Tanner had pretty much despaired of falling in love. The respectable women he met never captured his interest, and his string of mistresses quickly bored him. Both sets of women were more enamoured of his money than of him.

Marlena, on the other hand, had refused the help his money could offer her.

"Are you warm enough?" she asked.

"Yes," he responded in a quiet voice. "Sleep if you can, Marlena. With luck we will reach Edinburgh tomorrow."

The darkness and the silence did not help him fall asleep, however. He felt her warmth, heard her breathing, smelled the scent that was uniquely hers. He couldn't shift his position for fear of disturbing her sleep.

"Tanner?" Her voice drifted through the darkness. "What did you mean when you said you did not want my life on your conscience *as well.*"

He paused before answering. "That I will see you safe to Edinburgh, is what I meant."

She shifted, moving even closer to him. "No, you said *as well.* What did you mean, *as well?* Do you have a person's life on your conscience?"

He paused again, considering how to answer. "I did not kill anyone, if that is what you mean, but I caused the deaths of three people."

"How did you do that?" She asked the question in a soft voice, an accepting voice.

"Arrogance," he replied. She might as well know the sort of man he was. "Let us say, I coveted a prize so much, and fancied myself so clever, that I never thought my adversary would kill to win."

She touched his leg. "Then was it not your adversary who caused the deaths?"

The sensation sent need flashing through him. "I do not hold the man blameless," he admitted. "But neither am I absolved. Had I not decided to rub his nose in my superiority, he might be alive and the two others as well." It was surprisingly difficult to admit this to her. "They died because I cared only about winning."

She threaded her arm around his and leaned her cheek on his shoulder. "If only we could know what was to happen, we could decide very well then, could we not?"

He could only think how good it felt having her so near again.

"You are the best man I have ever known," she rasped.

He held her tightly. *There is no fixing this,* she'd said the night before. They would part in Edinburgh, but in his heart she would always be his marchioness.

"When I bring you to safety, I might deserve a piece of that regard," he said.

She groped in the darkness until she found his face. Holding his head in her hands, she guided him to her, missing his lips at first.

When she found his mouth, he pulled her on top of him. Into the kiss he poured all his terror at almost seeing her captured and his grief at losing her for good.

Marlena contented herself with kissing him, being held by him, touching him. It was like a gift.

She wished this castle still had its old bedchambers with big, old beds made of dark wood. Parronley used to have musty unused rooms where Marlena had pretended she was a maiden sought after by knights in chain mail and armour.

She sighed. Tanner possessed more chivalry than all the knights gathered at King Arthur's Round Table. Tears stung her eyes. She squeezed them shut, determined to defer the grief of losing him until after she sent him away.

Marlena had awoken several times during the night, each time savouring anew the bittersweet joy of feeling engulfed by him, of relishing the scent of him, of being soothed by the even cadence of his breathing. When she opened her eyes and saw light peeking through the cracks in the wall, her spirits plummeted.

He must have heard her stir, because he woke, too. His eyes were even more intense in the growing light, tinged with the same sadness that tore her apart inside.

"We must rise. Be on our way," he said.

But he made no move to leave. Instead he held her in a

long, warm, sheltering embrace, and she wanted nothing more than to remain for ever in his strong arms, a place of safety, refuge. Love.

Inevitably they had to depart. After they shed their extra clothing, Marlena repacked the bags. Tanner saddled the horses. Their two stalwart steeds seemed none the worse for spending a damp night in the castle and were even eager to continue the journey. Too soon Marlena and Tanner left the castle behind and headed north once more.

The ground, still wet from the rain, made their progress difficult. Marlena ought to have rued the slow pace, but instead it raised her selfish hopes for one more night with Tanner.

Tanner turned to her. "We should chance stopping at a village. Give the horses something proper to eat and ourselves as well." He smiled at her. "Unless you are not hungry."

She smiled back. "I am famished." Her smile quickly fled. "But what of Rapp? Dare we stop?"

His brows knit. "If we stay in this remote area, the chance of Rapp coming to the same village at the same time seems unlikely. We need food." He patted his horse's neck. "All of us." He gave her a reassuring gaze. "Let us look for a road to follow."

They found a path that wound around a hill and followed it, hoping it led to a road. The morning wore on without them finding a village.

"Will we make Edinburgh today, do you think?" Marlena asked at one point.

"I believe so," he said in a flat voice.

They fell silent, plodding along to the next hill, still no road in sight. The path widened enough for them to ride side by side.

Tanner looked over at her. "What happens when we reach Edinbugh, Marlena?"

She darted a glance at him, but quickly looked away. "We must part."

After a pause, he spoke again. "Am I to simply leave you, or is there someone waiting for you, someone to help you?"

She could barely look at him. "There is an old teacher from my school…" It was, she hoped, the last falsehood she would tell him. She knew no one in Edinburgh, but, then, she was counting on no one in Edinburgh knowing her.

His pained expression told her that he'd recognised her lie.

She changed the subject. "What of you, Tanner? Will you have enough money to get back to London?"

He frowned. "When I become the Marquess again, I will be able to get funds easily enough."

She was relieved, not wishing him to endure any more hardship on her behalf.

He spoke again. "I have been thinking. Before we part, we must set up a way for me to send you money—"

She broke in. "No, Tanner. You must not be connected to me ever again."

"I will not leave you destitute and alone." His horse jumped forward at his sharp tone.

"I will get by, Tanner," she called after him.

He increased his pace and she fell far enough behind to make further discussion impossible. Soon the terrain required all their attention as they climbed higher and higher to the crest of a hill. Marlena felt a *frisson* of nerves travel up her spine as they climbed, but she knew of no reason why.

When they reached the crest, he stopped and waited for her. As she caught up to him, Marlena scanned the vista. Low clouds gave a dreamlike appearance to the valley below until a sudden breeze swept them away.

In the distance was the sea and before it sat a great house

built of brownish-grey stone complete with turrets and towers and pointed rooftops. The house, once hazy from her long absence, was now all too clear in her vision.

Parronley House.

Each room, each view, every walkway in the garden, every furrow in the parkland, every rock in the cliffs beyond the house, rushed into her mind. Again, she and Niall ran through the rooms, frolicked in the garden, jumped from the cliffs into the deep pools of water in the sea.

"No," she cried, backing her horse away from the sight.

Tanner looked around him. "What?"

She caught herself and shook her head. "Nothing, Tanner. The house looked like a place where ghosts might dwell."

There was truth to that. Too many ghosts would inhabit this place, if only in her memory—her parents, her brother, the life she had left behind…

The living demons were who she must fear the most, however. She and Tanner had come directly to the place Rapp would think to look for her. *Parronley.*

Marlena pointed to her left. "I—I thought I spied a road over that way. Just a glimpse."

She knew there was a road there, a road that led away from Parronley, a road that could lead them on to Edinburgh, only about ten miles away. They must reach Edinburgh now. She would push him on.

At the bottom of the hill, exactly where she said it would be, was the road. When they reached it, the sun was high, near noon for certain. They came upon a signpost Marlena knew would be there. Kilrosa one way; Parronley the other. While her nerves jangled so severely she thought he would notice, he stopped to consult the map.

He pointed to Kilrosa. "This way."

She breathed a sigh of relief.

"We must stop at this next village," he said. "The horses are tiring and we all need food."

She wanted to tell him she was not tired. She was not hungry. She wanted to beg him to go on to Edinburgh.

They no sooner rode past the road sign when Tanner's horse began to falter. "Deuce," he said. "My horse has thrown a shoe."

Marlena's panic escalated. More delay.

Tanner dismounted and lifted the horse's hoof. "He needs a new shoe for certain. I hope he has not injured his leg. The village should not be too far."

About five miles away, Marlena recalled.

Five excruciating miles. Tanner had to lead his horse on foot and their progress seemed snail-like. Marlena expected every minute that Rapp would descend upon them.

She hoped no one in Kilrosa would recognise her. Surely her appearance had changed dramatically, and no one would look for that little girl in this plainly dressed woman with dirt splattered on her skirt and mud caking her boots. None of them, she hoped, would be expecting the Baroness Parronley in this disguise.

They came upon the church, which was just as she remembered it, made of the same stone as Parronley House. The buildings of Kilrosa would be made of that stone as well, so different from the buildings of London. Or Bath. Or Kent, where Corland's estate was located. So many memories came flooding back, of riding with Niall over these same hills, walking these same roads to the church on fine-weather days.

The village was soon ahead and it too sparked memories of the handful of times she visited it as a child. Parronley had been closer to her father's estate than Kilrosa and there had been few reasons to travel the extra miles to visit it. Still, as they entered Kilrosa, its winding main road with shops and the inn and smithy were familiar.

"Let us first find a stable and a smithy," Tanner said.

Marlena could have taken him directly to the stable, suddenly remembering one of the rare times her father allowed her and Niall to ride with him on some errand in the village. The local laird's property was nearby, she recalled, and her father had met the man in the local inn.

At the stable, a man approached them. Marlena held her breath, but to her relief, he showed no sign of recognising her.

"Good day to you," Tanner said to the man. "Is this your stable?"

"It is," the man said.

Tanner offered the man a handshake. "We've been travelling and my horse has thrown a shoe."

"Let me have a look at the fellow." The stableman lifted the horse's leg and examined its hoof. He rubbed his hands over the leg. "He's strained it, but he's not lame. You are lucky. I'll fetch the smithy and we'll tend to him, but you'd better rest the horse a day or two."

Marlena turned her head away as she dismounted, feeling as if every drop of blood had drained from her face.

She heard Tanner ask, "Is there an inn here?"

The man pointed to it, but Marlena could have pointed to it as well. "The Black Agnes. Not many folks come to stay there." He shifted from one foot to another. "Folks more often stay at Parronley, over yonder." He inclined his head in that direction. "When folks had business with the baron when he was alive. Poor devil. Not so much now."

"The baron?" Tanner asked conversationally.

Marlena thought Tanner must have known Niall as Baron Parronley once, from school or in London.

"Died of fever some time back, his boys with him." The man patted Tanner's horse. "Aye. Parronley has seen its share of troubles. There's worse—"

Marlena broke in. "I do apologise for interrupting, but I should like to go to the inn now." She had no wish for the stableman to go on about the sad tale of the baroness who killed her husband.

Tanner gave her a sympathetic glance, and took the bags from their saddles. "We'll be at the inn if you need to reach us," he told the man. "I'll check with you later, in any event."

The man peered at him. "English, are ye?"

Tanner laughed. "Yes. We are."

Marlena started to walk away. "May we go, please?"

Tanner bid goodbye to the man and caught up to Marlena. "You must be hungry."

"As must you." She hurried towards the inn.

They entered, but found no one in the hallway. Tanner stepped into the taproom and returned with a smiling older gentleman who looked so perfectly like an innkeeper Marlena could not tell if she had seen him before. She kept her face averted just in case.

"Sorry for not seeing ye come in," the innkeeper said. "My name is Gunn."

"Pleased to meet you, Mr Gunn." Tanner shook his hand. "Are you filled with guests or do you have a room for us?"

Perhaps Tanner's question was his way to check if Rapp could be staying at the inn. Marlena knew that if Rapp were this close—and she greatly feared he would be—he would stay in Parronley.

Gunn laughed. "As it is, you are our only guests. I'll show you the room, but I'd be obliged if you would sign the book for me."

Marlena relaxed a little bit. The Black Agnes in Kilrosa seemed safe enough for the moment.

Mr Gunn dipped a pen in ink and handed it to Tanner. Marlena glanced over to see what named he signed, so she would know who they were this day. *Adam Henry and wife*, after all the Henries in Shakespeare's plays.

She stared at his signature. *Adam Henry and wife*.

Under Scottish law a couple only needed only to declare themselves as man and wife in front of a witness to be legally wed. She and Tanner would be considered married the same as if they had been two impetuous lovers eloping to Gretna Green.

She would never claim to be Tanner's wife, except in her own heart. She touched the sapphire ring he had given her at Dutwood House. She would think of it as her wedding ring.

Mr Gunn took them up the stairs. "You can put your bags in the room and I'll start a fire."

"Can we get a meal in the taproom?" Tanner asked. "We have been on the road since morning."

"You may indeed," Gunn replied.

"May I have water to wash with first?" Marlena asked.

"And we had better change our clothes." Tanner added. "Is there someone who can brush the dirt of the road off them?"

Mr Gunn smiled. "You do have a wee bit o' mud on you, haven't you? I'll bring water directly and we'll launder what can be washed and also tend to the rest."

As soon as Gunn left, Tanner turned to Marlena, putting his hands on her shoulders. "Is anything amiss, Marlena? You've not said much since my horse lost a shoe."

Since seeing Parronley House, she thought. "I am tired and sore and hungry, that is all."

He kneaded her shoulders and wrapped his arms around her. "We may be forced to rest here a day or so, if my horse requires it. Would you mind very much?"

She hoped he didn't feel her tremble. She feared Rapp was in Parronley, or would be shortly. He might take it into his head to look for them in Kilrosa. If he found Tanner with her, Tanner would lose his chance to escape.

"I cannot like you being seen with me, Tanner, not with Rapp about."

He put his arms around her and held her against his chest. "We will take care." He pulled away. "Let us change into clean clothes so they can launder these."

They changed out of their mud-spattered clothing and Marlena sat on the bed to wait for the water.

Tanner touched her face. "I will go down to the taproom and discreetly inquire if anyone has seen Rapp." He gave her a reassuring smile. "Do you wish for me to come back up to fetch you?"

She caught his hand and held it to her cheek. "I'll come down to the taproom. Have them bring you your food as soon as you are ready."

When he opened the door to leave, he turned to her. "I do not regret that we must stay together longer."

After he left, Marlena lay down on the bed, exhausted from the ride and the worry. She closed her eyes and even her hunger could not prevent her from falling half-asleep.

A knock came at the door. "Your water, ma'am."

"Come in." Marlena sat up and rubbed her eyes.

The girl carried the water pitcher and some towels to a small table near the fireplace.

"Thank you so much." Marlena stood.

At that same moment the girl turned towards her and Marlena saw her face.

Fia Small.

Marlena gasped.

The girl's face went white. "Lady Corland."

The last Marlena had seen of Fia Small had been when Corland lay dead in a pool of blood, and her cousin had thrust the murder weapon into her hand.

Chapter Fifteen

The ale felt cool on Tanner's throat and greatly welcome. Gunn had reassured him that no stranger had been in the town for days. He could relax with a pint while he waited for Marlena. He'd built up a powerful thirst on that stretch of road. How long had it been since he'd walked five miles? Since he'd walked anywhere, come to think of it? His feet had held up tolerably well. Thanks to his bootmaker, he suspected. Hoby's cobbling skills were unsurpassed.

Gunn brought him a plate of bread and cheese and Tanner tore off a piece of bread and chewed on it.

He thought of strolling past Hoby's boot shop on St James's Street, of popping into Locke's for a new hat, of spending the afternoon at White's with other bored aristocrats.

He lifted the tankard to his lips and washed down the bread. The time he'd spent with Marlena meant so much more to him, even with all its discomforts.

A large man in an apron walked out of the kitchen, stopped abruptly and looked around.

The man turned to Gunn. "Where's Fia?"

The innkeeper inclined his head in Tanner's direction. "We have guests. Fia's tending to the room."

The young man swung around and stared at Tanner, suspicion and challenge in his eyes.

"Well, go ask the man if he desires another ale." Gunn made a shooing gesture with his hands.

The large man approached Tanner with a less-than-friendly demeanour. "Do you want more?"

Tanner looked up at him. "I do." He handed the man the tankard.

The man reached for it, looking directly into Tanner's face. Both his hand and his jaw dropped. "M'lord, what are you doin' here?"

Tanner looked around to see if anyone heard, but there was only one other patron in the taproom and he was sitting off in a corner his hands wrapped around a glass. Mr Gunn was busy behind the bar.

"You've taken me for someone else," Tanner said quickly.

"Nay, I have not." The big man's voice was still full of wonder. "You are the Marquess of Tannerton. I'd know you anywhere."

This man couldn't be more than thirty years, was definitely Scots, by his accent. He looked as if he'd stepped out from that Morier painting Tanner had seen once, the painting of the Battle of Culloden, hardly England's finest hour. Where the devil would he have met the fellow?

Tanner peered at him. "How is it you think you know me?"

"I was there, m'lord," the man said with reverence. "In Brussels after the battle. I saw what you did for the lads. No man worked harder for them than you, sir." He bowed.

Tanner glanced around again. "For God's sake, sit down, and keep your voice low."

The man sat, but stiff as the ramrod he'd probably carried in the battle.

"You were a soldier?" Tanner remembered the wagons of men that poured into Brussels after the battle. Men bleeding, missing limbs or eyes or entire faces, some crying for their mothers, some stoically helping others.

"71st Infantry," the man said.

The 71st helped send Napoleon's Imperial Guard packing, Tanner recalled. "What is your name?"

"Bram Gunn. This is my father's inn." He stood up abruptly. "I'll fetch your ale."

Tanner watched him carefully to see if he'd tell his father the Marquess of Tannerton sat in their inn looking more like a crofter than a marquess, but young Gunn only asked his father to draw another tankard of ale. Tanner blew out a relieved breath.

When Gunn brought the ale, Tanner again gestured for him to sit. The man stared at Tanner, his eyes wide, sitting as stiffly as if he'd been in Wellington's presence.

Tanner took a sip. "You are perhaps wondering why I do not at the moment look like a marquess."

Gunn nodded.

Tanner decided to tell the truth—but not all of it. The elder Gunn sauntered into the kitchen and the other patron was nodding off. No one would overhear.

"I am with a lady," he told young Bram. "She is in some danger, and I am escorting her to a safe place. I do not wish to call attention to myself." He gazed at the former soldier, trying to gauge his reaction. "Hence the clothing."

Gunn's eyes narrowed and he tilted his head slightly. "My father said our guests were a man and his wife. Would that be you and the lady?"

Taken a bit aback by the man's reaction, Tanner took another sip. "That is our disguise, yes."

Gunn leaned forward. "You are in Scotland, m'lord. Did you not know that if you say you are man and wife in Scotland, you are married?"

Tanner took a huge gulp. He ought to have remembered that fact. "It is all part of the ploy," he managed.

Tanner had inadvertently been granted his wish—to make Marlena his marchioness. The irony was painful, but marriage to Marlena pleased Tanner very much.

"So long as you know it," Gunn said.

Tanner gave him a direct look. "It is very important to me that this whole matter, who I am, who I am with, is not spoken of to anyone. May I trust you to say nothing of it?"

Gunn met his eye with a serious and determined look. "I'd do anything you ask, m'lord. Some of the lads you helped were like my brothers."

Tanner smiled at him. "First thing is to call me Henry, not m'lord. I am Mr Henry here, accompanied by Mrs Henry."

Gumm grinned back. "I'll do my best, m'l—Henry."

The door opened with a bang, and both Tanner and Gunn looked over. A well-dressed man swept in.

"Is there no one in this village?" The man spun around.

Hell, thought Tanner. He knew this man.

Wexin.

Who would have thought there could be two people who knew him in this tiny village completely surrounded by Scottish hills?

In his younger days, Tanner and Pomroy made the rounds of London's gaming hells with Wexin and others, but Wexin and his cronies gambled too recklessly for Tanner and Pomroy's tastes and the association ended. Tanner knew Wexin had married Strathfield's daughter when Tanner had still been in Brussels. He'd seen them from time to time at London social events.

Gunn stood up and the man came closer.

"I need the direction to Laird Hay." His head jerked back when he saw Tanner. "Good God, what are you doing here, Tanner?"

Tanner stood and inclined his head towards Gunn. "Passing time with Bram here. We knew each other in Brussels." He extended his hand to Wexin. "I might ask the same of you, Wexin."

Bram stepped back suddenly and knocked over a chair.

Wexin gave the young man a look of disgust and turned back to Tanner. "Business. At Parronley, you know."

Tanner did not know, but he had the feeling he ought to have known.

Wexin went on. "I am invited to dine at Laird Hay's and I do not know the direction." He snapped his neck again and looked Tanner up and down. "Why do you dress like a ruffian?"

Bram spoke up. "His lordship is wearin' clothes I found for him, sir, until his are cleaned and dry."

Tanner smiled. "I was caught in the rain. Everything I owned got wet." He fingered the cloth of his coat. "These garments are remarkably comfortable."

Wexin gave a sniff of disgust.

Bram glared at him. "If ye be seeking the laird, you must ride the main road out of town, about one mile. Follow the first fork you come to in the road and it will lead you to Laird Hay."

Wexin's brows lifted. "About a mile, you say?"

Bram nodded.

Tanner pulled out a chair. "Have a drink with us. The ale is quite nice, I assure you. Bram was about to get us both another pint."

Wexin's nose rose in the air. "I am expected at the laird's. When do you leave this godforsaken village?"

"Early on the morrow," Tanner said. "Too bad you cannot stay. I wanted to hear all the London news. How is your lovely wife, by the way?"

"She is well. I am anxious to return to her." Wexin's voice softened.

"Then I shall see you back in London," Tanner said. "Or have you and Lady Wexin retired to the country?"

"We remain in London." Wexin looked impatiently towards the door. "I must beg your leave."

Tanner waved his hand. "By all means. I would be grateful if you would refrain from informing Laird Hay of my presence here. I should like to avoid the delay of a dinner invitation."

Wexin sighed. "As would I. But I must be on my way. Do forgive me."

"Indeed. Good to see you." Tanner sat down again as Wexin left.

Bram stared at the man's back until he was out the door.

"Thank you, Bram." Tanner blew out a breath. "You saved my hide."

Bram watched Wexin through the window as he mounted his horse and rode away. "Is he a friend of yours?" Bram asked.

Tanner shook his head. "Not a friend. Merely someone I know." He peered at Bram. "Why?"

"I do not like the man," Bram replied.

Marlena rushed over as the maid's eyes rolled back in her head. She caught the girl before she fell and eased her across to a chair.

Fia bent over, her head in her hands. "I thought you were dead, m'lady. I was sure of it, because—"

Marlena spoke at the same time. "I feared you were dead, too. I feared he'd found you." She touched the girl's shoulder.

Fia sat up, some colour returning to her face. "I've been here in Kilrosa. I was a year here before I stopped being afraid he'd come. And now—"

"I am so glad." Marlena crouched down so her face was even with Fia's. She took the girl's hands in her own. "I am so relieved. I wanted you to be safe and not try to tell anyone what happened."

Fia's eyes widened. "You do not mind I did not tell what I saw?"

Marlena squeezed her hands. "He would have killed you."

Fia shuddered. "You will not tell anyone about me. Please?"

"No," she reassured. "I promise."

Fia looked at her. "Where did you go, m'lady? They were searching for you everywhere."

"A friend took me to Ireland to be her children's governess. But her brother came and recognised me. I—I had to leave there."

"Oh, m'lady, you had to be a governess?" The girl looked horrified.

"It was a happy time," Marlena reassured her. "Really."

Fia's eyes were still wide. "Why did you come here? This is not a safe place for you."

"We did not mean to come here. We wound up too far east." Marlena clamped her mouth shut before she revealed too much. It was better not to speak of her final destination.

"M'lady, are ye married again?"

Yes, Marlena thought. *To Tanner.* "There is a man helping me."

"But if you stay the night with him—"

Marlena knew. The marriage would be consummated.

They heard a horse outside and someone shouting in the street below. Fia's chair was right next to the window. She opened the curtain and peered out.

With a gasp, Fia drew back, her fist in her mouth as if to keep from screaming.

"What is it, Fia?" Marlena opened the curtain, but all she saw was a man's figure entering the inn.

"It is him." The girl rose from the chair and backed away. "Him."

Marlena crossed over to her. "Who?"

"Lord Wexin!" Fia's voice cracked and she trembled all over.

Marlena froze.

She had expected Rapp, not Wexin. He must have come to find her. Marlena dashed to the fireplace and grabbed the poker for a weapon. She stood by the door and listened, fearing to hear his footsteps approaching.

The next sound they heard was not footsteps on the stairs, but horse's hooves again.

Fia ran to the window. "He's riding away!"

Marlena released the breath she'd been holding and leaned against the door.

Fia turned to her. "When I heard he had come to Parronley, I thought it meant you were dead."

"It means he is looking for me, I fear." Marlena's mind was racing. What should she say to Tanner? Wexin must never know Tanner was here with her, but what if he'd seen Tanner here?

"If he finds me—" Fia's voice broke.

A knock on the door made them both jump. "Fia! Are ye in there?"

"It is Bram," Fia said.

Tanner's voice also came through the door. "Marlena?"

She hurriedly put the poker back by the fireplace.

Tanner opened the door, and a large man pushed past him to rush to Fia's side. "I've something to tell you, lass."

"I know…" she glanced to the window "…we saw him,

but, Bram, you will never guess." She extended her arm towards Marlena. "This is Lady Corland!"

Fia's Bram bowed. "My lady."

"I do not wish it to be known—" Marlena began.

Tanner turned to her. "Lady Corland?"

His eyes scanned her and her heart thumped painfully in her chest. She could just feel him searching his mind for where the name fitted into the puzzle.

His glance slid to Fia and her Bram. "I would like to be alone with her."

Bram bowed. "Of course, m'lord."

Tanner's expression did not change. "Take care, Bram. Say no more than that we are Mr and Mrs Henry. To anyone."

Bram glanced to Fia and back to Tanner. "May I tell Fia, m'lord? The lass has a right to know."

Tanner's gaze turned to Fia. "She knows more than I do, I believe," he murmured. He nodded, looking back at Bram. "No one else, Bram. This lady's—" he shot a glance to Marlena "—*Lady Corland's* well-being depends upon it." He spoke the name with venom. "Corland," he repeated in a near-whisper.

"Ay, you have my word—Mr Henry." Bram took Fia by the arm and whisked her from the room.

Marlena braced herself as Tanner faced her, not speaking. His expression told her he had put the facts together.

He knew.

He walked over to the window and looked out. "What was it the newspapers called you?" His voice was flat, devoid of humour, devoid of any emotion.

She felt sick inside. "The Vanishing Viscountess."

"That was it. *The Vanishing Viscountess.*" He nodded, still gazing into the street where Wexin had ridden off. "I was in Belgium, I believe. We were busy with other matters at the time."

A few weeks after her story reached the newspapers, the battle of Waterloo took over everyone's attention. That horrible news had erased her from the printed page, and she'd been largely forgotten.

"But I do recall a newspaper reaching us." He turned back to her. "Lord Corland was murdered in his bed, as I recall."

She straightened her spine. "He was."

He turned away. "Corland was your husband."

A shaft of pain pierced her heart. "I did not kill him," she added helplessly. "But you must see why I did not tell you."

He spun around again. "I do not see that at all, Marlena. Did you think I would not believe you?"

She straightened her spine. "You would not have believed me at first. Corland. Wexin. You knew those men. You would not have believed me."

His brows came together and he stared towards the window. "What has Wexin to do with it?"

"Wexin killed Corland. He placed the blame on me."

"Wexin?" He glanced back at her in surprise.

"He is very dangerous, Tanner." She spoke in an even tone. "He would kill you if he knew you were with me."

His expression turned sceptical. "Wexin?"

She took a breath and released it. "I knew you would not believe me. I would not have believed it myself if I had not seen what he'd done. I still have no idea why he did it. Wexin and Corland were friends, but Wexin—my cousin—set it up to look as if I had killed my husband." She shivered. "He is searching for me, Tanner."

He continued to gaze at her. "Why would Wexin search here?"

She gave a wry smile. "He assumed I would flee to Parronley."

His brows came together again. "Why?"

"It is my home, Tanner." She glanced away from him, seeing the house and land once again in her mind. "I spent my childhood in Parronley. When…" her voice faltered "…when my brother—you knew Niall, I think—and my two little nephews died, I became the heir. The title was such it could pass to daughters as well as sons."

"You are the Baroness?"

She shrugged. "I could not claim the title, of course, but, yes, the Baroness Parronley."

He pressed his fingers to his temple. "I do remember your brother. I remember reading about his death." His eyes, however, were filled with anger, not sympathy. "You had better tell me the whole now, Marlena. I would be obliged if you would trust me with the truth."

She told him all of it. Of coming upon Wexin dressed in her robe, holding her scissors, wiping Corland's blood on her clothing. Of seeing Corland, eyes staring, throat cut.

She told him how Wexin called for help and how servants came running. How when they waited for a magistrate, she escaped and ran to Eliza, who gave her refuge.

She told him everything except about Fia, because she had promised the girl not to reveal her part in it.

Tanner listened, but she could not read his stony expression. He stood still, taking in all she said.

As she spoke, she heard how ludicrous her version of the story sounded. Who would believe it? She'd always known Wexin had set up a brilliant plot against her.

When she finished, Tanner said nothing and still did not move. She could not bear any longer to watch him and she turned to lean on the nearby table, where the jug of water waited for her.

"You do not believe me," she whispered into the tense silence.

He lifted a hand as if to silence her. "That is not it,

Marlena." He backed away from her. "I need to be alone. I'll send food up to you. Stay in the room. Do not leave."

Before she could say a word, he was gone.

Marlena sank on to the nearest chair. She buried her head in her hands.

Chapter Sixteen

"You must tell what you know, lass." Bram held Fia's hands in his big strong ones.

Fia looked away. She hated Bram knowing how weak and cowardly she was.

They stood in the yard behind the inn. It was chilly outside, but she'd hardly felt anything since they'd left Lady Corland's room.

Lady Corland had found a strong man to protect her. A Marquess must be a grand man indeed. She did not need Fia to help her. Bram was strong, too, and he said he'd protect Fia, but she was still afraid.

"Think on it," Bram went on. "She's been hiding all this time, and so have you. You can go to the laird and tell him the truth. You'd both be free then."

She shook her head. "You do not know what Wexin can do, Bram. We'd have to go to London, and Wexin would kill us before we got there."

"I'd go with you, Fia. Naught would happen to you." He brushed a hand through her hair.

She pulled away. "Then he would kill you, too, Bram, and that would be worse!"

The door opened and Fia's aunt appeared in the doorway. "What're you two doin' out here? There's people wanting food and drink inside."

"We'll come now, Mam," Bram said.

Aunt Priss went back inside, the door slamming behind her.

"Come, lass, we must work." Bram held out his hand.

Fia hung back. "I want to go to my sister's house tomorrow, Bram. Will you take me? He won't chance to find me there."

Her sister was married to one of the laird's crofters. If Fia hid there, Wexin would not happen upon her as he almost had today. Bram could come fetch her when Wexin went away again.

Bram frowned. "If I can't change your mind, lass…"

They walked inside, passing through the kitchen, where Aunt Priss handed Bram a tray. "Some food and tea for the guest upstairs, Bram. Will you take it to her?" She turned to Fia. "There's people waiting in the taproom. What's got into you, Fia?"

"I'm sorry, Aunt Priss," she replied. "I forgot the time."

Bram, carrying the tray, followed Fia as she hurried into the taproom.

As soon as they crossed that threshold, Lord Tannerton stopped them. "Is that food for her?" he asked.

Bram nodded. "Aye."

The marquess glanced around and leaned forward, a fierce look in his eyes. "Will you betray her? Will you tell the magistrate that she is here?"

"Tell the laird? No!" cried Fia. "Don't say such a thing, m'lord."

"Call him Mr Henry, Fia," Bram corrected. "You have our vow. We'll not betray Lady Parr—we'll not betray her."

Tannerton nodded, but he blocked their way again. "Why? Tell me why you won't betray her."

"She did not do it," said Fia.

"You believe her?" Tannerton looked from one to the other.

Fia had been certain Lady Corland would tell the marquess about her seeing the murder and now it seemed as if she hadn't.

Bram gave her a glance. He turned to the marquess. "We believe her, sir."

Fia felt tears well in her eyes. Bram could have told the marquess right then about her seeing what really happened. He didn't, even though he thought the marquess was a very great man because of what he'd done in Brussels.

"Do ye not believe her, sir?" Fia asked the marquess.

"Of course I do," he answered sharply. His voice softened. "I merely wondered if I was the only one."

He thanked them again for agreeing to keep Marlena's secret and he returned to a table where a tankard of ale waited for him.

Fia reached for the tray in Bram's hands. "Will you let me take this to her? Will you care for the patrons 'til I'm back?"

"If you like." He gave her the tray.

Fia carried it up the flight of stairs and knocked on the door to Lady Corland's room. "It is Fia, ma'am."

Lady Corland opened it.

"Some food for you, ma'am." She set the tray on the table.

The lady looked pale and upset, and Fia felt a wave of guilt for not wanting to try to help her by telling the laird what she'd seen so long ago. She could not do it. She was so afraid inside she thought she might break in pieces.

"You didn't tell the marquess about me," Fia said.

Lady Corland looked at her in surprise. "I promised you."

"I thank you." Fia hung her head. "I—I want to go away. Is it all right with you, m'lady? Is it all right I don't tell what I know?"

The lady gave her a soft look. "It would be very dangerous to tell what you know, Fia. With my—my friend's help, I can go into hiding again. Then we both will be safe."

"Where will you be going, m'lady?" What place would be safe for her? Wexin was a rich man. He could go anywhere to find her.

Lady Corland's expression turned serious. "I'll not tell you, Fia. I don't want you to have the burden of knowing it, but you are not to worry. Eventually Lord Wexin will leave Parronley. You should be safe to live your life here with your young man."

Fia felt her face go hot. "Och, Bram is not my young man."

"Isn't he?" The lady smiled.

Fia was too embarrassed to answer. She glanced towards the door. "I'd best be seeing to the patrons."

"I understand."

"You can place the tray in the hall if you'd like it to be out of your way." Fia shuffled her feet. "I'll fetch it later."

"I will do that."

Fia walked to the door and opened it. "If I don't see you again, I wish you fare well."

"I wish you fare well, too."

Fia smiled because her ladyship spoke the words just like a Scotswoman. Fia hurried out of the room and down the stairs.

The first patrons Fia saw in the taproom were Erroll and Lyall Gibb. "Ho, you, Fia. We heard you had a guest in the inn. The man over there? Who is he?"

She remembered what the marquess asked of her. "He's somebody who got lost. What other reason has a stranger to come to Kilrosa?"

She glanced over at Bram who was working the tap at the moment. He had an approving look on his face.

"Now what do you want to drink?" she asked the Gibb brothers.

Tanner swayed a bit as he took the first step on the stairway. He grasped the banister to steady himself. Perhaps he should not have switched to whisky. Damned good drink, however.

He reached the room and entered with a clatter. Night had fallen. He'd intended not to wake her. He glanced to the bed, but it was empty.

Damnation. Had she run again?

He steadied himself on the edge of the bed, but he really wanted to pound his fist into the wall. Suddenly from the corner of his eye he saw something move.

She stood up from a chair near the fire.

Her hair was loose and flowed down to her shoulders. She wore the nightdress that the wife of that first innkeeper had given to her. After their nights together, he knew the feel of the cloth and the feel of her beneath it.

"You are still awake?" Idiotic thing for him to say. Of course she was.

"I rested some." Her voice floated across the room as if on the wings of angels.

He was waxing poetic. Must be jug-bitten.

"Sleeping is difficult," she added.

Her scent seemed to fill the room, the scent of soap and something indefinable, like a rare flower.

There he went again. Poetic. "Have you been in the room all this time?"

"I went below stairs to the necessary," she said.

He frowned. "All alone?"

"I was careful," she replied.

He winced with guilt. He should have checked on her; should have seen if she needed him. "I would have gone with you. Why did you not come to get me in the taproom?"

"I thought you did not want me there."

He wanted her wherever he was. Wanting her had consumed his thoughts while he'd been consuming multiple glasses of whisky. "I would not have minded."

He felt himself listing to the side, and grabbed hold of the bedpost. "Did you have enough to eat?"

"I did, thank you."

Blast it. He hated the caution in her voice. He desired hearing her voice filled with the same passion that burned inside him. That passion for her had remained constant even when faced with her unbelievable story.

No matter how preposterous her story, he believed her. He'd spent days with her. He'd lain with her. He *knew* her, knew the woman she was, no matter what name she went by, what story she told.

She should have trusted him. After that first time of lovemaking, she should have told him who she was—that she had been married. Blast the idea of protecting him.

"I knew Corland," he told her, as if she could follow the direction of his mind.

She lowered her head. "I presumed you knew him."

Tanner's throat went suddenly dry. "Did you love him, Marlena?"

She glanced up. "I thought I loved him at first. He was very charming."

"He was a damned fellow," Tanner said.

She met his gaze. "He—he was not unlike the man I invented in my tale for you."

Tanner gave a disgusted laugh. "The fictional jewel thief?"

She nodded.

"At least some of what you told me was true." He advanced towards her. "Corland was a bounder and debaucher. Did you not think I would understand—?" He stopped short of touching her.

She interrupted him. "Understand why I would kill him, do you mean?" She spun away from him.

He put his hands on her shoulders and turned her to face him. "You cannot think I do not believe you."

She avoided looking at him.

He lifted her chin with one hand. "I cannot abide thinking of you married to Corland, of your being in his bed—" He needed to brace himself on her shoulder.

"Tanner," she said breathlessly.

He shook his head. "You should have trusted me, Marlena. You've made me bring you to the place of greatest danger to you. Wexin is not five miles away."

She said nothing, merely looked into his eyes.

He released her, lifting both hands before placing one of them on the table for balance.

Did she think he would never discover she was the Vanishing Viscountess? During his stay in the taproom, he realised the crime made no difference to him. He could not leave her merely because it was not theft, but a murder charge on her head. He'd move all the mountains of Scotland to keep her from the hangman's noose. To protect her from Wexin.

"Wexin." He spat out the name. "The cursed villain! Why the devil did he wish to kill Corland in the first place? He gambled unwisely, but otherwise I would not have thought him capable of such tresh—treachery."

He swayed and lowered himself carefully into the chair next to him.

She sat on the opposite chair. "Are you drunk, Tanner?"

He tried to give her a composed look. "Merely a trifle disguised."

A smile teased at the corner of her mouth.

He smiled in return, but forced himself to at least look sober. "I was thinking we should go to France."

"France?" She sat up straighter.

He leaned on the table. "Instead of Edinburgh. Although we'll have to go to Edinburgh, I think, to get passage to France. The thing is, Wexin cannot get to you in France. You cannot be arrested in a different country. I should think Wexin would give it up with me protecting you."

"Wait." She touched his hand. "What do you mean *we* should go to France?"

His hand tingled at her touch, the sensation spreading through him. "I would not send you there alone," he managed to respond.

"Tanner—"

His mind was clear, even if the alcohol made him a trifle unsteady. He knew what must be done, what he wanted above all things.

"I worked this out, Marlena." He met her gaze soberly. "I'm not needed here. There is nothing for me to do but pursue pleasure. Gambling. Hunting. Other sport." Words were failing him and he wanted to make her understand." He winced. "The last time I amused myself, three people wound up dead—"

"The responsibility for that was not yours," she protested.

He waved a hand. "It was. No escaping truth. Thing is, I can help you. Have helped you. Might as well keep helping you—"

"Tanner, traveling with me to Paris will take time. Weeks, maybe. The more time you spend with me, the more risk there is of being connected with me and accused of helping me escape."

He laughed softly. "You do not know what I am trying to say. I would take you to Paris and stay with you. Live with you."

"No." She rose from the chair. "You cannot mean this."

"Of course I mean it."

"Tanner, you are a marquess." She gaped at him.

He wanted to pull her on to his lap and show her he was a man first, before a marquess.

She stepped away from him. "You cannot leave your responsibilities."

He waved his hand again. "That is just it. I can. I have hired a legion of workers who do an excellent job running the whole lot. That is my point, Marlena. *I* am not needed. My affairs have been set up to run well. For two generations the set-up has worked to perfection. I am the least important person in keeping them running well." He stood. "Oh, perhaps I may be needed for a signature or two, but documents can be couriered to me. You would be safe. We could have a life together." He touched her face, gently. "What do you say, Marlena?"

"Oh, Tanner." She wrapped her arms around his neck.

He seized her in his arms and captured her lips, kissing her with more hunger than when they'd gone without food. She was all softness, all curves, and his hands glided over her body, relishing where he touched, longing to feel her bare skin.

She pushed his coat over his shoulders and pulled on the sleeves until the garment fell to the floor. He wanted to laugh for joy, because she wanted him, too. She had thought of undressing him at the same moment he had thought of undressing her.

They were like two sides of a coin, he realised. Parts of the same whole, making no sense unless they were together. He wanted to show her, make her understand that they belonged together.

That he could not live without her.

This revelation had come to him in the taproom. *He could not live without her.*

She unbuttoned his waistcoat, and he shrugged out of it, pulling the shirttails out of his trousers next. Her delicate hands worked the buttons on the fall of his trousers, tantalising him, making him yearn for her fingers to touch where he was now so powerfully aroused for her.

Her fingers skimmed that part of him and again he had the fancy that they thought with one mind.

"Your boots," she murmured, urgency in her voice.

Damn the boots, he thought, not wanting to stop for such practicality as removing his boots. She knelt before him to pull them off, and his trousers after them. Her hands stroked his thighs as if wanting to come closer.

"Marlena," he rasped, unable to wait.

He pulled her on top of him, his hands under her nightdress, finding her breasts, feeling her nipples harden for him.

She moaned. "Can we do it now, Tanner? Here."

One mind, he thought. One passion. Never had he been with a woman so attuned to him. Never had he felt so complete as when joining with her.

"You and I can do whatever we wish." He felt more powerful with her than with all the trappings his title afforded him.

He positioned her on to him, entering her there on the chair. The moment of joining accelerated his joy and his need of her. They even moved as one, in perfect rhythm, their need growing in unison. He closed his eyes and let himself be lost in her, to relish this belonging to one person. To feel that this, above all else, gave meaning to his life.

They were as one in their moment of satisfaction, as well. He felt the release of his seed, the culmination of his pleasure at the same moment he felt her pulse against him. Their voices cried out together, and their last writhing of ecstasy came as if they were one.

He'd long abandoned the idea of leaving her in some god-awful place in Edinburgh without the intention of freeing her and coming back to her. Now he realised he did not want to leave her at all. It would be like leaving all that gave his life meaning.

He held her quietly on his lap for a few minutes until the reality of cramped muscles set in.

"I'm taking you to bed," he murmured into her ear.

She slid off his lap and pulled him to her as soon as her feet touched the floor. A kiss joined them once more, a uniting kiss.

He picked her up into his arms and carried her to the bed where they quickly disposed of her nightdress and his shirt and joined each other, skin to skin, under the covers. To his delight their passion rapidly rose again.

Afterwards she lay in his arms, and he savoured the smoothness of her skin against his.

He turned his head and kissed her on the temple. "You know what this means, do you not?" he said to her, his voice tinged with the joy that permeated every part of him.

"Mmm, what?" she murmured sleepily.

"We are married." He grinned and turned to her for a quick taste of her mouth. "We are in Scotland, claiming to be husband and wife, and we have just consummated our union." He swept a hand through her now tangled hair. "We are married."

"Married." She sighed.

In spite of all his drink, he lay awake while she drifted to sleep, his mind spinning with plans to reach Edinburgh. They would have to hide there somehow until he was able to access his funds and get enough money to set themselves up in France. He'd like them to be married properly, by clergy, if possible, but he could not feel more married to her than he did at this moment.

Soon he would be able to shower her with everything his wealth could provide her. He fell asleep, thinking of jewels and dresses and shoes and trinkets, every luxury he wanted to buy her.

Lord Wexin returned to Parronley in the dark after a deadly tedious meal with Laird Hay. He did learn a bit about how landowners were increasing their profits here in Scotland, by forcing out the crofters so there would be more land for sheep. The wool industry seemed to be doing quite well.

He frowned as he left the horse to a stable boy and found his way up the dark path to the great mausoleum of a house that smelled of years of being closed up. He could do nothing here until he inherited, and, unless Rapp located Marlena, that might never happen. He needed her to be found. Needed even more for her to be dead. Why the devil could she not have drowned in that shipwreck and her body wash up on shore? Everything would have been so easy that way.

He entered the house and found the elderly butler napping in a chair in the hall.

"Here, man!" Wexin said loudly. "Take my things."

The man woke with a snort and struggled arthritically to his feet. "M'lord," he mumbled, taking his hat and gloves and catching the top coat that was thrown into his arms. "Begging you pardon, m'lord, but a man arrived while you were out."

"A man?" Wexin raised his brows.

"Ay, sir," the old man said. "He said you would wish to see him this night. A Mr Rapp, sir."

"Why did you not say it was Rapp in the first place?" Wexin snapped.

The butler shrugged. "He waits in an anteroom near the kitchen."

"Is the drawing room lit with candles and a fire as I instructed?" Wexin demanded.

The butler bowed. "Ay, m'lord."

"Then bring me some brandy and have Rapp attend me there."

Wexin made his way across the hall, his heels clicking on the stone floor. The drawing room had none of the elegance and fine taste that his lovely Lydia had brought to their London townhouse, but he supposed it would do for the likes of Rapp.

A few minutes later Wexin was settled with a tolerable bottle of brandy. The butler announced Rapp, who strode in.

Wexin waited for the butler to close the door and for the man's receding footsteps to be heard.

"How did you know I was here?" Wexin demanded.

Rapp responded, "Your arrival was spoken of in Parronley. I am staying at the inn there."

Wexin waved an impatient hand. "Well, what is your report?

Rapp straightened. "I have seen her travelling in the company of a man. I am convinced she is coming here."

"You saw her and did not capture her?" Wexin huffed.

Two spots of colour tinged Rapp's cheeks. "She managed to elude me. Once in Liverpool. Once on the road outside Langholm, but I am confident she will not elude me a third time."

Wexin gave a sardonic laugh. "One woman managed to elude you twice? Three times if we count your losing her in the shipwreck?" He should have hired a more ruthless man to escort his cousin back to London, one who would have seen that a shipwreck ended her life.

"The man in her company came to her aid," explained Rapp.

Wexin glared. "And who is this man?"

Rapp pressed his lips together before speaking. "I have not seen his face. They change names at every stop. He may wear a signet ring, however."

"A signet ring?" Wexin's excitement grew. "Do you know the seal?"

Rapp lifted his chin. "Only that it included a stag and an eagle."

Tannerton's seal!

Wexin took a sip of brandy to disguise a smile. How many other gentlemen with a stag and eagle on their crest would be rusticating in this god-forsaken part of Scotland? It had to be Tannerton, and Marlena was with him. Wexin's hand trembled. He had been so close to her this very day.

He retained his composure. "This is all you have for me? That she travels in this direction with a man wearing a ring? I could have guessed as much."

Well, he would not have guessed she'd have a man with her, let alone a marquess, but it did make sense that she could not have come this far all alone.

"They travelled on horseback," Rapp responded, an edge in his voice. "That made it more difficult to follow their progress. They have largely remained off the coaching and toll roads."

Wexin waved a hand. "Go. You are dismissed. I'll have no further need of your services. Return to Bow Street and wherever else the deuce you belong."

Rapp frowned. "What of my pay, sir?"

Wexin eyed him with disdain. "No prisoner. No pay." He waved a hand. "Be off with you. I cannot abide incompetence and failure. I dare say you can find your way to the village. Do not show your face in this house again."

Rapp took one threatening step towards Wexin, but then he seemed to think better of it. He turned around and walked out, slamming the door behind him.

Wexin released a grin. He'd wait long enough for Rapp to be gone and then he would send for the men he'd brought with him from London, men who would not let a woman and a pampered marquess defeat them so easily.

He raised his glass in a toast. "To you, cousin Marlena. Soon we see each other again. Then you will meet your fate."

Rapp stormed out of the house and back to the stable for his hired horse.

Damned Wexin. He released a whole string of epithets towards this man who had not only cheated him out of his pay, but also the sum of money he'd spent along the road. He would show the ruddy man. There was still a reward waiting in London for the return of the Vanishing Viscountess. Rapp intended to collect that reward and Lord Wexin could go to the devil for all he cared.

Chapter Seventeen

Marlena awoke in Tanner's arms, with the delicious knowledge that each morning from now on she would awaken in the same spot. She'd never dared hope for happiness again, but Tanner had delivered it to her as surely as he had rescued her from the Irish Sea, impossible tasks both.

She ignored the twinges of guilt that teased at her conscience. She'd not asked Tanner to give up his life in England for her. He'd offered it. He wanted it. She pushed away the nagging thought that he would some day regret leaving his duties, his country.

She could not help but worry about the people of Parronley. Perhaps she could assume her title as Baroness when she was in France. Perhaps she could care for her people *in absentia* as Tanner planned to do.

At least they would not be under Wexin's care.

Another fear tugged at her sleeve. Would Wexin come after her even in France? Would she and Tanner still have to constantly look over their shoulders?

His eyes opened and gazed warmly into hers. "Good morning, wife."

She smiled. They were married. Could she really allow herself to believe that dream had come true?

Eliza, she thought. *Am I married to the Marquess of Tannerton?*

"Good morning," she responded.

He gathered her in his arms and kissed her, her body answering with the flushed excitement and yearning he always elicited in her, even in those days when she and Eliza were mooning over him.

She laughed softly. "Did you know you danced with me once, Tanner?"

His face screwed up in disbelief. "I would have remembered."

She touched his mouth with her finger tracing the outline of his lips. "At Lady Erstine's masquerade ball. I was dressed as a maiden from the time of King Arthur with a pointed hat and a flowing veil. And a mask, of course. You never saw my face."

His lips formed into a rueful smile. "I would treasure the memory—if I remembered it."

She laughed again. "I would never expect you to remember me. I was a very forgettable girl in those days, but my friend Eliza and I kept an account of you. We were quite enamoured of you."

"You jest."

She stroked his chin, loving how scratchy his growth of beard felt on her fingertips. "It is true, but a long time ago. A marquess was reaching too high for us. At the end of the season, Corland became my suitor and my brother declared he would make me a good husband."

Tanner's smile disappeared. He took a strand of her hair and twirled it in his fingers. "Your brother ought to have known better."

"Oh, I suppose Corland charmed Niall as thoroughly as he did me."

Tanner's brow furrowed. "Did you have any happiness with Corland, Marlena?"

She stared into his eyes, seeing flecks of brown in their mossy green. "Briefly, when I was too starry-eyed to know better, and Corland still had my money to spend." She cupped her palm against his cheek. "It never felt like this."

His eyes darkened and he placed his lips on hers again, giving her more in one kiss than she'd ever imagined a man could give.

"Marlena," he murmured, tasting of her lips again and again. "Wife."

She was certain of what love meant now. It meant how she felt about this man, how his mere whispering of her name sent shafts of desire through her, how his touch aroused her senses, how his smile filled her with joy.

She rolled on to her back and he covered her, worshipping her with his gaze, soothing her with his hands, thrilling her with his coupling. When he entered her it was all that she could do not to cry out in joy. He was hers. She, a fugitive everywhere else, was at home with him.

He moved with exquisite gentleness, making their passion grow. Though lost to sensation as the pleasure built inside her, one thought remained. She would belong to him like this for ever.

Sparkles of light seemed to dance behind her eyelids as he brought her passion to its peak. She imagined the light passing through her skin, becoming a part of her, belonging to her in a way she would never have to give up.

When she lay again in his arms, sated and safe, her joy turned to contentment.

She must have fallen asleep again, because when she woke, he was at the basin shaving, wearing only his trousers.

"Why did you not wake me?" she asked. The room was bright with sunlight. The morning well advanced. "It must be late."

He turned. "No need to do so. We have only ten miles to go by the map. An easy ride. I thought I would dress first and let you sleep."

She rose from the bed and retrieved her nightdress from the floor. Slipping it on, she walked over to him and hugged him from behind.

He turned and kissed her, then wiped the soap he left on her face with his thumb. "I think it best you remain in the room while I check on the horses. With any luck my horse will be fit for the journey."

"I do not mind." She loved their simple room in this humble inn. It was the site of her wedding, after all, and it felt safe.

She washed and dressed, finishing just as he was ready to go out of the door. As she started to pin up her hair, he gave her another swift kiss. "I'll be back. Before I head for the stable, I'll arrange for some food to be sent up for us."

After he left, she hurried to the window to watch him walk out of the inn, so tall, so commanding in his masculine stride. She felt as giddy as the girl she'd once been, watching him saunter into a ballroom.

Dare I be so happy, Eliza?

When he was no longer in sight, she finished dressing her hair and covered it with a cap. She straightened the bedcovers, her hand smoothing the linens, remembering how they had become so twisted and tangled with their lovemaking.

She had just finished tidying the room when Fia's Bram brought her breakfast.

He set the tray on the table. Such a big bear of a man, she

thought and smiled to herself, remembering Fia's protest about him. They were so obviously besotted with each other.

"How is Fia today, Bram?" she asked.

"Och," replied the large man, "I walked her to her sister's early this morn. That cursed flesher has her in a great fright, y'know. Best she hide for a bit."

Flesher. She had not heard that Scottish term for *butcher* in many years. It was an apt name for Wexin, she thought with a shudder.

"Whatever keeps her safe." She caught Bram's eye. "Wexin is a very dangerous man, Bram. You must be very wary of him, for Fia's sake."

A hard, determined look came over his face. "Aye, I'll keep her safe."

"Good." She smiled.

"Lord Tannerton will see you safe, as well, m'lady. He is a fine man. He'll see you to your destination without that demon finding you." He nodded his head in emphasis.

Marlena regarded him with curiosity. "From where do you know Lord Tannerton, Bram?"

"From Brussels, m'lady."

"Brussels?"

"Ay." He nodded again. "It was after the great battle. I was in the 71st, ma'am, who fought in the battle. After that day I was walkin' into Brussels with the wounded." He pushed up his sleeve and showed her a jagged scar. "I was not bad hurt, but others were dyin'. His lordship carried the lads from the wagons. He found houses to take the lads and tend them and he paid with his own money for the caring of them. Did it all day, m'lady. And the next. And the next."

"Lord Tannerton did that?"

"Aye, ma'am, and there were plenty lords who ran back to England that day, but not his lordship." His chest puffed out in pride as he spoke. "And then a year later I heard my officers talking that his lordship spoke in Parliament, to help the lads that came back, maimed and unable to work."

Parliament. The House of Lords.

Tanner had neglected to tell her that he had taken his seat in the Lords, but of course he would have done so.

Bram concluded. "Lord Tannerton is a great man."

"Yes," she agreed, her voice suddenly cracking.

Bram glanced to the door. "I'd best be going back to my duties, ma'am, if you are no longer needing me."

"No," she said distractedly. "I do not need you, but I thank you, Bram."

He bowed and strode out of the room.

Marlena grabbed hold of the bedpost, pressing her cheek against the smooth wood. She squeezed her eyes shut.

A great man, Bram had said. Tanner was a great man, a man who organised the care of the wounded at Waterloo. A man who spoke for those men in the House of Lords. He had said nothing to Marlena of this part of his life.

Marlena sank into the chair, but had little appetite for the food in front of her. She absently nibbled on a piece of bread, picturing Tanner's strong arms carrying men from wagons, seeing Tanner heedless of blood staining his clothes, thinking only of what must be done. She thought of him standing in the Lords, among all those important, titled men, his deep masculine voice booming to the far recesses of the room.

He was an important man.

There was another quick knock at the door, and Tanner walked in, a line of worry between his brows.

He smiled at her, though, and crossed the room to her, kissing her upturned face. When he sat down across from her, the worry line remained. "The horse needs another day of rest, the stableman tells me."

"I see," she responded.

He tilted his head. "I tried to barter for another horse, but the man did not think he could procure one before the end of the day."

"Could we walk or take one horse?" she asked.

He shook his head. "It slows us considerably. Should Rapp or Wexin encounter us, we'd have little chance of escaping." He lifted his palm. "I also thought about a carriage, but Bram said this village does not have a coaching inn. We would have to go to Parronley for it." He rubbed his face. "Wexin must be watching the coaching inn."

The fear felt like a hard rock inside her. "When can we leave?"

"Tomorrow, the stableman assures me." He reached across the table and took her hand.

She squeezed his fingers. "We can wait a day, can we not? We can hide in this room. Bram will warn us if anyone comes."

He lifted her hand to his lips. "That is the wisest course, I believe."

She poured his tea and placed some ham and cheese on his plate. She listened with only half an ear as he told her more particulars about the horse and his thoughts of what route they could take to avoid the more travelled roads.

"I spoke to Bram and he will draw us a map." He took a bite of ham.

Her heart began to pound faster. She tried to keep her voice calm. "Bram said he knew you from Waterloo, that you were in Brussels after the battle. He spoke of your heroic work with the wounded."

"Heroic?" He shook his head. "I assure you, I merely helped a little. There was nothing else to do."

What Bram described had been considerable, but Marlena did not argue the point.

"What were you doing in Brussels?" she asked instead.

The newspapers during that time had reported that some of the English had considered Brussels somewhat of a social event, the place to be, until Napoleon decided to be there as well.

"Pure accident, I was there." Tanner took a sip of tea. "I'd been at the Congress of Vienna. Assisting Castlereagh, you know. When he went back to England, I stayed. Helped Wellington for a bit and went on to Brussels when his Grace was called there."

Her jaw dropped. "You were at the Congress of Vienna?"

After Napoleon's first abdication, all the powers of Europe gathered in Vienna to decide the fate of the Continent. If Tanner had been there, someone must have considered his assistance very important indeed—important enough to be a part of deciding the fate of nations.

"Just helping out a bit. Castlereagh talked me into it." He chewed on a piece of bread.

She supposed Wellington had "talked him into" helping him as well. Marlena leaned back in her chair and stared at him. "Goodness, Tanner, what else have you done?"

"Done?" His brows rose. "I did not *do* anything. I merely assisted."

"Why you?" She lifted her cup.

He shrugged. "I suppose the Duke of Clarence suggested my name to Castlereagh."

"The Duke of Clarence!" The King's son. The Prince Regent's brother. She nearly spilled her tea.

"Friend of mine." He pierced another piece of ham with his fork and popped it in his mouth.

Although it seemed as if she could no longer breathe, she coaxed more out of him. He leaned his chair and balanced it on its back legs as he told her about his activity in the Lords.

His efforts seemed considerable to her, although he spoke of them as trifles. He shrugged his work off as no more remarkable or important than wagering on a horse race or playing at cards. Merely another means to relieve boredom.

The more he talked, the tighter the knot grew inside Marlena, the harder each breath came. It was plain as a pikestaff that Tanner did not see what was so very evident to a common man like Bram and to her. Tanner was a man capable of great achievement, not only because of the title he bore, but more so because of the man he was. He was capable of befriending Whigs and Tories alike, princes and common men, to charm them all with his affable manners, influence them with the sheer force of his personality.

Marlena swallowed against a rising sense of despair. If Tanner took her to France, if he remained with her, connected to her, what would happen to all those people he might have helped, the other men who might perish if he were not there to assume their burdens?

She choked back a sob.

He let the chair right itself again, peering at her with concern. "What is it, Marlena?"

"Oh." She blinked away threatening tears. "I suppose I am afraid."

He reached across the table and grasped her hand. "I'll make certain no harm comes to you. We'll make it to Edinburgh and to Paris."

You cannot let him do this, Marlena, the voice of Eliza seemed to warn.

I know it, she replied inside. *I know it.*

He smiled at her, eyes like a warm caress. "What shall we do to pass the time today, Marlena, confined to this room as we are?"

Her heart swelled with love for him, for his ready desire

to ease her fears. What frightened her now was more than her capture, however.

She tried to smile back. "I do not know, Tanner."

He rose from his chair, still holding her hand. "I shall think of something."

Wexin waited in the breakfast parlour, finishing his meal, while his lackeys had been dispatched to Kilrosa to discover if Marlena was indeed in residence there. Wexin had roused himself early and called his men to him to apprise them of his suspicions, ordering them to find her without delay. Now he had no choice but to wait for their report.

Wexin hoped his men would not tell him that she had fled already. The thought of her being so close and yet slipping through his fingers would drive him into a real fury. He wanted this business concluded quickly.

He took a deep breath, cautioning himself not to think in such a depressive vein. Marlena was in Kilrosa. He could sense it. All that was required now was a plan to capture her.

It was unfortunate that Tannerton accompanied her. Such a man would be a formidable enemy, one powerful enough to convince others of Marlena's innocence. And Wexin's guilt. Obviously, Tannerton must be killed, but the death of a marquess would arouse a great deal of undesired attention.

Wexin picked up a newspaper fetched for him by a footman the previous day. He supposed it would be several days old, having come from Edinburgh, but he needed the distraction.

A report caught his eye. *Packet Boat Wrecks.*

Wexin half-rose from his chair as he read the report of the boat Marlena had been on. Tannerton must have been on the packet boat, too. He nearly whooped with glee. Rapp said Tannerton and Marlena had been using false names.

Perhaps no one knew that the Marquess was alive. Wexin could dispose of him here in Scotland where no one would be looking. They'd assume he drowned.

The butler entered and Wexin refolded the newspaper quickly. "Well, what is it?" he snapped.

"Your men to see you, m'lord." The old man bowed.

Wexin straightened and gestured at the remnants of his breakfast. "Get rid of this and tell them to come in."

The butler bowed again and stacked up the plates in his hand. He reached for Wexin's tea cup.

"Leave me my tea, you fool." Wexin shooed him away.

Two of his men entered the room. Wexin signalled them to wait until the butler walked away with the dishes.

"What news, then?" Wexin asked, unable to suppress the eagerness in his voice.

Smith, as stout and solid as a powder keg, spoke up. "We've got nothing for certain, m'lord."

Wexin pounded his fist on the table.

The other man, Jones, shorter and leaner, but in a way that made him a good scrapper, broke in, "We are certain the woman is at the inn, m'lord. It is just that no one is talking about her."

"We saw the gentleman, though," Smith added. "He went to the stable. The man has two horses there, so she must be with him."

This sounded promising. "You left someone to watch the inn, I hope."

Jones nodded. "Oh, we did that, sir. Williams is watching the place."

Wexin stifled a laugh. Smith. Jones. Williams. Not real names, he'd wager a pony, but these were the sort of men who would get results, not incompetent asses like Rapp. He was well rid of that fellow.

He frowned again. They would be much too conspicuous, all of them, waiting and watching in the village. He must come up with another plan. "Can they be spotted leaving the village?"

"Unless they leave on foot," Jones replied. "There is only one road in and out."

Wexin leaned forward. "Here is what we do. Two men watch the road, one man watches the inn. We must attempt not to be conspicuous, however." His brow furrowed in thought. "I will accompany you." He would ensure they did not make some stupid mistake.

Smith piped up, "I overheard the stableman talking to the gentleman. One of their horses almost went lame and cannot make the trip until tomorrow. I think they won't go anywhere until then."

"We must assume nothing. We must watch them." Wexin drummed his fingers on the table. "If it were me, I would leave under cover of darkness." He felt energised with excitement. "Just in case, one of you must watch the inn all day; the others, the road, but when darkness falls, the real vigil begins."

Chapter Eighteen

The day with Tanner was a delight. They rarely left the room and did not leave the inn at all. Most of the time they remained in bed, making love or merely talking.

Marlena was hungry to know all about him, asking endless questions about his childhood, his thoughts, his secret wishes. He insisted his only wish was to be with her, but that statement only made tears prick her eyes again.

She soaked up tales of boyhood escapades, various larks that always seemed instigated by his friend, Pomroy, which took Tanner's cleverness to extricate them.

She told him about herself, about living at Parronley and leaving there for school, never to return. She told him about Eliza, how they were school friends and débutantes together. She told how Eliza took her in when she'd run to her, making Marlena a part of her Irish home, keeping her safe until Eliza's brother came to visit. Marlena talked about Eliza and her children becoming ill, and how Marlena tried so hard to keep her dear friend alive. Marlena talked about Niall, about his death, and the death of her nephews. Tanner held her when she finally could cry for them all and for herself.

And for him.

Time hung suspended, giving the illusion they would have all the time in the world to lie abed, talking. Loving. Then in an instant it was night, and desolation replaced the joy of her all-too-brief marriage to the Marquess of Tannerton.

The path she must take stayed in her mind while they talked and made love.

She knew better than to merely run. Tanner would find her and protect her, no matter what. Her only choice was to turn herself in, and he must not be a party to that. She must do it alone and never let it be known that Tanner had helped her.

The prospect of death lost some of its terror, at least. She had lived a lifetime in a few short days, more than some people live if they reach one hundred years. She'd known Tanner. She'd known love.

She wrote a letter to him in snatches, whenever he left the room to get them food, or to check on the horses. What he would think or do when he read it, she did not know.

In the letter she asked for his promise not to reveal that he had helped her, to give her the gift of knowing he would not share her fate.

She explained why she was leaving, to free him to do the good he was destined to do—nay, *obligated* to do with his personality and position. She reminded him of all the people they had met on their journey who needed him to look out for them. The innkeepers and stable boys, the blacksmiths and tavern girls, the caretakers at Dutwood, Bram and Fia, everyone who had helped them. She asked him to care for them in her name.

She wrote that it grieved her to know how much her leaving would wound him, but the more bound she felt to him, the more right it seemed. They had been born to duty, and his duty was to care for those who needed him. She would not allow him to sacrifice those people for her alone.

She closed the letter saying how much she loved him, and how grateful she was to have been his wife.

When they made love for the last time, each caress, each kiss brought pain as well as delight. She savoured every moment of the experience for herself, but there was more to it than that. This lovemaking was like a prayer, a prayer to give him happiness, to help him remember how greatly she loved him.

She lay in his arms afterwards, listening to his heartbeat and to each breath of air he took in. She could feel him drift to sleep as his breathing slowed. It was so tempting to close her eyes and join him in sleep, but she forced herself to remain awake.

She had watched the window, waiting for a glimmer of light. When it came, all too soon, she slipped from his arms and dressed herself. Her bag was already packed with her clothing, each item reminding her of Tanner. When all was ready, she placed the letter on the table where she knew he would see it, and took one long, last look at him, so peacefully unaware, his hair mussed, his handsome face still wearing a hint of a smile.

"I shall love you always, my husband," she whispered so quietly she was not certain she hadn't merely thought the words.

Turning the knob slowly, she opened the door, and walked away from the man she loved.

In the hall of the inn, she paused to don her cloak. As she stepped into the street, she saw a person rushing towards her. Marlena drew back to hide in the shadows.

It was Fia, hurrying to the inn's door as if she were being pursued.

Marlena stepped into the light. "Fia? What is wrong?"

The girl gave a sharp cry. "Lady Corland!"

"Has something happened?" Marlena looked at the girl with worry.

"Och, m'lady." Fia tried to catch her breath. "It is me that's wrong and I could not sleep for it."

"I do not understand." She took Fia's arm and led her away to where their voices would not so easily carry through the inn's windows.

Fia looked at the bag she had slung over her shoulder. "Are you and Lord Tannerton leavin' so early, m'lady? Because you need to hear what I say before you go."

It was too much to explain to the girl. "What is it, Fia?"

"I came to tell Bram I'm goin' to the laird. I'm going to tell Laird Hay what happened that night. I do not know what he can do, but he's the magistrate and I'm going to tell him." Even in the near-darkness, Marlena could see the resolute set of Fia's chin.

She held the girl by the shoulders. "No, Fia. It is too dangerous. Wexin—"

"I'm done with being afraid of Lord Wexin, m'lady," Fia cried. "It is wrong that he can go free and you have to hide." She paused, glancing towards the inn. "I cannot ask Bram to love me if I don't do something to stop this. Bram would do it in my place. I know he would."

"Fia, Bram would love you no matter. It truly is too dangerous." She gave her a little shake.

Fia twisted out of her grasp. "Nae, m'lady. I would not be worthy of his loving me. I woke my sister and told her I was comin' back. I'm asking Bram to take me to the laird. He'll believe us, I know he will. He's a good man, the laird is."

Marlena could hear the blood roaring through her body, ringing in her ears. She did not know if it was fear or excitement. She did not know if they could dare test the truth. Or dare to hope.

"I'm waking Bram for him to take me as soon as it is light. You cannot stop me." She leaned towards Marlena. "You should come with us—Lord Tannerton, too—the laird is sure to do something, if his lordship tells him to."

She gave Fia an agonised glance. "I'll go with you," she told Fia. "But Lord Tannerton must not be part of it. If this does not work, he could hang along with me."

"His lordship would not like you going without him, m'lady," Fia said.

They started to walk back to the door of the inn when two men jumped out of the shadows and seized them, clamping huge hands over their mouths. Marlena felt the point of a knife against her throat.

His breath foul with rotting teeth, the man holding her sneered, "You are coming with us. Do not make a sound or you both will be sliced to bits."

The other man made a high whistle and, as they were dragged behind the building and past the stable, two more men emerged from opposite directions.

One of them whispered, "Do you have her?"

"Take a look," Marlena's captor said, stuffing a dirty handkerchief in her mouth so that she thought she would gag.

The man came closer and peered into her face. He smiled, his teeth glowing white. "My dear cousin."

Wexin.

Her nightmare had come true, and Fia's, as well.

The knife still pointed to her throat, the man bound her hands.

"This other one said something about going to the laird," Fia's captor said.

Wexin turned and strode over to Fia, bound and gagged as well. Wexin gasped and squeezed Fia's face in his hand. "My good fortune is boundless this day." He turned to the men. "Quickly, before someone hears. Let us be off."

The men carried Marlena and Fia over their shoulders and quickly made their way out of the village. Marlena struggled to keep her wits about her, to look for an opportunity to escape and to free Fia.

The men had hidden horses outside of town. Marlena was thrown over a horse's back and bounced painfully against its withers as its rider put the horse into a gallop. She presumed they headed towards Parronley, to the home she had not been inside for over thirteen years.

She could see little but the horse's shoulder and the ground and she only glimpsed the entrance of Parronley when they passed through the wrought-iron gate and on to its cobbled road. She lifted her head and caught a glimpse of the house in the distance, lit from behind with the glow of dawn.

"This way," called Wexin. "The day grows light. We will lock them away until I decide what to do. Finding the girl puts this entire matter in a new light."

Marlena tried to keep her wits about her to make out which wing of the house the men were taking them, using the lightest part of the sky to tell her which way was east.

One of the men opened a door that creaked on its hinges. She and Fia were carried into pitch blackness.

"We need light," Wexin said.

She had not been able to determine exactly where they were. She had been so long away, and there were so many parts of the house unused even when she lived there.

Finally torches were lit and they were carried down a stone staircase and into what looked like a dungeon.

"In here." Wexin led the men to a room with a stone floor and stone walls and the smell of damp and decades of disuse. He put the torch in an iron bracket on the wall.

She and Fia were dumped on the floor like sacks of flour. The young woman thrashed against her bindings.

Marlena managed to sit up. She glared at Wexin.

He laughed. "I will remove that disgusting cloth from your mouth, my dear cousin. You may remember that no one can hear you in this place." He pulled out the handkerchief and held it in two fingers away from his body, dropping it on the ground. "There you are, my dear. I am certain that feels much better." He turned to the men who had captured them. "You have done an excellent job. Wait for me outside."

While their footsteps receded up the stone stairway, Wexin walked over to Fia. He pulled her hair, and she stopped struggling. Marlena could make out Fia's glaring eyes in the light of the torch. Wexin leaned down into Fia's face.

"It *is* you." His voice was triumphant as he removed Fia's gag. "You change everything, my sweet little maid. Who would have guessed I would find you here with her? I'd hoped you'd landed in a Cheapside brothel and died of the pox, but I could not depend upon it, you realise."

Fia twisted away from him.

"Why does she change everything, Wexin?" Marlena asked, more to take his attention from the girl than anything else.

He turned back to her. "I may be able to take you back to London for your trial and to weep for your wickedness as you walk to the scaffold, after all."

"What had you intended otherwise?" she asked, knowing he was capable of treachery much greater than taking her back for a sham of a trial.

"Well, to kill you, of course." He sauntered over to her. "I thought perhaps you might vanish, once and for all." He put a finger to his cheek. "Although that would delay the wealth of the barony passing to me. No, if you are hanged, then I shall have all of the Parronley lands for raising sheep. I assure you, I am in great need of the revenue that will earn. I just need to get rid of the crofters, but that is the fashion, I hear."

Marlena felt sick. What would happen to Parronley's crofters? Where would they go?

She glared at him. "Perhaps I shall escape again and deny you the pleasure of my death."

He tilted his head. "Believe me, it is no pleasure, cousin Marlena. It is a necessity, however. You and the maid."

She made herself laugh. "You have been so clever, Wexin. I never would have guessed it of you." Perhaps if she kept him talking, Fia could free herself from her bindings. Marlena worked on her own. "I always thought you merely followed in Corland's shadow—"

Wexin grabbed the front of her dress, lifting her off the floor as he put his face into hers. "I follow in no man's shadow." He dropped her back on to the floor. "Least of all your husband's. Corland was a fool and not at all a gentleman."

Marlena could not disagree. She sat up again and tried to keep him talking. "Is that why you killed him? Because he was not a gentleman?"

He laughed. "Yes. Yes. It was." He stared down at her. "Do you know what he threatened to do?"

"Beat you at cards?" she taunted. "Steal your mistress?"

She glanced at Fia and saw her trying to free her hands.

Wexin's eyes flashed. "Worse than that, Marlena. He threatened to call in my vowels." He looked skyward, as if remembering. "He'd gambled even more excessively than usual. He'd gone to the moneylenders and he could not meet their payments. So he called in my debt to him, so he would have money to pay the moneylenders. I did not have it."

Her eyes widened. "You killed Corland because you owed him money?"

He leaned close to her face again. "I killed him because he threatened to spread the word that I reneged on my duties as a gentleman. Lord Strathfield, you know, would look with great disgust upon any man who failed to pay a debt of honour. He'd refuse my offer of marriage to his daughter." He leaned back again. "That was a risk I was not prepared to take."

Marlena shook her head, unable to believe her ears. "You killed Corland because a man might consider you less of a gentleman?"

"That is the right of it." Wexin laughed. "But Corland's life had negligible value."

She tried to rise. "What of my life, Wexin? Did my life have no value? From the start you planned it so I would be blamed."

He sighed and rubbed his palms together. "Now that I do regret, but there was nothing else to do. I could not risk anyone thinking it was *me,* could I? Corland had given you so many reasons to do him in; you were the most logical choice." He turned to Fia again. "All would have been well if this little chit had not shared his bed that night."

He took a step towards Fia, but she lashed out, kicking her bound feet at him. He backed off again.

"I think I must kill you both." Wexin sighed. "I am too impatient to wait for a trial. I merely must ponder the best means of doing so." He sauntered to the door, then turned and touched his forehead. "There is the matter of Lord Tannerton, as well. He must also die."

Marlena went rigid with rage and it was all she could do to disguise it from Wexin. Her death mattered little, but Tanner and Fia must live.

Wexin paused again in the doorway. "I am not a heartless man, Marlena. I shall leave you the torch so you will not have to spend all of your last hours in darkness."

He closed the door behind him and turned a rusty key in the lock.

"My lady," Fia cried from the corner of the room. "Bram will try to stop him and he will get killed, too! We must escape from here."

Tanner, in that delicious moment between sleeping and waking, reached across the bed, expecting to pull Marlena's warm soft body next to his. He felt only cool sheets.

His eyes instantly flew open.

She was gone.

He sat up, heart pounding, knowing he would not find her in the room. "Blast it, Marlena. Why run from me now?"

He continued to swear as he jumped out of bed and reached for his clothes. When he pulled on his shirt, he saw the paper folded on the table. He grabbed it and read.

Forgive me, my love, the letter began.

Forgive her? He'd throttle her for putting herself in so much danger.

He read only far enough to see she was going to the laird. He threw the pages down and finished dressing, pounding his boots on to his feet as he rushed out of the door.

He ran down the stairs and into the taproom, looking for Bram. He needed the man's help.

Bram's stepmother jumped, dropping a spoon into a large pot of porridge. "Mr Henry, ye gave me a fright!"

"Where is your son?" he bellowed, scaring her more.

She placed a hand on her chest. "I do not know."

Tanner caught sight of the door to the back of the building and ran outside that way, rather than retrace his steps through the inn. As he reached the yard, Bram came towards him.

"Have you seen Fia, m'lord?" The man was white-faced. "She's left her sister's house."

"Lady Corland is gone," Tanner said, not answering him.

"Lady Corland!" Bram's stepmother stood in the doorway. "Bram, what is this? The baroness?"

Her stepson said only, "Mam, check if Fia is in the inn and be quick!"

She ran inside. Bram and Tanner followed, falling in step with each other.

"I walked to Fia's sister's house, wantin' to see her." Bram was breathing hard. "She'd left before dawn, her sister said."

"Lady Corland has gone to the laird."

They hurried through the kitchen when Mrs Gunn ran up to them. "Her room is the same as when she left it."

"They've both gone to the laird, then." Bram frowned, pushing his way towards the inn's entrance.

"What is it, Bram?" his mother cried. "Why do you talk of Lady Corland?"

"I cannot explain, Mam," Bram said as he and Tanner reached the door.

"To the stables," Tanner said. "We'll ride."

If Marlena and Fia had taken the horses, he would simply commandeer whatever horse was there. Both horses were there, however, already saddled as Tanner had requested of the stableman the previous day.

"Your steed is right as rain today, sir," the man said.

Good, Tanner thought. He might need to run the horse hard.

He lengthened Marlena's stirrups to fit Bram and within two minutes they were off.

"Show me the way," Tanner said.

As they rode, Tanner told Bram about Marlena's letter.

"I told Fia I would take her to the laird." Bram frowned. "I told her she must tell what she knows."

"What she knows?" Tanner asked.

Bram faced him as they rode. "She witnessed the whole

thing, m'lord. She saw what Wexin did to her lady's husband, and Wexin saw Fia."

"My God." Both women were in danger. "Let us hope they made it safely to the laird's, then."

Why the devil had Marlena left this time? Tanner fought against the pain of her running from him again. He needed first to know she and the maid were safe.

There was no sign of Marlena and Fia on the road. Bram led them to a comfortable country house with a well-tended park and good land around it.

They left the horses at the laird's front door. A footman answered the knock, greeting Bram by name.

"Has Fia Small and another lady come this day?" Bram asked the man.

"Fia?" The footman looked puzzled. "Call upon the laird?"

"Never mind that," Tanner said, striding into the hallway with Bram in his wake. "Tell the laird the Marquess of Tannerton wants to see him immediately.

The footman's eyes widened. "The who?"

"Do it. *Now*," Tanner barked.

It still seemed like precious minutes passed before they were ushered into a drawing room where an elderly man was still buttoning a brocade waistcoat, a white wig askew on his head.

Tanner strode up to him. "I am Tannerton. We need to know if Lady Corland and Fia Small have called upon you."

The man straightened his wig. "Lady Corland? Do you mean *that* Lady Corland? The murderess?"

"The accused murderess." Tanner tried not to lose patience. "We have reason to believe she and Miss Small intended to call upon you."

"Fia?" The laird shook his head in confusion. "No one has called this morning, I do not believe." He walked to the door.

"Lamont," he said to the footman. "Check with the staff if Fia Small has been here."

He glanced back at Tanner. "You are the *Marquess* of Tannerton?"

"Yes," Tanner replied.

The man's eyes looked uncertain. "May I offer you refreshment?"

Bram spoke up. "We cannot tarry, sir. We need to find them."

Tanner took the laird's arm and leaned close to him. "We may require your assistance. I must apprise you of this whole matter…"

As concisely as possible, he explained Marlena's situation, Fia's involvement and Wexin's treachery.

"Dear heavens." The laird collapsed into a chair. "Wexin dined with me two days ago. He seemed a decent fellow."

Tanner stood over him. "Are you saying you do not believe what I have told you?"

The man lifted his hands. "Oh, dear me, no. Who am I to dispute a marquess?"

"It is true, all of it," Bram put in. "Fia would not tell it false."

The footman returned. "No one has come here this morning."

"M'lord?" Bram turned to Tanner, his face white.

Tanner started for the door. "We are going to Wexin, Laird. I would be obliged if you would mount some men to come after us in case we need assistance."

Laird Hay stood. "I will do it."

Tanner and Bram ran out to the horses and were soon back on the road.

"Parronley is about seven miles, m'lord," Bram told him. He shot Tanner a pained look. "He has them, doesn't he?"

"I fear so."

Tanner prayed they would reach Parronley in time. He had no doubt in his mind that Wexin intended to kill both Marlena and Fia.

God, he prayed. *Do not let me have Marlena's death on my conscience. Save her. Take me, but save her.*

They set a fast pace, but had to slow down as they rode through Kilrosa; its people were now awake and busy and crowding the road.

"Where are ye goin'?" some shouted to Bram.

"I cannot explain now," Bram answered them.

Once out of Kilrosa, they put the horses to a gallop. Over a rise, however, a horseman approached.

Rapp, the Bow Street Runner.

"Whoa, there!" Rapp turned his horse sideways to block the road. "Not so hasty." He held a pistol and aimed it directly at Tanner. "You are not going anywhere."

Chapter Nineteen

Marlena struggled at the ropes that bound her wrists. "We *will* escape, Fia." She looked about their dungeon, trying to fix some memory with it. "Somehow."

The ropes were too tight to free her hands. She moved across to Fia. "See if you can untie me."

Fia wiggled her way closer to Marlena and they sat back to back, Fia trying to loosen the knot. "I cannot do it, m'lady."

"Perhaps I can untie yours," Marlena said. She found the knot and worked at it with her fingers. It would not loosen. "Let me try my teeth."

She manoeuvred herself so that she lay on the stone, her face in reach of Fia's hands. At least she could see the knot this way. It had been knotted several times. She pulled at the top strand with her teeth.

It formed a loop. She tugged at it until the loop loosened more. Quickly she swung around again and was able to get a finger through the loop, pulling one of the rope ends through it. She worked on the rest of the knot, first with her teeth, then with her fingers, until it came undone.

Fia hurried to untie her legs and then she worked on Marlena's bindings. In a moment, they both were free.

"I remember playing in the dungeons," Marlena said. "Niall and I. Wexin, too." She closed her eyes, trying to see it clearly in her memory.

When she was small Wexin had threatened to toss her in one of these rooms and throw away the key if she did not leave him and Niall alone. She later begged Niall to promise never to lock her in. Niall had hugged her and reassured her he would hide a key in all three of the dungeon rooms so she might never be locked in.

Did you hide the key, Niall? Marlena said to herself. *Show me. Please show me.*

She walked around the room, touching the wall, examining it, picking at stones that looked as if they might be dislodged.

"There should be a key hidden in here," she told Fia, who immediately began to search the other wall.

Niall would have made it easy, Marlena thought.

She ran to the door and examined its thick wood. There in a niche between two boards was a key. "Here it is," she cried. She could not pry it out with her fingers. The damp had rusted it and it was well lodged in its hiding place. "We need something to tease it out."

She pulled a hairpin from her hair and used it to pick around the key.

"Can you pry it out?" asked Fia, pacing behind her.

"I will," Marlena responded determinedly.

A sliver of wood broke off, giving Marlena sufficient space to hook the hairpin under the key. She pulled and the key moved enough so that she could grasp its end with her fingers.

It pulled free. "I have it!"

She put the key in the lock and turned, her heart leaping as the sound echoed in the chamber. Now if the old door would not creak so loud that their captors would hear it, they would be free.

Holding her breath, she pushed on the door. Its creaking sounded as loud as a demon's scream, but no one came.

Marlena turned to Fia. "There might be a guard at the outside door. We will have to go another way."

The dungeons hid a tunnel through the cliffs out to a tiny cove where the water was deep enough and still enough for a boat. It was a secret escape route for the laird should he need to get away by sea. Her old grandfather used to boast that his father had been prepared to use the tunnel to aid in the escape of Bonnie Prince Charlie, had the Prince come to Parronley. Marlena and Niall had been forbidden to play in it, so, naturally, they had explored the tunnel whenever they could.

Marlena grabbed the torch from its bracket on the wall. It was already burning low. "We must hurry."

She led Fia out of their prison chamber and turned away from where light peeped in from the top of a stone stairway.

"This way," she whispered. "There is a tunnel."

"A tunnel." Fia's voice was fearful but resolute.

As if Marlena had been there yesterday, she led Fia to the hidden entrance. Now they need only hope that the tunnel was still clear, that over the years the walls that had remained passable for three centuries had not collapsed. Debris that Marlena dared not try to identify crunched under their feet, and they heard the skittering of tiny animals, rats or mice, probably.

"How much further?" Fia gasped.

"I think not far," Marlena said, although there was nothing but darkness up ahead and the torch was burning out.

"I cannot believe my good fortune," said Rapp, still aiming his pistol at Tanner. "And, in case you decide you must play the odds that I will shoot and miss, I should warn you, this pistol has rifling in the barrel."

The man was reading Tanner's mind. Rifling made the ball shoot straight and true. "Rapp, stand aside and let us through. It is a matter of life and death."

"Life and death? Your life. Your death." Rapp leaned forward in his saddle. "I do not feel inclined to let you go, Mr Lear or whatever your name is. You have been harbouring and abetting my fugitive and I am going to see you pay the consequences. Now, where is she?"

"You ought not to speak to him that way," Bram cried, moving his horse closer.

Rapp gave Bram a fierce glance. "You had better stay where you are, or I will shoot him."

"Don't be daft, man," Bram went on. "It is a marquess you'd be shooting."

Rapp laughed. "Impersonating a peer, are you now? That will get you in more difficulty."

"He *is* a marquess," Bram said.

Tanner started to remove his glove. "I will show you my signet ring, if you wish."

"Bah." Rapp waved the pistol. "What do I know of rings? Besides, you may have stolen it."

Tanner lost all patience. He needed to find Marlena, to stop Wexin. "Listen, Rapp. I *am* the Marquess of Tannerton, and you will put that pistol down now. I need your help, not your interference."

Rapp frowned. "Do not try to trick me. I worked for Tannerton once. I would know—"

Tanner cut him off. "And you never met me, did you? You worked for me a year ago last summer, was it not? What was your task? To go to Brighton to find the whereabouts of Lord Greythorne? Or into the rookery to learn who might have killed two people? Or, perhaps you were one of those guarding the Vauxhall singer? Perhaps you were on duty that night when she and I were abducted from under your noses, but then, if you had been one of those men, you should recognise me now."

Tanner waited, glaring at Rapp, so furious, he felt like playing the odds and charging directly into the man. The ball might not hit a vital part of him. He ought to chance it.

Marlena's life depended upon it.

"Tannerton?" Rapp's arm lowered. He immediately raised it again. "It cannot be. You are not dressed like a marquess."

"Fool," Tanner bellowed. "I was in the shipwreck. Do you not remember me? I remember you. I remember you pushing your prisoner aside so you could take her place in the boat. You left her to die. May you be damned for it!"

Rapp bowed his head. "God help me." He glanced up again, but the pistol swayed in his grip. "You must understand. I have a wife. Children. She would have died anyway."

Tanner advanced on the man, moving his horse in slow, steady steps. "She will die now, if you do not let us through. Wexin has her. Wexin is the real villain. Wexin killed Corland—"

"Wexin?" Rapp's eyes widened.

Tanner nodded. "He made it look as if Lady Corland did it. She is innocent, Rapp. You saved yourself on the packet, leaving an innocent woman to die."

Rapp's face contorted and he let his arm drop completely, his shoulders shaking.

Tanner brought his horse next to Rapp's. "I need your help, Rapp, not useless bawling. Come with us to stop Wexin. Save her life now."

Rapp straightened his spine and nodded. He stuck his pistol back into his pocket, and turned his horse around. Bram started forward and shouted, "Let us go."

The three men galloped towards Parronley, and Tanner prayed they would not arrive too late.

The butler appeared at the door of the drawing room where Wexin was taking a cup of tea. The old man opened his mouth, but Jones pushed past him.

"Leave us," Wexin told the butler.

Jones watched until the man closed the door. He turned back to Wexin. "They are gone."

"Who is gone?" Wexin asked.

"The women."

"What?" Wexin jumped to his feet, knocking over the small table upon which sat his tea cup. "How could that happen?"

Jones slapped his hands against his sides. "I do not know. Williams went to check on them. The door was open and they were gone."

Wexin's fingers curled into fists. "You were supposed to be guarding them."

"We were," Jones protested. "We sat at the top of the stairs, right outside. They could not have got past us."

"Well, they did get past you, obviously." He started for the door. "We must search for them."

Wexin grabbed his top coat and the two loaded pistols he'd carried with him earlier that morning. He patted a pocket of the coat, feeling the knife he had also carried.

He and Jones hurried outside and around the house to the wing where they had imprisoned the women. Wexin descended the stone stairway and examined the room that ought to have kept them prisoner. Their bindings lay on the stone floor of the dungeon. The torch was gone.

He climbed back up the stairs. When he stepped outside to where Jones waited for him, Williams came running towards them from across the park.

At still some distance, Williams stopped and shouted, "We've found them!" He pointed in the direction of the cliffs and gestured for them to follow. Wexin ran, with Jones close behind.

The cliffs were nearby. Wexin soon saw Marlena and the girl silhouetted against the sky. They froze when they saw Smith and Williams advancing on them. They turned and ran back towards the edge of the cliff.

Wexin's worries were eased. The cliffs were at least twenty feet high, with nothing but water below. He had them trapped. There was nowhere for them to go.

He laughed in triumph as Williams and Smith caught up with the two women, but Marlena fought off Smith, and Wexin frowned again. If Smith released her, Wexin would have the man's head put on a pike. He wished like the devil that he'd killed the women right away. Their bodies could have rotted in that dungeon for as long as he needed to decide how to dispose of them. When he got his hands on them again, Wexin would not make the mistake a second time.

To his horror, Marlena, her hair loose now in the struggle, dug her fingers into Smith's eyes. Smith screamed and let go, clutching his face. She rushed to her companion and started fighting with Williams.

Wexin quickened his step. "Hurry, Jones. They must not escape."

Williams was teetering near the cliff's edge, trying to hold on to the maid, while Marlena was hitting him and pulling on his clothing. Wexin reached the struggle and, with a surge of strength borne of his anger, seized Marlena by the hair and pulled her off Williams.

"This shall be the end of you, cousin." He caught her in a firm hold.

"You idiot." She struggled. "How many servants do you think are watching from the windows?"

He glanced over at the house where the windows sparkled in the sunlight. Curse her, she was probably correct. If he was being watched, he'd have to keep them alive.

But not for long. Marlena and her maid would never reach London.

Williams now had a good hold on the maid and was dragging her back towards the house.

Wexin, sick of Marlena's nonsense, pulled out his knife and held it against her throat. "Come nicely with me, my dear. You know my skill with a sharp blade."

"I know it well." She ceased her struggling, but stood her ground. "Does your wife know this side of you, Wexin?" she taunted. "Is she as bloodthirsty? Your Lady Macbeth, perhaps?"

He pushed the point of the knife into her skin, drawing blood. He did not care how many servants watched. "Do not speak of my wife!"

At that moment, horses' hooves thundered in his ears. He looked up to see three horsemen advancing upon them. Jones turned and ran, one of the men on horseback turning to pursue him. Another made straight for the maid, and a third headed directly towards him.

Tannerton.

Tanner instantly took in the tableau in front of him, but his gaze was riveted on Wexin, who held Marlena at knifepoint close to the edge of the cliff.

When they had ridden up to the house, an elderly manservant had run out and yelled for them to head for the cliffs. They had barely broken speed to do so.

Tanner saw Marlena's hands gripped around Wexin's wrist, and she managed to break free of Wexin's knife as Tanner approached.

Tanner leapt off his horse, knocking Wexin to the ground, but the momentum sent Tanner rolling dangerously close to the cliff's edge. When he looked up, Wexin was advancing on him, eyes wild with fury.

"Give it up, Wexin," Tanner said, scrambling to his feet. "Your game is over."

Wexin, no longer holding the knife, reached in his coat and pulled out a pistol. He pressed the weapon against Tanner's chest.

"It is your game that is over, Tannerton," Wexin cried. "I will blow a hole through you."

Tanner lifted his arms and glanced over the cliff to see that the sea was a good twenty feet below them. Its waves sounded a steady rhythm, like a battlefield drumbeat. Tanner edged closer to the precipice.

"You will never get away with this," Tanner warned, his voice low with rage at this man bent on destroying Marlena. Tanner's feet were close enough to the edge to knock pebbles over the side.

Wexin's face was red. "I will take you to hell with me, and my cousin, too." He moved the pistol to Tanner's heart and straightened his shoulders.

"No!"

Tanner heard Marlena's cry the same moment she barrelled into him. As a shot pierced the air, Tanner and Marlena flew off the edge of the cliff.

"Mar—" Tanner managed before they hit the icy water and plunged into its depths.

It was as if a nightmare repeated itself. Tanner felt the same bone-numbing cold as the night of the shipwreck, the same disorientation, the same desperate need for air. He thrashed in the water, one hand still gripping Marlena's clothing. He'd be damned if he'd allow the sea to take her now, not after all they had been through. This time, daylight shone through the water like hope. Tanner kicked towards it.

They broke the surface and both gasped for air. Still holding on to her, Tanner swam in the direction of the tiny sliver of beach at the opening of what looked like a cave.

As they stumbled out of the water, Tanner took her in his arms and held her tight against him. "Marlena. We might have been killed."

"No." Her teeth chattered as she spoke. "I knew. Used to swim here. We escaped through the tunnel, Fia and I." She shivered. "So cold."

She made no sense, but Tanner could only think that he might lose her yet if he could not get her warm and dry. He glanced around, searching for a way out.

Wexin leaned over the edge of the cliff. "No! It cannot be!"

Marlena tried to pull away at the sight of him. Tanner covered her with his arms and backed towards the mouth of the cave. There were more shouts from above and the sound of a pistol shot rang through the air.

It is not over yet, thought Tanner.

At that moment, a man in livery, carrying a torch, appeared at the entrance of the cave. "This way," the man said.

Tanner lifted her into his arms. "I'm so cold, Tanner," she murmured. "I'm so cold."

Marlena woke in a familiar place, but one as disorientating as if she'd been transported to Van Diemen's land. She was in the room of her childhood, its walls and furniture the same as the day she had left it.

"Are you feelin' rested, m'lady?" Fia leaned over her, placing a hand on her forehead.

Events came rushing back.

"Tanner?" She sat up.

"Fear not. He is here. Below stairs with the laird and Bram and some others. They are sorting matters out."

"Wexin?"

Fia averted her gaze. "He is dead, ma'am. Shot himself after you and Lord Tanner climbed out of the water."

Marlena put a hand over her mouth, remembering Wexin's face the moment she knew he'd decided to shoot Tanner, the moment she ran and she and Tanner flew off the edge of the cliff.

Her memory was hazy after that. She recalled the icy cold water. She recalled Tanner pulling her on to the beach and carrying her through the tunnel. He'd carried her up the stairs to this room and had undressed her while shouting for dry clothes and blankets.

She looked down at herself. She was wearing an old night-dress that still smelled of cedar. "Are there clothes for me? I want to get up." And find Tanner, she could have added.

"Right here," Fia said. "I'll help you."

Fia helped her don a dress that might have once been her mother's, an old velvet gown in deep green.

"I'll help with your hair," Fia said, sitting her down at her old dressing table where Marlena's maid once plaited her hair and told her stories of Shellycoat and Selkies.

She opened the drawers of the table and found a forgotten ribbon in one and a comb in the other. Fia combed out the tangles in her hair.

"Tell me what happened, Fia."

Fia's brows knit. "Well, after you and Lord Tannerton went off the side, Lord Wexin ran to the edge. Bram was fighting the fellow who had me, and there was another man helping. A Bow Street Runner, Bram said."

"Not Rapp." Marlena's eyes widened.

"I do not know, ma'am, but he was helpin'." Fia worked the comb through a strand of Marlena's hair. "Lord Wexin must have seen ye come out of the water, because he yelled and then he took a pistol to his head and fired it." The girl shuddered. "It was an ugly sight, but I'm glad of it. I'm glad he is dead."

Marlena touched the cut on her neck, a small reminder of her cousin. "Is it over, then, Fia?"

"Aye, it is over and done, and we have naught to worry over. The laird came and I told him everything. Those men helping Wexin were all tied up, and some of the laird's men took them away. Lord Tannerton and the laird and some other men from Kilrosa are all below stairs talking about what is next to be done."

Marlena's cut stood out an angry red against her pale skin. "And you, Fia, were you hurt?"

Fia shook her head. "Nothin' to speak of, ma'am."

"And Bram?"

Fia's face filled with colour. "He is very well, ma'am."

Marlena smiled. "I am glad."

Fia's eyelids fluttered. "I am going to marry Bram, m'lady. He asked me after they took Wexin's body inside. He took me aside and kissed me. He knows all about me and still says he wants to marry me."

Marlena reached up to clasp her hand. "He is a very lucky man to have you."

Fia's face flushed with colour again as she tied the ribbon around Marlena's hair. Marlena slipped her feet into a pair of old silk shoes that must have also been her mother's. She and Fia walked down the stairway to the hall of Parronley House, another familiar site.

An elderly man approached her, bowing deeply. "Baroness."

"Forbes!" She recognised the old butler and threw her arms around him. "It is so good to see you."

When she let go of him, she saw tears in his eyes.

"It is good to see you, my lady." His voice was thick with emotion.

"Where are they?" she asked him.

"The drawing room, ma'am." He led the way, stepping inside the room first. "The Baroness Parronley," he announced.

A murmur went through the room as the gentlemen stood. Marlena caught a glimpse of Rapp, who averted his face from her. She would ask about Rapp later. When Bram stepped forward to take Fia's hand, Marlena smiled inside.

Then her gaze found Tanner.

He stood at the far end of the room, the apex of the group. The clothes he wore were old fashioned and even more ill fitting than those they had purchased in Liverpool, but, still, he had the air of command. The other men showed deference to his authority.

The other men bowed and addressed her as Baroness as she crossed the room. Tanner's gaze followed her progress, his expression a mixture of both tension and relief. As she reached him, his eyes glowed, warming her more than a blazing fire could do.

His arms opened to her and she stepped into his embrace.

"Gentlemen," she heard Tanner say, his voice deep and full of emotion, "may I present you to the Marchioness of Tannerton." His arms tightened around her. "My wife."

Heedless of their audience, Marlena wrapped her arms around his neck. "My husband," she murmured before his lips closed on hers.

Home, again. To stay.

Epilogue

March, 1819

Tanner stepped out of the Palace of Westminster, weary of sitting all day listening to the debates, tired to death of looking at the red walls, red chairs, red carpet. He was heartily sick of red. The bland beige of the buildings in the street was a welcome relief.

He chatted with Lords Heronvale and Bathurst. Lord Levenhorne walked by and nodded to him. Lord Levenhorne was Heronvale's brother-in-law and the heir presumptive to Wexin's title and property, waiting only for the widow Lady Wexin to give birth to the child she carried. Tanner did not know if Levenhorne cared much whether he inherited or not.

It was said Levenhorne was deeply affected by the scandal around Wexin's death, but the person for whom Tanner felt the most sympathy was Lady Wexin. She had withdrawn from society, from the prying eyes and loose tongues so quick to condemn her by association. Tanner had heard she was in debt, but she had turned down his offer to assist her.

Bathurst was in danger of rehashing the entire day's debate

if Tanner did not stop him. He turned to Heronvale. "I have heard horses from your brother's stables are fetching top dollar."

Heronvale beamed. "Indeed. If you've a fancy for a race-horse, you should pay him a visit."

Tanner held up a hand. "Not at the moment, but I would not be averse to placing a wager now and then."

"A wise bet," Heronvale said. "Devlin's breeding pro-gramme promises to produce winners."

Bathurst recalled seeing one of the horses race and he launched in to a stride-by-stride description. Tanner spied his carriage finally appear at the end of the queue of carriages waiting to transport the lords from Westminster to their homes in Mayfair. He begged leave of his companions and walked to the vehicle rather than wait for it to reach him.

He greeted the driver and the footman who jumped down to hold the door open for him. Tanner climbed inside.

"Hello, my darling."

To his surprise, Marlena sat inside, looking beautiful in the light that filtered into the carriage. She wore a splendid carriage dress in deep blue with a pelisse to match. Her lovely face was framed by a matching hat with a tumble of white feathers on its crown.

"Ah, you are a feast to my eyes," he said, leaning over to give her a long, hungry kiss. When he broke contact, he murmured, "What the devil are you doing here? You must have been waiting an age."

She touched his face and lightly kissed him again. "Not that long, I assure you. I was pining to see you and took it in my head to ride in the carriage."

He wrapped his arm around her and held her close. "Very nice for me."

"How was the session today?" she asked.

He groaned. "The whole day was spent on the consolidated funds. Tedious in the extreme."

She looked at him with sympathy. "I am certain there was some good reason for such a discussion."

Tanner well knew that Marlena considered his activity in the House of Lords to be of very great value. He'd never thought much about it. It was an obligation, like signing papers, attending balls, answering a summons from the Duke of Clarence. If he was lucky, he had the chance to speak up about something worthwhile. Occasionally the debates became so loud and rancorous that bets were taken whether fisticuffs would break out. Those were the fun days. Mostly it was a boring obligation.

"The cursed bill was good enough," he told her. "To increase funds available for public service, but why they had to prose on about it all day was beyond me." He shook his head.

She laughed softly. "My poor husband."

He grinned at her then and tasted her lips one more time. "How has my wife been today?" He pressed a hand on her belly.

She covered his hand with her own. "I've felt splendid today. No queasiness at all. I even received callers."

To Tanner's great delight and Marlena's astonishment, she was with child. That physician who long ago pronounced her unable to conceive had been proven utterly wrong. There was a baby growing inside her. Tanner's baby. A son, a daughter, he cared not which. To have a child with Marlena seemed nothing less than a miracle.

Tanner asked her who had called upon her, and listened with half an ear as she told him about the ladies, most new to her acquaintance, those she liked, those she suspected of wanting merely to befriend London's newest marchioness, those who came to see the notorious Vanishing Viscountess.

Tanner enjoyed the sound of her voice. He had no right to feel so happy, to have so much to live for. His wife. His child.

After Wexin's death, they had travelled back to London, to clear Marlena's name once and for all and to do what needed to be done for her to assume her title as Baroness Parronley. One of Tanner's first tasks had been to dispatch his secretary to procure a special licence. Within a week of their return to London, he and Marlena were married by clergy at St George's Church in Mayfair. Many members of the *ton* witnessed the nuptials, as well as the Duke of Clarence and Tanner's much-relieved cousin, Algernon. Tanner wanted it very clear that he was really and truly married to Marlena, in the sight of God and everybody else.

Even before the wedding Tanner had taken Marlena shopping. Not at open clothes markets like in Liverpool, but at the finest shops Mayfair had to offer. He bought her jewellery at Rundell and Bridge, perfume at Floris, confectionery at Gunter's. He took her to all the best modistes— Madame Devy, Mrs Walters and others—and the best milliner, Mrs Bell. Marlena ordered a wardrobe of fine gowns and Tanner paid extra for them to be made for her as quickly as possible. Gloves, stockings, there was no item he did not wish to share in the purchasing, to make certain she knew she could have anything she desired.

To think he used to leave the purchasing of gifts to his secretary. He'd never enjoyed more what his money could buy than when using it to indulge Marlena in shop after shop after shop.

A lesser woman might have been overwhelmed by his attention and the attention of all of society upon their return. It had been somewhat like being plunged into the icy sea water, totally engulfing, hard to breathe. The newspapers carried the story and everyone from Mayfair to Cheapside was talking about the return of the Vanishing Viscountess. Marlena withstood the furore with the same fortitude she'd shown on their journey to Scotland, and Tanner was fiercely proud of her.

The consolation of all the tumult had been spending their nights together, full of lovemaking, full of joy, a haven in the midst of a storm.

"You are not listening!" she accused him.

He gave her a chagrined smile. "I was woolgathering, I admit." But what precious wool. "What did you say?"

"I had a letter from Laird Hay, with a message from Fia and Bram. Fia is increasing, too. Is that not splendid?" She squeezed his hand.

"Very splendid."

Tanner had had his secretary send money to all the people who had helped them during their flight to Scotland. When he took Marlena back to Parronley this coming summer, to await the birth of their child, he would find out what else he might do for Bram and Fia. Their own house, perhaps. Their own land.

He closed his eyes as Marlena sighed and relaxed against him. The carriage swayed as it rolled along, reminding him of the rocking of a ship.

Tanner thought back to standing in the cuddy of the packet boat from Dublin. He thought of his despair, his lamenting of his useless life. He had no doubt he would have let the sea take him if he'd not needed to save Marlena. He held her tighter.

She had saved him.

He lifted her face and his lips touched hers once more. He poured all the love in his heart into the kiss. Afterward he pulled her on to his lap and clung to her.

"What is it, Tanner?" she murmured, caressing his cheek, undoubtedly sensing his emotion.

"Nothing," he said. "Everything." He fixed his gaze upon her. "Thank you, is all. Thank you, Marlena."

They rode the rest of the trip to their Mayfair townhouse in contented silence.

THE MYSTERIOUS
MISS M

Chapter One

~~~~~~~~~~~~~~~~~~~~~~~~

London, September 1812

Madeleine positioned herself on the couch, adjusting the fine white muslin of her gown and placing her gloved hands demurely in her lap. The light from the branch of candles, arranged to cast a soft glow upon her skin, enhanced the image she was bid to make. Her throat tightened, and her skin crawled from the last man's attentions.

This wicked life. How she detested it.

She checked the blue-feathered mask, artfully fashioned to disguise her identity without obscuring her youthful complexion or the untouched pink of her full lips. 'The Mysterious Miss M' could be any girl in the first blush of womanhood. It was Farley's contrivance that she appear so, and the men who frequented his elite London gaming hell bet deep to win the fantasy of seducing her. Escape might be out of the question, but at least the mask hid her face and her shame.

Unable to remain still, Madeleine stepped over to the bed, discreetly tucked into the corner and covered in lace-trimmed white-and-lavender linens like some virginal shrine. She perched on the edge of it and swung her legs back and forth, wondering how much time was left before the next gentleman had his turn. Not long, she surmised. She had taken more care in the necessary toilette than usual, thoroughly washing away the memory of that odious creature who had not departed too soon for her taste.

Male laughter, deep and raucous, sounded in the next room. Stupid creatures, seated around tables, as deep in their cards as in their cups, just waiting for Lord Farley to make away with their fortunes. The girls who ran the tables, tonight dressed as she was, like ingenues at Almack's, were meant to tantalise, but, for a select few, the Mysterious Miss M was the real prize.

Farley would not allow his prize to flee. She had learned that lesson swiftly enough. No matter. There was nowhere for her to go.

Voices sounded outside the room, and she blinked away the memory of how Farley had doomed her to her fate, or, more precisely, how she had doomed herself.

The next man, thankfully the last, would appear soon, and she had best be ready. She checked her hair, fingering the dark curls fashioned in the latest style to frame her face, a pale pink silk ribbon threaded through them.

Something thudded against the door. Madeleine hopped off the bed and hurried to her place on the couch. In staggered a tall figure, silhouetted against the brighter light of the gaming room. He stood a moment with his hand to his brow.

A soldier. He wore the red coat of a British uniform, festooned with blue facings and looped gold lace, unbuttoned to reveal the white linen of his shirt. If only she were a soldier. She would battle her way out of this place. She would be in the cavalry and gallop away at breakneck speed. How lovely that would be.

The soldier, who looked not more than five years older

than she, swayed as he swung shut the door. Lord Farley's generous supply of brandy, no doubt.

Madeleine sighed. He might be foxed, but at least he was not fat. With any luck, his mouth would not be foul. She hated a putrid-smelling mouth. With all his lean muscle, he looked as a soldier should, strong and powerful.

'Good God!' he exclaimed, almost tripping mid-stride as he caught sight of her.

'I am afraid I am not He, my lord,' she retorted. The candles illuminated a handsome face, grinning with such good humour she could scarcely keep from grinning back.

'Yes, of course not.' His green eyes twinkled. 'And fortuitous for me that you are not, Miss…?'

'Miss M.' A charmer. She had met charmers before. The charm wore thin after they took what they wished from her.

'"The Mysterious Miss M", I recall now.' He flopped down on the couch next to her. 'I beg your forgiveness. You quite startled me. I had not expected you to actually look like a young lady.'

'I am a young lady,' she said, playing her part.

'Indeed,' he agreed, masculine approval shining in his sea-green eyes and a dimple creasing his left cheek. 'I swear you are the vision of one. England does offer the finest ladies. I find I must apologise for this humble uniform.'

He presented her with his boot-covered foot and winked at her while she tugged on it. Though properly polished, her fingers felt the leather's scratches and scrapes. From the battlefield? she wondered. When his foot finally gave up the boot, he nearly fell off the couch. She rolled her eyes.

He laughed. 'Have I impressed you with my finesse, Miss M?'

'Indeed, my lord. I cannot recall when I have been so entertained.'

He chuckled softly and swung around, bringing his face close to hers, his expression more full of mischief than lust. 'And I thought you were here to entertain me.'

She felt a smile tickling the corner of her mouth. He placed his finger on her lip and traced the edge. His eyes filled with a wistful expression that surprised her. A heat she was not quite prepared to feel made her wish to fan herself. As she wiped the disturbing touch from her mouth with her tongue, he took a swift intake of breath and gazed into her eyes so intensely that she lowered them.

He was like the fantasy she conjured up in her loneliest hours. A knight on a huge white stallion, who faced the evil lord in the joust, winning her away. Or the pirate who fought the blackguard and sailed her away in a ship with a dozen sails. He was the soldier, riding in with sabre flashing, to rid her of Farley and keep her safe forever.

Such nonsense. He was none of these, for all the splendour of his uniform, dark, curling hair and sun-darkened skin. He certainly looked the part, though, with his eyes wondrously expressive and a face lean, as if honed by battle.

Once Farley had been a fantasy, when she'd dreamed he was taking her to a marriage bed instead of the one in this room.

The soldier shrugged off his coat, and his loose linen shirt revealed a peek of black chest hair. Madeleine's eyes fixed on the wiry patch and her fingers itched to discover how it would feel.

As if it would feel any different than the other lust-filled men who forced themselves so hard against her that she pushed on their chests to give herself room for breath. She placed a hand on her breast. What fancy had captured her to give way to such thoughts?

He grinned impishly at her again, the dimple deepening

in his cheek. 'You are a vision, Miss M. Like England herself, beautiful to behold. Nothing mysterious about it. In fact, I shall call you Miss England.'

'Do not be so foolish, sir. The fabric of my dress is Indian. The design is French and the style Roman. My mask is Venetian. My pearls are Oriental. I think my shoes are from Spain. There is nothing of England here.'

His finger traced the edge of the demure bodice of her dress where the fullness of her breasts was only hinted. He hooked his finger under the material and pulled it away from her skin, allowing a soft touch of what was underneath.

'I suspect,' he murmured, stroking her skin and gazing into her eyes, 'underneath you are pure England.'

'Not pure, my lord,' she whispered as his fingers did lovely things to her soft skin. 'Not pure at all.'

He slowly leaned closer so that she could feel his breath on her lips. With a gentleness she did not know existed, he placed his lips on hers and lingered there, moving so softly, she was only half-aware of him urging her mouth open and tickling the moist inside with his tongue.

She moaned and positioned herself closer to him. Her arms twined around his neck and her fingers played with the curls on his head. He tasted of brandy, but she decided she might like brandy the next time she was compelled to drink it.

He urged her down on the couch, covering his body with hers. The hard bulge of his arousal pressed against her. To her surprise, it pleased her.

Only once before had a man's arousal not filled her with revulsion. That day in the country when her father's house-guest, the Lord Farley her older sisters prosed on about, met her out riding and showed her what happens between a man and a reckless, unchaperoned fifteen-year-old girl. She had thought it a splendid joke to be the first of her sisters kissed by a man, but, all too easily, that kiss had led to delights she had not imagined.

The soldier's muscles were firm beneath his grey wool trousers. His mouth played lightly on her cheek, and Madeleine's long-suppressed desire tugged at her again. She must not allow herself the weakness. She must control her sensibilities.

His kisses trailed down the sensitive skin of her neck, and she said her rehearsed lines: 'Shall we go to the bed, my lord?'

Immediately he rose, grinning his dimpled grin. 'Whatever you command, my lady.'

He gallantly extended his hand to assist her up. His grasp was firm and warm, even through her lavender-kid glove. As she led him to the bed, he kept hold of her hand, the gesture unexpectedly setting off a storm of yearning inside her.

Vowing to get her feelings under control, Madeleine continued her duties, turning back the covers on the bed and facing the soldier. She slowly pulled off her gloves, one finger at a time. Her fingers free, she unlaced his shirt, caressing his warm bare skin as she pushed it off his shoulders. When she unfastened his trousers, the bulge therein attested to the success of her endeavours. She tried not to watch his green eyes darken with passion.

A guttural sound emerged from his throat. Madeleine collected herself and proceeded with the task she was bid to perform. This was the moment for him to pounce on her. She must temper his lusting, so that her dress not become ripped from his impatience.

Even completely free of his clothes, he did not pounce. Instead, he simply gazed at her. All the unwanted cravings of her body rushed back as she gazed at him in return. Usually she avoided a view of the men who bared themselves before her. When Farley first seduced her, she had been too shy to look, but her gaze freely drank in this soldier's body. He was more beautiful than the drawings of Greek statues in her father's books. Her eyes widened with surprise at the pleasure of seeing him.

'Good God, Miss England,' he exclaimed. He moved toward her. With gentle hands on her shoulders, he turned her around and fumbled with the laces of her dress, his progress painfully slow.

He chuckled. 'I am woefully out of practice.'

With a resolute purse of her lips, Madeleine spun back to face him and made quick work of the laces. The dress fell to the floor. She tackled the corset next. When she let her shift drop from her body, his gaze was as rapt as hers had been, and her resolve to simply perform her task fled.

His eyes met hers. 'I feel home at last.'

He ran his hand over her breasts, his fingers barely skimming the soft flesh. Her breasts ached. How could they ache? He'd barely touched them.

'Wh—where have you been?' She would distract herself. These feelings were too disturbing. 'In the Peninsula?'

'Last at Maguilla.' His manner turned solemn and his sparkling eyes lost lustre.

Maguilla. So exotic a name, like a magic kingdom far away. But what had happened there to cause his change in mood?

Sadness lingered in his eyes, but he smiled. 'I have been too long at battle and not long enough at home to have seen what I most have missed.'

'I do not understand you, my lord.' She chewed on her lip. 'What have you most missed?'

His gaze travelled up and down the length of her.

'England,' he said in a reverent voice. 'Every hill, curve, and thicket. All lush beauty and honest comfort.'

Madeleine felt herself blush. She stilled the impulse to cover her most female parts. 'Well,' she said, 'shall we proceed, my lord?'

Quickly she climbed on the bed, her mouth set in a determined line. He followed her, more slowly than she would have guessed. That he was not so eager to slake his desire unsettled her, but not so much as her own yearning. When he climbed in the bed and positioned himself over her, she nearly burst with excitement. It felt too much like what had brought her to ruin, but she wanted this soldier. Wanted him very much.

She stiffened and panic raced through her.

He halted immediately, searching her face. 'What is wrong?'

Her heart pounded. 'Nothing. Nothing is wrong.'

He cocked his head sceptically. 'You are frightened. I do not understand. What frightened you? Did I hurt you?' He shifted to lie beside her.

She avoided the puzzled look in his eye. 'No, you did not hurt me, my lord. I am not frightened. You may proceed.'

His hand grasped her chin and brought her face closer. 'I'll not *proceed*, as you say, until you explain.'

She could not explain what she did not understand. Even when Farley had seduced her and her body responded so wantonly, she had not felt like this. So...so excited and breathless.

Was this what young women felt when they loved the man they bedded? Was this a feeling she could never have or deserve?

A tear trickled down her cheek. As it appeared from beneath her mask, he wiped it away with his finger. 'There now,' he murmured, stroking her cheek. 'No need to cry.'

'It is of no consequence,' she said, stifling a sob, furious at her tears. Farley would be even angrier, if he knew.

Weeping was not in the carefully fashioned script. 'Please don't tell Lord Farley about this.'

'Now, now.' He sat up and settled her in front of him, wrapping his arms around her. 'Why would I ever do that? Come. Tell Devlin what troubles you.'

'Devlin?' His arms felt like a warm blanket around her. She wished she could remain cosseted within them and never, ever leave.

'That's my name. Lieutenant Devlin Steele of the First Royal Dragoons. Youngest brother of the very honourable Marquess of Heronvale. At your service, Miss England.' He cuddled her closer to him. 'Tell me what is wrong.'

She released a deep, shuddering breath. 'Sometimes…sometimes I wish to be what I appear, not what I am.' The tears came in earnest now, soaking the feathers of her mask.

If only she had not gone riding that fateful day. If only Farley had not seen her scandalous attire, her brother's old clothes already too small for her. If only she had known that kissing a man could lead to so much more.

She fingered the damp feathers of her mask, hoping they would dry without losing shape or she would be punished.

'Shh, now, it will be all right,' he whispered.

No, nothing would ever be all right again.

The lieutenant held her and rocked her and murmured comforting words into her ear. It was a long cry, longer than any she had allowed herself since the night she'd learned Farley had other plans for her besides marriage.

Soon enough, though, she recovered. She pulled away from him and turned so he could not see her face as she removed the mask to wipe her eyes with the linen sheet. When she turned back her mask was in place.

'Now have you finished, little watering pot?' he asked, his lovely green eyes the kindest she had ever seen.

She nodded.

'Silly goose.' He tapped her on the nose and slid off the bed to grope on the floor for his clothes. Still unsteady, he stumbled and bumped against the bedpost.

'What are you doing?' she asked.

He laughed softly. 'Getting dressed. Do not worry, miss, I will forgo your favours tonight.' He cast her a long glance, a woeful expression on his face. 'Though it may be more difficult than piquet duty in freezing rain.'

'No, you mustn't.' She pulled him back, trying to urge him back on top of her. 'It would not suit. I am expected to perform.'

'No, sweet Miss England. You have performed enough tonight.' He stood again.

Madeleine stared at him, trying not to be transfixed by the flexing of his well-defined muscles as he groped for his trousers. She could not bear it if he should leave so soon.

He turned that mischievous grin upon her, his dimple emerging. 'We must, of course, give a show for the others in the next room. Create proper noise. Make the poor buggers envious.'

She giggled.

'Not laughter. Passion. Like this.' He let out a loud moan. 'More! More! More!'

'Yes! Yes! Yes!' she returned. They both burst out laughing, holding their mouths to keep it silent.

He collapsed on the bed. 'Stop. It hurts to laugh.' He grabbed his side. 'Ow.'

She pulled his hand away. To the side of his abdomen there was a scar, jagged and still pink from recent healing.

'You were injured at…at…?' She traced the scar with her finger.

'At Maguilla? As you would say, it is of no consequence.' He smiled, but without joy. 'We chased a regiment of French

cavalry until the tide was turned and their reserves chased us.
I made a foolish attempt to rally the men. A Frenchman met
me with a lance instead. The wound is healed now. In two
days' time I return to my regiment.'

'Back to the war?'

'Of course. It is a soldier's duty.'

Two days and he would return to war. He could be injured
again. He could lose his life. Never again see his precious
England. And, if she knew Farley, Devlin Steele would also
return to war penniless.

'Lieutenant?'

'You must call me Devlin.'

She waved her hand dismissively. 'Devlin, then. Have you
won at cards tonight? I mean, in addition to winning me?'

He laughed. 'Will you be in search of my money next?'

This offended. She had principles, after all. 'I want none
of your money, but you must refuse to play further. Make
some excuse.'

'Whatever for?'

'The game is not honest.'

The silly men who lost fortunes to Farley while trying to
win a second chance with her never comprehended. No one
won her twice in a night.

'The devil,' he mumbled. 'I never thought to inquire of
Farley's reputation. I should have known better. I shall
make my excuses to him. I am indebted to you. You are
quite a lady.'

'Don't elevate me, sir. I am just as I seem.'

He laughed. 'You seem quite like the misses in the
marriage mart. A young lady of quality.' He smiled. His eyes
turned kind and his voice tender. 'Indeed, that is what you
are. A young lady of quality.'

Her face grew hot with shame. 'No.'

He struggled to get into his trousers, hopping on one foot and making no progress.

She did not wish him to leave. 'Lieutenant?'

'Devlin, remember?'

'Devlin. Will England win the war?'

He momentarily ceased his struggle. 'Without a doubt. It is nearly done, I think.'

'Wellington will see to it, will he not? And you soldiers who fight the battles with him?'

'Worry not, little miss.' He ran his finger over her brow. 'England will endure.'

Madeleine reached out and placed her hand over his scar. 'Lieutenant?'

'Yes?' He had become still, too, looking directly into her eyes.

'I wish to make love to you.' She slid her fingers up his chest.

'Miss England, it is not necessary.'

She reached behind her head and untied her mask. With trembling fingers, she removed it. His eyes darkened.

She moved closer. 'I will make love to you. It will be my gift, because you must return to battle.' With one hand stroking his hair, the other moved downward. Farley had taught her where to touch to arouse. This time, with Lieutenant Devlin Steele of the First Royal Dragoons, it gave her pleasure.

He moaned, softer this time. She clasped her hand behind his head and brought him uncomplaining to her lips. Urging him atop her, she gasped as the firmness of his body bore down on her. Her heart beat faster. She would truly make love to this soldier, this kind man who had been willing to comfort her.

He eased himself inside her with exquisite gentleness,

and what typically caused her to deaden all emotion gave unexpected delight. She thrilled to the feel of him filling her, revelling in each stroke, each scrape of his chest against hers, each breath on her face. The only sound she heard was the clap of their bodies coming together and their panting breath. She matched his rhythm, stroke for stroke, press for press, and the sensations he created in her became urgent, spurring her on with each thrust. His pace quickened and her need grew. She would burst with pleasure, she was sure. She would shatter into a thousand sparkling shards. She would escape herself, this life she was forced to lead, the dismal future, in this brief space of time with Lieutenant Devlin Steele.

He collapsed on top of her, his need satisfied with hers. Sliding off, he lay facing her, his eyes half-closed, his skin aglow with a sheen of sweat. Madeleine let her gaze wander languidly over his face, memorising each feature, committing each curve and line to memory. She needed to remember him. She needed to dream of her Dragoon returning victorious from the war, coming to whisk her away. She would need for him to come to her tomorrow and the next day and the next.

The fantasy would comfort, though it would never come true.

'Sweet England,' he murmured. 'Thank you.'

She kissed him again, boldly giving him her tongue, tasting him. Brandy would never again taste so vile. It would be how *he* tasted. She inhaled his masculine scent, filling her lungs and memory with it, as his seed had filled her. She entwined her legs with his. He moved away from her kiss and grinned at her as she arched her pelvis to his.

'Ah, England, you shall be most difficult to leave.' As she placed her finger in the dimple on his cheek, he pressed his fingers into the soft flesh of her buttocks. She felt his passion flare back to life and she made a primitive sound deep in her throat.

As he entered her for the second time, Madeleine whispered. 'Lieutenant Devlin Steele. I shall remember you.'

Chapter Two

London, April 1816

Devlin Steele glanced up from the cards in his hand. The acrid smoke and dim light muted the gaudy red velvet of the gaming room. He reached for his glass and set it down again. The prodigious amount of brandy he had already consumed threatened to fog his brain.

His months back on English soil were as hazy as his present thinking. Snatches of memory. His brother, the imperious Marquess, rescuing him from the dirty makeshift hospital in Brussels. Days drifting in and out of consciousness at Heronvale, his sisters hovering around him, dispatched there to return him to health. Eventual recovery and a flight to London for a frenzy of dissipation meant to banish images of blood and horror and pain. Thus far, Devlin had managed to gamble and debauch away his quarter's entitlement. What capital he'd possessed had gone to money-lenders, but at present his pockets were flush, an unexpected surprise at Lord Farley's table.

'Your bet, Steele?' Farley's smooth voice now had an edge. His foot tapped the carpet.

Devlin stared at his cards, blinking to focus on the hearts and spades and diamonds. He had avoided Farley's gaming hell until this night, preferring an honest game, but damned if the man had not sought him out at White's. Predictable, Devlin figured, after he'd been tossing blunt all over town. Ripe for fleecing, by all accounts. A perfect pigeon for Farley.

He smiled inwardly. Farley had not yet heard the River Tick was already seeping into Devlin's boots. All the fleece had been long shorn.

'I'll pass.' Devlin barely glanced at the man seated across from him, concentrating instead on keeping his wits about him. Knowing Farley dealt a dishonest hand gave Devlin a slight advantage, if he could but hold on to it.

The cards were too good, though. Farley must be seducing him with a run of luck. He bet cautiously, against the cards, and avoided losing the successive hands. Farley's brow furrowed.

Rumour had it that Farley had lost a fortune in bad investments. Moreover, Napoleon's exile to St Helena had brought an end to the lucrative smuggling business everyone knew he ran. Farley was mortgaged to the hilt, a situation to make a man desperate—and desperate men made mistakes. War had taught Devlin that.

Farley indeed became more reckless, and Devlin stacked his chips higher.

Farley dealt the next hand, and Devlin carefully watched his expression. The man could still be considered handsome, though hard living had etched lines at the corner of his mouth and eyes. With his thin elegant nose, hair once fair, now peppered with grey, he had the look of the aristocrat he was, though his family fortunes had been squandered by an ancestry of fools. Typical of society, Lord Farley might not be a welcome suitor to the daughters of the *ton,* but, in the world of gentlemen who enjoyed his brandy, his card tables, and the young woman whose favours he doled out to the select few, Farley was top o' the trees.

Farley's fingers tapped a nervous tattoo on the table. 'Steele, I believe I could allow you some time with our Miss M. She is delightful tonight. A Spanish maiden. Perhaps she will remind you of your service in Spain.'

Devlin peered over the fan of cards in his hand. 'I have no wish to be reminded of Spain.'

He placed his cards on the table, and Farley blanched, pushing another stack of chips to Devlin's side.

The man plastered on a smile, but a nervous twitch had commenced under his right eye. 'I think you might recollect you won a time with Miss M once before. I assure you, she remains in good figure and has added to the delights she may offer.'

Devlin remembered her. Indeed, memory of her lovely face, so pale against her dark hair, had often warmed lonely nights as the British waited for Napoleon's army to attack. Her spirit and sensibility had intrigued him more than young ladies in drawing rooms could do. Not that he had mixed in society to any great degree. Good God, he'd never even set foot in Almack's.

Devlin smiled at his host. 'I'm sure I'd be delighted to renew my acquaintance, sir. Perhaps after a hand or two.'

How long ago had he shared that memorable space of time with her? Three years and more? Just after Maguilla. What had her life been like under the thumb of this man?

Farley's brow broke out in beads of sweat. Devlin suppressed his smile. The man was in trouble. Throwing caution to the wind, Devlin made a hearty bet. The tic in Farley's eye quickened.

The cards were called, and the man on Devlin's right let out a whoop. So intent on besting Farley, Devlin had forgotten the other player. As Devlin gave up half his stack of chips, he vowed not to continue such carelessness.

'Enough for me, gentlemen. I think I shall stop before Barnes here takes my whole stack.'

Barnes bellowed with laughter. 'I'd be pleased to do that, Steele.' He gathered his winnings, leaving Farley with a scattering of chips too small to stack.

'Another time,' Devlin said, standing.

'One more hand.' Farley's voice was thick and tense. 'Don't deny me the chance to recoup, Steele. One more hand is all I ask.'

It would hardly be civil to refuse. Devlin bowed slightly and sat back down. One more hand couldn't break him, though that last loss had hurt a bit. Farley would have been wiser to quit. The man had lost all card sense. Devlin doubted he could even cheat effectively at this point. Barnes, too, was flush with his winning streak and eager to extend it.

Play was fierce. Devlin bet moderately, intent only on preserving his present winnings, but the cards came like magic. Was Farley setting him up, or had true luck shone upon him?

Caution be damned, he thought. Life's the real gamble. Devlin bet deep.

And won.

Barnes good-naturedly laughed off his losses, still ahead with his one spectacular hand. Farley slumped back in his chair, his face drained of all colour.

'You will accept my vowel, sir?' Farley's question did not demand an answer.

'But of course,' Devlin replied amiably.

As Farley wrote out his vowel, Devlin gazed around the room, into the dark recesses where Farley's girls, looking like Spanish tarts, ran the tables.

'Shall I make Miss M available to you?' Farley asked, his voice flat.

Devlin considered, sweeping his gaze over the too-opulent room. Had this place truly impressed him three years ago with its wainscoting and brocades? Now it appeared as false as glory.

Perhaps it would be preferable to seek the relative silence of the street and preserve The Mysterious Miss M as a memory.

A shout came from outside the parlour. The door opened and a burly man dragged in a girl who was beating at his chest and kicking his legs in protest. She wore a mask.

'Lord Farley,' the huge man said, 'she's brawling again.' He dropped the girl at Farley's feet. Her pale delicate fingers grabbed the edge of the table to pull herself up. She lifted her head regally and smoothed the skirt of her red silk dress. Black sensuous curls tumbled to her shoulders in a tangled mass. The lace mantilla had slipped off and hung on one of her shoulders.

'I have no patience for this,' Farley growled. 'What now?'

'She refused a patron.' The man tossed her a scathing look. 'She bit him in…a most unfortunate place.'

The girl faced Farley with her chin held high, her face half-covered by a red leather mask. 'I warned you I would do so.'

Farley shot out of his chair and with a loud clap struck his open hand against her cheek.

'The devil!' Devlin sprang from his seat to catch her before she hit the floor. Both her hands clutched her head, and Devlin supported her with an arm around her waist.

'Farley, I must protest. That was most poorly done.'

'I'll thank you to stay out of my business, Steele,' Farley snarled. 'You have no say in the matter.'

'If you strike her in front of me, I claim the right.' Devlin spoke through clenched teeth. 'You might hear her out.'

Farley rubbed his face. 'I have treated her with more consideration than she deserves, and she still defies me. I'm done with her. You found her pleasing once. Take her in lieu of my debt.'

Devlin combed her hair away from her mask with his fingers. He would leave no woman to suffer such treatment. He leaned close to her ear. 'What say you, Miss England?'

She blinked uncomprehendingly, her eyes unfocused. Suddenly her vision seemed to clear and she stared at him, the bright red imprint of Farley's hand remaining on her cheek. She smiled faintly and flung her arms around his neck.

He gazed over the top of her head to Farley. 'Your debt is settled, sir.'

A half-hour later Devlin paced the pavement in front of Farley's establishment, cursing himself. In the space of a moment, he'd tossed his winnings away and incurred further expense. All for a lightskirt with whom he'd once spent a pleasant interval. He could almost hear the Marquess ring a peal over his head. 'Brother, how many times must I caution you? Think before you act.'

Ah well, he could not very well leave his Miss England with Farley, could he? Perhaps she had some family. His winnings ought to be sufficient to send her wherever she wished to go.

At least the money bought him a little more time. Only two months left before his brother released his quarterly portion.

Two cloaked and hooded figures hurried from the alley. Devlin instinctively kept a watchful eye on them. In this neighbourhood one could easily be set upon and relieved of one's winnings. Indeed, Farley might attempt to recoup his losses. The two shadowy figures came to a stop in front of him, one carrying a large portmanteau.

'We are ready, my lord,' the other one said, breathing hard.

Devlin peered at her. In the lamplight, her face was all but obscured by the hood, and she was wrapped entirely in her cloak, clutching some bundle beneath its folds. Still, he could not mistake his Miss England.

'We?' he asked, one eyebrow arching.

'Sophie accompanies me. I will not leave her.' The resolute tilt of the young miss's head was the same defiant gesture she'd made to Farley. 'Please, we must hurry.'

'She is your maid?' Mentally, Devlin doubled the expense facing him.

'Yes, but more so she is my friend.' She glanced about nervously. 'Truly, haste is in order.'

'Haste?'

'We did not secure Lord Farley's permission for Sophie to accompany me, but I'll not leave her.'

The other woman was a wisp of a thing almost overwhelmed by the portmanteau. Devlin massaged his brow.

What the deuce. In for a penny, in for a pound. 'Very well, Miss England.' Devlin glanced around the street for a hack. 'Shall I relieve you of your bundle?'

She shrank from him. 'If you could take the portmanteau from Sophie, sir, I would be most grateful.'

'Indeed. Sophie, allow me to carry that for you.'

The maid hesitated, backing away as if it were a precious burden unsafe to hand over. He nearly had to wrestle it from her grasp. The portmanteau weighed a ton. Surprising she had strength to lift it off the ground.

'Where is your carriage, sir?' Miss England asked.

Devlin laughed. 'You mistake me for my brother, the Marquess. Perhaps we can find a hack hereabouts.'

'Please, let us remove ourselves.'

He led the way, and the women fell in step behind him, like sari-clad females of India, keeping a respectful distance.

Perhaps he should have cast his lot with the East India Company. There were fortunes to be made, to be sure, but he had no wish for foreign shores. Not after Spain and Belgium—truth was, he had no idea what to do with his life.

Devlin glanced behind him, checking on his two shadows. The memory of his Miss England's soft lips and bold tongue drifted into his mind.

A hack ambled to a stop at the end of the street, and Devlin quickened his step to arrange its hire. He assisted the women into the conveyance, and the driver stowed the portmanteau.

Devlin sat opposite his cloaked companions. 'Where shall I instruct the driver to deliver you?'

The little maid huddled against Miss England's shoulder. Miss England faced him, but he could barely make out her features. 'We have nowhere to go,' she murmured.

He rubbed his hands. 'Is there no relation who might be persuaded to take you in?' The coil he'd gotten himself into had just developed more tangles.

'There is no one.' She turned her head, but held it erect. 'Leave us where you wish.'

Indeed, drop them into the street? They would be gobbled up in a trice. How long could he afford to put them up at some inn?

At that moment, the bundle in Miss England's arms emitted a squeak. Two small arms poked out of the wrapping and wound themselves around her neck.

'Deuce,' Devlin said.

The cloak opened to reveal an equally small head with a mop of hair as dark as her own. The child cuddled against her chest, fast asleep.

'This is my daughter, Lieutenant.' Miss England faced him again and spoke in a trembling voice, both wary and defiant. 'Linette…England.'

'Good God.'

Miss England spoke again. 'I do wish you would order the hackney somewhere away from this place. I care not where.' She grasped the child more firmly. 'Lord Farley might have a change of mind.'

Devlin instructed the driver to take them to his address. Where else could he take two women and a child when his brain was foggy with brandy and fatigue?

The passengers lapsed into silence. Miss England pointedly avoided conversation, and Devlin, angry at himself for his rash behaviour, clamped his mouth shut.

The thin light of dawn seeped through the London mist as the hack pulled up to a plain, unadorned building near St James's Street. His rooms were at the edge of the unfashionable district where the rent was cheaper. It was an area best known for housing Cyprians of the *ton* and, therefore, acceptable for a gentleman.

His entourage spilled out into the street, the little maid grabbing the portmanteau before Devlin could reach it. He began to chuckle. To anyone passing by at this hour, the women would appear as two more fancy pieces under protection. As long as the bundle in Miss England's arms remained covered, that is.

Devlin walked to his entrance halfway round to the back. Wait until Bart saw what he had won at cards. The sergeant's face when they came in the door would make this whole escapade worthwhile.

Devlin had once saved Bart's life on the battlefield. Ever since, the older man made it his mission to take care of him. Primary among Bart's self-imposed duties was tempering Devlin's rash, impulsive nature—a task at which he was doomed to fail.

Live for the moment. As a creed, it was as good as any.

Hmmph, more like a curse, Devlin thought. That particular creed had gotten him sent down from a school or two, but, from the time his late father had purchased his colours, it had meant survival. Now, however, it meant he had the charge of two women and a child.

He glanced over his shoulder. The women were not following. They stood on the spot where the hackney had left them, looking as lost as waifs.

Devlin cursed himself. They presumed he would abandon them. When had he ever passed by a creature in need? In his youth, one of his impulsive habits had been collecting stray animals which he'd then had to conceal from his father.

He walked back to the women. Three more strays to add to his collection.

'This way, if you please.' He wrested the portmanteau from the maid again. 'My abode is humble, to be sure, but will have to do.'

Miss England stood her ground. 'You need not trouble yourself, Lieutenant.'

'Nonsense,' he replied. 'We shall contrive something. The streets are too dangerous for you.'

With halting steps she followed him through the narrow alley. Her maid crept close behind. The sky had brightened, showing signs of becoming a magnificent day.

Devlin knocked on the door and only a moment passed before it opened. 'Good morning, Bart,' he said in a cheerful manner. 'I trust you have not been up all night waiting for me.'

'Half the night is all, then I consigned you to Jericho and took to—' Pale brown eyes in a weathered face widened.

'I've brought guests.' Devlin smiled as he dragged in the portmanteau. Bart's astonished expression was as rewarding as he could have wished. 'Not guests, really. Charges, you might say.' He stepped aside to let the women enter. 'Bart, may I present my charges.' He swept his arm in a graceful gesture. 'Miss England and Sophie.'

The little maid stepped forward cautiously and curtsied.

Devlin tossed Bart an amused glance as he shrugged off his coat. 'Where are your manners, Bart? Take the lady's cloak.'

Bart, mouth open, did as he was bid.

Devlin turned to Miss England. 'Allow me to assist you.' He stepped behind her and unclasped the fastening under her chin, removing the garment.

As the cloak fell away, the child in Miss England's arms whimpered in her sleep.

'My God,' exclaimed Bart.

Devlin laughed. 'This is Miss England's daughter...um...'

'Linette.' Miss England turned to face Devlin, and he had his first good look at her.

His memory had not failed him. Her face was almost regal in its loveliness. Her skin shone like fine porcelain, except for finger-shaped splotches of blue. Her lips were the identical colour to a rose that had grown in his mother's garden. Her lush mahogany-coloured hair cascaded down her shoulders, the perfect frame for a perfect face. She met his appreciation with a bold gaze, her intelligent blue eyes reflecting both youthful innocence and knowledge far beyond her years.

Devlin's breath left his lungs.

'I...I do not know your true name...' he managed, feeling his throat tighten at the vision of so much beauty.

She paused, her eyes searching his face. 'My name is Madeleine.' She added a faint smile. 'Madeleine England.'

He remembered the feel of her bare skin next to his, the lushness of her full breasts, and the ecstasy of her passion. His eyes swept over her as his body came alive to her again.

The child sleeping against her shoulder brought him back to his senses, a tiny girl, a miniature of the mother, very much resembling the wax dolls on his sisters' old toy shelf. The child's feathery long lashes cast shadows on the rosy cheek that lay against Madeleine's shoulder.

What the deuce was he to do with the lot of them?

Bart broke out into guffaws of laughter. 'Cast yourself into the briars again, have you, Dev?'

Madeleine lifted her chin, refusing to let it tremble in disappointment as she regarded the two men. At Farley's, her vision blurred by Farley's blow, she'd thought she dreamed Lieutenant Devlin Steele. Lord, she'd dreamed of him often enough. But when she'd blinked her eyes, it truly had been he.

She understood too well the look he'd given her a moment ago. It spoke of wanting to bed her. Foolish of her to forget this would be his motive for rescuing her. He could not be the brave and gallant dragoon of her fantasy. It had always been a silly fancy, after all, even if visions of him riding up on a tall stallion had comforted many a night.

Especially the nights Lord Farley came to share her bed.

The lieutenant ran his hand through his hair and replied to the other man's remark. 'I've not quite worked out what to do.'

She knew what he would do. He would cast them off as soon as he could. He must dislike her bringing Sophie and Linette. Perhaps if she'd come to him alone he'd have been content to keep her.

No matter. She would go nowhere without her daughter and her friend. They depended upon her.

She avoided looking at him. 'We shall not trouble you, sir. It is light outside. I am sure we may be safely on our way.' She reached for her cloak. 'Come, Sophie.'

The slight figure was in mid-yawn, her lank yellow hair falling across her face. The other man reached out an arm for her as she staggered.

'The lass is dead on her feet,' he protested.

The lieutenant rubbed his brow, as Madeleine struggled with her cloak. The child squirmed and started to whimper. The cloak slipped to the floor. She tried to comfort Linette, swaying to and fro with her as she had done since her infancy.

'Do not be foolish, Miss England.' He picked up the cloak and tossed it out of her reach. 'You confided you have nowhere to go.'

'It is none of your concern.' She attempted to pass by him to reach her cloak.

He stepped in her path and put his hand on her arm. 'You will stay here.'

She wrenched her arm away. The child started to whimper.

'You have made her cry,' Madeleine said. Much easier to be angry at him than to worry about where she would go if they did walk out the door. What would happen to Linette out there in the streets?

'I have made her cry?' His eyebrows lifted. 'Do you believe she will fare better if I allow you to leave? Do you have money enough to take care of her?'

She could not meet his eye.

He gently took her chin in his hand and made her look at him. 'You do not have money enough even for a hackney coach, do you?'

Her little girl stopped crying and stared with wide eyes at the man. 'Coach?' the child said.

Madeleine clucked at Linette, taking advantage of the opportunity to turn her back on Devlin. Inside panic reigned. Where would they go? Not back to Farley. Never back to Farley, but where? 'I do not need your concern.'

He marched around to face her again, and his voice became quieter. 'I beg to differ with you. If you will recall, it was I who intervened when Farley struck you.' He reached toward her cheek.

She shrugged him away, refusing to let him touch her. 'What does that signify? It is not the first time he has hit me.'

His hand remained poised in the air, his expression conveying acute sympathy. She should not allow herself to believe he truly cared, no matter how much the fantasy of that very thing had sustained her these few years.

The child squirmed in her arms and pulled away to grasp his fingers. The child giggled. Devlin stepped closer, and the tiny girl tugged on his neckcloth. This time when he touched Madeleine's bruised cheek, she did not draw away. Could not draw away. Speech became impossible.

'He will not hurt you again,' he murmured.

He became the hero of her daydreams again. How could she believe in him? Other young men had vowed to place her under their protection. They never returned, or, if they did return, never spoke such a promise again. Farley had seen to it. Why had Farley allowed this man to take her? Was it some sort of trick?

She glanced at her lieutenant. His eyes were warm and full of a resolve she would at least pretend was real. His face again became the one in her weary daydreams, conjured up after her toils were done and she was free to seek her bed alone. He always smiled at her in her dreams, his dimple winking at her.

Now his manly face filled her with excitement. The memory of his gentle kiss and peace-shattering lovemaking returned and agitated her. It was acceptable to dream and remember, but to let herself feel again? To hope? No, her only hope was to contrive to support Linette and Sophie, two people she could depend upon because they needed her so.

Linette tore out the folds of Devlin's neckcloth as he leaned down. His lips came closer. Madeleine's heart thudded against her chest.

'I settled the lass in my cot.' The voice of Devlin's servant, Bart, broke in, full of indignation.

Devlin smiled at the man. 'In your cot, Bart? Quick work.'

'I'll harbour no insults, if you please.' This man did not speak as servant to master. 'If you've managed to get us any funds, I'll see about some food. Some milk for the wee one.'

Devlin marched over to the table and emptied his pockets. 'Good news. We shall eat well.'

Bart picked up a few coins and shoved the rest back to Devlin. 'See you try to hold on to these for a bit.' He reached for a coat on a hook and went out the door, closing it silently.

'He is your servant?' Madeleine asked, conscious of being alone with him once more.

As if reading her thoughts, Devlin regarded her with smouldering eyes. 'More than that, I suppose. We managed through Spain and Belgium together.'

'Belgium,' she murmured. After news of Waterloo, for days she had pored over the names of the dead, weeping in relief when she finally found him listed among the wounded.

No matter. Now that his servant had absented himself, her lieutenant would soon wish payment for her rescue.

Her heart pounded. She must not feel this excitement at being near him. She must expect him to be as selfish and capricious as other men. Madeleine adjusted her hold on Linette, who rubbed her eyes and flopped her head on Madeleine's shoulder again.

Devlin came near to her again. 'The child must be getting heavy for you. Come. It is time for bed.'

Devlin led her into his bedchamber, acutely aware of blood

thundering through his veins. By God, she was more desirable than that first, magic time with her.

As she regarded the room with dismay, he saw it through her eyes. A smallish room, furnished with a tall double chest of drawers in a style long out of fashion and a large four-poster bed with faded curtains. His old trunk was tucked in the corner, clothing spilling out.

Her gaze rested on the bed. What might it be like to share that bed with her? To tangle with her in its sheets?

This would not do. She appeared as if she would collapse at any moment. The child was no infant, nearly three years old, he'd guess. A sturdy bundle, and Madeleine had not let go of her for nearly an hour.

'Where shall Linette sleep?' she asked nervously.

'In the bed, where else?'

She straightened, her defiant chin lifting. 'My lord, I am prepared to repay you for your generosity, but I must insist on privacy for Linette. She must not be in the same room, let alone the same bed.'

He raised his eyebrows. Did she think him unmindful of the child? Did she think him so base as to take advantage of her?

'And I'm loath to leave her alone in a strange place,' she continued, her mouth set in firm determination.

He stared into her blue eyes and the breath left his lungs. He let his gaze travel down the length of her. Her red silk dress clung to her form and the weight of her daughter pulled its low neckline down lower. The attire was pure tart, but her bearing regal. The combination set his senses aflame, though he had no intention of acting upon them, ill timed as they were.

A smile not absent of regret spread across his face. 'I meant for you and the child to share the bed. Did you think I meant otherwise?'

She blushed, bringing a most innocent pink to her cheeks, her eyes downcast. 'You know very well what I thought.'

He stepped behind her and put his hands on her shoulders. The little girl's curls tickled his fingers. For a moment he let his fingers caress Madeleine's soft flesh. He held her against him, inhaling the scent of lavender in her hair. From behind her, he planted a chaste kiss on her cheek and gave her a push toward the bed.

'Sleep well, Madeleine.'

Chapter Three

The damp chill seeped through Devlin's clothing. His twisted limbs would not move. Pain had settled into a constant ache, made worse with each breath, worse still by the rancid stench of blood. Of death. Moans of the dying filled the night. The sounds grew louder and louder, until they merged into one piercing wail. An agonised sound. The sound of fear and horror and pain.

Coming from his mouth.

He woke, his heart pounding, breath panting. His vision cleared, revealing faded red-brocade curtains made moderately brighter by sunlight. What were brocade curtains doing at Waterloo?

He sat up, his mind absorbing the round mahogany table in the corner with its decanter of port, the mantel holding one chipped porcelain vase. His back ached from contorting himself on the settee. It had been the dream. He hung his head between his knees until the disturbing images receded. Had he cried out in his sleep?

The wail again sounded in his ears, coming from the bedchamber this time, not from his own soul.

He leapt from the settee and flung open the door. Madeleine paced the room, clutching her little girl. The child cried and struggled in her arms. Madeleine's red dress was creased with wrinkles. That she'd not bothered to undress before sleeping moved him to compassion. How exhausted she must have been.

The child gave a loud, anguished cry, and Madeleine quickened her pace.

'What the devil is going on?'

She spun toward him, her youthful face pinched in worry. 'She is feverish.'

'She is ill?' Devlin's head throbbed from the previous night's excess of brandy.

'Yes. She coughs, too.' Her voice caught. 'I have never seen her so ill.'

'Good God,' Devlin said. 'We must do something.'

'I don't know what to do!'

Tears glistened in her eyes. The child's wailing continued unchecked. He had not bargained for a sick child.

'Bart!' he yelled, rushing back into the parlour. 'Bart! Where are you?'

Bart emerged from his room, Madeleine's small companion like a shadow behind him. The sergeant, his craggy eyebrows knitting together, protectively held her back. The gesture irritated Devlin. Did Bart think him dangerous to young females?

'What in thunder?' A scold was written on Bart's face.

'The child is sick. We must do something.' He stood in the middle of the room, doing nothing.

'The wee one is sick?' parroted Bart, standing just as paralysed.

'Linette!' Sophie rushed past Bart and ran to Madeleine, who had followed Devlin into the room. She frantically felt the child's forehead.

'She is burning up!' she exclaimed. 'Maddy, sit down. Let's loosen her clothes. Mr Bart, if you please, some cool water and some clean rags.

'Clean rags?' Bart said, still immobile.

'Make haste!'

At Sophie's words, Bart sprang into action, drawing water from the pump and bringing it to the women, both fussing over the child. Finding clean rags was more of a challenge. He finally brought a stack of towels and bade them to cut them up, if necessary. Sophie dipped one towel in the water, wrung it out and placed it on the child's chest. Madeleine mopped the little girl's brow with another.

The child seemed to settle for a moment, but, before Devlin could relax, broke out in a spasm of coughing.

'Deuce,' said Devlin, barely audible and still rooted to the floor.

Madeleine flashed him an anxious look. 'I am attempting to quiet her, my lord.'

'I did not complain,' he protested.

Her eyes filled with tears. 'I am at a loss to do more.'

'I would be honoured to assist, if someone would instruct me.' No one heeded him.

Madeleine sniffed and patted Linette's head with the damp cloth.

Her friend regarded him with a wary expression. 'We could try to give her a drink of water.'

Before Devlin could move to the small alcove that served as the kitchen, Bart delivered Sophie a cup of water.

'Let me try to give her a sip,' Madeleine said.

Linette flailed her arms, jostling Madeleine, who spilled the water on her daughter and herself. Devlin walked to the cupboard, removed another cup, and placed in it a tiny bit of water. He handed this to Madeleine.

'Try a bit at a time,' he suggested.

She did not look up to acknowledge his act, but she was able to pour a small amount into the child's mouth. He took the empty cup and poured a bit more from the fuller one. Again the child accepted the drink.

Devlin was feeling rather proud of himself at having been so useful, when the child began another spell of coughing. Madeleine sat the little girl on her knees and leaned her over to pat her gently on the back.

The child promptly vomited the water all over Devlin's stockinged feet.

'Damn.'

Madeleine gasped. Sophie grabbed the wet towel and wiped his feet, kneeling like a slave girl. Bart glared at him as if he were somehow solely responsible for the child's ill health.

'Enough. Enough.' He stepped away from Sophie's ministrations. She burst into tears and ran from the room.

Bart glared at him. 'Now look what you've done. You've frightened the lass.' He rushed after her.

Devlin reached for his head. Bart, he supposed, would not be inclined to brew the remedy for his excess of brandy. The child wailed again.

The sound triggered memories. Voices of dying men. His knees trembled, and he feared them buckling underneath him. The dream of Waterloo assailed his waking moments. With it came the terror that had only been too real.

Clamping down on his panic, he rushed into his bedchamber and pulled fresh stockings from the chest. He shrugged into his coat, and retrieved his boots from the parlour where he'd left them. Without a word, for he could not guarantee his words would be coherent, he rushed out of the apartment, slamming the door behind him.

Madeleine flinched at the sound and held her coughing

daughter against her shoulder, still patting gently. Well, good riddance to Lieutenant Devlin Steele, she told herself, battling the disillusionment of his abandoning her at such a time.

'Was that the door?' Bart asked, coming back into the room.

'He left,' she said, shrugging her shoulders.

'Hmmph.' The man pursed his lips.

Linette settled into a fitful sleep. Though her skin burned like a furnace, Madeleine could not let go of her.

The stocky man surveyed her. Not as tall as the lieutenant and a good ten years older, he seemed solid as a rock.

His gaze softened when lighting on Linette. 'Ma'am, would you and the lass be all right if I went out for a bit? I've a mind there are some things we may be needing.'

A rock that easily rolled away. She sighed inwardly. It was foolishness to hope for assistance from any man.

But Devlin had assisted her in the most consequential way. He had rescued her from Farley, when he need not have done. He was under no obligation to assist her further, however. After Linette's distress he would surely wish them speedily gone. Madeleine's lips set together in firm resolve. He would have to put up with all of them until Linette became well.

If Linette became well.

Her throat tightened. Her child meant everything to her. She'd risked Farley's wrath to give birth to Linette and to keep her. Her daughter was the only worthwhile part of her life.

Sophie appeared at her side. 'Mr Bart went out. Do you think the master will return soon?'

'Lieutenant Steele?' Madeleine would not call him master. 'I very much doubt it. I fear Linette's illness displeases him.'

'Is Linette better? She's quiet.' Sophie leaned over and brushed the child's dark curls with her fingers.

'She sleeps fitfully and is so very hot.' She dabbed at the child's face with the cool cloth.

Sophie wandered about the room aimlessly, and Madeleine watched her, needing some distraction. The room was comfortably fitted to double as parlour and dining area, but its once-fashionable furnishings showed signs of wear. The carpet had lost its nap in places, and the cushioned seats looked faded and worn. Had not Devlin said his brother was a marquess? Perhaps the family had more title than blunt. Not that it at all signified. It was far superior to Farley's richly done-up rooms.

Unbidden thoughts of home came, mahogany tables polished to mirror finish, sofas and armchairs covered in rich velvet. No threadbare furnishings there. She could see herself bounding through the rooms, her scolding governess in hot pursuit.

Linette stirred and Madeleine's attention immediately shifted to her. It never did any good to recall those days, in any event.

'Should I unpack our clothes, do you think?' Sophie asked.

Perhaps if they appeared settled in, they might delay an eventual departure. 'That would be good. I fear I cannot help you, though.'

'Oh, Maddy, do not trouble yourself. You have your hands full.' Her waiflike friend smiled at Linette. 'You ought to lie down with the babe.'

Her arms ached from holding Linette, and she had slept only a couple of hours before the child's cries woke her. 'I suppose you are right. I will bring her into the lieutenant's bed.'

She carried Linette to the bedchamber, placed her in the centre of the bed, and climbed in next to her. The sheets and pillow held Devlin's scent as they had the night before. She had dreamed of him walking toward her to a bed like this. He would gently brush the hair from her face and lean to kiss her. She had dreamed of this Devlin many times.

It took no more than a moment to fall exhausted into sleep.

* * *

The banging of the door woke her. She immediately felt for Linette's forehead, still too hot.

'Where the devil is she? I've brought a doctor.' Devlin's voice came from the other room. 'Where's the child? Has the fever broke? Deuce, I've been to Mayfair and back. Found the doctor three houses down.'

As the door of the bedchamber opened, Madeleine had a glimpse of Sophie skittering away. Devlin charged in, a short, spry figure behind him. He had mentioned a doctor. For Linette.

The doctor wore a kindly smile in a round countenance. His coat was shabby and the leather satchel he carried was battered and worn. He came directly to Linette. 'Is this our little patient? Here, let me have a look at her.'

Madeleine rose quickly and handed Linette over to him. He sat in a wooden chair and spoke softly to the child as he peeked into her mouth and examined her all over. Madeleine watched the doctor's expression for a clue as to his thoughts. She chewed on her lip. Devlin came to her side and put his arm around her. Needing his strength, she leaned against him.

Finally the doctor handed Linette back to her. 'She has a putrid throat. Nothing to signify under ordinary circumstances, but I cannot like her fever. How long has she suffered thus?'

'This…this morning,' Madeleine stammered. Devlin squeezed her closer.

The doctor smiled, kind crinkles at the corners of his eyes. 'Well, she seems a sturdy child. A little bleeding may suffice to throw off the fever.' He rummaged in his bag.

'Bleeding?' Madeleine said warily.

'Yes, just a little. Come hold her.'

Madeleine sat on the bed and placed Linette in her lap. The doctor opened a small container and, with long pointed tweezers, removed the ringed worm.

'Hold her arm, if you please.'

Devlin stood his ground, though every impulse shouted at him to flee. He recalled the doctors placing such creatures on his arm. The memory belonged to the time of delirium and pain, when he fancied the leeches would consume him alive. Madeleine sat so composed, so resolute in assisting the doctor.

His arms prickled with the sensation now being experienced by the little girl. She was too weak to struggle, as limp as his sister's dolls when they carried them about, as he had been those months ago in Brussels.

The child will feel better after the bleeding, he reminded himself. It had been so for him.

Finally the leech fell away, satiated, and the doctor placed the creature back in its container. He packed up his bag while Madeleine tucked Linette into the bed.

The doctor took Madeleine's hand. 'You have taken good care of her thus far. Try not to lose heart. I have some powders that may assist, as well.'

Madeleine nodded, looking unconsoled. The doctor frowned worriedly at Devlin and gestured for him to follow out of the room. Devlin escorted the doctor out.

When outside, the doctor paused, glancing worriedly back into the apartment. 'The child's fever is very high. Only time will tell if she will recover.' He handed Devlin a packet of powders and gave instruction how to use them. 'I shall return tomorrow to see how she fares.' He patted Devlin's shoulder.

Devlin pushed some coins into the man's palm. The doctor placed them in his pocket, not glancing at the amount. Smiling reassuringly, he took his leave.

Devlin returned to the bedchamber. Madeleine stood beside the bed where the child slept.

'He told you it is hopeless, did he not?' she said, rubbing her arms.

Devlin attempted a smile. 'Indeed, he said no such thing. He gave me the powders and told me how to mix them. He will return tomorrow to see how she fares.'

'She will not die?' Her voice trembled.

He walked over to her and gently brushed the hair off her face. 'She will recover. You are overwrought. Come, sit. I will wager you have not eaten.' He found a chair and brought it next to the bed. 'Where did your friend and Bart go?'

'Her name is Sophie, Lieutenant.' Her voice still shook.

'And mine is Devlin.' He tapped her nose with his finger. He gazed at the little girl. 'The child will sleep, I think.'

'*Her* name is Linette.'

Devlin touched a lock of the child's hair. 'I know.'

He heard the door open and went into the other room. Bart entered, carrying pieces of wood.

'What's all this?' Devlin asked.

Bart cleared his throat. 'I took the liberty of procuring a bed for the wee one. A rocking chair, as well. The poor babe needs a place to sleep.'

Devlin smiled at him. Bart was a practical man. 'Well done, my friend.' He had not thought of such a necessity.

Madeleine stood in the doorway. 'A bed for Linette?'

'Aye, miss. And a chair to rock her in.'

The look she gave Bart was almost worshipful. Devlin's skin grew hot. By God, he was jealous. Of Bart. He wanted Madeleine's gratitude all to himself.

'Set the bed up in our room for now, Bart,' he said and received not a glance from her.

Sophie peered out from the closet where Bart slept. 'Can I help you, Maddy? What would you have me do?'

'Prepare some food for Madeleine,' Devlin said. Sophie shrank from his voice, but scurried to do what she was told.

Devlin sat Madeleine at the small table and took a seat

across from her. He poured a small glass of port. 'This will fortify you a bit.'

He sat so near to her, Madeleine again became aware of the scent that had surrounded her in his bed. The lines in his face were clearly visible and told of years spent on battle-fields. Her heart gave a lurch. He was too much like her dreams.

'Drink,' he commanded, handing her the glass.

Madeleine obeyed. The sweet liquid warmed her throat, but Devlin's solicitude frightened her. The doctor must have given ominous news indeed.

He continued to speak to her in a kind voice. 'We will put the child into her bed as soon as Bart has put it together. Sophie can see to the linens. You must try to eat something, Madeleine.'

Sophie scurried from the scullery. Madeleine sipped her port, keenly aware of Devlin's eyes upon her.

Bart announced the bed to be ready, and Devlin accompanied her to the room. She placed Linette gently into the small wooden bed and carefully tucked the linens about her. The child settled, and Devlin took Madeleine's arm and urged her away.

When she returned to the table, Sophie put a plate in front of her with a fat slice of bread and cheese. Madeleine ate, because she did not know what else to do.

When darkness fell, Devlin lit the candles in the bedchamber to dispel the gloomy shadows that had crept into the room. The soft glow of the candlelight illuminated Madeleine, who looked vulnerable as she sat by Linette's bedside. She had barely moved from the little girl's side all day, though he could not fault her. Little Linette was an appealing child and it pained him to see her suffering.

Madeleine glanced at him. 'Do you go out this evening, my lord?'

He put his hands on the arms of her chair and leaned over her. 'My name is Devlin.'

'Very well. Devlin.' Her eyes drifted back to the child.

He pulled up a chair next to her. 'Now, how could I go out when our babe is ill?'

She gave him a sharp glance. 'You are not obligated to stay. I would not hold you.'

'Fustian,' he said.

She rocked gently. He wished he could convince her all would be well. He'd been trying to do so all day, but she did not believe in reassurances.

Devlin heard Bart's deep voice coming from the next room. He smiled to himself. The old sergeant was taken with that mouse of a female. It was amusing. Devlin always imagined Bart would shackle himself to some sturdy country girl to match the farm he used to dream of owning. To make a fool of himself over a wisp of a city chit amused Devlin no end.

'Devlin?' Madeleine's voice was barely more than a whisper.

'Yes?'

'I have never thanked you for…for the doctor and for… allowing us to stay.'

'Deuce, Madeleine. What do you take me for?' Tossing her out, indeed. 'Did you think I'd send you back to Farley?'

She twisted around to face him, alarm lighting her face. 'You would not!'

He stroked her cheek. 'Of course I would not.'

She turned back to Linette, but her hand went to the place he had touched. Devlin leaned back in his chair, balancing it on its back two legs. 'How the devil did you come to be at Farley's? You are too young, surely.'

She rocked at a faster pace. 'I am old enough.'

'Nonsense, you are hardly out of the classroom.'

She tossed him an insulted look. 'I am eighteen.'

'Eighteen!' he cried, unbalancing the chair and nearly pitching over. Linette stirred, whimpering.

'Shh.' Madeleine reached for the child, rubbing her back.

'Good God.' He lowered his voice. 'How old were you when you came to him?' He'd made the computation in his head, but could barely believe it. She'd been so young, and he'd made love to her. How could he have done so?

'I was fifteen.'

'Damnation!' So painfully young. He had left her there when she was younger than the silly chits making their come-out, the ones he thus far had successfully avoided. 'The man's a damned reprobate.' Devlin had bedded her, as well. What did that make him?

She gave him a sideways glance. 'You assume me the hapless victim, Devlin. Don't make me so good.'

'You did not join him willingly.' He would not believe it.

She continued her rhythmic rocking. 'Is this any of your concern, my lord?'

'Not a whit.' But that would not stop him. 'Why did you join that cheating lout, then?'

She sighed. 'This is a sordid story. Hardly of interest.'

'Of interest to me,' he persisted.

'Very well.' She paused to stroke Linette's hair. 'He seduced me. I was ruined. What else could I do?'

She made being ruined sound like getting a soiled spot on her gown. This was a rum story if ever he heard one. Farley was forty, if he was a day. Seducing a girl of her tender years—abominable. Devlin ought to have rescued her from him back then. Saved her from that abominable life.

She adjusted the blankets around the child, the candle

behind her placing her profile in silhouette. His breath caught. She was a beauty. As fair as a cameo. As exotic, with her thick black curls, as a goddess from foreign shores. As skilled in the sheets as would fuel any man's dreams.

Her fingers gently touched the child's forehead. When she drew them away, they covered her face. Shame on him. Her child's life hung by a fragile thread, and he thought of bedding her.

'She will recover, Madeleine. Do not fear.'

She leaned back in the rocking chair and closed her eyes. Her silence stretched into the night, and Devlin felt guilty and useless. He watched her rock slowly back and forth in the chair. Back and forth. Back and forth.

'Devlin?' Her voice came as if from a great distance.

'Yes?'

'Do you believe God punishes sinners?'

Chapter Four

Devlin woke sharply, still sitting in the chair. The candles had burned down to stubs and the peek of dawn came through the windows. Madeleine cradled the child in her arms. The child was still.

'My God, is she…?' No, it was unthinkable.

'She's sleeping.'

Devlin's heart started beating again.

Madeleine shuddered. 'Her fever broke and she fell asleep. I thought I would lose her, Devlin. It is what I deserved.'

'Nonsense.' Weak with relief, he stretched his stiff limbs. 'She is through the illness, then?'

She nodded, her cheeks wet with tears.

While she had kept her anxious vigil, he had fallen asleep. Damned if he was not a useless sot. He stood up and, with a tentative hand, stroked the child's hair.

He kissed the mother on the forehead. 'Now you can get some sleep, as well. To bed, Madeleine, the babe can lie with us.'

He urged her up by her elbow and put an arm around her waist as he escorted her to the bed.

She looked about to protest.

He grinned. 'Now don't get in a twist. I'm too tired to remove my clothes and so are you. We will be as proper as peas.'

She removed her slippers and laid Linette on the bed. Devlin's boots had long been tossed into a corner, as had his coat and waistcoat. He turned down the covers, and she crawled in. When he took his place next to her, he tucked her against him and promptly fell back to sleep.

When Madeleine woke, she was alone in the bed.

Linette. Where was Linette? She scrambled out of the covers and ran to the door.

Opening it, she saw Devlin seated at the table, Linette on his lap. The child giggled as she pulled on Devlin's nose. Two dark curly heads so close together.

Devlin turned his head to escape the assault on his nose. He spied Madeleine. 'Good morning, sleepyhead.'

'Deddy's nose,' cried Linette, pushing Devlin's head back with two chubby hands on his cheeks. Devlin pretended to resist.

'Would you like some nourishment, miss?' asked Bart, pulling out a chair for her.

She glimpsed Sophie perched on a stool near the kitchen alcove, looking smaller and more childlike than ever. Sophie jumped down and disappeared into the scullery.

'Our girl has made a remarkable recovery, wouldn't you say, Maddy?'

Hearing Devlin say 'our girl' gave her heart a lurch. Nor did the familiarity of him calling her Maddy escape her notice.

'She seems fit,' she agreed.

'Mama!' Linette scrambled off Devlin's lap and flung herself into Madeleine's. 'I got Deddy's nose!'

'I saw, sweetling.' She kissed the top of Linette's head and felt her forehead with her hand. It felt blessedly cool.

Bart brought a tray of tea things, followed by Sophie carrying a plate of biscuits. He set the tea service beside her and poured her a steaming cup. 'Do you want some tea, Dev?'

Devlin nodded.

Linette pointed to the biscuits, 'I want one.'

Madeleine placed a biscuit on a plate and lifted Linette on to the other chair to eat it.

'Maddy, you're a sight.' Devlin blinked at her over his cup. 'That awful dress.'

She glanced down at the crumpled red silk.

'Would you like Bart to fill you a bath? We have a tub here-abouts, don't we, Bart?'

'I believe so,' Bart responded.

Before Madeleine could think of what she wished to reply, Bart fetched the large tub, carrying it into the bedchamber while Sophie put on more water to boil. When they began to carry buckets to fill the tub, Madeleine offered to assist, but Devlin would not let her. Even Linette helped, carrying small pitchers of water, spilling more than made it into the tub. It felt all wrong to be so pampered.

When the bath was filled, Devlin brought her into the bed-chamber. Bart and Sophie took charge of Linette, but Devlin remained. Madeleine began to understand.

Devlin closed the door and leaned against it. 'Shall I play lady's maid for you?' His voice was velvet.

It was time for her to pay for his kindness. Farley had taught her how.

She cast Devlin a demure look under her lashes and strolled over to the bath. 'As you wish, sir.'

He moved closer, as smooth a motion as a stalking cat. Presenting her back to him, she lifted the long tangled curls off her shoulders. His hands slid up the length of her back. Slowly he undid her laces, his fingers light and dextrous. She remembered him fumbling with her laces all those years before. Her body lapsed into a languid state. His hands slipped under her dress and ran over her skin like warm liquid.

The wrinkled red silk dress fluttered to the floor. Next came her shift. When she was fully naked, she knew he would wish to see. She turned to face him.

As she expected, his eyes feasted on her, darkening with arousal. She had learned to stand still for a man's visual pleasure.

He took time to regard her, longer than she thought she could bear. His gaze disturbed her. Not precisely as the ogling from Farley's clientele had done, but in an indefinable, unsettling way. His eyes finally reached her face.

'You are lovely.' The corner of his mouth turned up, and his dimple deepened.

The next move belonged to her. She stepped toward him and reached out her hand to caress his neck. She had not intended to kiss him, but he leaned down, and she had only to rise on tiptoe to reach his lips. He crushed her against him, standing wide-legged so she could feel his arousal pressing into her. For a moment she forgot her role and simply revelled in the strength of his muscles, the sweetness of his mouth, the feel of his hands pressing into her back, sliding down to hold her tightly against his groin. She did not realise how quickly she removed his shirt, how efficiently she freed him from his trousers, how she clung to him as he carried her to the bed.

'Madeleine.' His voice was a groan as he placed her on the bed and climbed atop her. His lips feathered her cheek and neck, soft, warm, and hungry. Her heart raced in excitement.

His tongue circled the pink of her nipple, and all her senses sprang to life. She ached with wanting him.

She was spiralling out of control at the precise moment she ought to check herself. She had succumbed to the ecstasy of Devlin's lovemaking once, but that interlude belonged to daydreams. She must shield herself, protect herself from feeling, just as she'd done when required to endure the attentions of other men. The Mysterious Miss M could not be hurt, or humiliated, or betrayed, because The Mysterious Miss M felt nothing at all.

The Devlin of her daydreams was not the same Devlin whose hand now stroked the flesh of her belly, whose mouth rained kisses over her breasts. She would not be fooled, no matter what kindnesses he chose to make. Ultimately, all men served their own needs, and demanded payment for any small favour they bestowed. If they were refused, they could be very cruel.

It had been that way after the enchanted night with Devlin so many years ago. Farley had come afterwards to claim his pleasure, but Madeleine refused him. He went into a rage that left her bruised and in pain. The next day, Farley departed on one of his mysterious long trips. By the time he returned, Madeleine knew herself to be with child.

Now Devlin's hands and lips threatened to engulf her in sensation. She remained still, resolving to repay him for rescuing her, for taking in Sophie, for snatching her child from the clutches of death, but she would not allow herself to feel anything.

She pushed on his shoulders, and he lifted his head.

'Shall I pleasure you now, my lord?' She modulated her voice to a velvet smoothness, as she'd rehearsed many times.

He leaned on his elbow, his expression puzzled. 'Pleasure me?'

She deliberately slithered out from beneath him, facing

him instead. She ran her finger in circles on his chest. 'I wish to please you. Tell me what I must do to pleasure you.'

He grabbed her hand and searched her face. 'What the devil…?'

She laughed, making a throaty sound Farley insisted she learn. 'Oh? Would you like me to be wicked? I can be wicked, my lord, if that is what you wish.'

He dropped her hand and sat up, rubbing his face.

She pretended to look wounded. 'What is amiss, my lord? I shall do whatever you desire.'

'Stubble it, Maddy.' He swung his legs over the side of the bed and grabbed his clothes.

'Do not be vexed.' Retaining her velvety voice, she pressed herself against his back. 'I would not wish you unhappy.'

His muscles stiffened. 'And I do not wish to play this game of yours. We are not at Lord Farley's establishment, Miss M.'

'Game?' She sat back, blinking in confusion.

He shoved his arms into the sleeves of his shirt and groped around for the rest of his clothes, donning each piece as he came to it. 'You are acting like cheap Haymarket-ware.'

She blinked at him, covering herself with the bed linens. 'I do not know what that means.'

He glared at her. 'It means lightskirt, Cyprian, dolly-mop. Shall I continue?'

Her eyebrows knitted together. 'But that is what I am.'

He grabbed at the linens covering her and yanked them away. Before Madeleine could protest, he picked her up and dumped her into the now-tepid bath water.

'How dare you!' she shouted before she remembered that men did not like it if you showed them anger.

He lunged down at her face, and she drew back, fearful of the price he'd exact from her show of temper. Only an inch lay between their lips.

His voice became disturbingly low. 'You cannot fool me, Maddy. You wanted me as much as I wanted you.' As quickly, he strode out the room, slamming the door behind him.

Dripping with water, Madeleine burst into tears, but she did not know if it was because she had angered him or because what he'd said had been only too true.

'Can you make it fit, Sophie?'

Madeleine stood in the centre of the bedchamber while her friend pulled on the strings of her dress. Though her hair, now in a braid down her back, remained damp, all other signs of the bath had been removed. Not from Madeleine's mind, however, where Devlin's angry eyes continued to haunt. She rubbed her temples.

Sophie tugged on the material of the dress. 'It is too small, Maddy, and the seams cannot be let out.'

'Oh, bother,' she mumbled.

The door slammed. Footsteps sounded in the outer room. 'Bart! Bart!'

Madeleine felt the blood drain from her face. Devlin had returned.

'Where is everybody?' He entered the bedchamber.

Sophie shrank back to a corner. Madeleine braced herself.

Surprisingly, he wore a grin on his face. He walked briskly over to her, lifted her off the ground, and swung her around. 'I have a surprise for us. Where is Bart?'

'Here I am, Dev.' Bart appeared in the doorway, holding Linette's hand. Linette had her thumb in her mouth.

Devlin released Madeleine. 'We're moving. Right now. We have to pack.'

'Did you get us tossed out of here?' Bart asked, his eyes narrowing.

Devlin clapped Bart on the shoulder, smiling broadly. 'No,

I've merely secured lodging spacious enough for the lot of us.'

Madeleine's hands flew to her face. For all of them? What of sending them away?

'Explain yourself, lad.' Bart said.

'I have procured the lease to Madame LaBelmonde's apartments,' Devlin responded, grinning.

'Madame LaBelmonde?' Madeleine raised an eyebrow.

'Two bedchambers above stairs and two below. A parlour, dining room, and a proper kitchen.' He placed his hands on his hips in satisfaction. 'It should do very well.'

'A sizeable rent, I suppose?' Bart pursed his lips.

Devlin shook his head. 'Not beyond our touch, once my quarterly portion is in hand.'

Bart clucked his tongue. 'How do we pay until then?'

Devlin tossed Madeleine a broad wink before answering Bart. 'I wagered the first month's rent on a roll of the dice and won. My recent winnings should pay the second.'

'You wagered the rent?' Madeleine gasped. Visions of foolish, ruined men, their faces bleak and despairing, leaving Farley's gaming rooms flashed through her mind. She remembered the sounds of angry words, overheard years ago outside her parents' bedchambers.

'Lord Devlin is a sad gamester, ma'am,' Bart told her.

'What else was I to do with my time but play cards?' Devlin countered. 'We shall go on very well, I promise.'

Madeleine wondered about more than the rent. 'Who is Madame LaBelmonde?'

Devlin smiled at her. 'A close neighbour.'

'Close?'

'Indeed. She has found a new protector. Lord Tavenish, I believe. He purchased a town house for her. She leaves her furnishings.'

'Lord Tavenish,' Madeleine repeated. A frequent visitor at Farley's, Lord Tavenish had been well over fifty with sagging skin, and a sour smell. Would a town house be worth such a man?

Bart blew out a breath. 'Well, what is done is done.'

'Indeed.' Devlin grinned. 'We have not a moment to lose. There is a tenant interested in these rooms.'

'These rooms? Already?' Bart asked.

'The matter is completely settled. I called upon our landlord and made an arrangement with him. If we move out today, our debt to him is forgiven.'

Little Linette let go of Bart's hand and tottered over to Madeleine. 'Up, Mama.' She reached her hands up. Bart turned on his heel, muttering about setting to the task and hot-headedness. Sophie quietly crept along the wall until she, too, reached the door.

Devlin turned to Madeleine, his smile taking her breath away. She spun to face the wardrobe, gathering Devlin's clothing to pack in the trunk.

'You rented these accommodations to include us?' She could not believe it. There must be some mistake.

He put his hands on her shoulders and turned her to face him again. 'Yes, to include you. We could not get on here, all of us, in this small space.'

She dipped her head, hiding her face from him. 'You are not obliged to house us.'

He tilted her face to him, his fingers under the soft skin of her chin. 'I am obliged.'

Not that he understood it, but Devlin felt keenly responsible for them. What would happen to them otherwise?

She shook her head.

He held her gaze. 'As you have said, you have nowhere else to go.'

She cast down her eyes.

'Madeleine, you are no prisoner here, if you wish to go.'

Her glance flew back to him. 'I do not wish to leave. You are correct. There is no place for me.' Her voice cracked.

His finger drew a line down her cheek. 'Let us not speak of this now. We have much to do.'

He watched her turn away, stooping down to hand Linette some clothing. 'Put them in the trunk, Linette.'

The laces on the back of her dress were undone. 'Let me lace you,' he said, reaching for them as she stood up again.

She twisted away from his hand. 'It is no use. The dress no longer fits.'

'Change to another then. I will leave the room if you desire privacy.'

She kept her eyes on her daughter, a doll-like miniature of herself. 'I have no other dress.'

'No other dress?'

'Well, there is the horrid red one, but Sophie washed it and it is quite wet still. I must have grown out of this one since last wearing it.'

He studied the frock, and it did indeed look unfashionably old and slightly girlish. 'A long time ago, I collect.'

'The day Farley brought me to London.'

Devlin heard the edge in her voice. How had she come to be in Farley's clutches? 'You brought only one extra dress?'

'I did not want Farley's clothes.'

Devlin raked his fingers through his hair. He had not calculated on having to purchase a wardrobe. Did the little maid and the child need to be clothed as well?

Madeleine regarded him, her eyes serious. 'Do not worry. Sophie will know how to alter it. She is clever at such things. In the meantime, if I go out, I shall wear my cloak. It covers everything.'

'We will get you clothes, Maddy.'

She lifted her eyes to him before walking over to Linette.

Later that afternoon, Madeleine held Linette's hand as she walked through their new rooms. Linette chattered, and she answered automatically, trying to stay out of the way of Devlin and Bart, busily carrying in trunks and boxes.

She had feared Madame LaBelmonde would have furnishings as gaudy and garish as in Farley's establishment, but these rooms were genteel, the golds, reds, and greens muted and beautiful. She might have chosen them herself. Would it not be lovely if this really were her house? She the mistress, and Devlin...

No, she must not pretend. But as she strolled through the rooms, she could not help herself.

She entered the parlour and ran her finger across the polished mahogany and silk upholstery. She pictured herself seated on the couch, and Devlin, on the nearby chair, reading the latest newspaper. Linette sat at her feet, playing with a doll. She ought to be doing something in this fantasy, but what? Her attempts at embroidery used to wind up in tangles, and she had never paid enough attention to sewing to know how to mend.

Sophie walked in the room in such high spirits her usually pale face was flushed with pink.

'Oh, Maddy, it is the loveliest set of rooms I have ever seen. Do you think we may really stay? Look at the furniture. I should like to keep such nice tables polished. Do you think lemon oil or beeswax would do?'

Madeleine stared at her, not having any notion of what best polished wood, nor whether they might stay.

Sophie did not seem to notice she had not responded. 'I shall ask Mr Bart.' Sophie swept out of the room as quickly as she had come in.

'Mama, I want Mr Bart!' Linette pulled at her hand to follow Sophie.

'No, Linette. Mr Bart has much to do right now. He's moving boxes.'

'I want boxes, too.'

'Let's explore the kitchen, shall we?'

She led Linette to the kitchen where the little girl opened cabinet doors, momentarily distracted by new discoveries within. Madeleine ran her hand over the cupboard, imagining life inside this kitchen. She saw herself kneading bread, and Devlin entering, kissing her cheek, and asking for his meal.

Folly! She knew not the first thing about making bread, nor how to cook a meal.

Devlin entered the kitchen, carrying a big wooden box. 'Maddy, is the kitchen well supplied?'

She opened a cupboard. 'There are things in here. Do you suppose it is adequate?'

Devlin stood next to her and peered in the open cupboard. 'Hmm. Well, Bart will know.' He set the box down on the table and walked out.

Much later, the five of them sat around that rough wooden table, having finished a hastily prepared meal of bread from the nearby bakery and hard cheese. Devlin poured each of them another glass of wine, giving Linette, seated on his lap, a small sip from his own glass. The little girl puckered her lips at the taste, and he laughed.

Madeleine gazed at all of them. She pretended they were a family, without a care, sharing a simple meal and pleasant conversation. The thought made her smile.

Devlin caught her eye and winked at her. 'I propose a toast.' He raised his glass.

'I want toast,' Linette said.

'To our new abode,' Devlin said.

'New 'bode,' Linette parroted.

'Hear, hear,' Bart responded.

'It is a lovely place.' Madeleine sipped her wine and swept her gaze from corner to corner.

Devlin gave her a smile. He'd had no idea that pleasing her would make him feel mellow and strangely content. He raised his glass again while Bart sliced a piece of cheese and handed it to Sophie. Little Linette banged on the table with both hands.

The mellow feeling returned. 'Tomorrow, ladies, we shall visit the mantua maker. Outfit you properly.'

Panic came over the shy Sophie's face. 'Oh, no, my lord.'

Devlin at last saw an opportunity to befriend the skittish young woman. 'Would you not like a pretty dress or two?'

Sophie shook her head and dared to glance up at him for a moment. 'No pretty dress. Nothing pretty. A bit of fabric will do, if it is not too dear. I do not presume to ask, my lord.'

'Sophie, you are part of our household. You deserve decent clothing.'

'Yes, my lord.' She slid off her stool and cleared the dishes.

Devlin rolled his eyes and caught Bart's disapproving look before the man followed Sophie out of the room.

'Do not mind her, Devlin,' Madeleine said. 'She does not want presents, I think.'

He took a gulp of his wine. Linette relaxed against his chest, still at last.

'She is afraid of you.'

He gave a dry laugh. 'Indeed.'

'It is because you are a man.'

He ran a finger through Linette's hair, brushing it off the child's forehead. 'Bart is a man, I've noticed.'

'True.' She looked quizzical.

'Well, Maddy, shall you and I visit the modiste or do you choose to be your own dressmaker, too?'

He meant to be good-tempered, but she responded with a wounded look.

'I cannot sew.'

Lord, women were difficult.

'It is of no consequence,' he said, hoping to return to her good graces. 'I'm sure we can find a skilful mantua maker. I would be pleased to see you in a pretty new dress.'

Her countenance changed, as if he had said something of great importance that had never occurred to her before. 'Of course. I understand perfectly.'

He wished he understood. Devlin poured himself more wine and drained the entire contents of his glass. It was easier to evade the musket balls of an entire French battalion than to navigate a simple conversation with a female.

'Linette is falling asleep. I need to make her ready for bed.' Madeleine rose from her chair.

'I'll carry her.' Devlin lifted Linette, and the little girl relaxed against him, a warm bundle more than comfortable against his shoulder.

He followed Madeleine into the bedchamber where they had set up Linette's bed. A connecting door joined the two upstairs bedchambers. He wanted to think of Madeleine knocking softly on that door and coming to him in the night, but, after the morning's débâcle, he was sure she would not do so.

Madeleine pulled out a tiny nightdress from the bureau. Linette's meagre supply of clothing barely filled half a drawer, and Devlin vowed to ensure the child, as well as the mother, had a pretty new wardrobe.

'Place her on the bed, please.'

He did so as gently as he could. 'Toast,' Linette murmured, opening her eyes momentarily.

Madeleine glanced at Devlin and smiled. How pleasant it felt. He had no idea domesticity could be so comfortable.

After she settled the child into bed and kissed the soft pink forehead, Devlin wrapped his arm around her and squeezed. 'She's a fine child, Maddy.'

'She is everything to me.' Her voice shook with emotion.

Madeleine leaned her head against Devlin's shoulder. His strong arm felt so comfortable, she could almost imagine he belonged to her and they were gazing upon their own—

No, she must not lapse into that particular fantasy. She must remember that Devlin wished to see her in pretty dresses, just as Farley had. She must remember that she owed him for his kindness.

'Shall I ready myself for bed as well, sir?' She modulated her voice as she had been used to doing for these last years.

He placed her away from him and looked into her face. Madeleine knew how to control her expression. She smiled, half-demurely, half-seductively. She gently caressed his neck, leaning forward so when he glanced down, a peek of the rounded shape of her breasts was clearly visible. She led him to the connecting door, pulled him into the other room, closing the door behind her.

'Shall I kiss you?' she purred, wrapping her arms around his neck. Not waiting for his answer, she stood on tiptoe and touched her lips to his.

Yes, she could do this, she thought, keeping her body in firm control. She could indeed pleasure Devlin and repay his kindness without ever pleasuring herself.

Devlin wound his arms around her and pressed her against him. Desire flared inside him, and he deepened the kiss. She reached her hands around to loosen the already loose strings of her dress. It fell to the floor, leaving only her corset and shift. He ran his hands across her bare shoulders.

So lovely. So soft. Like honey. He wanted her. Wanted to plunge into her, join himself to her and not feel so alone.

'Shall we go to the bed, my lord?'

The words echoed in his mind, from long ago.

He released her, watching as she moved toward the bed. She tossed a seductive glance over her shoulder.

She climbed onto the bed and turned to face him. 'Come, let me remove your clothing.'

He rubbed the back of his neck. And stood his ground.

'Come,' she purred, reaching her arms above her head, arching her back. 'Come, my lord.'

Devlin spoke quietly. 'You must call me Devlin. Did you forget that, Maddy?'

She rolled to her side and stared at him.

'This is not Farley's establishment.' He stared back.

She twisted the sheet in her hand.

'Go to your room, Maddy. Your daughter might need you this night.'

She sat up. 'No.'

'I do not want your favours.' Something else from her, perhaps, but not what Farley required of her.

'But you must.' A desperate look came over her.

'No.'

She scampered off the bed and gathered her dress, holding it in front of her, covering herself with it. 'Please, Devlin, you must let me make love to you. You must.' Her words came out between laboured gasps.

'No, Maddy.'

He walked to the door and opened it.

'Devlin, I am used to this. It is not difficult. I will pleasure you. It will be pleasant, I promise you.' Tears sprang to her eyes.

With every sensation in his male body, Devlin wanted to

accept her offer, but he could not bear the emptiness in her seductive words. He well remembered what had passed between them that first time and this was not it.

She rubbed her eyes, now red and swollen. Her nose had turned bright pink. 'I…I wish to show you my gratitude.'

'Gratitude? Do you think I desire your lovemaking out of gratitude?'

Confusion wrinkled her brow. Devlin suspected that was not part of her practised repertoire. She clutched her dress in her hands. 'You want me, I know you do. Men like to…to… You liked it, too.'

He had indeed, but not when her eyes stared vacantly and her words were rehearsed.

'Go to bed, Maddy. Your own bed, not mine.'

She dropped her dress to the floor and wound her arms around his neck, kissing wherever her lips could reach. At least her rehearsed seduction had fled, but her desperation was no better. None the less, his body flared to life. He picked her up and she sighed in relief, nuzzling his neck. He carried her through the doorway and dropped her on to the large bed in the other room.

'No, Devlin.' She grabbed the front of his shirt, trying to pull him back. 'You do not understand. I must do this.'

He moved her hands away, trying to be gentle, but not succeeding. The demands of his body were making him harsh. 'You do not need to bed me. It is not something I demand of you.'

'But it is the only thing I can do.'

Madeleine watched him turn away from her and walk toward the door. 'You do not understand,' she whispered. 'It is the only thing I can do.'

He did not look back, but closed the door behind him, leaving her alone.

* * *

Devlin fled down the staircase and out into the damp night air. He strode through lamp-lit streets until reaching the nearest gaming house. Instead of sounding the knocker, he stood staring at the entrance. What would he find inside? Cigar smoke? Bad brandy? The luck of the draw? It was not ennui he sought to dispel this night, but the turbulence left in Madeleine's wake.

Why not accept her gratitude and bed her? He'd rescued her from Farley's, hadn't he? Taken in her child and her mouse of a maid. Provided them proper lodgings.

Devlin turned from the door of the gaming establishment and walked back to the street. When he had first met her, she had come to him, not with gratitude, but desire. Almost like loving him. He had never forgotten.

He wandered slowly through the streets, until he found himself back at the door of his expensive new rooms. The place was quiet as he entered, a single candle providing light. He glanced toward the back of the place where the two other bedchambers were located and wondered what might be occurring behind those closed doors. Was Bart holding the frail Sophie protectively, lest the 'lord' attack her in the night? Had Sophie offered her body to Bart, as well? Had he accepted?

Devlin would bet a month's blunt Bart had not made a mull of things as he had, and that, on the morrow, the little maid would gaze upon Bart's craggy features with adoration.

Devlin entered Madeleine's room quietly. The dim illumination of the street lamp shone on Linette's sleeping figure, her thumb in her mouth. Devlin smiled and gently pulled out her thumb. The little girl stirred, her long dark eyelashes fluttering. She popped the thumb back in.

Madeleine's bed was empty, and he felt a moment's anxiety, until he spied her curled up on the windowseat, sound asleep, as innocent and vulnerable as her daughter.

They were both beautiful, these charges of his, and totally dependent upon him. It frightened him, worse than leading men into battle. Soldiers knew the stakes were death, but they had the tools to fight. If he failed Madeleine and Linette, they would be at the mercy of creatures like Farley and would have no weapons with which to protect themselves.

He would not fail them, he vowed. He would see to their needs no matter what the cost.

Devlin gathered Madeleine in his arms, her weight surprisingly like a feather. He carried her to the bed.

'Only thing I can do,' she murmured, resting her head on his shoulder, much like her little girl had done earlier.

'Hush, Maddy,' he whispered. 'You'll wake Linette.'

'Linette,' she murmured. 'All I have.'

'Not any more, Miss England.' Devlin laid her carefully on the bed and tucked the covers around her. 'Now you have me, as well.'

Chapter Five

Madeleine held tightly on to Devlin's arm as they strolled the pavements of London in the bright morning sun. She pulled the hood of her cape to obscure as much of her face as possible. Still, she felt exposed.

'You will not take me to a fashionable modiste, will you, Devlin?' The thought of walking down Bond Street filled her with dread.

Devlin regarded her with an amused expression. 'No, indeed, Maddy. Would I subject you to such a terrible thing?'

That made her laugh. 'Do not tease me. It is merely that I would not want to be seen.'

'Do not worry, goose. You were always masked, were you not? No one will recognise you.' He patted her hand comfortingly.

'Of course. So silly of me.'

She took a deep breath. He did not understand. Farley's patrons did not concern her, but perhaps those she did fear encountering would not recognise her either. Surely the years had altered her?

'Where are we bound, then?' She gazed up at Devlin, so

tall and handsome. His green eyes sparkled in the sunlight, like emeralds on a necklace a young man had once bestowed upon her before Farley snatched it away. If necessity bade her to walk in daylight, it pleased her to be beside him.

'Bart found a dressmaker only four streets from here,' Devlin said. 'How he should know about dressmakers foxes me.'

She laughed. 'Bart is very clever, isn't he? He and Sophie. I do believe they can do everything.'

'Unlike me, I suppose.' He smiled, but the humour did not reach his voice.

'You are the hub around which all revolves.' She spoke absently, transfixed by a coach rumbling down the street. 'Oh, look at the matched greys. How finely they step together. They are magnificent, are they not?'

'Indeed,' he answered.

She watched the coach-and-four until it drove out of sight. 'Oh, my.' She cast one last glance in the direction it had disappeared. 'What were you saying, Devlin?'

'I was remarking about how utterly useless you find me.'

She glanced at him. 'You are funning me again. What would have happened to me and Linette without you, Devlin?'

Madeleine felt her face flush. She should not have spoken so. To suggest he had any obligation to her was very bad of her. She had awoken in her own bed this morning. The only service she could render him, he'd refused.

'It is I who am useless, not you, Devlin.' She sighed. 'I am skilled at nothing…well, nothing of consequence.'

A curricle drawn by two fine roans raced by. Madeleine stopped to watch it.

'Do you like horses, Maddy?'

'What?' She glanced at him. 'Oh, horses. I used to like horses.'

'Not now?' His mouth turned up at one corner.

'I have not been on a horse since…for many years.'

'You ride, then?'

She had careened over the hills, giving her mare her head, clearing hedges, sailing over streams. Nothing unseated her. She outrode every boy in the county and most of the men. When she could remain undiscovered, she spent whole days on horseback.

Had she not been out in the country on her mare, unchaperoned as usual, she might not have met Farley, might not have succumbed to his charm. Never riding again was fitting punishment for her fatal indiscretion.

She blinked away the regret. 'You might say I used to ride horses as well as I now ride men.'

'Maddy!' Devlin stopped in the centre of the pavement and grabbed her by the shoulders. 'Do not speak like that. I ought to throttle you.'

She tilted her chin defiantly. 'As you wish, sir.'

He let go of her and rubbed his brow. 'Deuce, you know I will not hit you, but why say such a thing?'

'Because it is true. I know what I am, Devlin. There is no use trying to make me otherwise. It is my only skill. Bart and Sophie can do all sorts of useful things. You, too. You can win at cards and go about in society. You have fought in the war. What could be more useful than that? But me, there is nothing else I know how to do.'

He extended his hand to her, wanting to crush her against him and kiss her until she took back her words. Though the kissing part might not prove the point, exactly, he admitted. He dropped his hand and, putting her arm through his, resumed walking.

After a short distance in silence, he said, 'That's what you meant last night. Saying it was the only thing you could do.'

She did not reply.

Devlin held his tongue. This was no place for such a conversation in any event. Besides, each time some handsome
equipage passed by in the street, she slowed her pace a little.

He chuckled. 'Horse mad, are you?'

She pointedly turned her head away from him.

'Now do not deny it, Maddy. You are horse mad. I recognise the signs. I was myself, as a boy. Why, I liked being with
the grooms better than anyone else. My brother, the heir,
could not keep up with me when I rode, though he's a good
ten years my senior. Nothing he could do but report to Father
that I was about to break my neck.'

He threw a penny to the boy who had swept the street in
front of where they crossed.

'Oh, look at all the shops!' Madeleine exclaimed. 'I had
not reckoned there to be so many.'

Like a child at a fair she turned her head every which way,
remarking on all the delicious smells and sights.

'You have not been to these shops?'

She laughed. 'Indeed not. I always wondered what the
London shops would be like.'

'You've been in London three years and have never seen
the shops?' This was not to be believed.

'Lord Farley did not take me to shops.'

This time Devlin stopped. 'Do you mean that devil did not
let you out of that house?'

'Not as bad as all that, I assure you.' She patted his hand
and resumed walking. 'When Linette was big enough, I was
allowed to take her to the park across the street. But only in
the morning, not when other people might be about. And
there was a small garden in the back of the house. Sophie and
I were allowed to tend it, though I mostly had the task of
digging the dirt, because I did not have the least notion how

to make the flowers grow. I enjoyed feeling the soil in my hands, though.'

Such a small space of geography in which to spend more than three years. 'I wish Farley to the devil.'

She gave him a look. It struck him as almost the same expression Sophie bestowed on Bart.

As they stood at the entrance to a shop with an elegant brass nameplate saying 'Madame Emeraude', Madeleine shrank back. Devlin had to practically pull her into the establishment. She held her fingers to the hood of her cloak, covering her face.

A modishly dressed woman emerged from the back. 'May I be of assistance?'

Since Madeleine had turned away, Devlin spoke. 'Good morning. Madame Emeraude, I collect?'

The woman nodded.

Devlin gestured to Madeleine. 'The young lady is in need of some new dresses.'

'Certainly, sir. Shall I show you some fashion plates, or do you have certain styles in mind?'

It irritated Devlin that the dressmaker addressed him directly instead of Madeleine, as if Madeleine were his fancy piece to dress as he wished, but, he supposed, in this neighbourhood, her clientele were almost exclusively from the demimonde.

'Shall we step into the other room?' She gestured elegantly.

He pulled Madeleine along to the private dressing room in the back. 'The young lady is in somewhat of a fix. You see, she has only the dress she wears and we were hopeful to purchase something already made up.'

Understanding lit the woman's eyes. 'Let me see her.'

Since Madeleine was acting like a stick, Devlin had no choice but to treat her that way. He turned her toward the dressmaker and removed the cloak that obscured her.

'Oh,' said the woman in surprise. 'Miss M, is it not? How delightful to see you again.'

'How do you do, ma'am,' Madeleine murmured politely, though Devlin did not miss the splotches of red on her cheeks.

'Deuce,' said Devlin.

'Why, I believe I have a dress ready for you,' said Madame Emeraude helpfully. 'Do you recall we fitted it not a fortnight ago? Wait a moment and I shall see—'

'No!' Madeleine cried.

Devlin interceded, putting his arm around Madeleine. 'We do not wish that dress.'

Madame Emeraude looked from the one of them to the other. 'I see. It is a new day, is it not? Well, I am pleased for you, miss. That other one was charming, but I shall have no business with him, I tell you, until he pays—' She caught herself. 'I beg pardon. I only meant I wish you well, Miss M.'

'Thank you,' Madeleine said, continuing to look miserable.

Madame Emeraude smiled and began to consider her, stepping around her. 'Oh, my,' she said as she saw the open laces of Madeleine's dress. 'This dress does not fit. No, no, no. This will never, never do.'

'You see our predicament.' Devlin smiled. Madeleine fixed her interest on the floor.

'Let me show you a few things I have on hand.'

Madame Emeraude signalled an assistant, who carried in one dress after another. Madeleine seemed to regard each garment with horror. They were, Devlin thought, merely dresses. A little fancy, perhaps.

As Madame conferred with her assistant, Madeleine whispered to him, 'Devlin, please do not make me wear those dresses. This one I have will do, or Sophie can make me a plain one.'

'What is wrong with them?'

'They are not...respectable.'

He regarded her, rubbing his chin. 'I see.'

When Madame Emeraude came back to them, Devlin took the woman aside and spoke to her. Madeleine watched them, the modiste nodding and looking her way. She dearly wished to leave this place where the proprietress knew her as Miss M.

Devlin came back to her. 'Madame Emeraude is ordering a hack. She has given me the direction of another dressmaker where we will go next.' He held her cloak open for her.

'I do not wish to. Let us go home, please.' This short excursion had already been mortifying.

'We will try this other place first. You need clothes, Maddy.'

In the hack she continued trying to persuade him. 'I believe Sophie could teach me to sew, Devlin. A piece of cloth would be enough.'

He would not listen. He did not understand. Though it was exciting to be out among the carriages and shops, it was frightening, as well. She would always be face to face with what she was.

Madeleine peeked out at the passing scenery, the bustle of London with the pedestrians so intent on their destinations and the tradesmen so occupied with peddling wares. She could not hide forever. How could she rear Linette if she hid? Her daughter would have to go out into that world, too. She was determined that Linette's life be respectable, though nothing could ever change what Madeleine was inside.

If Devlin Steele was determined she should have clothes, she was determined they be respectable ones.

'Are you taking me to Bond Street?' she asked, meaning to sound merely curious, but her voice shook.

He smiled at her. 'Not to Bond Street. We are directed to a modiste who dresses the worthy daughters of our bankers and merchants.'

'Very well.' Not the fashionable part of town. No chance of encountering members of the *ton*.

They discovered a goldmine. The wealthy daughter of an East India merchant had abandoned her trousseau for one made at a fashionable address. The young woman was of Madeleine's size, and the dresses were exquisitely tasteful attempts by the modiste to expand her clientele.

Madeleine quarrelled with Devlin over the number of dresses he would purchase, wanting no more than two or three. She adamantly refused to let him include even one evening dress and would not even discuss the riding habit. His easy acquiescence in these last two matters made her momentarily suspicious, but he whisked her off to the milliner next door and a new set of arguments became necessary.

As he made arrangements for the delivery of his final purchase of several bonnets for Madeleine and one very plain one for Sophie, Madeleine gazed in the mirror.

She wore a pale lilac muslin walking dress adorned only by vertical tucks in the bodice edged by a plain purple ribbon. A blue spencer, lilac gloves, and a modest straw bonnet, simply adorned with a blue bow, completed the ensemble. She even carried a reticule.

Studying herself in the glass was like gazing into the distant past.

Devlin's image appeared behind her. 'You look very well, Maddy.'

She swallowed the surge of emotion that had risen in her throat. 'It seems like too much…'

He held up his hand. 'No more of that. We still need to stop by the shoemaker.'

She opened her mouth to protest, but as he took her hand and tucked it in his arm, he quickly added, 'Do you suppose we could convince Sophie to be measured for new shoes?'

For all his generosity to herself, his thinking of Sophie most touched her heart. She cast him a smile. 'Perhaps we should charge Bart with such a task.'

He laughed as he escorted her out the door to the street. 'Very wise idea.'

Madeleine had an illusion of being transported to the town of her childhood. The pavement was more crowded, indeed, and the shops more varied and numerous, but it was a most respectable street, and her dress indistinguishable from other young ladies shopping. Or so she thought. She still received many curious looks.

'Devlin, are you sure my appearance is acceptable?'

Devlin had noticed the admiring glances of the men and appraising looks of the women. He could not help but be proud to be Madeleine's escort. Beautiful even in her own ill-fitting frock, she quite took his breath away in her new walking dress.

'You look lovely,' he whispered back.

This news did not appear to cheer her. She furrowed her brow. Too bad some choice piece of horseflesh did not come into view to distract her.

Devlin caught sight of a shop window. 'We must go in here.' He pulled her into the shop. 'Must not forget our girl.'

They entered a toy store with shelf after shelf of dolls, toy soldiers, and miniature coaches and wagons. An exquisite wax doll with real hair as dark and curly as Linette's caught Devlin's eye. He vowed he must purchase it for Linette. Madeleine adamantly refused, saying the child was too young to care for such a treasure. He settled instead for a porcelain-faced baby doll, a ball and blocks. As he finished giving the direction for the toys to be delivered that afternoon, he spied a carved wooden horse and, thinking perhaps the little girl might be horse-mad like her mother, added it to his purchases.

Back on the street, a handsome carriage drawn by a set of matching bays approached in their direction. Devlin frowned as he spied the crest. The carriage stopped next to them. As Madeleine shrank back, Devlin stepped forward to greet its passenger.

'Devlin, it has been too long,' the fair-haired lady at the carriage window exclaimed.

'How are you, Serena?' His sister-in-law was a good creature, well intentioned, eminently correct, with classical looks and very little in common with Devlin except a connection to his brother.

'I am well, as usual,' she responded in her soft voice. 'And you, brother? We do worry when you do not call.'

'I have been shockingly remiss, but I'm fit, I assure you.'

His sister-in-law gazed curiously at Madeleine. It had never entered his mind that he'd be required to introduce Madeleine to anyone, least of all his sister-in-law, the Marchioness.

He pulled Madeleine forward, needing to exert a little physical effort to do so. 'Serena, may I present Miss England. Miss England, the Marchioness of Heronvale, my sister-in-law.'

Madeleine executed a very correct curtsy.

'Have we met before, Miss England? I do not recall.'

Madeleine, with her eyes downcast replied, 'No, madam.'

'Well, perhaps I may convey you both to your destination? I would be pleased to do so.'

Devlin suspected Serena would be very pleased for an opportunity to find out who her brother-in-law escorted unchaperoned through this shopping district. He felt Madeleine painfully squeeze his arm.

'I believe Miss England has one or two more shops to visit, but that was kind of you, Serena.'

'Are the shops worthwhile, Miss England? I confess I have never visited the ones on this street.'

'They suit me very well, madam,' responded Madeleine in a quiet voice.

'Perhaps you could recommend one to me,' the Marchioness persisted. Devlin knew her inquiry to be meant in a friendly way, but he also knew his brother's wife was nearly as fixed on him securing his future as was his brother. She wanted nothing more than to see him happily married; the Marquess wanted merely to keep his brother's fortune secure.

'I would not presume to.' Madeleine looked miserable. Only his firm hold on her arm kept her from bolting, he suspected.

A hackney coach came from behind, its driver shouting for the carriage to move on.

'Oh, dear,' said Serena. 'We had better go.'

'Indeed,' replied Devlin.

'Please call soon, Devlin. My pleasure, Miss England.' The carriage moved forward and these last words faded with distance.

'Devlin, may we please go home now?' Madeleine raised a shaking hand to her bonnet.

'No,' he said mildly, determined for her not to be made uncomfortable by her encounter with Serena. 'We need to have you measured for shoes and I must not return without cloth for Sophie.'

'Oh, yes, I quite forgot Sophie's cloth,' she murmured. A racing phaeton whizzed by. She did not even notice.

'Maddy, were you made uncomfortable by my sister-in-law?'

They walked a few steps before she answered. 'It was very improper to introduce me to her.'

'I disagree. It would have been ill-mannered not to introduce you. An insult to you.'

He glanced at her, seeing her brows knitted together and
her bottom lip trembling slightly. 'A fine lady like the Marchioness should not be made to converse with one such as
me.'

'Maddy, I refuse to allow you to speak so. You have studied
your appearance. You could not be more presentable.' He did
not yet know the story, but he would wager she'd not chosen
her life with Farley. But who would choose such a life? Only
a woman with no other choice.

'My appearance does not alter the fact that you should not
have introduced a marchioness to...to Haymarket-ware.'

'I refuse for you to speak so,' he said.

She did not look at him. 'I will endeavour to obey you, my
lord.'

He yanked open the door to the shoemaker.

After he'd ordered various pairs of shoes for her, he
seemed relaxed again. By the time they'd selected several
pieces of material at the cloth merchant's shop, they were
back in temper with each other.

Devlin hailed a hack. As he negotiated with the driver,
Madeleine noticed a gentleman across the street looking at her.

Farley.

He saw her look in his direction and tipped his hat to her.
Her heart pounded wildly, and she feared she might vomit.
She felt Farley's eyes on her the entire time it took for Devlin
to lift her into the hack.

As they pulled away, he saluted her once more.

Lord Edwin Farley watched the hack start off down the
street. He had taken to frequenting a tobacconist on this row,
one of the deplorable economies he was forced to make in

his constrained financial circumstances. At first he'd noticed the young lady in the lilac and blue with a connoisseur's appreciation, but when he saw it was Madeleine, he froze. All that beauty, and he'd let her fall into the hands of Devlin Steele. It irritated him beyond belief.

He'd hoped to recoup from his recent bad luck by playing until Steele owed him a bundle. The Marquess of Heronvale would have redeemed his little brother's vowels, even if the sum had been large. Everyone knew the older brother doted on the younger one. But Farley had lost instead. If that were not bad enough, he'd impulsively used Madeleine to settle his debt. Damned Steele.

The hack turned the corner and disappeared from his sight. He resumed his stroll down the pavement. Madeleine had looked quite fetching in that lavender confection. His body stirred merely thinking about her.

He'd have her back, he vowed. He'd unpeel those layers of clothing from her and bed her like she'd never been bedded before. He'd make her beg for him, make her pant with wanting him. She'd been easy to seduce as a girl. He'd only had to say a few pretty words to her, and she'd been his. He laughed, remembering how easy it had been to entice her to his room that night, her father bursting in at the perfect moment—when she'd been naked on top of him.

Yes, he'd get her back, he vowed. This time without the child she was stupid enough not to prevent. Perhaps he could make some money on the child. He knew men whose tastes went to ones as young as that. A little beauty like her mother, she would likely sell at a good price.

What revenge ought he to exact upon Steele? It would give him added pleasure to give that matter some thought.

Humming and jauntily swinging his walking stick, Farley continued on his way.

Chapter Six

The packages from their shopping expedition arrived that afternoon amid much excitement. The wide eyes of little Linette as she opened hers made all the extravagance worthwhile. Sophie, whom Devlin did not expect to break out in raptures, reverently fingered the cloth they had purchased.

'Thank you, my lord,' Sophie whispered, though she did not meet his eye while saying it.

'You did tolerably well, Dev,' Bart said, watching Sophie's every movement.

'Indeed?' He laughed. 'I am unused to such high praise from you.'

'The lass is happy. Mind you do not tease her, now.' Bart shook his finger in warning.

Devlin tried to stifle his grin. 'I shall endeavour not to.'

Madeleine was unusually quiet. She excused herself, saying she wished to unpack her dresses. Thinking of it, Devlin realised she had been just as solemn on the ride back home.

Linette held the horse up to Devlin, pulling on his trousers as she did so. 'Horse! Horse!' she said excitedly. It was inevitable. The horse captured the little girl's attention and the expensive doll was ignored. Devlin sat down on the floor.

'Shall we build a stable for your horse, Lady Lin?' He gathered the blocks together and started building.

'Wady Win,' Linette parroted.

'How much did all this cost, might I ask?' Bart's voice was deceptively casual.

'I think you had better not ask,' Devlin said ruefully. 'I thought I might pay a visit to my brother tomorrow.'

Madeleine walked back into the room. 'You will visit your brother?'

She did not need to know he intended to ask his brother for a small advance. 'I promised my sister-in-law, as you recall.'

'Oh.' She sat on the settee and watched Devlin and Linette build the promised stable with the blocks.

'Would you like me to make tea, Maddy?' Sophie asked, dropping her fabric back into its box.

Madeleine popped up. 'I will do it.'

'You, Maddy?' Sophie said. 'It is not necessary.'

'I want to. It is not so difficult, is it?'

'Neigh! Neigh!' Linette galloped her wooden horse, trying to make it jump over the blocks. The blocks tumbled.

'Now, I was building that.' Devlin ruffled the girl's hair, making her giggle. He kept an eye on the mother.

'I will do it, Maddy. Do not trouble yourself.' Sophie started for the kitchen.

Madeleine insisted. 'No, *I* will do it.'

'It is my job,' Sophie said, visibly upset.

Madeleine put her hands on her hips. 'I would like to make it. I am tired of being waited upon as if I am no use at all.'

'But, but…' Sophie burst into tears and ran out.

'That was badly done, miss.' Bart gave her a stern expression. 'The lass wishes to serve you. She credits you with sparing her much hardship.' He marched after Sophie.

Madeleine glanced at Devlin, her hand rubbing her throat. 'I did not mean to make her cry.'

Devlin understood. She wanted to feel she had some use beyond the bedchamber. He had even less to offer, except the money his brother controlled, if he could get it. If Madeleine wished to make tea, what was the harm?

He turned back to the blocks. 'Maddy, if it would not be too much trouble, would you make me some tea?'

The next morning Devlin walked up to an impressive town house on Grosvenor Square and rapped with the shiny brass knocker. The heavy door opened and a solemn-faced butler almost broke into a smile.

'Master Devlin.'

'Barclay, you never change.' Devlin did smile. 'I trust you are well?'

The man took his hat and gloves. 'Indeed, I am, Master Devlin.'

'Is my brother here?'

'He is expected directly, my lord. Shall I announce you to her ladyship?'

'If you please.'

He followed Barclay to the parlour, decorated with Serena's usual perfection, couches and chairs arranged to put visitors at ease. A moment later, the Marchioness came through the door.

'Devlin, you kept your promise. How good to see you.' She reached out her hands to him.

He clasped them warmly and kissed her cheek. 'Serena, you are in excellent looks, as usual.' His brother's wife had the cool beauty of the fine china figurines gracing the mantelpiece, disguising her warm-hearted nature. Her reserve and unceasing correctness could so easily be mistaken for coldness.

She coloured slightly. 'Do sit with me and tell me how you go on. I've already rung for tea.'

He joined her on the couch. 'I am well, Serena.'

She peered at him worriedly. 'Are you sure? You look a little pale. Do your wounds still pain you?'

He laughed. 'I am quite well. Thoroughly recovered and there is no need to fuss over me. Where is Ned?'

'Attending to some business.' Her brows knit together. 'Are you in trouble, Devlin?'

'Good God, no, Serena.' Her solicitude rivalled his brother's. 'I have something to discuss. Nothing to signify.'

The tea arrived and she poured with precision. He sipped the liquid, brewed to perfection, and thought how different this cup was from the strong, leaf-filled concoction Madeleine had made the day before.

Serena spoke. 'It was pleasant seeing you yesterday.'

'Indeed.'

'That young lady—Miss England, I believe—was lovely. Who is she, Devlin?'

He should have expected this question. He gave Serena a direct look. 'An acquaintance.'

Her eyebrows raised.

He held her gaze.

Serena glanced down demurely. 'Does she interest you?'

Did Madeleine *interest* him? Keeping her safe interested him. Making love to her interested him, but he would not explain that to Serena. At least Serena must not suspect Madeleine to be anything but a well-bred young lady, unchaperoned though she had been. She would not have mentioned Madeleine at all if she had thought her to be Haymarket-ware, as Madeleine called herself.

'She is an acquaintance, Serena,' he repeated in a mild voice.

She tilted her head sceptically, but was much too well bred to press any further.

They sat in awkward silence.

'I should tell you I have moved, Serena.'

She peered at him. 'Moved? For what reason?'

Devlin paused. 'No reason.'

'Some difficulty with the rent?'

'No.' Devlin hid his impatience with a small laugh. 'Why do you suppose I should have difficulty with the rent? You and Ned. I cannot say who is the worse. I am not in difficulty. I am well able to take care of myself. At six and twenty I should know how to go on. I survived Napoleon's army, if you recall.'

Serena looked stricken. 'But you were so badly injured. We feared you would not live. You do not realise how close a thing it was.' She fished a lace-edged handkerchief from her sleeve and dabbed her eyes. 'And you have been gambling so. Ned was concerned because no one has seen you for days.'

'Ned can go to the dev ' This was too much. 'Good God, what does he do, scour the town for news of me?'

Serena's eyes glittered with tears. 'I believe he hears word of you at White's,' she replied in all seriousness.

Devlin burst into laughter. He sat down next to her and put his arm around her, squeezing affectionately. 'Dear sister, I beg your pardon. I do not mean to upset you. I know you and my brother mean well, but you forget I'm out of leading strings.'

She blushed and straightened her posture. 'I am sure we do not.'

'Tell me how you and Ned go on? Is my brother still managing the family affairs to perfection?'

Serena lifted her chin protectively. 'Ned has much on his shoulders.'

Devlin gave her a kind smile. 'Indeed he does. He is a man to admire, Serena. I mean that.'

'I have heard from your sisters and brother. They are excellent correspondents.'

Unlike himself who wrote little and visited less.

'Indeed? What is the family news?'

Serena, with a wistfulness in her voice, chattered on about the trifling activities of his nephews and nieces. Percy's son, Jeffrey, the eldest, at Eton. Rebecca, Helen's daughter, learning the pianoforte. All the little ones merging into a blur. He listened with as interested an expression as he could muster. Serena doted on all the children. By far she was their favourite aunt. And he, the Waterloo Dragoon, was their hero uncle, even though he had difficulty keeping their names straight.

What a pity Serena had not had a child. Fate had no notion of fair play. She would make a perfect mother, and a loving one, as well. He suspected her disappointment in that quarter was immense.

'And you, Serena? How do you go on?'

'I am well.' A sad look came over her face.

Devlin gave her another hug. She would not wish to speak of her disappointment at not presenting the Marquess with an heir.

'Dear sister,' he murmured.

She recovered herself. 'Ned will be here directly. Will you wait for him?'

He had little choice. 'Serena,' he said, surmising a change of conversation was in order, 'do you suppose Ned would mind if I borrowed a pair of horses some morning? I've a notion to ride.'

'You will ride again?' she said brightly. He had not been

on a horse since charging the French, east of the Brussels road. 'Indeed he will not mind. He will be glad of it, and I will personally ask Barclay to instruct the stable to provide any horse you wish.'

'Any two horses. I…I wish to have Bart join me.'

'Two horses it is.' She smiled.

The parlour door opened and the Marquess strode in at a quicker pace than was his custom. Devlin stood to greet him.

'Devlin, how good to see you.' Equally uncharacteristic of him, he embraced Devlin heartily.

This idol of his childhood, his oldest brother Ned, usually did not betray emotion. Ned always could be counted on to remain unflappable when his youngest brother came begging for his help out of the latest scrape. Because of those days, Devlin always felt in awe of that tall, ramrod-straight figure. He always expected to crane his neck to look at Ned. It never failed to be a shock when he found himself half a head taller and his brother going grey at the temples.

'What brings you to call?' Ned asked with such surprise, it suggested he had given up altogether on a visit from Devlin.

'I wished to see you and Serena, of course, but I also have a matter of business to discuss with you, if it is convenient.'

Ned regained that strict composure. 'Indeed. We shall go into the library. You will excuse us, Serena?'

With a nod to his wife, he preceded Devlin out the door. Devlin followed dutifully, feeling much like that little boy, in a scrape once more.

Inside that book-lined room, Ned poured two glasses of port. Devlin glanced at the shelves and had the incongruous thought that Madeleine might enjoy a good book. Not the sort of book to be found in this room, he supposed, but perhaps a Miniver Press novel such as his sisters had read when they sat by his sick bed.

Ned handed him his glass. 'What did you wish to discuss?'

Devlin sipped and paced the room, trying to figure out the best way to present this.

'Are you in trouble?' Ned's voice was low and steady.

Devlin flashed him an irritated glance and muttered, 'You and Serena.' Speaking more firmly, he said, 'I am not in trouble.'

His brother's face remained impassive.

Devlin took a gulp of port. 'I have moved.'

'Yes?'

'To a larger place.'

'You required a larger place?' A disapproving tone crept into his brother's speech.

'It was too good an opportunity to pass up. On the same street, but a much better situation.'

'And?' One of Ned's eyebrows rose.

Devlin took a deep breath. 'I am short of money as a result. I would ask if you would advance me some additional funds until next quarter.'

His brother did not drop his gaze, nor did his expression change, even a muscle. Devlin knew he was considering, weighing the matter silently in his head.

As a child, this silence had been a comfort. It meant Ned was reckoning a way out of his difficulties. As a man, he was less certain.

His brother stared implacably into his port. 'How wise was this move?'

'Devil it, Ned, the move is made. Whether it was wise or not is moot.'

'You engaged in this impulsively.' This was not a question but a statement of fact, a disapproved-of fact.

Devlin put his glass down on a table and faced his immovable brother. 'It is done, Ned, and I need some money to get through to next quarter. Will you give it or not?'

Ned sat in a nearby chair and casually crossed his legs. 'You have been gambling heavily, little brother.'

Devlin knew that was coming. 'As your spies have reported? I do not suppose they were present when I won back my losses?'

Ned's cronies would never have been present at such an unsavoury place as Farley's. If they had, his brother would be discussing what else Devlin won that night.

'I have heard your losses to be steep. This gambling must stop, Devlin.'

If his brother had not ordered him to stop gambling, he might have informed Ned that he'd come to the same conclusion. Now he would not give his brother that satisfaction.

'And what else might I do, Ned? What is there for me to do? The war is over, and I'm damned if I'll go anywhere else in this world to fight. India? Africa? The West Indies? I'm no longer keen on dying on foreign soil.'

Ned swirled his port and tasted the rich, imported liquid. 'It is time you took your rightful place in the family.'

'Rightful place?' Devlin prowled the room. 'What the deuce is my rightful place?'

Calmly his brother spoke, 'You need to assume the control of your estate. It should not fall to our brother Percy, who has enough of his own to oversee.'

'You know I cannot.' Devlin glared at him. 'You and my father saw to that. I cannot take control until I marry. I must subsist on what you obligingly provide me until I marry a suitable woman of whom you approve. Good God! What possessed you and my father to contrive that addle-brained plan?'

'You know why.' Ned spoke in the most reasonable voice possible. 'You lack control. You have always been devil-may-care. Father had the wisdom to know you would cease your wild ways when you had another person dependent upon you. A wife.'

'Damn it, Ned, would you have me marry merely to get my fortune? Would you have married under that fancy bit of blackmail?'

At least Devlin had the satisfaction of seeing his brother betray emotion. Ned's cheek twitched. 'Leave Serena out of this.'

Devlin felt a pang of guilt for speaking of his brother's marriage. He never knew for certain if his brother loved Serena, though he suspected she loved Ned. When he saw Ned and Serena together, there was such a reserve between them, who could tell? Had Ned married her out of duty? Pity Serena, if he had. Their father was behind the match, of course, and Ned would never have gone against their father's wishes. Two peas in a pod, his brother and father.

'I am not speaking of Serena,' he said more mildly. 'I am speaking of myself. I have no desire to marry at the moment, but I am more than ready to assume control of my property. Indeed, I long to run it. Let me take the task from Percy and work the farm. I do not give a damn if the rest of the money is under your thumb.'

It would be an ideal solution. Bart and Sophie would fit in neatly on the estate. Madeleine and Linette would be a bit more difficult to situate, but he was sure he could contrive something.

Ned regained his damned composure. 'Doing so would deprive you of an opportunity to make an advantageous match. The Season has begun and there are all manner of eligible young ladies from whom you may choose.'

Devlin clenched his fist. 'I have no desire to marry.'

Ned rose and walked to the desk by the window. He fussed with papers stacked there, glancing through them, and re-stacking them. Devlin would have liked to think his brother was considering his proposal, but he suspected Ned was simply showing him who was head of the family.

Ned did not look up from the papers when he spoke. 'Our father's wishes will continue to be honoured. You will receive your allotted portion on the quarter, not before. When you marry an acceptable young lady, your estate and your fortune will pass to you, and I will have no more to say of it.'

Devlin leaned down, putting both hands on the desk, forcing his brother to meet his eyes. 'Both you and Father were mistaken, Ned. You could at least let me work. As it is, you and our dear departed father have deprived me of any responsibility at all and have kept me as dependent as if I were still a schoolboy. Had I something of value to do, I might have reason to be steady. As it is, I have nothing.'

'You will have everything you desire if you marry.' Ned spoke through clenched teeth.

'But I do not wish to marry.'

The two men glared at each other.

Devlin swung away from his brother. 'You and Father never trusted me to find my own way. You knew, did you not, that he almost refused to purchase my colours?' He fingered one of the volumes on the shelf. 'I would have enlisted as a common foot soldier had he done so. Father could not force me to do anything and neither can you, Ned.'

'You are being foolish, Devlin. This is for your own good. You have always been too wild by half and too wilful to behave with any sense.'

'You dare to say such a thing to me? Do you forget what I have been doing these past years? Do you think I have been on a lark?'

The Marquess stood. 'I know it killed our father to have you traipsing all over the continent risking your neck.'

Devlin shook with rage. 'Unfair, Ned.'

'You should have been seeing to your duty to the family.' Ned raised his voice.

'I *was* seeing to my duty to the family. How well do you think the family would have fared under Napoleon?' Devlin matched his brother's volume. 'Go to the devil, Ned.'

Ned stepped from behind the desk and faced his brother. 'Our father worried every day that you would meet your death. Not only during the war, but every day of your sad youth. You have been a rash care-for-nobody and it is past time you became a grown man.'

Devlin clenched his fists, standing nose to nose with his older brother. 'I fought for my life before I ever went to war. To be a man means more than following the dictates of a father who thought he could pull a string and have all his bidding done. When will *you* assume manhood, Ned? Have you ever had a thought of your own?'

'You are addressing the head of the family, little brother.'

'I am addressing my father. You may as well be him, Ned. You always did whatever he said. You and Percy and our sisters. You all blindly did his bidding. If he said jump, you jumped. If he said marry this young lady, you made the offer.'

'Leave Serena out of this!' Ned's eyes blazed. He shoved hard against Devlin's chest.

Devlin automatically shoved back, his soldier's reflexes operating. With his greater height, youth, and war-honed strength, he knocked his brother to the floor. 'Leave me to live my own life! I will choose when and who I marry.'

'Indeed you shall, you insufferable ingrate.' Ned picked himself off the floor and, to Devlin's surprise, came at him with a swinging fist that connected smartly to Devlin's jaw.

'Deuce,' yelled Devlin, lunging back at him, toppling them both to the floor. They rolled, grunting and punching, knocking down a small table and sending the wine decanter crashing to the floor, red wine splashing.

'Stop this! Stop at once!' Serena cried from the doorway.

The two men paid her no heed. On their feet now, they smashed into a bookcase and books rained down from the shelves. Blood dripped from Ned's nose and Devlin's coat ripped.

'Barclay! Barclay!' Serena screamed for the butler as she ran over to her husband and brother-in-law. She pulled on Devlin's back to get him off Ned.

'Master Devlin. Master Ned.' A voice of authority seemed to boom directly from their childhood. White-haired Barclay entered the room. 'You ought to be ashamed.'

They stopped fighting at once.

Ned recovered first, dabbing his nose with the lace-edged handkerchief Serena offered him. 'Thank you, Barclay. We are quite in control again. Your help is no longer necessary.'

Devlin felt a pain in his stomach that was not the result of a punching fist. How had he wound up brawling with his older brother? He'd seen Percy and Ned in a scrap or two, always carefully kept from their father, but it was unthinkable that he should actually strike this man who'd searched all through the wounded and dying in Brussels until he found his younger brother.

'Ned, I—'

'Enough, Devlin.' The Marquess folded the handkerchief.

Serena looked as if she might swoon at any moment, filling Devlin with more guilt. Her face was pale as she righted the toppled table and tried to pick up the glass fragments. How could he have distressed her like this?

Ned straightened his clothes and brushed himself off. He glanced at his wife. 'Serena, would you leave us, please?'

'I would not wish—' she began.

'Leave us. We shall not come to further blows.' Devlin had not thought his brother could speak so softly.

With a worried look at them both, she left the room, one hand covering her mouth.

Ned composed himself and returned to his desk, showing no signs that they had been rolling on the floor moments before. 'Serena tells me you were in the company of an unchaperoned young woman.'

Devlin rolled his eyes. He might be standing before his father again. Too many times his father ignored what Devlin tried to say and went directly to whatever would hurt him most.

'Your point, Ned?'

'Did you introduce my wife to your fancy piece?'

Amazing. Ned managed to provoke his anger again. 'Ned, I assure you, I would not do anything to embarrass my sister-in-law. I have the highest respect and sympathy for her.'

'What do you mean "sympathy"?' Ned sounded ready to punch him again.

'I meant nothing.' He meant he was sorry she had not conceived a child, but this was not the time to address Ned on that subject. He had no notion how the wind blew for his brother on that score.

'Who was the woman you were with? Do you have a lightskirt who costs you?'

Good God. Did Ned wish another jab in the nob? 'She is an acquaintance who does not deserve your insults.' Devlin would say no more. He merely wished to get away from his brother. 'Ned, we have said more than is prudent. I will beg your leave.'

'Indeed? We have resolved nothing.' Ned looked like a stranger. No, he looked like their father, not at all like his adored older brother.

'It doesn't matter. I will wait for my money to come due.' He walked to the door.

Ned's mouth set into a thin, grim line. 'When your money comes due, it will be half the amount.'

'What?'

'Half the amount.' The Marquess studied his papers before glancing up at Devlin. 'You need to search for a wife. Perhaps penury will serve as an incentive.'

Devlin fought the rage that erupted inside him. How would he care for Madeleine? How would he feed little Linette? 'Damn you, Ned. You have no idea what this means.'

'Remember who is the head of the family, little brother.'

'I'll not forget.' He spoke through his teeth.

Devlin hurried out of the library and almost ran into his sister-in-law, who was walking back and forth in the hall.

'Devlin, what happened? Why were you fighting?' she whispered, her voice filled with anxiety.

He stroked her arm. 'A brothers' quarrel, nothing more. Do not worry, sister.'

She looked unconvinced. He gave her a long reassuring hug and let her weep against his shoulder a little. 'It was entirely my fault, Serena. You know how I can provoke Ned. Do not cry.'

The library door opened. An icy voice such as Devlin had never heard said, 'Unhand my wife and take your leave.'

Chapter Seven

Misery assailed Devlin as he walked through the doorway of Ned's town house. He'd made a mess of things. What a colossal fool, provoking his brother, though he could not precisely remember what he had said to set Ned off. They had disagreed reasonably for a short time. How had he ended up punching Ned in the nose, for deuce's sake?

Worse than bloodying the nose of the Marquess of Heronvale was jeopardising Madeleine's future and that of her child. How would he care for them now?

What a damned coil. What a fool and idiot.

He set a slow pace in the direction of St James's Street.

He ought to have conserved his money, not rented the bigger apartment, not purchased as many lengths of fabric for Sophie, as many toys for Linette. He should not have purchased an entire wardrobe for Madeleine when she argued for only two or three dresses. Most of all, he should not have lost his temper with his brother. He should have remained calm. He should have rehearsed several cogent arguments why his brother should advance him the money. Instead, he'd allowed Ned to goad him until they came to blows.

He might laugh at rousing emotion in his brother, if only the result had not been the halving of his funds. Ned's calm, dispassionate control, so comforting to him as a child, irritated him as a man. To think he used to shake with fear when Ned and Percy pummelled each other with their fists, Ned as out of control as Devlin so often was. It had been like watching the foundations at Heronvale crack and crumble.

This time it was his own would-be estate that crumbled—Edgeworth, twenty miles from Heronvale and ten from Percy's estate. His father had aimed to keep them close, tied to the land that he'd purchased from neighbours who let their property slip through their fingers.

'Land, my boy.' Devlin could hear his father's firm voice, his fist pounding the dinner table. 'If a man has land, he has a future.' His father would gesture to Devlin's plate. 'Land gives you good food and drink to fill your belly. Mind, you have never been hungry in my house.'

True, but Devlin had known hunger on the Peninsula where supplies were often low, and he had known thirst when wounded at Waterloo, waiting twelve hours in the mud to be found.

Devlin was ready for the land his father bequeathed him. Ready for work. He longed for hard physical labour. He yearned to work next to the men in the fields, as he had fought beside their brothers. Wouldn't that give Ned apoplexy!

Devlin stopped in the middle of the pavement and rubbed his brow. What good did it do to think of Edgeworth? He needed to think of Madeleine.

It would not be at all difficult to find positions for Bart and Sophie somewhere in the family. Percy, especially, had a kind heart for a person in need. Indeed, anyone would be fortunate to hire Bart. And, if he knew Bart, the man would care

well for Sophie. As for himself, he could plague Ned by
visiting one sister after another, never complying with the
Heronvale dictates. What prime sport that would be.

But what about Madeleine and Linette? He would go to
the devil and drag Ned with him before he'd allow Madeleine
to return to the only profession she knew and her daughter
with her. Damn, he needed money to save her from that fate.
Enough money for her to live comfortably and to rear Linette.

Devlin's mind spun round and round. The only thing he
knew with a certainty was that he was a damned fool and had
failed the people who depended upon him.

Failed Madeleine.

Too soon he neared the lodgings. With a heavy heart, he
turned the knob of the front door.

Madeleine stole a surreptitious glance at Devlin during
dinner later that evening. He was unduly quiet. Something
troubled him, and she did not know what. Did she even have
the right to inquire?

If he were like other men, she would not care what problems
he had. But he was not like other men. Would another man be
so kind to her daughter? When it had been time for Linette to
go to bed, it had to be Devlin to carry her up and tuck her in.
For a moment she worried about leaving Linette to a man's
care, but that was foolish. Devlin would not harm her.

Indeed, he should not be so kind. It made her feel she could
depend on him. It was dangerous to depend upon anyone.
They fooled you, then tricked you into doing what they
willed.

She cast her gaze on Devlin again, and made an attempt at
conversation. 'Did you have a pleasant visit with your
brother?'

He glanced up and paused so long she thought he would

not answer. 'I spent an agreeable interval with my sister-in-law.'

What did that mean?

'Scrapped with your brother, did you?' Bart snorted. 'That explains your black looks.'

Devlin did not banter back at Bart as was usual. Instead, he rubbed his forehead and stared down at his plate. Madeleine frowned. Bart should leave off scolding this time. Something was indeed wrong.

Sophie, her usual wary expression on her face, popped up to gather the dirty dishes. She had a cat's sense for danger.

Little had been eaten from Devlin's plate. 'Leave the dishes a bit, Sophie. I wish to speak to all of you.'

Madeleine's pulse accelerated. No good news could be forthcoming.

'Let us clear the dishes first,' Madeleine suggested. 'It will be more comfortable.' And it would delay the inevitable.

Devlin released a breath. 'Very well, remove the dishes, but return promptly, if you please.'

'I will help.' Madeleine picked up her own plate and Devlin's.

'I can do it, Maddy,' Sophie said.

'I want to help,' Madeleine countered. She was able to clear dishes, at least. No special skill needed for that. Besides, it helped quiet her nerves to be busy.

Madeleine returned to her seat next to Devlin. He had poured small glasses of port for all of them and his eyes held such a pained expression, the fear rose in her once more.

What other kind of bad news could there be, except she, Linette and Sophie would have to leave? She clenched her hands together in her lap.

Devlin toyed with his glass of port. He cleared his throat. 'I visited my brother to request an advance of the money due me in two months' time. We have wound up a little short—'

'Because of my dresses.' Madeleine moaned, misery and guilt swirling inside her.

He held the glass still. 'Not only your dresses, Maddy. My mismanagement is primarily the blame.'

'Now, lad…' Bart began, an uncharacteristic soothing tone in his voice.

Devlin cleared his throat. 'You see, I had decided the way out of our difficulties was to make the request of my brother. Unfortunately, I had not counted on the Marquess refusing.'

'The man refused?' Bart's thick eyebrows shot up.

'I fear so.'

'No worry, Dev. We shall manage.' Bart nodded his head as if convincing himself as well as the others. 'We can practise some economy. We shall do nicely.'

Devlin gave a dry laugh. 'You have not yet heard the worst of it, my friend. Not only did my brother refuse an advance, he cut my allowance in half. I do not see how we can go on at all.'

Bart's mouth opened. 'Half?'

'What does it mean, Maddy?' Sophie leaned over the table to whisper to her.

'It means you and Linette and I must leave.' Madeleine's hand went to her throat. She thought her words would strangle there.

'No,' Devlin protested. 'It does not mean that.'

'Oh, perhaps not today,' she went on. 'We should have a little time to make other arrangements. Nothing hard-hearted about it.' Her voice trembled now.

'Maddy.' Devlin grabbed her hand. 'It does not mean you must leave.'

She met his gaze. Along with pain, she saw a tenderness that took her breath away.

'I do not know how, Maddy, but I will take care of you.'

She blinked.

He turned back to Bart and Sophie. 'I think I should be able to find you both positions with some member of my family.'

'I will not leave Maddy,' Sophie cried.

'And I will stay with you, lad. We have endured worse than this.' Bart lifted his glass in a salute.

Devlin looked from one to another. 'We did not have women and a child to care for in those days.'

'We will take care of ourselves.' Madeleine lifted her chin in a show of bravado she could not feel.

'How, Maddy?' Devlin said. 'You have no means of income.'

Bart stood and held his glass high. 'We are in this together, do we agree? We solve it together.' He stared at them until they all lifted their glasses in return.

'I could take in laundry,' Sophie said in a quiet voice.

Devlin laughed. 'I hope it does not come to that, little one. I thought I might speak to some people I know tomorrow. Perhaps someone can find a use for me.'

'If there's labour to be done I can do it,' Bart said.

Madeleine toyed with her glass. 'There are three or four men who would pay much for time with me.'

They all stared at her.

'It should not be difficult, I think. I can give you the names and you can find out how to communicate with them.'

'Good God, Maddy.' Devlin's face drained of colour.

Madeleine gave him a surprised look. 'It would pay handsomely, I am sure.'

He spoke through clenched teeth. 'I do not give a deuce how well it would pay, you will not bed other men on my behalf.'

'Not on your behalf, but for us all.' He could not prevent her from doing her part, not when she was the cause of the problem.

He slapped his hand on the table. 'I will hear no more of this.'

Sophie's eyes grew wider. With a nervous glance, she slipped off the chair and skittered into the kitchen. His arms crossed against his chest, Bart regarded Madeleine and Devlin with a disapproving expression.

Madeleine continued. 'I believe it would bring in a good sum of money.'

He stood up and leaned over her. 'No.' He strode out of the room.

She followed him. 'Why not?'

He wheeled around to face her. 'You have to ask?'

'Devlin, it would not be difficult for me to do this. It is not as if I have not done it before.'

His eyes flashed.

'What objection can you have? It is the perfect solution.'

'You will allow me to solve our problems, Maddy. You will not do it by lying on your back.'

He did not need to speak to her in such a crude manner. 'It is what I do best, if you recall.'

'Deuce,' he said. 'And where shall you perform this lucrative act? In this house? With Linette in the room?'

'Of course not!' How dare he suggest such a thing. 'I have always kept Linette out of the way. Sophie would take her.'

'Much more proper,' he said, the corner of his mouth turning down in contempt.

'I have told you, I am not proper.'

'And where would Bart and I be? Collecting the money at the door?'

'Do not be absurd. I cannot talk to you. You do not see reason.' She stalked off.

How could he not see she must resolve the difficulties she had placed him in? She owed him that much. It was not that she wished to bed anyone, except…except… No, he must recognise how much she was indebted to him. He had rescued her from Farley. For that she would do anything for him. Anything.

She ran up the stairs, but he came right behind. At the top of the stairs, he caught her by the shoulders and spun her around.

'We will finish this, Madeleine. We will not solve our financial woes in this way, do you hear? You will not speak of this again.' He dug his fingers into her shoulders.

'How is it that you could object, Devlin? You know what I am.' She lowered her voice.

He made a strangled sound. 'Do you think I wish to think of another man's hands all over you?'

She stared at him. The hands of many men had touched her.

His fingers slid down her arms. 'Do you think I could accept money for another man to bed you?'

She swallowed. 'Farley did.'

'I am not Farley, Madeleine. I thought you understood that.'

He stood so close, all she needed was to stand on tiptoe and touch her lips to his. She could smell the port on his breath and the taste of it resonated in her mouth. The wish to taste it on him was almost too difficult to bear. He made no move to close the gap between them. It was clearly her choice.

His hands rested gently on her arms. Those hands had once caressed her bare skin. She craved the joy and terror of his body joined to hers. Her feet arched and raised her higher. He uttered a guttural sound and closed the gap between them, his mouth plundering as if he were a man starved. Her own hunger surged as she pressed herself against him and wound her arms around his neck. His lips travelled to her neck, sending sensations straight to her soul.

She wanted him again with all the wantonness of her

wretched body. The body that had betrayed her and led to her deserved ruin. She had learned to erase all thought and all feeling in order to play the role Farley bid her play, but Devlin made her tremble with longing. He tore away the safety of her detachment.

She struggled to speak. 'Do you want me, Devlin?' Her voice sounded more controlled than she felt. 'Do you wish to bed me?'

He stilled. Straightening, his eyes narrowed. Her knees began to shake as his silence grew longer.

Finally, he spoke, his tone cold. 'Am I able to afford you, Miss M?'

He turned and hurried down the stairs and out the front door.

At the town house in Grosvenor Square, the Marquess of Heronvale pushed food around his plate. The cavernous dining room echoed with the clink of his silver fork against the china.

He glanced at his wife. She looked absorbed in her own thoughts, the corners of her eyes pinched with unhappiness. A ball of misery sat in his stomach where food should have been.

He had disappointed her once again, more inventively this time. Indeed, rolling on the floor, trading punches with his youngest brother could hardly have lowered him further in her estimation. Especially since he had lost the fight.

Humiliating.

She had probably championed Devlin, in any event. He could not blame her. She was at ease with his brother in a way she was not with him. There was so little emotion between Serena and himself he would have been surprised if she had taken his side. Serena undoubtedly would think him too severe with Devlin, that a marquess should wield his power with more compassion.

But Devlin had infuriated him with those comments about his wife. Success with women came as easy to Devlin as riding, shooting, gaming. His youngest brother did everything without effort, as well as without thought, while he, the bearer of the title, had laboured for every accomplishment.

How well he remembered Devlin's birth. He had been home on school holiday, old enough at ten years to take charge of Percy, Helen, Julia, and Lavinia during his mother's confinement. He smiled inwardly at his less-than-learned explanation to his sisters and brother of exactly what would transpire during the birth. From the moment he'd held the newborn baby in his arms, Ned had been full of pride in this littlest brother. He made a solemn oath, that day, to always protect and defend him.

Devlin had made keeping that vow a challenge. A more reckless individual had never been born. It had been no surprise to Ned that Devlin joined the cavalry. Had Ned not been heir, he might have served his country as well, fighting at his brother's side, but all he could do was bring a near-dying Devlin back home.

'Ned? Is something troubling you?' Serena's sweet voice broke through his reverie.

'What?'

'I thought you might be troubled.' She averted her eyes.

'No, I am not.' She would think him weak, for certain, if she knew his thoughts.

'I beg your pardon,' she murmured.

He wished more to beg pardon of her, for his abominable behaviour, but did not know quite how. It seemed to him the silence between them was a condemnation.

'You disapprove of my dealings with my brother,' he blurted out.

Her eyebrows flew up in surprise. 'I would not question your judgement.'

'You think me too harsh.'

'I would not presume…'

He dismissed her words with a shake of his head. With trembling fingers, she picked daintily at her food.

After eight years of marriage, his wife remained a stunningly beautiful woman, her restraint the epitome of what became a lady. He could not complain. She was biddable, even when he pressed his carnal urges upon her, something he did as rarely as he could tolerate. The marital act was too painful for her sensibilities, but she craved children and he wished to give them to her.

Another failure on his part.

Ned drained the wine from his glass for the third time. 'Do you go out tonight, Serena?'

She jumped at the sound of his voice and barely glanced at him. 'No.'

It was his turn to be surprised. She had lately developed the habit of accompanying friends to the evening entertainments, the ones from which he begged off with increasing frequency.

She pressed her fingertips against her temple. 'I shall retire early. I…I have the headache.'

He had made her ill. He poured another glass of wine, wanting to express his concern, to offer to get her headache powders, to escort her up to her room and help her into bed.

He did none of those things.

'If you will excuse me…' She rose and, without waiting for a reply and probably not expecting one, left him alone in the room.

A footman entered and moved quickly to clear the table. Ned gestured for him to take away the plate from which he had barely eaten. When the man set the brandy in front of him, Ned began to see how much of that bottle he could finish.

Chapter Eight

Devlin picked a secluded chair at White's far from the bow window. He intended to sip his brandy in peace, away from the curious passers-by in the street. He wished to steel himself before circulating among the gentlemen of the *ton* in another attempt to procure employment. But what reason was there to expect this afternoon to differ from the last two weeks? He had made inquiries with the few of his senior officers still alive and exploited every imaginable family connection.

He might as well have bivouacked in a field. In fact, he would have preferred it, sharing cold, damp nights and bawdy soldier's tales with men who knew life could end with a musket ball the next day.

'May I join you?'

Devlin glanced up. The elegant figure of the Marquess stood before him. He shrugged his assent.

His brother signalled for a drink and settled in the comfortable chair across from him. 'How do you go on, Devlin?'

How did Ned think he went on? He and Bart had counted every coin that morning. They had a few days' escape from the River Tick, no more.

'Tolerably well,' he said.

Ned regarded him with a bland expression. What lay beyond that inscrutable countenance was a mystery. Devlin could wait out the silence, even if his brother never spoke.

Ned did not betray a thought, let alone a feeling. 'I understand you have inquired about employment around town.'

Devlin cocked his head, ever so slightly.

The waiter placed a glass before Ned. 'Without success, I recollect.'

Devlin favoured him with an ironic grin. 'I am pleased you are so well informed. Unfortunately, there seems to be a surplus of men such as myself. Soldiers needing work.'

'A pity.' Ned raised his glass to his lips.

'It does not help that the men from whom I seek employment instead contrive to introduce me to their daughters.'

'Indeed?'

Damn his brother's implacability. 'It was not you who spread the tale of our father's peculiar arrangement for me?'

Ned's eyes flickered with surprise, not guilt.

Devlin laughed. 'Not you, I collect. A sister, perhaps?'

Ned's control returned. 'Helen is a likely suspect.'

'Likely,' Devlin agreed. 'She has a crony in town, I believe.'

'And meddling proclivities.'

For a moment the ease between them returned and Devlin could almost forget that his revered brother had unwittingly placed a young woman and her innocent daughter in jeopardy. Ned would disapprove if he knew of Madeleine, but would he be less tight-fisted? Pride prevented Devlin from revisiting his monetary request on his brother. He was less sure why he did not confide about Madeleine.

'How is Serena?' he asked instead, seeking neutral ground.

The Marquess's eyes narrowed. 'Well.'

Serena was not neutral ground, then. Had Ned's anger something to do with Serena? Devlin studied him. The Marquess's bland expression had a hard edge.

'Good God, Ned. Is there some trouble between you and Serena?' The sudden thought burst into words.

Ned's face turned to chiselled granite. 'Mind your loose tongue. Your voice will carry.'

'I am sorry,' Devlin mumbled. Deuce, he had managed to blunder into more disfavour. If others had heard his ill-conceived words, the rumour-mill would carry the tale throughout the *ton*. He glanced around the room, but no one seemed to have given them the least heed. He hoped.

Ned had not looked around, but maintained his damnable composure. What a soldier he would have made, thought Devlin. He would bet Ned could face down a battalion single-handed without flinching. But would he be able to muster enough emotion to strike? A soldier eventually had to tap into rage. Until their fisticuffs of a fortnight ago, Devlin would not have believed Ned capable of rage.

Devlin felt light-headed. He ought not to have imagined battle. Images, sounds, and smells enveloped him. The thud of horses' hooves, the cry of battle, the smoke and smell of musket fire. Men screamed. Horses squealed. Metal clanged against metal before thrusting into flesh. Blood sprayed and the stench of death grew stronger.

Devlin pressed his fingers to his temple.

'Are you unwell?' Ned's voice held genuine concern.

Beads of perspiration dampened his forehead, as if the day had not been cool. The incessant thunder of French cannon echoed through his brain and his vision blurred into smoke-filled chaos. He could see the men, the shapes of their noses, the yellowed colour of their teeth, the stunned expressions as his own sabre sliced their throats.

'Dev, you are white as death. Let me summon a doctor.'

At his brother's voice, the images dissolved as suddenly as they had come, leaving his emotions in tattered pieces. Devlin suppressed an urge to laugh. As in childhood, his brother had rescued him, this time from his own personal demons.

'No doctor.' Devlin's voice was not quite steady. 'I was wool-gathering for a moment.' He stood. All notions of grovelling for employment fled. 'Would you excuse me, Ned? I must leave.'

The brow of the Marquess wrinkled slightly. 'Are you sure you are not ill?'

Devlin's mouth lifted at the corner. 'Poor, perhaps, but not ill. You needn't worry.'

'I have my barouche. I will take you home.'

'Not necessary, brother. The walk will do me good.' His heart still pounded and his hands trembled. All Devlin wished to do was flee. He touched Ned on the shoulder and hurried away.

A light rainfall greeted him on the street and he closed his eyes for a moment, savouring the cool droplets pattering on his upturned face.

'Good day, Steele. Been at White's, I see.'

Devlin opened his eyes and met the affable grin of Lord Farley. He merely nodded and made to continue on his way.

Farley put a hand on his arm. 'Pray, what is your hurry? Come with me to my establishment. I shall buy you a drink.'

'I think not.' Again Devlin tried to leave.

'Come. You may give me news of Madeleine,' he persisted. Devlin shrugged off the man's hand. 'I think not.'

Anger flashed through Farley's eyes for a moment before the amiable expression reappeared. 'How does she go on? I hope she still pleases you, but perhaps you have tired of her.'

Devlin's emotions were ragged enough to plant his fist squarely in the centre of Farley's face. He pushed past.

The man fell in step with him. 'I say, Steele, I hear you are seeking employment. Consider working for me. I could use a skilled gamester, and, I promise you, I would compensate you generously. I am again flush in the pockets, you see.'

Devlin stopped, his fingers still curled into fists. He'd heard the tale of Farley's change in fortune. 'Tell me, would my employment include fleecing green boys—like young Boscomb? He put a pistol to his head after a visit to your tables, did he not?'

Farley's eyes narrowed but his grin remained. 'An unfortunate incident.'

Devlin attempted to walk on, but Farley kept pace. 'Perhaps, if you are in need of funds, you would return Madeleine to me. In return for the money you won from me, of course.'

Devlin's fists tightened. If he'd had his sword in his hand, he would relish the sound of its steel plunging into Farley's gut. Devlin gritted his teeth. 'Do not speak of her.'

'Oh?' Farley remarked casually. 'She has become troublesome to you, perhaps? She has a habit of doing so. I assure you, I know precisely how to deal with her.'

Devlin spun toward Farley and, with the strength of both arms, shoved him away. Better that than attacking and killing him. Farley fell, splashing into a puddle on the pavement.

Farley struggled to rise. 'You have ruined my coat.'

Devlin leaned over him. 'I'll ruin more than your coat if you dare speak to me again, Farley.'

He turned his back and crossed the street, not heeding the stares of others walking by.

Madeleine stood in the hall, pushing the broom here and there, wondering how one contrived to get all the dust into one spot so that one could use the dustpan. She decided to experiment on a little pile of dust, but couldn't work out how to hold the broom and the dustpan at the same time. Linette sat in the corner galloping her wooden horse back and forth, while her doll sat abandoned on a parlour chair.

Bart had accompanied Sophie to the dress shop. How could any of them have guessed that little Sophie would be the only one to find paying work? Bart searched each day for labour, coming home talking of scores of veterans like himself lining up for one job. And Devlin. More lines of worry etched his face each day.

When Madeleine and Sophie took some of her new dresses to the dressmaker in the hope that they might return them, Sophie came home with a large package of piecework, Madeleine with the dresses she had sought to sell.

She struggled with the sweeping. She was determined to do her part. While Sophie sewed and Bart and Devlin searched for work, she would care for the house.

Madeleine tried a different way to hold the broom, sticking it under her arm and levering it against her hip. She pretended to be a simple country housewife. She cleaned the house and tended the child while her husband—Devlin, of course—tilled the earth. Their lives were a quiet routine of hard work, peaceful evenings in front of the fireplace, and nights filled with loving. Madeleine leaned on the broom and sighed. How wonderful it would be.

She should not waste time in fancy. This silly habit of hers did not do her credit. She needed to solve her problems such as they really were. She needed work. Employment as a housemaid would not be the means, she supposed, although housework had never seemed difficult for the housemaids she once knew. They sped through chores with no apparent effort.

She jabbed at her pitiful pile of dust with the broom, scattering it everywhere except into the dustpan. 'Deuce.'

As she uttered this unladylike but Devlin-like epithet, the

door opened and Devlin walked in, his head bent and his shoulders stooped. When he saw her, he smiled, but his eyes remained sad. 'What the devil are you doing?'

'Sweeping.' She looked down at the floor. 'Or trying to do so.'

'Deddy!' Linette popped up from her corner and propelled herself into Devlin's arms.

'How's my little lady?'

Linette wrapped her little arms around Devlin's neck. 'Deddy play?' She batted long lashes and smiled sweetly.

'Not now, Lady Lin.' He put Linette down and the child ran back to her toy horse. Devlin rubbed his forehead. He turned toward Madeleine and again smiled.

She stepped over to him to take his hat. 'You are wet.'

'It is nothing. A little rain.'

'Let me help you remove your coat.' She reached for the lapels. He held her arms and stared at her a moment before clutching her to him.

She could hardly breathe, he held her so tight.

'Do not worry so, Devlin. We shall come about.' She wound her own arms around his neck.

Linette ran to them, arms raised. 'Me! Me!'

Devlin scooped her up and enveloped them both in a hug, the kind of coming-home greeting she had imagined a moment ago, but infused with pain instead of pleasure.

'Come into the kitchen, Devlin. I'll make you a cup of tea.' She liked the sound of that, the housewife giving comfort to the labourer.

'I want biskis!' Linette cried.

Devlin, holding them both more loosely now, gave her a perplexed look. 'Biskis?'

'She means biscuit. I believe we still have a good number that Sophie made.'

He smiled. 'Tea and biskis it is, then.' Still carrying Linette, he followed her into the kitchen.

Bart and Sophie entered from the rear door as Madeleine poured Devlin's tea. Devlin merely raised his eyebrows to Bart, who shook his head.

'These are hard times.' The sergeant frowned.

Madeleine bade Bart and Sophie sit for tea and 'biskis', and, amid Sophie's protests, she served them all. Linette had climbed upon Devlin's lap. While the others traded news of their efforts of the day, she surveyed the scene. Their situation was dire, but the moment filled her with peace.

Her family, she thought. She put a hand to her brow. She must not think of family.

'Perhaps I have something of value to sell,' Devlin mused. 'I must have a stick pin or something with a jewel in it. Or perhaps my sword would fetch a good price.'

'You must keep the sword.' Bart nodded his head firmly. 'To honour the others.'

'You are right.' Devlin's voice was barely audible.

'I could try another shop to sell the dresses,' Madeleine offered.

He winced. 'Yes, you could.'

Sophie rose and dropped a few coins into Devlin's hands. 'My earnings, sir.'

Madeleine watched the look of pain flash over his face, replaced by a gentle smile for Sophie.

'Thank you, indeed, little one. This is a welcome contribution.'

Sophie flushed with pride.

He stood, having drained the contents of his cup and set Linette upon a chair. 'If you all will pardon me.'

Madeleine watched him walk out of the room, his tall figure ramrod straight. A moment later the front door closed.

* * *

Later that evening when she was putting Linette to bed, she heard Devlin's footsteps on the stairs. He entered his bedchamber. Half-listening for sounds from his room, she sang softly to her sleepy daughter. Within a few minutes, the child's eyelids fluttered closed. She kissed Linette's soft, pink brow, tucked the covers around her, and tiptoed over to the chest. Quietly opening the top drawer, she removed a small package wrapped in cloth.

Madeleine tapped lightly at the connecting door between her room and Devlin's. Without waiting for an answer, she entered.

He sat on the edge of his bed, bare-chested, his elbows resting on his knees, his hands clasped together. He glanced up.

'May I speak with you, Devlin?'

He nodded.

She walked over to the bed, handed him her parcel.

'What is this?' He took it in his hand.

'Something for you to sell.'

He unwrapped the cloth and lifted a delicate gold chain with a teardrop pearl. In the cloth were matching pearl earrings.

'These are lovely. Where did you get them? From Farley?'

'No,' she said, indignant that he should think so. 'They were mine before I met Farley. You may sell them.'

He stared at the jewellery and at her. 'Not quite yet, Maddy. Keep them for now.'

She carefully rewrapped the package.

'I have been thinking.' He rubbed his hands together. 'I have depended upon all of you too long. Poor Sophie, her fingers sore from sewing. You, ready to sell your treasures. Bart, searching for labour I'd not ask an enemy to perform.'

She stroked his cheek. 'I have caused you this trouble.'

He clasped her hand and held it.

Suddenly shy under his gaze, she glanced down. Her eyes rested on his chest and widened. 'Devlin, you have scars.'

His torso was riddled with them. Now, thinking about it, she realised she'd felt rough areas on his chest, that day she had touched him and almost made love with him. She had not looked, however. Now, so close to him in the candlelight, she recognised the long scar from the injury in Spain, but there were so many others, short and jagged.

'It is repulsing, is it not?' he said.

She touched one of the scars with her finger. 'Oh, Devlin, how could you think such a thing?' With gentleness, she traced it, still pink from healing. 'What happened to you? How did it come about that you have so many?'

'Waterloo.'

She placed her palm against his firm chest. 'I know it was at Waterloo. I should like to hear what happened to you.'

He rose, walking over to his window. 'The tale is not fit for fair ears.'

'Fustian. Nothing about me is fair.' She followed him. Standing behind him, she marked the scars on his back with her fingers. 'You had to endure this. It cannot be worse for me to hear of it.'

He turned to face her. She placed her hands on his shoulders as he gazed at her. The green of his eyes turned soft as moss. 'I have a proposition for you, Miss England.'

She stiffened, pulled away, but he held her firm.

'Not that kind of proposition.' He took her chin between his thumb and fingers. His expression turned serious again. 'I will tell you about Waterloo on one condition.'

'What condition?' She could imagine no other condition but bedding him. He meant a proposition, after all, no matter how he coloured it. When he touched her like this, she dared hope for it.

He gave her a light kiss on the lips, which merely gave her an urge to kiss him harder in return. 'I will tell you about Waterloo, if you tell me about how you came to be with Farley.'

She pulled away and rubbed her arms. 'Nonsense. I told you already that he seduced me. What else is there to tell?'

He crossed the room and picked up the cloth wrapping her necklace and earrings. 'I want to know how a girl who owned these came to be in Farley's gaming hell.'

She turned away. She had never spoken of her past to anyone, not even Sophie. In fact, she chastised herself if even a thought of the past invaded her mind.

She faced him. 'Very well, I will tell you, but not this night. I do not wish to speak of it this night.'

'You have a bargain, Maddy.' He returned to her, kissing her on the cheek. 'I do not wish to speak of any of it tonight.'

The chaste kiss disappointed her. She wished something else from him. She wished to pretend she was the farmer's housewife readying for bed with her husband. There was no Farley, no Waterloo, no shortage of money. Just days full of useful toil and nights filled with love.

He walked back to the window and stared out at the street for countless minutes. She knew not whether to stay or leave, but she did not want to leave him, especially with the weight of all their problems on his shoulders.

'Sophie is teaching me to sew.' Her voice sounded foolish in the face of his troubled silence.

But he turned to regard her with a kind look in his eye. 'That is very well. Had you not learned before?'

'Oh, I was taught, but I did not heed the lessons.'

He chuckled. 'Your head too full of horses?'

She smiled. 'Sadly, you are right. I never could keep my mind on much else.'

He sat on the window seat, his long legs stretched out before him. 'I know precisely what you mean.'

She sat next to him, tucking her legs beneath her and leaning against him. His arm circled around her shoulders. 'It is a pity that I could not procure employment in a stable. I could do all manner of things there.' She sighed.

He became silent again, and she struggled to think of some other topic to converse upon. She rested her hand on his knee and in a moment, he covered it with his own warm, strong hand.

'No, I shall find the way,' he murmured.

She snuggled against him, the moment acutely precious.

Devlin lifted his hand to her hair, stroking gently. Her locks felt like spun silk beneath his fingers. He inhaled the faint scent of lavender in her hair, and recalled that fragrance from his first meeting of her. After Waterloo, when fever made him delirious and his sisters bathed his forehead with lavender water, his Miss England swam through his dreams.

He had never expected to see her again, and here she was, more wonderful than he could have believed.

He snuggled her closer. She tilted her face to him, the pupils of her eyes wide, her pink lips moist and irresistible.

He kissed her, tasting the sweetness of her, wanting to remove every pain and care from her life and resolving once again to do so. No matter what he must bear.

As his lips gently rested against hers, she whispered, 'Devlin, I…'

He moved to the tender skin beneath her ear.

'I will make love to you, Devlin.'

He stopped and searched her face. 'Only if you truly wish it.'

She cast her gaze down. 'I do wish it. I know it is wicked of me.'

Lifting her chin with his finger, he forced her to meet his eye. 'It is not wicked.'

'But it is,' she insisted. 'I know it is.'

'Well, then, I must be damned indeed.' He ran his lips over her brow. 'I wish that much to make love with you.'

Her face flushed pink. 'It is different for a man.'

'And how is it different, sweet goose?' He pulled the pins from her hair, freeing it to tumble over her shoulders.

'It is no shame for a man to take his pleasure.' Her countenance was solemn. 'Men even boast of it.'

The truth of her words shamed him.

He drew his fingers through her hair. 'Women are made to feel the pleasure, too, Maddy. They are merely expected not to speak of it.'

'Do you truly believe so?' Her wide eyes made her appear as innocent as a young virgin. As she must have been, before Farley.

He smiled. 'I do indeed.'

She gazed at him, a dreamy look on her face.

'Come.' He led her to the bed.

She followed almost shyly, like a bride on her first night. He was determined that she should feel every pleasure he could provide for her. He wanted to show her that lovemaking could be beautiful. Enlightening. Forgiving.

He undid the laces of her dress and gently peeled the cloth from her skin. She released a long breath. Next came her corset. As he pulled her shift over her head, she raised her arms, bringing them down again around his neck. Clinging tightly to him, she kissed him.

Though he throbbed to mate with her that instant, he kept his kiss light. He sensed she also could succumb to the passion of the moment, but he held her back. All she'd known was frenzied, impersonal coupling. He wished to show her more. He wished to show her love.

And he wished to savour each moment of it.

She unfastened his trousers and slid her hands under the cloth until she'd pushed them down to his ankles. As she stood again, she slid her hands up his legs, torso, and shoulders, nearly causing him to abandon his resolve to proceed slowly. He captured her hands in his own and tasted her lips at leisure.

Lifting her on to the bed, he settled beside her, letting his eyes drift down the naked length of her.

Miss England, he had called her that first time, half in jest. She was still so very much like the homeland he loved. Peaceful and pleasing. Exciting and teasing.

He slid his tongue down her neck and covered the rose of her nipple with his mouth. She moaned and arched toward him.

Not yet, Miss England, he thought. This must be a journey with so languid a pace every part would be savoured and committed to memory.

As dawn tried to poke its fingers through the thick morning mist, Devlin sat in shirt and trousers, staring out the window. Madeleine rolled over in the bed, making endearingly incoherent sounds as she did so. His attention shifted to her.

Her beauty took his breath away, as it had that first moment he'd seen her in Farley's gaming hell. Her dark hair such a contrast to her fair skin; her long eyelashes, so like Linette's, full against the pink of her cheeks. He memorised her image, just as he had done before returning to Spain.

The eyelashes fluttered and she opened her eyes. The smile she gave him, so peaceful and satisfied, tugged at his heart.

He would see that peace stay with her forever, no matter what the cost to him.

'Good morning,' she said, sleep making her voice raspy.

'Did you sleep well?' He already knew her reply. While he had hardly captured two winks all night long, she had slept as sound as a kitten.

'Indeed.' She stretched, arching her back and extending her arms above her head. 'And I have the feeling that this will be a lucky day. Today you will find the solution to our problems.'

'I have done so already.'

She brightened, sitting up straight. 'You thought of it in your sleep?'

Sleep, indeed. 'I thought of it last night, but I only decided this morning.'

She sprang from the bed and rushed over to climb into his lap. With her arms around him, she rested her head against his chest. 'What is the solution, Devlin?'

He closed his eyes. As if lances were piercing his skin again, he steeled himself against the pain.

'I must marry.'

Chapter Nine

Madeleine's heart pounded. Marriage had figured too prominently in her fantasies of late.

'It was my father's plan.' Devlin's voice vibrated through her body, but it did not soothe. 'And it is the only means I have of solving our problems.'

He held her more tightly. 'You see, Maddy, I am a wealthy man. My father bequeathed me a fortune, as he did my sisters and second brother. Ned, of course, has the title and all the entailed property and is as rich as Croesus, but my father saw that each of us would prosper.'

'I do not understand. You are wealthy, but your brother refuses you money?' He made no sense.

He laughed drily. 'There is the rub. My father thought me unfit for my property and wealth. Ned controls the lot until I marry a lady of whom he approves.'

She buried her face into his chest so he would not see. Her fantasies had indeed been foolish. He must marry someone of whom his brother approved. A lady such as the beautiful Marchioness. Not one who came as the prize in a game of cards.

She took a deep breath. 'So you must marry.'

'Marriage shall steady me…or so Father believed. I have resisted, Maddy. It seems an abominable reason to marry.' He squeezed her, his strength conveying his frustration. 'It is too soon for me, in any event. I have just done being a soldier. I do not wish—' He broke off.

Madeleine pulled away and retrieved her clothes from the floor. Suddenly conscious of her nakedness and ashamed of even more that that, she donned her shift, aware of his eyes upon her. She glanced at him and he averted his gaze. Tossing her hair over one shoulder, she slipped into her dress and fumbled with the laces. Devlin came and tied them for her, the light touch of his fingers sending shimmers of pleasure down her back.

'It is because of me…' She felt sick inside, unsure if it was because Devlin would once again pay the price for her freedom, or because he might think of bedding her, but never, never would he think of marrying her. 'I will not allow it.'

'You have no choice.' His voice was bleak.

'I could leave here.' She set her chin firmly. 'You would not need to marry, then.'

He turned her around and held her arms firmly, forcing her to look at him. 'You would be driven back to Farley. Or worse. Believe it, there can be worse.'

'I will never go back to him.' She shuddered at the thought. 'I will find employment. I am already learning to sew.'

He regarded her with tenderness. 'Yes. I am proud of your efforts, but, even if you attain Sophie's skill, it is but a pittance to earn. I counted her money, you recall.'

'I will contrive something.'

'No, you will not. I have been around this in my mind in all manner of ways.' He released a ragged breath. 'I must marry.'

Someone else. Some other woman. A lady.

'You are not responsible for me,' she continued, struggling to keep the misery at bay.

He brushed a lock of hair off her forehead. 'But I am, Maddy. I am responsible for the lot of you.'

'I could walk out. You could not stop me.' She glared.

He shook his head. 'Do not be foolish. You must think of Linette.'

She closed her eyes. He was correct. She would sell her soul to spare Linette a future like hers.

Pulling away, she went to Devlin's bed and smoothed the covers they had disordered, trying not to recall the wanton pleasure of loving him. Her carnal pleasure had come at great cost.

He spoke from behind her. 'I will see to both of you, Maddy. A snug little house for you. Whatever you want. School for Linette. I will make her future secure, and you will not want for anything.' He turned her around to face him. 'It is the only way. I will not permit you and Linette to suffer.'

His countenance, so sincere, with a look so loving, caused tears to prick her eyelids. 'I cannot like being a burden to you,' she said lamely.

He gathered her in his arms, holding her tightly against his chest. 'You will never be a burden. My wealth is such that I may easily afford to provide you and Linette a life of ease.' He took a deep breath and his chest rose tighter against her. 'But I must have a wife to do so.'

He would be that rich? But he had been satisfied to count pennies and seek common employment. Why had he done so?

Her mind seized on an anxious thought. 'Is there a woman for whom you have already spoken?'

He petted her hair. 'No, my sweet, there is no one else.'

She glanced up at him. His green eyes were soft, though tiny lines of worry etched their corners. She lifted her fingers to feel the rough stubble of his beard. Her childish fantasy of a pirate whisking her away flashed through her mind. Would that it could be true, that this unshaven, half-dressed, hot-blooded man would whisk her away. Not send her away, as fate decreed.

His eyes darkened with passion. Adjusting his hold on her, he captured her lips. The kiss, rough and as yearning as her heart, sent fire through her. She uttered a deep, needful sound and grasped at his shirt, wanting to tear it away from where her hands longed to touch.

His hands untied the laces of her dress as he backed the two of them against the bed. She let her dress slip to the floor, not caring if she stepped on it. He lifted her on to the bed and moved back to rid himself of the shirt and unfasten his trousers. She lifted her shift. He climbed atop her and she relished the weight and nearness of him. His male scent filled her nostrils along with the more primitive smell of desire.

He kissed her again and she arched to him, wanting to join with him, the need more urgent now that she knew this golden time with him would end. She whispered for him to proceed with haste, and he made ready to comply.

'Mama!' Linette's plaintive cry sounded through the door.

'Deuce,' Devlin muttered.

'I have to see to her.' Madeleine said, fighting her body's craving to do otherwise.

'I know.' Devlin sighed and moved off her, grabbing her dress, which she hurriedly donned. He worked the laces as she headed for the door.

He stopped her at the door with a quick, regretful kiss. 'See to the child. I'll come below stairs soon.'

With one glance back, Madeleine opened the door to her

room and headed for the outstretched chubby arms of her daughter.

Devlin dragged his hand through his hair and stared at mother and child, desire still churning through him. He closed his eyes and took deep breaths. Arousal faded little, but calm did not return.

He watched Madeleine tend to her child with confidence, efficiency, and calm good humour. How could she manage that when his body still throbbed with wanting her?

Lord, he did not want to leave her when their passion flamed like this. Marrying would not have to cause this to end, would it? He could continue to visit her, still warm her bed.

He quietly shut the door.

No, he would not see her again after the damned marriage. It would be too cruel to this hapless future wife for their marriage to include a mistress.

The wretched course he had decided upon was the correct one. The only one. But it sickened him all the same. To damn another lady to a future without love merely to secure his fortune was detestable, but not to do so meant damning Madeleine and her child to a living hell.

He prowled the room, unable to quiet the storm of emotion inside. He must give up Madeleine. It was the only way to ensure her a good life. Marriage was his only choice.

The walls of the room closed in on him, and his breathing quickened. He shut his eyes and yearned for escape, for freedom.

Until Waterloo, soldiering had been his freedom. Living by his own wits with men who understood what was essential in life. Making the most of each day. Grateful for food, shelter, the occasional warmth of a willing woman. Laughing and drinking and sleeping under the stars. Surging with excitement, raging against the enemy. Testing skill, courage and luck. He would trade everything to go back to those days in Spain.

What blithering nonsense. Those days had vanished with Waterloo.

A heavy fatigue overtook him, but he proceeded to shave and dress. He would put the best face he could on this day, for Madeleine's sake.

Below stairs, he walked past the dining room and smiled. Their little household rarely supped at the table there, except for the last meal of the day. He liked the informality of the kitchen where they gathered as equals in this venture to survive.

That would vanish, too, with his decision. When his money flowed again, he would be master.

As he neared the kitchen door he heard Madeleine's voice.

'Sit, Sophie. Please do. I will tend to the meal.'

Sophie's inevitable protest dissolved into a fit of coughing.

Madeleine looked up as he entered. Linette clambered over the chairs to get to him.

'Deddy!' The little girl jumped into Devlin's arms.

'Devlin,' Madeleine said, 'please tell Sophie to sit and allow me to do the work. She is ill.'

'I am not ill.' The little maid, sallow-faced with dark circles under her eyes, choked on her words and turned her head to cough some more.

Devlin opened his mouth, but had no chance to speak.

'I cannot see how she fooled Bart. He never would have gone out had he known.' Madeleine fussed at putting bowls on the table.

'Deddy play?' Linette batted her long lashes at Devlin.

Madeleine whirled to the child. 'No, Linette, sit here and eat.' She swept over and took the child from Devlin's arms.

She put Linette back in her chair, raised high by a wooden box upon which Linette now stood, not sat. Madeleine continued, 'Dev, please do something. Sophie will not listen to me.'

As if to prove Madeleine's words, Sophie pushed her hands on the table to raise herself. Devlin pressed his fingers to his brow.

'All of you, sit!' he commanded.

The three sat, like obedient soldiers.

He glared from one to the other. 'Linette, do as your mother says. Eat. Maddy, stop fussing. If you wish to ready the meal then bloody do it.' He softened his voice for Sophie. 'Little one, do not exert yourself. It is foolishness when Maddy is capable of a simple breakfast.'

Sophie did as she was told, coughing softly, eyes downcast.

Madeleine rose to pour a cup of tea for Sophie and Devlin. 'You need not have snapped at me.'

He glanced at her, regretting his burst of temper, but her eyes held the hint of a smile and a softer expression that spoke of what had passed between them the previous night.

'I apologise.' His eyes held hers for that moment. He hoped she knew he was sorry for more than a fit of temper.

Between coughs, Sophie said, 'I need to tend to my sewing.'

Madeleine started to protest, but Devlin shot her a glance to keep quiet. She spooned him a bowl of porridge.

'You need sew no longer, little one. We have had a change in fortune. In fact, I intend to return your earnings to you.'

Sophie's eyes grew wide. 'We have money?'

'We will by this afternoon, I expect. I will call on my brother again. He will give me the money this time.' He cautiously took a spoonful of the lumpy porridge. Perhaps by the morrow they would be feasting on boiled eggs and ham.

'You see, I will do as my brother wishes and he will advance me the money.' Devlin would leave further explanation of their change in fortune to Madeleine, not knowing how to tell Sophie about his need to marry.

'May…may I continue with the sewing?' Sophie asked, her eyes darting warily.

He leaned to her and placed his hand on her arm. 'You may do whatever you wish. I do shout and bluster, but you are a free woman, Sophie. Not mine to command.'

Madeleine stood behind him with the pot of tea. She brushed against him as she poured.

'Where the devil is Bart?'

'Gone to find work,' Madeleine said.

'Deuce, you did not stop him?'

'He left before I came down.'

Bart would be out searching for some sort of back-breaking labour, or something so dangerous, only a few of the out-of-work war veterans would compete for the job.

'He went to a lead factory in Islington,' Sophie said, before a cough stopped her.

'When?'

She held her throat, as if that would hold back another coughing spell. 'An hour or more, I think.'

He could hire a hack and catch up to him. Devlin took a quick sip of his tea and rushed off to warn his sergeant not to risk his neck another time for Devlin's sake.

He found Bart at the factory door where he and others hung about, hoping to be chosen for a job. The factory billowed black smoke and flecks of black ash covered the pavement and buildings. How could anyone abide such dismal surroundings?

'Come on, Bart. Let us get you out of this damned place.' He gestured his friend over to the hack.

Bart did not leave his place in the ragged line that had formed. 'It is honest work, Dev, and pays well.'

'You no longer need to break your back. Our fortunes have changed.'

Bart stared at him, hands on his waist. After a moment he abandoned the line and walked over to the hack.

Devlin explained the whole business as they rode back. Bart responded with a grim expression. 'It is right enough, Dev, but I do not like it all the same.' He shot Devlin a suspicious glance. 'Are you certain you have thought this through?'

Devlin nodded, frowning. 'This is not one of my impulsive acts. I have sat up half the night figuring this. We are mere days from having no blunt at all. What else can we do?'

The two men stared at the buildings passing by, the only sounds the horses' hooves on the cobblestones and the shouts of vendors selling their wares.

'When the time comes,' Devlin said at last, 'I want you to stay with Madeleine.' He did not have to explain what he meant.

'We have not been apart since Spain. I'll not desert you now.' Bart's thick brows knitted together in one straight line.

Devlin regarded his friend with a wan smile. 'Sophie will not wish to leave Madeleine, I expect, and I doubt you will wish to leave Sophie. Am I correct?'

Bart did not answer, but neither did his craggy brows move from their stern expression.

'I can only do this if I know they remain safe.' Devlin's voice became low and insistent. 'I must depend on you to look out for them. I will not be able to see to it myself.'

Bart stared at him as the hack neared St James's Street. 'I will do as you say.'

That afternoon, Madeleine was alone in the house. Linette napped. Sophie, who had insisted herself fully recovered, went to return her sewing to Madame Emeraude and get another batch. Bart accompanied her, so she need not carry the basket.

Devlin left to see the Marquess, to announce his decision to seek a wife so as to release his allowance.

Madeleine hated this solitude. Busy all morning, she had given herself no time to think of Devlin searching for a wife. And leaving her.

Now there were no distractions.

The only fantasy she could muster was of Devlin in a church with a beautiful lady like the Marchioness at his side, saying his vows. If she shook off that unwanted reverie, she saw him facing the same lady in his bed.

She grabbed her sewing and settled herself in the parlour's window seat. The day was clear, the kind of day she once might have spent on horseback, galloping over the hills near her home. Those days felt as unreal to her as her fantasies about Devlin. She frowned over her stitches. Sophie had helped her design an apron to protect her dresses during the day. They had found an old bedsheet to make it with. Stitching was laborious, but she was determined to finish the garment when she was not needed helping Sophie with the dresses.

Sewing simply did not occupy enough of her mind, and this morning of all mornings she did not wish to think. Devlin would marry and she would be sent away.

She supposed she should be grateful that he intended to take care of her and Linette. It was a good fortune, a perfect solution to all their problems. Perhaps Devlin would visit after he wed. Lots of men kept mistresses, she knew. Several had offered her a *carte blanche*, but Farley inevitably found out and they never offered again.

She refused to rank Devlin the same as those odious creatures who used to drool over her. He was not like them. Being with him was so different than being with other men. So wonderful. Devlin was a man like no other.

She turned back to her stitches. Perhaps if she became truly skilled at sewing, she and Sophie could earn enough for a little place to stay, enough to feed and clothe themselves and Linette.

Devlin would be free.

Madeleine concentrated on speeding up her sewing, necessary for a seamstress. She tried very hard to keep the stitches the same size and close together. Sometimes she would forget to use the thimble and push on the needle with her bare finger. More often, she poked herself with the needle's point instead of moving her fingers away.

For a few moments, the effort consumed her mind, but a noise in the street distracted her. A shiny barouche with a splendid pair of matched bays pulled up in front of the house. The horses were as fine as any she had ever seen. What stable had bred them? she wondered. They were identical in size, their markings so similar one would suppose they had been twins. She wished she had seen them in motion.

The knocker of the door sounded, and she jumped. She peeked out the glass to see who knocked. An unknown man stood there. The driver of the elegant equipage?

She opened the door.

The man who stood before her was more refined than any she had ever seen. His buckskins and driving coat were so finely tailored they looked moulded to his well-formed frame. His eyes, regarding her with a startled expression, seemed familiar, as did the set of his chin.

'I was given this as Lord Devlin Steele's direction.' He eyed her as men usually did, but without the typical prurient gleam.

'Lord Devlin is not presently at home,' she said.

He stepped past her, across the threshold, though she had not given him leave to do so. Her heart beat in alarm and she was acutely aware of being alone in the house.

She straightened her posture. 'Perhaps you would wish to leave your card.'

He removed his hat. 'I wish to wait.'

She bit her lip. She dare not betray being alone. His eyes still carefully assessed her.

'Who are you?' His question was more like a command.

She bristled. Smiling with bravado through her nervousness, she said, 'Forgive me for not introducing myself. I had thought it proper for visitors to announce themselves first.'

His eyes flashed at her insolence. She supposed he was not one accustomed to having his behaviour questioned. She smiled again and cocked her head as if waiting.

'The Marquess of Heronvale,' he said impatiently.

Her smile vanished. Devlin's brother.

'You are?' he commanded again.

She waved her hand as if his question was foolish, but curtsied politely. 'Miss England at your service, my lord. I am the... the housekeeper.'

'Indeed?' His eyebrows lifted in a top-lofty expression and his eyes flicked up and down her person once more.

She took a breath. 'Lord Devlin intended to visit you this afternoon, my lord. Perhaps you might find him at your residence.'

He made no move to leave. 'I will wait for him.'

She took his hat and showed him into the parlour, where he stood continuing to watch her. She scooped up her sewing from the window seat and twisted the material in her hand, wishing she had finished the garment so it could cover her pale yellow muslin dress.

'I shall bring tea.' It sounded like what a housekeeper might do. He still stood, watching her.

As she moved to leave, his voice stopped her, sounding less imperious. 'Tell me, Miss England. My brother...is he well?'

An odd question. 'Yes, he is. Very well, my lord.' She curtsied again and hurried out the door.

The Marquess watched the retreating figure, wondering what to make of this surprise in his brother's household. Housekeeper, indeed. The young woman—lord, she looked more like a girl—was a breathtaking beauty with startlingly blue eyes and dark unruly hair. Where had Devlin found her? He had heard no rumours of his brother forming a liaison.

He strolled around the room, intrigued, as well, with the genteel furnishings. The place must have commanded a respectable rent. With this 'housekeeper', it was easy to see why Devlin wished to move. And he could see why his little brother had overspent his due. A woman of Miss England's face and figure would not come cheap, as her tasteful new attire could attest.

He'd not reckoned on his brother living with a mistress, had not conceived the notion even when Serena reported seeing Devlin with a woman. Devlin had introduced Serena to her as if she were respectable. Devlin should have told him about her.

He should not be surprised Devlin had not. Ned wandered over to the window. He would have disapproved. He would have given Devlin a list of cogent reasons why keeping a mistress was irresponsible and he would have reminded Devlin of his duty.

Ned had often thought about keeping a mistress himself. There were times when his masculine urges raged in a manner he could not inflict upon his delicate wife, and a willing woman would have easily slaked his desires.

But he had not.

In any event, Devlin had no business keeping a woman. He had no fortune of his own to command. Ned stood again and peered out the window. He had planned merely to assure himself Devlin was not ill and be on his way. He pulled on the bell cord.

Miss England appeared at the door. 'Yes, my lord?'

At least she played her role of housekeeper well. Puzzling, she spoke like an educated miss. Still, her youth did not make sense. She could be no more than nineteen.

'Please have someone instruct my tiger to walk the horses.'

'Yes, my lord,' she replied.

He watched from the window to see it done and was surprised when Miss England went from the house to speak to his tiger.

A few minutes later, she entered with a tea tray. She poured the tea prettily and offered some lemon cakes, as well. He noticed tea leaves swimming in his cup.

He could not resist baiting her. 'Tell me, Miss England, how long have you been in my brother's…employ?'

'Not long, sir,' she replied, an edge to her voice.

'He had not spoken to me of having a housekeeper.'

She did not lower her gaze at this question. She smiled instead. 'Indeed? Do gentlemen discuss such matters?'

He narrowed his eyes, 'Was it you whom my wife met with Devlin—Lord Devlin?'

Her cheeks flushed. 'Yes, my lord. She kindly spoke to me.'

He ought to wring Devlin's bloody neck. How dare he put Serena in such a position, to speak to one such as this Miss England? He glared at her.

But at the moment she looked more like a timid young girl, nervous and uncertain. It was difficult to maintain his anger.

'May I be excused, my lord?' Her cheekiness had fled, at least. He wished to ask more questions, but could think of none.

'Deddy?' A small voice sounded from the doorway, and Miss England turned pale.

Ned turned to come face to face with a tiny child, no more than a baby, rubbing her eyes and yawning.

The very image of his brother.

Chapter Ten

Ned stared at the child, a doll-like little girl who clutched a wooden horse in her hand. Even the toy was like one Devlin had carried with him at that age. She had blue eyes instead of green. Even so, this little girl was a female version of Devlin twenty-five years ago. The child stole a wary glance at him and ran to Miss England, who scooped her up in her arms.

'I want Deddy,' the child said.

Miss England flushed.

'Daddy?' Ned asked, raising an eyebrow.

The young woman blinked rapidly.

'The child's word for papa?' Perhaps the child had picked up the Scottish term from the faithful Bart.

Her eyes darted. 'No, indeed, for a…a…toy.' She looked at the girl. 'Go above stairs now, sweetling. Mama will be up directly.'

The child flung her little arms around Miss England's neck. 'No!'

Ned remembered that feeling. Chubby arms clasping his neck, the awesome knowledge that such devotion could be

directed at him. His littlest brother, following him everywhere when he was home on school holiday. Worshipping
him. Needing him.

'She is Devlin's child.' He did not ask.

A panicked look flashed across Miss England's face. She
recovered quickly, meeting his eye. 'She is *my* child.'

Her child? She looked barely old enough.

The little girl studied him with wide lash-fringed eyes.
'Who zat, Mama?'

'He is the Marquess,' she responded.

His title would mean nothing to the child. But it would
warm his heart if he again heard a childish voice call him Ned.

The little girl squirmed and her mother set her down.

Ned squatted to the child. 'And what is your name?'

'Winette,' the shy little voice said, a thumb popping into
her mouth.

'Winette?' He looked to Miss England.

'Linette,' she said.

Ned smiled at the child. 'That is a splendid horse you
have, Linette. May I see it?'

Linette thrust the hand holding the horse in Ned's face.

'A splendid horse, indeed. Does your horse have a name?'

She released her thumb. 'Deddy's horse.'

Ned glanced at Miss England. Her hand had flown to her
mouth. With a halting gesture, he touched Linette's dark
curly hair. His brother used to run to him for comfort, he
recalled. Ned would mop up his tears and stroke his hair just
like this.

'Markiss play?' the little girl asked, cocking her head and
batting her eyelashes.

Ned laughed and ruffled the child's hair, a smile lingering
on his lips. Yes, he would like to play again, to sit on the floor
and gallop a wooden horse.

He stood instead. 'I shall take my leave, *Miss* England. Please tell my brother he shall hear from me.'

'Yes, my lord.' She hurried to fetch his hat and gloves and to open the door for him. The child hovered behind her, and he gave the little girl a final smile as he walked out of the door, his barouche pulling up in front of the house.

Linette ran out the door, pointing. 'Horse! Horse, Mama!'

Miss England rushed out to grab her. Ned caught the child first and held her until Miss England took her hand. Regretting he had to leave the child, Ned continued towards the barouche. He stopped, a thought interrupting the plan half-formed in his head.

He turned back. 'Miss England?'

She hesitated. 'Yes, my lord?'

'Are you married to my brother?'

Surprise flashed across her face and she blushed deep red. 'No, my lord.'

He continued on his way, climbing onto the barouche and snapping at the rungs while his tiger leapt on to the back.

From an alleyway across the street, black eyes watched the retreating vehicle and glanced back at the mother and child re-entering the house.

What was meant by that tender scene? Lord Farley wondered. The Marquess of Heronvale going all mawkish over Madeleine's child? Perhaps the man's fancy ran toward young ones. Rumour said he had no fancy for his ice-maiden wife.

Farley tried to calculate what small fortune a marquess might spend for the rare chance to dally with such a child. He rubbed his hands at the thought.

Perhaps he should have sold the child to settle his debts instead of giving up Madeleine. Madeleine had become so much more difficult since the child was born. He should have got rid of it straight away.

Cursed chit—Madeleine had vowed to slit her own throat if he so much as touched the child, and he'd decided to keep her happy. He'd counted upon her being grateful enough to come willingly to him, like the first time when she'd been flushed with delight. That was what he desired again.

Farley leaned against the lamppost. He removed a pinch of snuff from its box and inhaled it. After a spasm of sneezing, he glanced back at the door she'd walked through, recalling the sway of her hips. She was made for seduction. If ever there was a woman created for passion, it was Madeleine.

So why did she withhold that passion from him? It enraged him. He thought he'd taught her a lesson when he forced her to become the bribe in his crooked games. He'd intended to offer her only a few times, but she'd made him a tidy profit. Men would come to his establishment every night, hoping to win time with her, especially if he offered her only every now and then. Then they returned often, losing more blunt each time.

While she was fat with child she'd earned him nothing. If he'd been in London he'd have dealt with her before it had grown too big to get rid of, but one did not refuse an emperor's summons or, to be more accurate, one from an emperor's emissary. Not when the emperor paid well for information gleaned from brandy-loosened tongues and gentlemen desperate to settle gambling debts.

He should have taken her to France with him, but that night before he left she'd angered him, and it had suited him well enough not to set eyes on her for a while. Besides, she'd become something of a patriot. More than once he discovered her poring over newspapers filled with stories about the war. If she had discovered his business dealings with

Napoleon, she might have been stupid enough to pass the word to some fool willing to put country above fortune.

Stepping out of the alley onto the pavement, Farley gazed once more at the apartments where Madeleine lived with Devlin Steele. He thought of her naked beneath Steele, and his own loins ached.

He'd have her again, even if he had to kill to get her.

Madeleine paced the floor, wishing Devlin would hurry home and dreading when he would.

What could be worse for Devlin than the Marquess of Heronvale learning of her existence and that of her child? She knew what could be worse—his suspecting the child to be Devlin's.

Oh, she should never have opened the door. He would have gone away none the wiser had she not.

Linette walked up to her. 'Mama? Where's Markiss's horse?'

'Gone, Linette,' she said for what seemed like the hundredth time. Linette had not stopped speaking of those cursed horses. They were beautiful animals, she had to admit.

After what seemed like hours but could barely have been more than one, Devlin walked in. Linette reached him first and was lifted into his arms.

'Markiss's horse! Markiss's horse!' Linette chattered.

Madeleine tapped her foot in impatience.

Devlin frowned at her. 'My brother was not at home, so we remain penniless.'

'He was here.'

Her words were drowned out. Linette grabbed Devlin's cheeks and yelled, 'Markiss's horse!' as if getting louder would help.

'What the deuce is she talking about?' Devlin asked.

'I told you. Your brother was here. He came here, Devlin. He saw Linette. Markiss. It is her way of saying the Marquess.'

'Good God,' Devlin said. 'What did he want?'

'To see you.'

'For what purpose?'

She lifted her arms in frustration. 'I do not know. He did not confide in me.'

'Good God. He met you?'

'Of course he met me.' Her voice went up an octave. 'I have told you.'

She knew it was a terrible thing for Devlin's brother to learn of her existence. Still, it stung to realise Devlin thought so, as well.

Devlin set Linette down, putting his hand to his brow.

'You need not worry.' She lifted her chin. 'I told him I was the housekeeper.'

He threw his head back and laughed, the sound bouncing off the walls of the hallway.

Madeleine glared at him. 'It is not a jest, Devlin.'

Grinning, he drew her into his arms, even though she tried to pull away. 'You are nothing like a housekeeper.'

She pushed at his chest. 'Be serious. What are we to do?'

Linette ran up with her toy horse. 'Deddy play!'

'Not now, Lady Lin.' Devlin continued to hold Madeleine. Linette pulled at his trousers.

'We do nothing, Maddy,' he said. 'Ned would know of us sooner or later. My brother always discovers my secrets.'

Madeleine settled against him. As long as her presence remained a secret, she had an easier time pretending. In the full light of day, however, her existence was a shameful one.

Madeleine rested her head against the comforting beat of Devlin's heart.

'Are Sophie and Bart here?' His deep voice resonated in his chest. It was like feeling the sound, as well as hearing it.

Madeleine did not move from his warm, strong arms. 'They went to Madame Emeraude's, but that was a while ago. I believe they may be dallying.'

He chuckled, producing more interesting vibrations. 'They are the unlikeliest pair.'

No, she thought. *We* are. A man of Bart's class may marry a girl, no matter what her reputation. A lord may not.

The next morning Devlin woke, tangled in Madeleine's embrace. He stared at her face, inches from his and, in sleep, looking innocent as a lamb, so very young and vulnerable. His heart ached with tenderness for her.

She had not come to him in the night. He'd been restless and eager, desire heating his loins until he could wait no longer. He crossed the room, opened the door, and lifted her into his arms. She'd not protested when he carried her to his bed.

He intended to make love to her this morning. More than once, if the child slept long enough. Knowing he must give her up made him hungry for her, as if he needed to get his fill of her while he could. Enough to sustain him for the rest of his life.

Her eyes fluttered open, immediately filling with tenderness. A heartbeat later those eyes registered alarm and then, slowly, carefully, turned blank.

'Shall I make love to you, Devlin?' She spoke in that sweet voice that sounded as if it came from someone else. Her hand slid across his scarred chest and descended, nearing to where he was already hard for her.

He caught her wrist. 'Do not trouble yourself, Miss M.'

He had not expected to see this side of Madeleine again. He'd resigned himself to a limited time with her, but he expected her passion. Had not that much passed between them?

It angered him, made him want to teach her a lesson. He could show her how a man takes what he wants. He could climb atop her and force her to love him, before their time ran out.

Devlin sat up and ran a hand raggedly through his hair. His heart pounded and his throat tightened so that he could not take a breath. The walls of the room closed in on him and he heard the beat of the French drums, the pounding of horses' hooves charging. Retreat! he thought. Run. Ride. Gallop until your lungs feel like bursting and you are safe behind the line.

He swung his legs over the side of the bed and searched for his clothes.

'What are you doing?' Madeleine's modulated voice trembled a bit.

He could show her his anger, but he would be damned if he would let her see this panic that so frequently beset him.

'I am going out.' He left the room, still buttoning his trousers.

Madeleine, her breath coming rapidly, waited a few moments before donning her nightdress.

The previous night had been more than her daydreams could have imagined. He created sensations in her that she'd not known possible. Her body had responded to him, and she had performed all the tricks she had been taught to perform. But this time she had *meant* them. She had wanted to share her pleasure with him, wanted to feel him under her hand and her lips, wanted to bind him to her forever.

She must not allow herself to love him. She must give up foolish dreaming and prepare for leaving him. She must hope that the lady he wed would be worthy of him, and that he would eventually fall in love with her and be happy.

Such a thought was too miserable by half.

Madeleine opened the door connecting her room and Devlin's. Linette still slept, but in a short space of time the sun would send its fingers through the window to poke her awake. Madeleine hurried to dress herself and to drag a comb through her unruly curls. In the scratched mirror, her lips looked swollen from Devlin's kisses. She lightly touched her breast, remembering how his hand had felt there the night before, remembering the ferocity of their lovemaking.

Her body sprang to life. The light from the rising sun increased its brilliance. The sounds of Linette's breathing grew louder. From the open window, she could smell dampness in the cool morning air. She could not afford to feel so alive again. She vowed to tame the desire he aroused in her and to become dead again. As she had been at Farley's.

After all, leaving Devlin would be a little like dying.

Devlin strode through the streets with only one thought in his mind. To run. To ride. To be on horseback again with the sensation that nothing could catch him. No man, no musket ball, no blue eyes that stared blankly through him.

He quickened his pace as he neared his brother's stable. Entering, he called a 'halloo' and walked past the gleaming berlin carriage, a well-sprung curricle, and what appeared to be a brand new barouche. The smell of hay, so long missed, came back to comfort him.

A squat, wiry figure emerged from the most distant stall, wiping his hands on a rag. 'Yes, sir. What is it, sir?'

Devlin peered at him as he walked closer. The man was about his age and familiar. 'Jem, is that you?'

The man broke into a wide smile. 'Lord Devlin, well I'll be. Good to see you again, sir.'

They had grown up together at Heronvale, separated by their stations in life. Jem had been born to the stable, while

Devlin belonged in the great house with its portrait hall of ancestors, its armour and family silver. When he and Jem met in the horses' stalls, however, they were of one mind. Horses. They could spend hours talking of horseflesh. On horseback, they rode for miles.

Devlin reached out his hand, which Jem accepted with hesitation. 'What are you doing here, Jem? By God, I have not seen you in years.'

'Yes, sir, since you went off to fight the Frogs.' Jem glanced around proudly. 'His lordship gave me the running of the stable here.'

'Indeed?' Devlin surveyed his surroundings again. 'Well done, Jem. He could not have chosen a better man. How goes it with you? You are well, it seems. What of your mother?'

'Passed away two years ago, I'm sad to say.' Jem's mother had worked in Heronvale's kitchens. She had been a jolly, generous soul.

'I am sorry. I had not heard.' Devlin felt guilty for not having known, not having even thought of her in that many years.

'I'm married now, sir,' Jem said, a proud expression on his face. 'I have a son and another babe on the way.'

'That is excellent news.' It was on the tip of Devlin's tongue to tell all about Madeleine, Linette, Bart and Sophie, but it could not be right to do so. Jem had a real family. His was not.

They stood awkwardly for a moment before Jem asked, 'And how can I be serving you today?'

Devlin had almost forgotten his purpose, though it now seemed less necessary to thunder away on horseback at breakneck speed. 'I had a fancy to ride this morning. Did the Marchioness send word of me using the stable?'

'She did, m'lord.'

Devlin clapped the man on the back. 'Show me your animals, Jem, and help me select the best bit of blood.'

As they toured the stable, Devlin selected Ned's black gelding, the only horse to truly tempt him. He spied another spirited animal, a mare.

'Jem, I have another request…'

From the kitchen where she washed the morning dishes, Madeleine heard the front door open. Devlin's voice roared, 'Bart!'

She ignored it and returned to her chores. Sophie had become more accustomed to Madeleine's insistence on helping with the work. The little maid's success as a seamstress helped her relinquish her hold on every menial task that needed to be done. That and the fact that her cough had become no better.

Linette came barrelling into the kitchen.

'Mama! Mama! Horses. *Horses*.' The little girl pulled her by the hand and there was no refusing. Madeleine followed, though she preferred to avoid Devlin.

Linette led her out the front door to where Bart was holding the reins of two of the most beautiful horses she had ever seen. The gelding was so black the sun on its coat reflected blue. The mare was a rich chestnut. The steeds' eyes shone with intelligence and good breeding. Their superior long legs impatiently pounded the cobblestones of the street.

She noticed the mare was saddled for a lady to ride.

Linette squealed something incoherent, and it was all Madeleine could do to keep hold of the child's hand.

'What are you about, Bart?' she asked.

'Dev asked me to hold them.' Bart scooped Linette up in his free arm, cooing to the child, 'Now, lass, pet the nose gently.'

Linette was in raptures, hardly able to be contained in Bart's arm.

Madeleine smiled at her daughter's enthusiasm. 'What is this?'

Devlin appeared at her side, responding to her question in a low voice. 'Have you forgotten what riding horses look like, Maddy?' He reached for Linette.

He was dressed in riding gear: buckskins clinging to his muscular thighs, top boots gleaming with polish, a riding coat of deepest blue. Her heart caught in her throat and she turned away from him.

'Horses, Deddy!' the child cried.

'Indeed, Lady Lin.' He grinned at Linette and placed her on the back of the black horse, holding on to her as he did.

Linette looked tiny atop the huge steed. 'Devlin, please take her off. She is too little—'

He spoke stiffly. 'I'll not let any harm come to her.' Without turning toward her, he continued, 'Madeleine, you will accompany me for this morning ride?'

The lady's horse was for her? A thrill rushed through her, replaced by trepidation. She should not spend time with him.

'I have no clothes.'

'Yes, you do. On your bed is the riding dress.'

She had refused the riding dress at the modiste. He had ignored her. 'I told you I'd have no need of riding clothes.'

'You were wrong. You need them now.'

More useless money spent on her. Perhaps if he had simply given her the money he spent on clothes, she could have found her own place to live and he would be free not to marry for her.

She crossed her arms in front of her chest. 'What else did you buy that I asked you not to?'

'The evening dress.'

'The evening dress!' Her voice became shrill.

'And shoes to match.'

She gritted her teeth. 'Useless waste of money.'

Devlin spoke firmly. 'Madeleine, change into the riding dress and return here forthwith. We will ride.' It was a command straight from a battlefield.

'Yes, my lord.' She turned and made sure she did not rush up the steps and into the house.

Once out of his sight, her anger blazed. She stomped into her room, and saw the riding dress laid out on her bed. It was an elegant outfit, a deep crimson, the colour rich and luxurious. She fingered the fine weave of the cloth and could not help but admire the garment's excellent cut.

She picked up the matching hat. A single feather adorned it, curled into a crescent to accent her chin. The hat had netting she could pull down over her face.

She had never expected to ride again. Indeed, she had settled in her mind that giving up horses was fitting punishment for fate to bestow upon her. When Lord Farley had first seen her on horseback, she had worn her brother's outgrown breeches and shirt instead of a proper riding dress. His old clothing was tight on her newly emerging curves. Now she knew how such garments must have inflamed Farley's senses, and she'd had no sense to restrain herself.

Yes, it was a fitting punishment to never ride again.

She walked over to the window and peered out. Devlin was now astride the black horse with Linette seated in front of him. He urged the horse into a sedate walk and she could hear through the closed window Linette's squeals of delight.

Devlin looked as if he were born to the saddle, and, as he held Linette protectively in his arm, Madeleine felt her heart yearn for him.

No. She must refrain from such feelings. She would ride,

as he commanded her to do, but she would not allow herself to feel a thing. Not for him. Not for anything, except her daughter. She would not allow herself to care about how the horse felt beneath her, how the hooves pounded in her ears, how the wind beat against her face.

She turned back to the bed and began undressing.

A quarter-hour later, she allowed Bart to toss her into the saddle. She remained silent while Devlin handed Linette down to Bart and they cantered through the London streets.

They made a solemn pair as they rode next to each other through neatly kept streets, still quiet at this early hour. The shops made way for rows of houses, each larger and more elegant as they progressed. She did not ask where they were headed.

Devlin finally spoke, though more to himself than to her. 'I have not been on horseback since…since Belgium.' His voice was flat, expressionless.

Her mouth dropped open in surprise. She must have tugged on the reins because the horse broke its gait. She hurriedly righted it again, but remembered the battle's evidence on his chest and back. In spite of her resolve to be angry with him, her throat tightened with emotion.

'We are here,' he said. They had stopped in front of a large stone gate.

Hyde Park.

Beyond the gate was a landscape of green, a fantasy of countryside in the midst of a city. 'Oh, my,' she gasped.

'It is early. No one will heed us at this unfashionable hour.' His horse led the way.

So many years ago, it had been her girlish wish to gallop down Rotten Row in Hyde Park, while her sisters had merely aspired to sedate afternoon drives.

As she and Devlin rode, Madeleine tried to imagine row after row of fashionable equipages with beautiful ladies and finely dressed gentlemen perched on the seats. The less prosperous would stroll along the pavement. She admitted to curiosity about such a sight, even though she had disdained the role of passenger. In those innocent days, however, she had never expected to feel like a trespasser in a world to which she no longer belonged.

Devlin led her to a dirt path where it was clear they could let the horses have their heads. Rotten Row. There were a few other riders, and Devlin ignored them. Madeleine pulled the netting of her hat over her face.

'We will race.'

He was back to giving commands, was he? Well, she would do as he commanded. She would race.

She did not wait for his command to begin. She pressed her knee into the horse's side. The mare leaped into motion. Madeleine leaned forward almost flat against the horse's neck. She inhaled the mare's scent, heard the panting of the mare's breath and the pounding of her hooves. Madeleine's heart ignored her bidding to play dead and leapt with delight. For the first time in years, she felt exhilaratingly free.

Other hooves sounded and Devlin's horse, neck pumping, pulled alongside. She glanced at him. His beaver hat was gone, and his hair blew wildly around his head. His eyes, too, blazed with excitement.

She urged her horse faster. Joy overwhelmed her and she laughed out loud. She glanced at Devlin, his horse neck to neck with hers. He grinned. They ended the course together.

They slowed their horses to a walk. Devlin, breathing as hard as his horse, circled around Madeleine. He gazed at her. To Madeleine, the green of the park faded and was replaced by the green of his eyes. She held his gaze, memorising it.

No matter what her resolve, she vowed to remember the passion she saw in his eyes, the passion that mirrored her own.

A slow grin came over his face. 'Shall we do it again?'

Before she could figure out what the *it* could be that they would do again, he launched into a gallop. She recovered quickly and urged her horse on his heels. He smiled proudly at her when she caught up. Again they finished the course together.

'I won,' he said, a smug look on his face.

'You did not,' she countered. 'I would have been a length ahead if not for this infernal saddle.'

His brow wrinkled. 'Is something amiss with the saddle?'

She felt herself redden. 'No, I…I am accustomed to riding astride. Or I used to be.'

His expression turned solemn and she suspected he could imagine the scandalous picture she made in those days.

A bird fluttered noisily out of a nearby bush, startling Devlin's horse. He quieted the animal and glanced at Madeleine. Her face was flushed and her blue eyes sparkled. No matter what happened to him from this day forward, he would never regret this moment with her. Nor would he forget.

They remained that way, staring into each other's eyes, their mounts restless underneath them. Neither looked away.

More riders arrived in the park. Some greeted Devlin and tossed curious glances toward Madeleine. She held her head down.

'Perhaps we had best head home,' he said.

'Perhaps.'

He rode to retrieve his hat and led them to the gate. She followed closely.

They returned through the most fashionable streets, to streets full of shops, to their own nearly respectable address.

Madeleine spoke, 'Why did you hire horses today?'

He glanced at her. 'They belong to my brother.'

'The Marquess?' Her voice was anxious.

'Yes, but do not worry, Maddy. I have my brother's permission.' It was not entirely accurate, but he had Serena's permission, and Ned would never counter her wishes.

They lapsed back into silence.

Soon they neared their street. Madeleine asked, 'Why did you do this?'

'Fetch the horses?'

'Make me ride with you.'

He frowned. How could he explain what he did not truly understand? He had not meant to invite her. At first he had meant to escape her. 'I did not wish to ride alone.'

'You could have taken Bart with you.'

To Bart horses were like tools, a means to get a job done. His wish to ride was more ephemeral. A last chance for freedom? Bart would never have understood.

He had not even thought of Bart, though. He had wanted Madeleine. Who else would understand the need? The pleasure?

'I wished it to be you.' His voice had turned low and he was not sure if she heard him.

As they rode up to their apartments, Linette's face disappeared from the window. A moment later she was out the door, tugging away from Bart's firm grip.

'Horse! Horse! Mama. Deddy.'

'Hello, my darling,' Madeleine called to her.

'Me, too, Mama. Me, too.' Linette cried, squirming to get free. Even a strong man like Bart could barely hold her.

'Bring her here, Bart.' Devlin reached down and scooped the child into his arms, holding her securely in front of him. 'Maddy, come with us.'

Devlin, Madeleine, and Linette rode sedately to the end of the block, quiet at this hour, and back again. The little girl's delighted laughter filled the street.

'More. More.' Linette shouted.

'Enough for today, Lady Lin.'

Bart reached for the child. Devlin slid easily off the horse and turned for Madeleine, holding her firmly by the waist to assist her to dismount.

She looked him directly in his eyes and whispered, 'Thank you, Devlin.'

He held her there, suspending the moment.

When he finally slid her down his body to touch the pavement, Madeleine blinked, turned and took Linette from Bart. She allowed Linette to pat the horses and say goodbye to them.

'Would you return the horses, Bart?' Devlin asked.

Bart nodded, taking hold of the reins. 'Dev, a note was delivered for you. It is on the table inside the door.'

Devlin, his emotions in a tangle, ran up the steps and into the house. He had not wanted that time with Madeleine to end. He removed his coat, gloves and hat, and picked up the envelope.

Madeleine and Linette came inside, and Linette ran to the window for her last glimpse of the horses. 'Bye bye, horses!'

'What is the note?' Madeleine asked as she pulled off her hat. Her hair tumbled down to her shoulders.

He handed her a piece of paper.

Her eyes grew wide. 'It is a voucher for Almack's!'

'Serena certainly lost no time procuring it for me.' He wrinkled his brow. 'The other paper is an invitation,' he said, though she was paying little attention. 'No, a command, really.'

'A command?' She gingerly fingered the voucher.

'We are commanded to dine with my brother and his

wife this evening, at their town house.' He tapped the card against his palm.

'You are?' She said absently.

'*We* are,' he corrected. 'You and I.'

Her face turned pale. 'No.'

Chapter Eleven

'Oh, yes,' Devlin said. 'The invitation is very specific. It is for us both.'

'I will not attend.' Her voice sounded as if she were being strangled. 'I will not expose myself to…to a society dinner where I do not belong.'

Devlin saw the rising panic in her eyes. 'It is a private dinner. You and I are to dine with Ned and Serena, *en famille*.'

'No.'

Devlin rubbed his brow. What the deuce could Ned be thinking of? It was not like his brother to play games. Impossible to believe he would invite Madeleine to his home to dine with his wife. Ned might not love Serena, but he certainly would never deliberately cause her any discomfort. And, then, there was the matter of the voucher to Almack's. An invitation to bring his mistress to dine, and a blatant entry into the marriage mart in the same package. It made no sense.

Madeleine stared at him, her chin now tilted in defiance, anxiety lingering in her eyes. He looked back at the card, not so much to read it again as to collect his thoughts.

He wrinkled his brow. 'I think the voucher must mean Ned

intends to give me the money, but…' he glanced up at her '…I cannot understand why he wishes us to dine.'

'I will not go.'

'I do not think there would be any harm in it.'

She crossed her arms over her chest. 'I will not go.'

Devlin attempted a cajoling smile. 'You would find use for the evening dress.'

She threw the voucher at him and fled up the stairs.

As he bent to retrieve it, Linette toddled in from the parlour where she had been on sentry duty at the window. She pulled on Devlin's sleeve, her little mouth turned down and her big blue eyes mournful. 'Horses gone.'

Devlin almost smiled, even amidst his confused thoughts. He picked her up. 'That's right, Lady Lin. Horses gone.'

Linette flung her chubby arms around Devlin's neck. He clung tightly to Linette. The freedom and joy of the ride with Madeleine receded. Walls blocked his escape and the air seemed in short supply.

Run, he heard himself shout. *Run*. He was on horseback again, this time screaming for his cavalry to withdraw. They had gone too far, drunk with the carnage they'd wrought on the French, still swinging their sabres into retreating backs, until the pounding of fresh French cavalry sounded in his ears.

He opened his eyes and caught a glimpse of himself in the hallway mirror, Linette's curly dark head leaning trustingly on his shoulder.

He took a deep breath. 'Come on, Lady Lin. Let us see if Sophie left us some lemon cakes in the kitchen.'

Madeleine flung herself dramatically on the bed. As a child, she might have indulged in a fit of angry tears, but now she knew tears achieved nothing.

She rose and unbuttoned the riding dress, choosing her

yellow muslin to wear. After fastening the laces, she picked up the riding dress again and held it to her nose. It smelled of horse. She closed her eyes. The ride had been glorious. The exhilaration, the freedom of speed, Devlin, hatless and grinning beside her.

Another memory to store. She pored over every detail, fixing each in her mind. With another whiff of the lingering scent, she laid the garment carefully on top of the trunk at the foot of her bed. Later she would brush it off as she had seen Sophie do, and she would hang it up to air out.

The door opened. 'May I come in?'

She stiffened at his voice. 'You might have knocked first.'

Devlin closed the door and leaned against it, his legs crossed at the ankles. 'You might have refused me entry.'

She picked up the riding dress and brushed it off with her hand. It was something to do, to look busy.

'May we talk, Maddy?'

He looked appealingly long limbed, taut with strength, but infused with gentleness. She did not wish to see him thus. She closed her eyes, but that only brought the memory of him wild-eyed on a galloping horse. She shrugged.

'First, let me assure you that the decision is yours. I will not mention this matter again, do you understand?'

She nodded, but did not look at him.

'I do not know why my brother made this invitation, but I cannot believe he would mean any harm. He is a good man.'

'I am not so certain of that.' The Marquess represented danger to her, even though he had been gentle with Linette.

Devlin continued, choosing not to argue the point, 'The invitation must have something to do with Ned advancing my money, or else why would he include the voucher? I think that in order to get the money, we must do as he says.'

She stiffened. 'I do not have to do as he says.'

He softened. 'Of course you do not. But I wish that you would. Nothing is more important to me than securing your future. And Linette's and Sophie's and Bart's.'

'Why?'

He looked surprised.

Her vision blurred with useless tears. 'Do you wish to go to Almack's and search for a wife?'

She watched one of his hands clench into a fist, then relax again. 'I do not *wish* to do so, but I must.'

'I cannot like it,' she said lamely.

One corner of his mouth turned up in an ironic smile. 'I cannot like it either, but we must do it for Linette's future.'

Did he mean this, or was he saying it because he knew she would do anything for Linette's sake? Her child was more important than all the rest of it. Even more important than Devlin's happiness, though it killed her to have to make that choice. She truly wanted to believe that Devlin cared so much for Linette, but men had said many things to her over the past years and she'd learned not to believe any of it.

'Linette is my concern, not yours.' She strode to the window and looked out.

He came behind her and put his hands on her shoulders. 'I have told you before. You all are my responsibility. You. Linette. Sophie. Even Bart. What kind of man would I be if I did not see to your well-being? But I need the means to do so.' He gently rubbed the tender skin of her neck with his thumbs. 'My brother controls the money, so I must do as he says for the time being. It is the price of my independence and your survival.'

'He is making you marry and you do not want to do so!' she blurted out. 'And the fault is all mine.'

He put his fingers to her lips to silence her. 'I choose to do this. Ned does not make me. Just as I will not make you go to this dinner, though I want you to do so.'

With all her heart, she did not want to go. She did not belong in polite society, and she did not trust the top-lofty Marquess, even if he did show a soft spot for her daughter.

It was unfair of Devlin to ask her to do such an unsuitable thing. How would she endure it? Madeleine pursed her lips. She had managed more unendurable things. She could manage this.

'Very well, I will attend your brother's dinner. For Linette's sake.'

'That is also why I attend,' he murmured, gazing into her eyes with a softened expression. 'Madeleine,' he whispered, his lips inches from hers. His fingers gently stroked her cheek.

The passion flared inside her, making her ache for him here in the middle of the day with the whole household up and busy. She had lost all claim to respectability with her wantonness. Worse, she had tied herself to him with her body.

He leaned closer. She felt his breath on her own mouth. She wanted him again, felt urgent for his kiss. She considered how to loosen his buckskin breeches.

Small steps pounded on the stairs. 'Mama, Mama!'

Devlin took a step back, a rueful smile on his lips. 'In here, Lady Lin.'

The Marchioness of Heronvale felt uncommonly nervous as she waited with her husband for the arrival of their dinner guests. She was anxious that her new guest approve of her, a silly worry. Since when did one concern oneself with the approval of a…such a woman?

Her husband's plan filled her with excitement, but she was afraid to even think of that, so huge were the hopes that could be dashed. So she thought instead about how scandalous it was to invite to their respectable home a woman whose attachment to a man involved carnal matters. Serena put her fingers to her cheeks to conceal her blush. What would Devlin's woman be like? What would be different about this woman that she could hold a man by bedding him? Serena felt almost unbearably wicked for pondering such things. What would Ned think of her if he knew?

Rarely did Ned require her to face the carnality of the marriage bed. When he did, all she managed to feel was anxiety that she would displease him. Displease him she always did, though he was too much of a gentleman to tell her so.

She wondered if Ned would look upon this mistress of Devlin's in that sensual way she had often glimpsed at the opera, where young dandies eyed gaudily dressed women in the pits. It frightened her unbearably that Ned might do so, just as it frightened her to think he might have a mistress of his own. He gave her no signs of doing so, but how would she know?

As usual when she let herself dwell on such matters, she felt her eyes sting and her throat tighten. Ned would not approve if she looked as if she might cry. She steeled herself to assume a placid expression.

'My brother is late.' Ned stood at the mantel where the clock had chimed the half-hour.

Ned was always prompt, sometimes embarrassing Serena when they arrived first at a social gathering. She could never convince her husband that the time on the invitation was not the time one was expected to arrive.

She opened her mouth to make an excuse for Devlin, but shut it again. For some unknown reason, Ned lately became angry whenever Serena spoke on Devlin's behalf.

She was glad, though, that Ned had decided to advance Devlin his allowance, but it puzzled her why Devlin had now decided to pursue a wife when he was obviously involved with this mysterious woman, Miss England. It was hard to reconcile the idea that the pretty girl she'd met with Devlin was a wanton demimonde sharing his bed.

Barclay appeared at the door. 'Lord Devlin and Miss England,' he announced.

Serena rose, her heart pounding with excitement.

Devlin entered, looking handsome in his evening attire. It had been a long time since she'd seen him dressed so. His plain coat of black superfine complemented his dark hair and superbly fit his soldier's broad shoulders. Still, he managed to wear the formal clothes in that careless manner so typical of him. Serena fixed her gaze upon the young woman who stood a step behind him.

She was dazzling. Her hair, as dark as Devlin's, was piled high on her head. Natural curls framed her face and caressed the nape of her neck. She wore a delicate pearl necklace and matching teardrop pearl earrings. Not at all the jewellery one would expect of a mistress, more like a set Serena had received on her twelfth birthday.

The gold silk evening dress Miss England wore was cut in classical lines and free of adornment except for matching gold beading around the neckline and hem. Serena had seen more revealing necklines on the *ingénues* at Almack's, but this young woman's figure was such that a man's eye would certainly be drawn to that part of her. Serena glanced hurriedly at Ned, to see his reaction. He merely lifted an eyebrow.

'Ned. Serena. How good to see you!' Devlin spoke with cheerfulness. 'Let me formally present to you Miss Madeleine England. Miss England, the Marquess and Marchioness of Heronvale.'

The young woman curtsied perfectly to each of them and then stood regally, directly meeting their gazes. 'I am pleased to renew your acquaintance.' Her voice was cultured and correct, indistinguishable from one who'd had a respectable upbringing.

'Good of you to come,' Ned said stiffly. He turned to Devlin, just of hint of worry in his eyes. 'Are you well, brother?'

Devlin rolled his eyes. 'Good God, Ned, I am no longer at death's door, you know.'

Serena watched Miss England glance in surprise at Devlin's comment, concern flashing across her face. Devlin caught the look and disarmed it with the hint of a smile.

Serena was fascinated.

Barclay entered with a tray of aperitifs. They were still standing. Serena was embarrassed at her lapse of manners.

'Barclay, Miss England and I will sit on the sofa. Come, Miss England, let us sit and become better acquainted.' Serena led her guest to the sofa. The two women sat and accepted the small crystal glasses from the butler.

Serena had no idea how to converse with this beautiful young woman. 'I hope our coach brought you here satisfactorily.'

Miss England smiled cordially. 'It was kind of you to send it.'

'Well, we could not have you walk, and Devlin could not hire—' Serena stopped. It was poor manners to refer to Devlin's lack of finances, especially since Ned was the cause.

Miss England seemed to ignore her embarrassment. 'Indeed. It was most generous.'

Serena listened carefully to the expression in Miss England's voice. She was not sure what she expected—for the girl to be nervous? She did not seem so. For her to be insolent and mocking? There was none of that. Miss England seemed perfectly composed.

'I must also compliment you on your appearance,' Serena said, searching for conversation. 'Your dress is lovely.'

Miss England blushed at this and seemed for the first time to look ill at ease. What woman was not pleased with a compliment to her clothes?

'Thank you,' the girl murmured.

Serena's distress increased. She was not handling this well at all. She glanced to see if Ned noticed, but he was deep in conversation with Devlin. It pleased her to see the two brothers not slamming fists into each other. Ned loved Devlin more than he did anyone else in the world, Serena knew.

'They had a disagreement, I believe,' Miss England said, turning her head toward the two men.

The directness of this statement surprised Serena. She would never have mentioned the topic to anyone. 'Yes, they did.'

Miss England gave a faint smile. 'Perhaps Lord Devlin lost his temper with his brother.'

'I believe my husband provoked the trouble,' Serena said. 'It seems forgotten now.'

Barclay announced dinner.

'I will escort Miss England,' Ned said, bowing to her and holding out his arm. Serena felt a pang of jealousy. The young woman took the offered arm and waited until Serena, escorted by Devlin, walked ahead of her.

Devlin gave Serena a brotherly squeeze. 'Tell me, Serena, what is this about?'

She blinked. 'What is what about?'

He frowned at her. 'You know very well. This invitation.'

She bit her lip. 'We...that is, Ned... We wished to see you.'

He tossed her a sceptical glance. 'Fustian,' he whispered. 'Why did you invite Maddy?'

'So you would come?' Her answer came out like a question.

They entered the formal dining room with its crystal chandelier glittering from the candle flames. Serena wished they had set up a small table in one of the more cosy parlours, but Ned had wanted Miss England to see the opulence of the house. It was odd, though, that the young woman seemed to accept the frescoed ceiling, long mahogany table, and multi-piece silver service as a matter of course. Serena had instructed the servants to set the table so that they sat at one end. Ned at the head, of course, and she to his right. To his left sat Devlin and Miss England.

Serena watched the young woman throughout dinner. Miss England never hesitated over her choice of cutlery, and she seemed completely at ease with having servants present the food. The conversation was confined to topics of general interest, upon which Miss England conversed easily, but Serena noticed that she never spoke unless she was addressed first.

Serena also watched Devlin. He checked Miss England often, concern or pride alternating in his face. She looked at Ned, whose expression never changed. Serena was struck with a pang of envy so strong she feared she might burst into tears right over the chocolate truffle.

When the port appeared, Serena was relieved to leave the dining room to the men and return to the parlour with Miss England.

Miss England selected a single chair, waiting politely for Serena to sit first. A small fire had been lit in the fireplace to ward off the chill of the damp spring night, its hiss and sputter loud in the silence between the two women.

'Would you like tea?' Serena asked finally.

'No, thank you, ma'am.' The young woman remained composed, her hands folded in her lap.

'I do wish you would call me Serena.'

Miss England glanced at her in surprise. 'I would not presume.'

'But you are Devlin's friend, and he is so dear to us.' Serena fingered the lace trim on her dress.

Madeleine's nerves were beginning to fray. She had

managed the role of guest long enough. 'I am not Devlin's friend.'

This pretence seemed even more dishonest than those she was forced to enact for Farley. It was shameful for her to even set foot in this house, more flush with money than Farley could have wrested out of her in one hundred years. She wished she could excuse herself and run.

Instead she regarded the Marchioness. What could have induced this high-born, titled lady to entertain her? To ask for the intimacy of first names? There was no sense in it.

The beautiful blonde woman in her pale blue dress edged in delicate lace looked even more uncomfortable than Madeleine. Madeleine suspected the Marquess was behind this visit, and his wife compelled to go along. But why?

It certainly did not help matters that the Marchioness looked as if she might cry at any moment. 'I apologise, ma'am. I did not mean for my words to distress you.'

The Marchioness smiled faintly, blinking. 'Do not concern yourself about me. I fear I am proving a poor hostess.'

Madeleine blinked in surprise. 'Why should you be a good hostess? You ought not be compelled to entertain me at all.'

Her hostess looked up. 'Compelled? I assure you I was not compelled. It was my idea to invite you to dinner.'

'Why?' It was presumptuous of her to ask, but the word simply burst out of her.

Distress again pinched her ladyship's brow, and she gave Madeleine a pleading look. Madeleine felt a different kind of shame for distressing such a lady. Lady Heronvale had truly laboured to be kind. There had not been a moment when she had shown even a hint of the disapproval Madeleine deserved.

Madeleine glanced around the room, her eyes lighting on the figurines on the mantelpiece. 'They are Meissen, are they not?' she said, trying to find something comfortable to talk about.

'What?' The Marchioness still looked distressed.

'The figures on the mantel. They are Meissen.'

'Why, yes they, are.' Her ladyship's eyes widened with surprise.

Madeleine smiled. 'They are lovely.'

After nearly half an hour of more awkward conversation, Ned and Devlin entered the parlour. The brothers looked congenial. Madeleine did not know if this boded good or ill. In any event, what more pain could the Marquess inflict than making Devlin leave her? Devlin would leave her no matter what. The Marquess could not, after all, know her identity.

Ned surveyed the parlour and elected to stand near the mantel, upon which he leaned casually. The leg nearest the fire felt too much heat, but he ignored the discomfort. He had a good view, a position of power.

He had been pleased to be able to converse with his brother in an amicable way, though he sensed Devlin's wariness. He glanced at his wife and perceived her discomfort, as well. Miss England was more of a puzzle. She seemed serene, poised, untouched by the tensions crackling throughout the room.

Ned rubbed the elegant carving of the mantel with his thumb. The time had come. He met his wife's eye. She inhaled sharply. He would bring Serena her heart's desire.

He looked down on the young woman who should never have been invited to his wife's home. 'Miss England,' he began in a mild voice, hoping it sounded friendly.

She lifted her gaze to him, the impassive expression still in her eyes.

'What think you of our house here in town?'

A flicker of surprise showed in her face, but she quickly changed her expression to one he could not read. Mocking? Melancholic? 'It is a magnificent home, my lord. Very fine.'

He smiled. 'I am pleased that you think so.'

She returned his smile. 'I did not realise you sought my good opinion.'

That statement must be sarcasm, but he could not tell for certain. He ignored it, clearing his throat. 'This house pales in comparison to Heronvale. Heronvale is a piece of heaven.' Ned glanced at Devlin. 'It was a marvellous place to be reared, was it not, Devlin?'

Devlin's eyes narrowed suspiciously. He lounged in a chair, but one leg crossed over the other swung with nervous energy. 'It had fine stables.'

Ned laughed, hoping to dispel his brother's tension. 'My brother saw little of Heronvale except on the back of a horse. Did you know that, Miss England?'

The smile was fixed on her face. 'Indeed.'

This woman gave up little of her feelings, Ned thought.

'Miss England is an accomplished horsewoman,' Devlin said.

'Is that so?' Ned remembered the child's excitement seeing the horses of his curricle. He had assumed her passion for horses had come from her father. 'You and my brother have that in common, then.'

Miss England shrugged her reply.

This was like fencing with an opponent reluctant to reveal his skill. Perhaps he should begin the attack.

He strolled over to a decanter of claret, lifting it to offer its contents to the others. Devlin shook his head and Serena mumbled 'No, thank you.'

'I should like some,' Miss England said, and Ned had the foolish impression that they had each chosen their weapons. He handed her a glass and poured one for himself. He took a sip.

First lunge. 'Did you know my brother is a wealthy man, Miss England?'

Her glass pressed against her lips and her taste of the wine was long and delicate. 'Is one wealthy who has no money to spend?' Parry.

Riposte. 'You know, then, that Devlin must marry?'

Her brows lifted. 'For his wealth, he must marry, unless you declare otherwise.' Well parried. Too well parried.

'He must marry. His heritage demands it. Do you understand?'

She stared at him, bringing her glass to her lips again.

Ned abandoned the fencing and indulged in a rare display of anger. 'His behaviour with you has been irresponsible. Unbecoming in a gentleman—'

Devlin rose from his chair. 'Enough, Ned. These are words to be spoken to me in private. I will not have you do so in front of Madeleine.'

Ned took a step toward his brother. 'You took a mistress when you knew full well you could not keep her in clothes or jewels—'

'She does not want—'

Ned closed the distance on his brother. 'You involved a child, Devlin. A child. How irresponsible is that?'

Serena gasped.

'You know nothing of this matter, Ned. I have said I will find a wife, what more do you want? I'll accept my bloody heritage and be damned, but you owe Madeleine an apology.' Devlin's eyes blazed with anger. 'She has done nothing to deserve these words of yours.'

'She has borne a child, has she not?' Ned paced back to the mantel. Devlin stood his ground. Turning to face them again, Ned saw the alarm in Serena's face. Miss England looked on, alert.

'The home you have contrived is no place for a child,' he said. 'The little girl needs comfort and education and a solid moral foundation. You cannot give that to her, Devlin.'

'I can and will take care of the child. Why do you think I agreed to marry? You've left me no other way to take care of them, have you? Well, brother, you may bet on it that Madeleine and Linette will be well cared for.' Devlin's fists were clenched and his body poised for a fight. 'By me.'

Ned paced the floor. 'You cannot provide her a good home. What will the child learn of life in a household like that, with you arriving at odd hours to warm her mother's bed?'

'Damn you, Ned. You have stepped too far over the line.' Devlin's face became a rigid, angry mask. Ned thought this might be how he appeared galloping toward a company of bayonet-wielding Frenchmen.

'Ned?' Serena's fingers crushed the fabric of her dress.

He glanced from Serena to Miss England, her hands folded demurely and her gazed fixed on them. Damn his brother for compromising that young woman.

And damn himself for being glad of it.

He would not back away now, not when he had come so far. He slowed his breaths and moderated his voice. 'I do apologise. I did not intend to ring a peal over your head.'

Devlin's hands curved into fists.

'Serena and I wish to help. It is why we invited you here.'

Miss England raised her head.

'We believe it would be advantageous to everyone, if you agree with our proposition.'

Devlin still glowered, but showed a hint of curiosity, as well.

Ned went on. 'We wish to adopt the child and raise her as our own…'

Chapter Twelve

'Good God, Ned.' Devlin turned away from his brother and drew a tense hand through his hair. Ned wanted the child? 'What right have you to propose such a thing?'

He heard the Marquess take a deep breath. 'I am head of the family, you might recall.'

'What the deuce has that to do with it?' Devlin swung back to him.

Ned made no effort to respond, simply staring back.

Devlin's mind reeled with his brother's words. Ned thought he had seduced Madeleine. Thought she pined for dresses and jewels. Thought he could take Linette from her.

'Serena and I realise—' Ned's voice was steady and reasonable '—that there may be talk about our raising your child, but we are prepared—'

'*My* child?'

'Linette.' Ned went on. 'Such talk would disappear as soon as something more interesting came along. So I would not—'

'My child?' Devlin repeated, raising his voice.

'Of course,' Ned glanced at him and continued talking. 'It would be no time...'

Devlin stared at his brother, impeccably dressed in white breeches and superbly cut black coat. His hair, flecked with grey, remained neat and orderly. Did his ever-perfect brother think he'd seduced Madeleine, got her with child, then abandoned her to go off to war? Only a cad would do such a thing.

Devlin longed to explain to Ned he was not that sort of man. Explain that Madeleine had been Farley's prize. That the child might be anybody's. Serena might blush, but how scandalised could she be? An occasional tumble with such a woman was expected of young men. His brother might lift a disapproving eyebrow, but he could not damn Devlin's character. Yes, all that was needed to clear his name was to expose Madeleine's life under Farley and shame her in front of Ned and Serena.

Devlin tried to keep his voice steady. 'What causes you to think the child mine?'

Ned gave him a look of exasperation. 'She looks like you.'

'She looks like Maddy.' A vision of Linette flashed through Devlin's mind. Her curly dark hair always falling from its ribbon. The clear blue innocence of her eyes. The pouty mouth when she did not get her way. So much like Madeleine. From his first glimpse of the child, his heart had reached out to the little girl. She was Madeleine as a child.

'She is the image of you at that age,' Ned countered. 'If you do not believe me, come to Heronvale and check the family portrait in the music room. She is even named for you. She was obviously conceived during your leave from Spain. The timing is correct. How you supported them in your absence is a mystery, but there is no mystery about the fact that she is your child.'

'My child.' Stunned, Devlin made his own calculation. His one brief encounter with Madaleine. The child's age. He'd never considered.

Madeleine stared down at her lap, her knuckles turning white as she gripped her hands. The Marquess's words echoed as if emerging from a distant cave. Saying he wanted to take Linette. Saying Linette was Devlin's child.

She stood and spoke with cold rage. '*My* child.'

These men were no different than Farley and the ones he had sent to her bed. They all wielded power over her. The power to control her life, to violate her body…and to steal from her all that was dear. This rich Marquess controlled with his title and money. What chance had she against such weapons? Even Devlin, for all his pretty words, held her life and her daughter's in his hands. He could crush them both in an eye blink. He could cast them into the street. Abandon them to his brother.

Send them back to Farley.

Madeleine's body trembled. Panic mixed with rage. Three sets of eyes stared at her. The Marquess's with a look of impatience. His wife's with tears rolling down her cheeks. And Devlin's with confusion and surprise.

Madeleine held herself erect, lifting her chin high. These people would not see she feared their power. Indeed, she would not fear it. She would defy it. No one would take Linette from her. No one.

She let a faint smile cross her face and spoke again, her voice mild. 'Linette is my child.'

And, as they stood poised to hear more, she bolted. She ran out the mahogany parlour door, down the white marble stairs and through the hall, glittering with gilt. She heard Devlin shout her name. Heard the Marchioness wail, and the Marquess call for someone to stop her.

No one did. She flung open the front door and ran out into the street. She cared not that she held her skirts high away from her ankles, nor that the silk slippers scuffed roughly against the pavement. She would get to Linette first. She would grab Linette and Sophie and run.

She had only a vague notion of which direction to take, but trusted that her need to protect Linette would lead her home. Shouts sounded from behind her. She dared not look back. She'd always been fleet-footed. None of the lads she'd grown up around could best her in a race and no one would best her now.

'Maddy!' It was Devlin's voice.

She ran faster, past the elegant houses and neatly swept streets, ghostly in the lamplight. Ahead was a jumble of carriages, polished and shining, clogging the street. Elegantly liveried footmen milled about. Candlelight blazed from a house and, as she neared it, Madeleine heard sounds of music and revelry coming from the windows. She also heard Devlin's shoes pounding behind her. Coachmen and postilions glanced curiously in her direction. There was nothing to do but head straight for them. She plunged into the crowd.

Devlin's lungs strained and his legs ached as he pushed himself into greater speed. His months of recovery had robbed him of more strength than he had known. Madeleine was in sight. He gained on her slightly when she disappeared into the throng of vehicles and men lounging in front of the elegant town house. A satisfactory crush by the looks of it, but he had been out of society so long he could not even remember whose house it was. He only knew Madeleine would draw attention to herself in her flight. He must catch her before danger befell her. What could she be thinking of running into the night alone and unprotected?

He slowed, trying to get a glimpse of her in the confusion.

'Lord Devlin?' A man panted as he came up behind him.

Devlin greeted him with relief. 'Jem. Help me find her.'

Bless Jem. He asked no questions, but immediately ran to

search from the edge of the line of carriages. Devlin headed through the jam where he'd seen Madeleine disappear. The commotion ahead of him told him he was close.

'Hey, missy, what is your hurry?' Men's voices laughed. 'Stop now, missy.'

Would she appear to be a lady to them? The coachmen and postilions would be whiling away the hours of waiting with a bit of drink. Boredom and drink were dangerous companions. He glimpsed her, seeing only a bit of her gold silk before men closed behind her, calling after her. Were they grabbing at her? Please no. They would not molest her here in Mayfair. St James's Street was the danger. Not Mayfair.

She turned, giving Devlin an anguished look. Jem had circled behind her. He caught her in flight.

'It's all right, Maddy. Jem is a friend,' Devlin said to her, as she struggled to get free. 'You are safe with us.'

'Let me go,' she cried. 'Let me go.'

Jem did let her go, but not until Devlin had her firmly in hand, one arm encircling her waist.

Devlin saw one of the footmen look curiously in their direction. He thought it prudent to avoid further trouble. 'Come, let us get away.'

Jem led them to the entrance of an alleyway. Madeleine thrashed and kicked as Devlin half-dragged her into the alley. 'I want to go.'

Devlin kept his arm tight around her waist. 'Jem, can you send the carriage? I assume you made it ready for us.'

'Yes, sir.' He ran off.

Madeleine squirmed and struggled in Devlin's arms. 'Let me go,' she cried feebly. 'Let me go.'

He leaned her against the cold stone wall and secured her with his body, his arms embracing her. Her struggles quieted, but she trembled against him, her breath ragged.

'You are safe now, Maddy,' he whispered in her ear. 'I will not hurt you.'

'You will let him take Linette,' she cried.

'No, I will not,' he spoke soothingly in her ear.

'He will make you do it,' she insisted. 'Just as he makes you get married.'

The truth in that statement stung. Ned held the power over his fortune, and he needed that fortune to safeguard Madeleine and Linette. Devlin had no means to combat him.

A few weeks ago Devlin would have bet his entire fortune that his brother would never to do anything so dastardly. Now Ned was like a stranger, capable of anything.

Trying to sound confident, he assured her, 'Ned will not take Linette from you, I promise.'

'I am sick to death of gentlemen's promises.' She spat out the words. 'Promises mean nothing.'

'Mine do,' Devlin insisted, offended and hurt that she would think him like other men, after all they had been through.

She met his eyes, her own a challenge. 'Do they?'

What was the use? She would not believe him. He cursed Farley and every man who had failed her. He cursed himself. It had not occurred to him to take her away from that life when he first met her. Had he done so, she'd have been spared years of suffering, of rearing her child in such a scandalous place.

Her child. His child, perhaps? Had he left his own flesh and blood to Farley's evil whims? Perhaps Ned's ill opinion of him was well deserved.

Her struggles ceased, but though his body was pressed against hers, he felt her distance.

The carriage pulled up with Jem on the box beside the driver. Devlin walked her to it.

She looked up. 'I will not ride in *his* carriage.'

'Do not be foolish, Maddy. Let us get out of here.' Curious bystanders started to gather, doubtless trying to see the crest on the side of the vehicle.

'No.' She tried to pull away.

'Enough of this,' Devlin said, more to himself than to Madeleine. He picked her up and tossed her into the carriage, jumping in behind. 'Go!' he shouted to Jem.

The carriage lurched, and Devlin fell against her. She pushed him away. Crossing her arms over her chest, she huddled against the side of the carriage, as far away from him as possible. A tear trickled down her cheek.

Feeling miserable, Devlin rubbed the back of his neck. Her dress was wrinkled and dirty, her shoes near tatters, her hair half-tumbled from its pins.

She glanced at him briefly before turning back to the curtain.

'Maddy?'

She did not respond.

Devlin took a breath. 'Linette…is she…is she my child?'

Madeleine shut her eyes and focused on the rhythmic sounds of the horses' hooves against the cobbles. She had intended for this moment never to come.

She turned to him. 'I do not know.'

There was little light in the carriage, and she could only dimly see his face. She could not read his expression.

She continued, 'She could be your child.'

He made a sound, an aching one. 'How? From that first night, I suppose, but how could you know?'

He meant how could a woman who had been with countless men say that one of them fathered a child? She winced.

'I do not pretend to know.' She had promised herself never to believe Devlin fathered her child. She'd always told herself naming her Linette was in memory of a man who had been kind to her, nothing more. But sometimes, when she gazed upon her daughter, she believed otherwise.

'It is possible, nothing more.' She felt her throat tighten. The memory of that night, both with him and afterward, was etched in her mind.

'I was a foolish girl. You undoubtedly will think me so.' She attempted a light tone to her voice. 'When you left that night, I did not do as I was supposed to do. I did not wash myself. I fancied it would keep you with me a little longer.'

She heard his breath quicken.

'And when Farley came to me, I refused him.' She winced at this part. 'I had never refused him before, and he beat me soundly, but he did not bed me. The next day, he left. He was gone a long time, more than a month.'

Those rare times when Farley left had been the best her life had to offer in those days. She was guarded against running away, but none of his lackeys dared touch her and the gaming hell ran without her as the prize.

'Maddy.'

He reached for her, but she twisted away. 'By the time Farley returned, I knew I was with child. I hid the fact from him as long as possible. He wanted to get rid of the baby, but I threatened to kill myself if he did.'

'Maddy, I'm sorry.' Devlin reached out to her, but she pushed his hand away.

'Linette has been reward enough. I ask for nothing more.'

'I should have been there to help you.' He sounded anguished.

How like a man to be sorry for what he had not done, though he probably gave not a thought to it until this moment. Did Devlin think his regret made any difference to her? He had not believed Linette to be his child and looked for excuses not to believe so now. His words were empty.

'I will not let the Marquess take Linette,' she said. 'Sophie and I will take her away this night. You need not trouble yourself further with us.'

'You will not leave, do you understand?' He spoke sharply. 'It is not safe for you.'

'You cannot make me stay.' She twisted toward him. 'Unless you plan to hold me prisoner like Farley did. Under guard every moment.'

'He kept you under guard?'

'At first. After Linette was born, he guarded her.'

'Damn.' The word barely reached her ears.

They rode in silence, the creaks of the carriage and the sounds of the horses' hooves filling their ears until the carriage came to a stop. Jem hopped down from the box and opened the carriage door. Devlin lifted Madeleine out.

'Wait for me, Jem,' Devlin said.

'You are going back?' Madeleine said, fear creeping back.

'I need to speak to my brother.'

They would plot the stealing of her child. Devlin would give Linette to the high-minded Marquess and flawless Marchioness.

'Do you keep me here? Do you alert Bart to guard the door?'

He attempted to take her by the elbow, but she pushed him away and ran hurriedly to the door. He caught up with her there, pulling the key from his pocket. He gripped her arm with his other hand as they entered the house. The hallway was lit with two candles, the rest of the house, quiet.

Devlin took her by the shoulders and forced her to look at him. 'Nothing is changed, Maddy. I promised you that I would take care of you and Linette, and I will fulfil that promise. I will not take Linette from you, nor let my brother do so. I promise you on my honour.'

She glared at him and tried to back out of his grasp. 'More talk of promises.'

He kept his grip on her shoulders and kept in step with her. 'You must stay here, Maddy.'

'You do not command me, my lord.' She backed into the wall.

He moved towards her still. 'I must command you in this. There are dangers out there for you and Sophie and Linette. Men like Farley and far worse. You would not be safe if you left, and I would not be able to protect you.'

'I am not safe here.' He was too close now, his hands on the wall and his legs spread apart like a cage entrapping her. 'You would give my child away.'

He gave an exasperated bark. 'Damn it, Maddy. I will not.'

She stared at him as he loomed over her. His features blurred in the dim light. More vivid was the scent of him, the warmth of him.

He rubbed his cheek, rough with stubble, against hers and brought his lips near her ear. 'You may not believe my promises, but I will believe yours. Promise me you will not run away. You will stay here until I have the means to set you up in your own house, wherever you wish.'

Her breath quickened, swelling her chest so that it touched his with each breath. She wanted to believe him. Wanted to believe he was the soldier returned from the war to rescue her, to whisk her and her daughter to a pretty little cottage where they would live happily forever.

His lips touched the sensitive skin of her ear. 'Promise.'

She squirmed under the sensations his lips created, making her press against his pelvis. She forced herself to place her back flat against the wall.

She also forced herself to think realistically. It was more likely he would barter her child to his brother. Linette would be wrenched from her arms and sent to live in the Marquess's house, and Devlin would be free to pursue whatever pleasure he wished. Linette would have sugared treats and pretty clothes and a pony of her own. There would always be a fire warming her room and food filling her belly. She would learn to call the kind-hearted Marchioness 'Mama' and the Marquess, who had looked upon her with such tenderness, 'Papa'.

A sob escaped her lips. Devlin gathered her into his arms and she soaked his jacket with her tears.

'Promise you will not run away,' he murmured. 'Let me keep you safe.' He lifted her chin and placed his lips on hers.

For a moment she melted into him and allowed him to pet her and taste the tender interior of her mouth. For a moment she believed him. Catching herself, she struggled in his arms, wrenching her face away from him. He released her, pain written on his face.

She ran up the stairs without a backward glance.

Devlin returned more than two hours later. The candles in the hallway were burned to nubs. He pinched them out before ascending the stairs. His heart pounded in his chest.

Had she stayed?

When he had arrived back in Grosvenor Square, his brother and Serena still sat in the parlour. Serena's eyes were red with crying. She twisted a damp handkerchief with her fingers. His brother poured from an almost-empty decanter of brandy.

Serena had gasped when he reappeared.

'She is safe at home,' he announced.

He then endured his brother's lecture, watching the clock on the mantel pass midnight, wondering all the while if Madeleine waited for him, or if she had run. He declared to Ned that he, not the Marquess, would care for Madeleine and the child, had explained that their care was his whole motivation for marrying. He accepted Serena's shocked protests regarding such a marriage plan and allowed his brother to exact from him a promise to disengage from Madeleine and her child after his marriage. Ned rang another peal over his head about the destructiveness of debauchery and the necessity of relieving Madeleine of the disreputable status of mistress. Devlin had resisted the temptation to tell Ned the promise was unnecessary. Ned renewed his offer to adopt the child. Serena even proposed the unlikely option for Madeleine to become the governess.

Before Devlin bid Ned and Serena goodnight, Ned had discussed with him the financial obligations of engaging in courtship. They had come to agreeable terms.

Now, as Devlin mounted the stairs to where his two charges should be sleeping, his pockets were weighted with gold coin and a promise had been extracted from him to accompany Serena to Almack's the coming evening. All of which seemed of no consequence at all.

Devlin paused upon the top step, trying to sense if he would find Linette's little bed unoccupied, drawers void of contents, trunks bare.

Madeleine gone.

He knocked gently on Madeleine's door and opened it. The lamplight from the street provided dim illumination to the room. The light rested on Linette's bed.

The little girl slept peacefully. Her long lashes brushed the tops of her chubby cheeks and her little pink lips moved around the thumb tucked securely in her mouth.

He leaned over to watch her. My child? he asked himself.

He still could not see it. The little girl looked like a tiny, innocent Madeleine, before she'd encountered life's ugliness. Devlin reached out his hand and brushed his fingers through the child's dark curls.

Did it matter to him if she were his child or not? Would he feel the same ache in his heart at the prospect of losing her if he knew her to be from the seed of some other man?

He would never know.

Devlin glanced toward the larger bed, expecting to see Madeleine looking similarly peaceful in sleep, but the bed was empty. His heart accelerated and panic rushed back. Had she gone? He pressed his fingers against his temple.

And felt the point of a sword sharp in the small of his back.

Chapter Thirteen

'You will not take my child, Devlin.'

Madeleine pressed the point of the sabre into Devlin's back.

She had waited in the shadows of the room for over an hour. Each moment he had been away convinced her he was plotting with his brother to take Linette. She was furious with herself for being too cowardly to grab her child, wake Sophie, and flee.

She had finally decided that if Devlin returned home and went directly to his room, he was worthy of her trust. But if he entered her room, thinking her asleep, it would be to take her daughter. And she would be ready for him.

She had taken the sword from where it rested against the wall in his room, unsheathed its curved blade, and waited in the darkness. When he entered, she moved like a cat, silent and predatory, until the sword's point rested against his back.

'Maddy.' He started to turn.

'No!' She pushed on the sword. Its sharp point pierced the cloth.

He became still. 'I was not attempting to take her.'

'I do not believe you.' She kept pressure on the sword.

'I kept my word to you. Remove the sword.'

Her hand trembled. His coat ripped.

'You are piercing my skin, Maddy.' His voice was mild. Deceptively so, she thought.

'Why did you come in this room, if not to take her?' Madeleine's voice quavered. She had not truly intended to draw his blood.

He did not answer. He remained very still for what seemed to be an eternity. 'I merely wished to look at her.'

Something wistful sounded in his voice, and Madeleine faltered. Perhaps it mattered a trifle to him that Linette might be his child. Her grasp on the sabre relaxed slightly.

Devlin whirled around, his movement so swift she was not sure how he achieved it. He grabbed her wrist and wrenched the sabre from her grasp, catching the hilt of the falling sword in his other hand.

She cried out.

He whipped the sword to point at her. Madeleine shrank back. His face held no expression at all.

'If you must use the sabre, Maddy,' he said in a rumbling tone, 'it is not for stabbing, but for cutting and slicing.'

The sword whirred as he cut and sliced the air, fluttering the lace of her nightdress. He pointed the sword inches from her nose. Her heart hammered painfully against her chest.

Ever so slowly, his eyes not leaving hers, he lowered his arm so that the blade pointed to the floor.

'Now, heed me, Maddy.' His eyes narrowed. 'I offer you my protection. That includes Linette and Sophie, as well. You may accept or leave. You know the world you face if you spurn my offer, but perhaps you would prefer the dangers of the street…' he paused and blinked '…to me.'

Madeleine's heart slowed and she allowed herself to breathe, her thoughts a hopeless muddle.

She dreaded the idea of leaving him. Dreaded the thought that he would marry. She had persuaded herself he would steal Linette from her. How could she have thought that? He had rescued her. He planned to marry to support her and Linette. But how could he not have accepted the offer his brother had made? Linette would receive everything as the child of the Marquess.

'What is your wish?' he snapped.

Her wish? What she could not have. Her throat constricted, with frustration and despair. 'I will stay with you.'

He whipped the sword blade up into a salute, then turned and left the room.

Madeleine collapsed on to her bed and squeezed her eyes tight. She had cut him and made him bleed. She had torn his clothes.

She heard him slamming and banging things in his room, as well as the muffled sounds of swearing. She lay in the darkness and listened. What would happen in the morning? The one time she had totally defied Farley he had beaten her senseless. She had done so much more to Devlin. His forgiveness was impossible.

The cuirassier rode his midnight-black steed over a mass of writhing blue-coated bodies. Sunlight glinted off his metal breastplate and the sharply honed blade of his sword. The wind whipped the horsehair plume on his helmet while his black moustache quivered. The Frenchman laughed, and the sound echoed, merging with the moans of the wounded. The stench of war's carnage filled Devlin's nostrils, and he struggled to run, to retreat, but bloody hands clasped his ankles, holding him fast. Escape was impossible.

The huge Frenchman, a grin showing his yellow teeth, slowly raised the sword over his head and brought it down, closer and closer—

'No!' Devlin cried.

Hands grabbed him and shook him.

'Devlin, wake up! You are dreaming. Wake up!'

He fought, bucking and rearing and pushing the hands away. The voice became more urgent. 'Wake up!'

He opened his eyes, expecting to see each face of each man he had ever killed.

He saw Madeleine. She was straddling him, her nightdress hiked above her knees. Her hands were clasped around his wrists and he pushed against them, trying to free himself.

'It was only a dream, Devlin,' she said, her tone soothing.

He stared at her. *Madeleine.* Was she real? Perhaps she was the dream and if he closed his eyes again, the faces of the dead would return. He widened his gaze. His sheets were damp with sweat and his heart pounded like the drums of the French.

'There is no danger now.'

Madeleine. He ought to be furious at her, he dimly recalled, but he was so damned glad she was here. He relaxed his arms and, by so doing, caused her body to lie flush against his nakedness. As the last wisps of the nightmare evaporated, he turned his face from her, ashamed of his terror.

Madeleine stroked his hair. 'There, there.' She spoke as to a child awoken by dreams of goblins. 'It is all gone now. Nothing to signify.' Her lips touched the sensitive skin of his neck. Her body was warm, like a blanket.

'It will never go away,' he mumbled.

The first light of dawn shone through the window and the clatter of workmen's wagons testified that ordinary life proceeded, in spite of his private horror. His eyes moistened. Madeleine took his chin in her hand, turning his head to face her and kissing each eyelid.

Relief and gratitude washed through him, leaving him

drained. He lifted his head to kiss her and tasted the salt of his tears on her lips. If only his world could consist solely of this. Why could life not be as simple as a man and woman making love?

She moaned softly and opened her mouth, giving, yet demanding more. Devlin pulled her nightdress over her head, his hands sliding against her smooth skin and full breasts. He was hard and urgent beneath her and desperate to feel the comfort she offered. He lifted her slightly and, as if she anticipated his desire, she gave him access.

Devlin's world became simple. Madeleine was here and his body pulsed with the sensation of her. Her hair tumbled forward, her curls tickling his face. Her pink lips parted with passion and her eyes half closed. She felt warm and smooth beneath his hands, her breasts soft on his chest. He grasped at her, feeling greedy and fearing she, like all that was beautiful, would disappear and he would fall into the cauldron of destruction and death from which he would never escape.

'Madeleine,' he growled, his need for her primal.

She gasped, and he felt her convulse around him. He exploded inside her, pleasure and peace filling him.

She relaxed, lying next to him and gazing at him. Devlin wanted nothing to break this moment.

Her blue eyes searched his, concern filling them.

He attempted a smile. 'I am quite all right now.'

Her concern did not disappear. 'I have heard you restless in your sleep before this.'

The nightmare came often enough. 'And you did not offer this comfort?' he joked.

The familiar masked look came over her and her body tensed. 'You had only to ask, my lord.'

'Shh, Maddy,' he whispered. 'I meant only a poor jest. Do not spoil this moment.'

She slipped away and reached for her nightdress. The moment had been spoiled. 'Your dream,' she said, thrusting her arms through her sleeves. 'Was it of Waterloo?' Her tone was almost conversational, but she had brought back the horror with the word.

Waterloo.

'I do not wish to say.' He spoke through clenched teeth.

'You promised you would tell me of Waterloo,' she reminded him. It sounded a scold.

'You promised me you would tell me of Farley,' he countered, mimicking her tone.

'I will,' she said. 'But first you must tell me of Waterloo.'

He turned his back on her. He felt her move toward him on the bed. Her fingers touched the sabre cut she had inflicted.

He wished to run from the memories, as he tried to run from the visions that plagued him at odd moments during the day and the dreams that tortured him at night, the ones drinking and debauchery had never quite erased.

'And if I do not, do you impale me with my sword again?'

She inhaled sharply, then kissed the wound she had made. 'I am sorry, Devlin.'

His words made him feel small.

'You carried the sabre that day, did you not?'

Damn her. She would not leave it alone. Well, she would hear it, then. All the horror. She would see what kind of man had lain with her.

'It is not a story for delicate ears.' Let it not be said he did not warn her.

'My ears have heard much that is not delicate.'

He had forgotten for a moment that her world had contained its own version of hell.

He took a deep breath. 'First there were the guns…'

French cannon had thundered and pounded destruction

through the allied ranks before the relentless rhythm of the drums signalled the first French infantry assault. Devlin again heard the screams, and saw bodies being torn apart.

Wellington's motley mix of untried Allied troops was far outnumbered by the thousands and thousands of French, resplendent in new glittering uniforms, eager to bring glory to the emperor who had miraculously returned to them.

By the time the order came for the cavalry to charge, Devlin and his men lusted for French blood. They became drunk with vengeance, wreaking destruction on French infantry who broke and ran. He remembered the exhilaration of slashing his sword at men who were merely trying to run to safety. The air reeked of blood and sweat, gunpowder and grass. He told Madeleine how he rode over bodies and their severed parts, over men still moving and men who would move no more.

She listened. He sat facing her, his legs crossed in front of him on the bed. She kept her eyes on his, but he saw nothing but the memories.

'The killing did not last,' he said.

She reached over to him, placing her hand on his arm.

'The cuirassiers came.' He closed his eyes, again seeing them, hundreds of them mounted on fresh horses, shiny in their gold-tasselled uniforms. 'They rode slowly at first, then picked up the pace, like rocks tumbling from a cliff, faster and faster, until, raining down so fiercely, they bury you. I called out for the men to retreat, but they did not hear me.'

She squeezed his arm.

He met her gaze. 'Our horses were blown. We were no match for them. The cuirassiers had their revenge. My men screamed and died as the French infantry had done at our hands.'

'You watched this?' she asked, her voice hushed.

If he shut his eyes again, he would see it still. 'I was alone for the moment, the dead on the ground around me. Only for a moment...'

'Oh, Devlin.' Her hand stroked his arm, sending shivers.

'I was not alone for long. A French officer mounted on a huge black horse headed toward me. There was no escaping him. I was hampered by the dead and dying, you see. My horse could not manoeuvre.'

Devlin could still recall the man's chipped and yellowing teeth, each pockmark on his face, the glee of victory in his near-black eyes.

'Did he attack you?'

Devlin gave a dry laugh. 'He attacked my horse.'

Poor Courage. Courage had been a clod-footed, stout-hearted animal with an instinct for battle. The horse had saved his life more than once.

'That is the best means of crippling cavalry.' He gave a half-smile. 'We are nothing without our horses.'

Madeleine did not smile back.

He rubbed his hands. 'The Frenchman slashed at my horse with his sword. Skilful job, it was. Threw me off. Almost lost my sword, I managed to recover it, but he'd already had a go at me.' He fingered one of his scars. 'I cannot fathom why he did not finish me off. He jabbed at me. I rolled in the mud to escape him, while my horse screamed and stumbled nearby. Not exactly a heroic end.'

'But it was not the end,' she said.

'He meant it to be. I can still hear him laugh at my feeble attempts to fend him off. I kept rolling, until I rolled into an irrigation ditch. He slipped at the edge and tumbled down on top of me, impaling himself on my sword.'

She gasped.

'I heard the Frenchman draw his last breath, and my horse fell dead across the ditch, entombing me with my dead enemy.'

'Oh, my.' Her hand went to her mouth.

Devlin, suddenly chilled, wrapped the bed's blanket around him. Again he felt the cold mud seep into his back and the still-warm blood of the Frenchman soak his chest.

A tear trickled down Madeleine's cheek. Devlin was surprised at the tear's effect on him. Something near pain, near pleasure.

He would spare her the real horror. The sounds of the battle raging above him. The cries of the dying and wounded. The cold bleakness of the endless night, looters rustling above him. The stark terror that he would be discovered and killed for his silver buttons and leather boots.

'Bart found me the next day.'

'How did he find you among so many?' she asked, her voice raspy.

He gave her an ironic smile. 'I was quite hidden from view. He found my horse.'

'Your horse?' Her eyes widened again, this time with surprise.

'I had remained in the ditch, under the horse, under the Frenchman.'

'Devlin...' she whispered, reaching to stroke his cheek.

He moved away, not from her sympathy but from the memory that provoked it. 'I do not remember much of the rest. Bart carried me to Brussels. Then Ned came. Days had passed, I've been told. Ned brought me home on the yacht, to die at Heronvale.'

'But you did not die,' she said, as if that had been of some significance.

'That is it,' he whispered. 'Why did I not? Why great numbers of other men and not me? I killed many. Why did that damned Frenchman not kill me?'

Madeleine watched his face break. He squeezed his eyes

shut and grimaced. She wrapped her arms around him and pressed his head against her breast. Sobs racked his body and his breath came in heaves.

'So you could save me,' she told him. 'That is why the Frenchman did not kill you. So you could save *me*.'

He drew away from her and stared, stunned.

Madeleine looked upon him and filled with tenderness. She memorised each line on his face. She repeated his words in her head so she would never forget what he had endured. The incident at his brother's faded. She pushed it from her mind. There was no stabbing him with his sword, no conspiring to steal her child. There was only the need to ease his suffering, his pain and guilt. And to think of how close she had come to losing him.

He leaned back against the bedboard and took a deep breath.

'Do you feel better?' she asked.

He nodded.

'Nothing helps more than a good cry.' She smiled. A good cry had never helped her, but it seemed the proper thing to say.

He smiled back, this time wide enough for the dimple to crease his cheek. His eyes were still red and puffy, and his nose bright pink. She thought, perhaps, he had never looked so appealing. She smoothed his hair, her heart tender for him.

There was a jiggle at the connecting door and it opened. 'Mama?'

Linette stood in the doorway rubbing her eyes. Devlin hurriedly wrapped the blanket around him. 'Mama?' she said again, finally finding Madeleine.

She trotted to the bed and climbed atop it. Madeleine gathered her in her arms. 'Good morning, my darling.'

'I heard you and Deddy.' The little girl peered at Devlin who clutched the blanket around him. Linette touched his damp cheek and looked puzzled. 'Deddy cry?'

'A little,' explained Madeleine. 'He had a bad dream.'

Linette scrambled out of her mother's arms and into Devlin's, giving him a big hug. 'There, there,' she said, patting his back. 'All gone now.'

Devlin's gaze caught Madeleine's, his eyes moist again.

'Thank you, Lady Lin,' he said. 'I think I am better now.'

Linette grinned in triumph. Devlin fingered the dimple in her cheek.

'Young lady, shall we get dressed for breakfast?' Madeleine asked, her throat tight with emotion. 'Bart and Sophie will be expecting us.'

The child jumped off the bed. 'Deddy come, too,' she said imperiously as Madeleine took her hand.

'I'll be down directly.'

Madeleine glanced over her shoulder before walking back to her room. He remained on the bed, staring back at them.

A half-hour later, Devlin entered the kitchen. He overheard Bart asking, 'Did his brother advance him the money?'

He sat at the table. 'Indeed he did, my friend.'

Madeleine spooned some porridge into a bowl and poured him some tea.

Devlin glanced at the bowl with dismay. 'Today you must replenish our larder, Bart. Bacon and boiled eggs for breakfast tomorrow.'

'Bacon, bacon, bacon…' sang Linette, a white moustache of milk on her lip.

'And wages for you both,' Devlin continued.

Sophie, whose eyes had remained downcast when he entered the room, looked up with awe.

Bart turned red. 'Now, I was not asking about my wages, but there is a matter I wish to discuss.'

'What is it?'

Sophie slipped out of her chair and retreated to a stool in the corner.

Bart fidgeted with his spoon and for once avoided glancing toward Sophie. 'I…er…um…'

'Out with it, man,' Devlin insisted.

'I wish to arrange for the banns to be read.' He gripped the spoon. 'For Miss Sophie and myself.'

Except for Linette's incessant song about bacon, the room went quiet as the significance of the words penetrated.

Devlin glanced at Madeleine, who had frozen, looking pale.

'Well,' gulped Devlin. 'I see.'

Poor Bart and Sophie stared at them warily and Sophie looked about to cry.

'Why, it's wonderful news!' Madeleine jumped out of her seat and rushed over to hug Sophie. 'We were taken by surprise by it, were we not, Devlin?'

'Yes, surprised,' he agreed. He followed Madeleine's example, clapping Bart on the back. 'God help our Sophie, marrying this crusty fellow.' They all laughed except Sophie, who rarely expressed that much emotion. She did manage to smile.

Devlin reached into his pocket and pulled out a pouch of coins. He counted out a generous amount. 'Here you are, with extra for a betrothal gift.'

'No, it must be three times what you owe,' Bart protested, pushing the stack of coins away. 'You must save the money, Dev. We mustn't go short again.'

'Nonsense.' Devlin pushed the stack of coins back and sat in his chair. 'Now that I intend to assiduously follow my brother's wishes, he will continue to fund me.'

Linette, attracted by the coins, climbed on Devlin's lap, now singing nonsense words. She peeked inside the pouch. Devlin let her pour the coins on the table.

'See? We are flush in the pockets again.' Devlin gestured to the pile of coins.

'Fush,' Linette said, intently concentrating on stacking the coins as Devlin had done.

Madeleine watched Devlin finger Linette's soft curls, the expression on his face soft and tender. She stared as he gingerly kissed Linette on the top of her head.

'If it is agreeable to you, we should be about the business.' Bart had spoken. Perhaps he had spoken before, but she had not heard and, apparently, neither had Devlin.

'By all means,' said Devlin. He pushed a few more coins to Bart. 'Here. This will pay to fill our cupboards and settle our accounts. Will you see to it?'

Bart laughed and, as tenderly as Devlin behaved with Linette, reached out his hand to Sophie and assisted her from the stool.

'I want to go, too!' Linette cried when she saw Bart and Sophie leaving.

'No, Lady Lin,' Devlin crooned to her, holding her on his lap as she tried to propel herself out of it. 'Stay with me a bit. Would you like a walk in the park while your mother cleans up?'

'I want to ride your horse.' Linette turned to face him, and she played with his neckcloth and gave him her most appealing expression.

'The horses cannot come today,' he said. 'But we might see some in the park.'

Madeleine felt a chill run down her back. She did not wish to believe he might be conspiring with his brother, but the park would be an excellent place to hand over Linette.

She took a deep breath, deciding to trust him. 'You will have a lovely time, Linette.'

Chapter Fourteen

Devlin stood at the entrance of Almack's with Serena on his arm. He had never attended the assembly room, too occupied with Spanish battlefields or, when in town, with pursuits of a baser nature. The room itself was unexpectedly plain, but the pale-coloured dresses of the *ingénues* gave it the appearance of a formal flower garden in full bloom. In his youth he might have relished the prospect of gathering a bouquet, but, on this night, one suitable flower would be sufficient.

Dozens of female eyes fixed upon him, the older ones coldly calculating, probably tallying what they'd heard his fortune to be. Younger eyes might be assessing other attributes as well, but would likewise not be insensible of his monetary worth.

Devlin thought he heard the pounding of cavalry hooves, but his mind played tricks on him. The sound was merely the buzz of so many voices over the music. Perhaps the analogy to an impending battle was more apt than a flower garden. He certainly felt like the target of a frontal assault.

Truth was, he entered this room with as much intent as the

flowers before him. He only hoped it was possible to find a biddable female who would welcome marriage to a man whose heart was engaged elsewhere.

Madeleine.

She had offered to play valet for him, but he had undressed her as quickly as she tried to dress him. He could still feel the heat of her body next to his, still feel the raw rush of pleasure as he entered her—

'Devlin?' Serena shook his arm.

Serena had been speaking. He forced himself to attend to her.

'We must greet the Patronesses first of all.' Serena led him into the room, seeming to know in just what direction to go. Had Serena met Ned in these rooms? Perhaps Ned had scanned the flowers with as much detachment as Devlin, since his blossom had been previously selected for him.

Serena led him to where the Patronesses held court. Three in attendance this evening, all looking more ordinary than he had expected. He would not have picked them from the crowd, except perhaps for their vigilant eyes.

'Dear Serena,' one said as they approached. The woman extended her hands to Serena and seemed genuinely glad to see her.

'Maria, how glad I am you are here,' Serena responded in kind. She nodded to the two other ladies who were busy scrutinising Devlin.

He hoped his neckcloth had remained in place and that they would not notice the mended place on his long-tailed coat. He had insisted Madeleine repair the damage she had done, although she begged to have Sophie do it. Devlin wanted to assure Madeleine that her sewing was equal to the task. She had laboured hard to learn the stitches, after all.

Serena urged him a step forward. 'Lady Sefton, Lady

Cowper, Mrs Drummond-Burrell, allow me to present to you Lord Devlin Steele, who is Heronvale's youngest brother.'

Devlin bowed to the ladies and managed to push a little charm into his smile. 'It is an honour, ladies.'

'We have not seen you here before, Lord Devlin,' Mrs Drummond-Burrell said, her eyebrow raised suspiciously.

'I have not previously had the pleasure.' Devlin met her gaze and tried to sound sincere.

Serena spoke quickly. 'Devlin—Lord Devlin—was with Wellington. He is recently recovered enough to come to town.'

Serena had drilled him in the proper topics of conversation, which were pitifully few. He hoped oblique references to war wounds were included as acceptable. Not that he wished to speak with these ladies of such matters.

'Indeed. I believe I recall the story,' Lady Cowper said. 'Heronvale fetched you from Brussels. Is that correct?'

'Yes, ma'am, I am indebted to my brother.' Talk of the battle was thus avoided by mention of the rescue.

Lady Sefton took his arm. 'I am certain Lord Devlin did not come here to discuss such unpleasantness. He came to meet our young ladies, is that not so, sir?'

'I am found out.' He smiled.

Mrs Drummond-Burrell tilted her chin in the direction of an exquisite blonde creature surrounded by a group of fawning gentlemen. 'Amanda Reynolds is the current Diamond, I believe. She is not within your touch, however.' The Patroness sniffed. 'Your brother might have tempted her, but not an untitled younger son.'

'You spare me from wasting my time. I am grateful to you.' He bowed.

The Diamond would not have tempted him in any event. The fire within such a lady was as much an illusion as the sparkle of a gem. Devlin preferred the burning passion of a dark-haired woman with fine blue eyes.

But he must not think of Madeleine while here. If he did, he would never find a woman needing marriage and not much else.

'How about Lady Allenton's daughter?' Lady Cowper suggested, glancing pointedly at a plump, rather frightened-looking girl.

'Hmmph!' snorted Mrs Drummond-Burrell. 'She lacks wit, sense and beauty. Her fortune is impressive, but that is the end of it, and Lord Devlin has no need of her funds.'

'Come, my lord.' Lady Sefton, still holding his arm, pulled him away. 'We shall introduce you to many young ladies before the night is over. I suspect they will be eager to add you to their tally of partners.'

So Devlin met many agreeable young ladies, danced many pleasant dances, and gradually felt more and more depressed. Some of the *ingénues*, particularly the youngest ones, were insecure and full of anxieties, others blatantly forward, as if already composing an engagement announcement. None were Madeleine, however, and all suffered in the comparison. He longed to be at Madeleine's side, even if merely seated in the parlour watching her struggle with her sewing. He longed to bounce Linette on his lap and hear her delighted squeals.

That morning he'd held Linette up next him at the mirror, their heads together. He saw identical shapes of the brow, identical dimples. For his child and her mother he would perform his duty.

He begged leave of the forgettable creature who had partnered him in the last country dance and joined Serena, seated with Lady Sefton among the matrons.

Serena regarded him worriedly.

Lady Sefton smiled. 'You are doing very well, Lord

Devlin. I believe you have made an impression on our young ladies.'

'They are quite lovely.'

She laughed. 'Charming, sir! You shall have your pick, I am sure.'

He frowned. 'This is my first evening among society, ma'am. I mean only to enjoy myself.'

Serena avoided his eyes. He supposed she knew he was lying. Or perhaps she continued to disapprove of his decision to marry.

'Would you ladies like some refreshment?' He may as well be useful.

'An excellent idea.' Lady Sefton nodded.

Devlin walked to the room where the refreshments were served. The ladies had requested lemonade.

'Steele! Upon my word, it is you.'

Devlin turned to see who spoke to him. A slim man in an impossibly high collar and tiers of intricate neckcloth grinned at him.

'Duprey.'

The young man smirked. 'Steele, I have not seen you since you were sent down from Oxford, I declare. Been up to no good, I expect.'

Robert Duprey had been a particular stickler at school, always eager to turn in a pupil who deviated from the rules.

'I've been in the army, Duprey.'

'Indeed? Well, I suppose that makes sense. Keeps you out of trouble, eh?' He laughed the same squeaky laugh he'd had in school.

'You have the right of it.' Devlin picked up the two glasses of lemonade.

'I say, have you tried the orgeat? Dreadful stuff.' Duprey took a sip.

'I beg your pardon,' Devlin said, stepping around him.

Duprey followed him into the ballroom. 'I say, who is that creature seated with Lady Sefton? She is perfection.'

'My brother's wife.' Devlin strode away. He served the ladies their lemonade and idly surveyed the room.

Duprey sauntered over to converse with a young lady dressed in a pale yellow gown. Devlin watched her as she spoke to his old schoolmate. She seemed familiar to him, the way she moved, the expression on her face. She had brown hair, facial features of no distinction, a passable figure. There was no reason he should recall an acquaintance with her.

Devlin walked back to Duprey and stood at his side.

'I did not mean to leave you so abruptly, Duprey,' he lied. 'I thought you meant to follow.'

Duprey gave a snorting laugh. 'I say, I would have appreciated a presentation to that exquisite angel; that is, before I knew who she was.'

The young lady attended this conversation composedly, pale blue eyes resting on each speaker.

Devlin favoured her with a smile, and received one in return. 'Perhaps you would present me…?'

Duprey clapped the heel of his hand on his forehead. 'Oh, indeed.' The man waved toward the young lady. 'My sister, Miss Emily Duprey. Or I should say, Miss Duprey. Our other sister finally legshackled some viscount a year or so ago. Piles of blunt. Emily, Lord Devlin Steele.'

'Miss Duprey.' He bowed to her.

'Lord Devlin,' she murmured through downcast lashes.

Miss Duprey was at least in her twentieth year, Devlin guessed. Perhaps if she had seen one or two unsuccessful Seasons, she might welcome an offer such as his with pragmatism.

'Do you enjoy yourself this evening, Miss Duprey?' he asked.

'Oh, yes, indeed,' she replied. 'Almack's is always agreeable, don't you think?'

'I have not had the pleasure of attending before this night.' He smiled at her, sure now he'd not met her before.

Her brother piped up, 'Steele was at Oxford with me, Em. That is, until he was sent down and joined the army.'

Leave it to Duprey to place him in a negative light. The lady's countenance remained complacent, however, so hopefully his less-than-pristine past would not disfavour him in her eyes. Devlin secured the next waltz with Miss Duprey and took his leave of her.

When he presented himself to Miss Duprey for the dance, her mother took far more interest in him than the daughter had, but the dance was pleasant enough. They made predictable conversation. Devlin knew Duprey stood to inherit a barony, not a lofty title. He knew little else about the family. If they had married one daughter well enough, there might not be a need to seek a title for the other.

The rest of the night dragged on. Devlin was surprised to see the Diamond, Miss Reynolds, eyeing him curiously. Perhaps she had not yet heard he was a younger son. Everyone else seemed to know his situation and fortune, accurate to within a pound. Devlin ran into a couple of acquaintances, including one fellow officer he had known slightly when in Spain. He supposed the few officers left alive would be, like he, searching for a wife. There was little else for a former soldier to do.

When Serena had finally indicated that they might leave without disgrace, Devlin was grateful. As they waited for their carriage, Devlin found himself standing next to the Diamond. Serena, acquainted with the aunt who chaperoned Miss Reynolds, made the introductions.

'You did not seek a dance with me, Lord Devlin,' the Diamond said, while her aunt and Serena chatted together.

'I am afraid I was warned that the competition would be too stiff,' he replied.

She laughed and grinned conspiratorially. 'A dance with any gentleman serves to cause worry to those truly in the running.'

Her carriage arrived and he bid her goodnight.

When he and Serena finally were seated in her carriage, Devlin breathed a sigh of relief.

Serena glanced at him warily. She hesitated before speaking. 'I hope the evening was to your liking.'

He gave a sardonic smile. 'It was up to my expectations.'

'You did well,' she faltered. 'You danced many dances.'

'I did indeed.' He crossed his arms over his chest and retreated into his own thoughts of the evening, thoughts he would not dare speak aloud to Serena. How boring the evening had been. And how he hated himself for performing his expected role, when he would have rather been with Madeleine.

Serena glanced at Devlin, sitting silent and sullen next to her in the carriage. She had detested this evening, having agreed to accompany her husband's brother only because her husband wished it. She could not help but think of the beautiful young woman Devlin had brought to their house and how Devlin had gazed at that beauty throughout the evening. Miss England seemed perfectly suitable to Serena. She was polite and well mannered and obviously educated. Surely those things would make her suitable? What did it matter if she had come from trade or something equally as shameful?

Serena wished she could discuss the matter with her husband, but she dared not. He had been in such a temper about his brother, she might aggravate the situation if she interfered. Besides, she never interfered with her husband's affairs. She never even knew what they were.

Ned would not understand if she talked with him of her conviction that Devlin loved this mere girl whom he had kept secret for so long. Ned should make Devlin marry the girl. Surely it would not be too scandalous for the family for a younger son to marry a mistress who had already borne him a child? Why did Ned not consider it Devlin's duty to marry Miss England?

She feared she knew the answer to that question. Ned still wished to adopt the child. Of course that was the reason. He still hoped to convince Miss England to give him her little daughter, because his wife could not bear a child of his own.

Tears welled up in Serena's eyes. Sniffing the tears away, she fussed in her reticule to find her handkerchief.

Devlin turned, looking concerned. 'What is wrong, sister?'

'Nothing,' she mumbled.

'Fustian,' he said. 'Tell me what is upsetting you.'

He put his arm around her and leaned her against his shoulder. The comfort almost opened the floodgates, but Serena refused to give in to the impulse to weep.

'I...' She searched for something to say, something other than the real reason for her tears. 'I...I cannot like this search of yours for a wife. Your heart is engaged elsewhere, I am convinced. It...it seems dishonourable.'

He stiffened. 'I have no other choice. I need to support her and the child. How else may I do that? Your husband controls my money, so I must do as he bids.'

'I still cannot like it,' she murmured.

'I cannot like it either.' He gave her arm a fond squeeze. 'I promise you I will be honourable to whomever I marry, Serena.'

'Oh, Devlin!' she sighed.

The carriage pulled up to the Marquess's town house. Devlin hopped out and turned to assist Serena.

He walked her to her door. 'Thank you, sister, for accompanying me. I could not have endured this evening without you.'

Serena did not know what to say in return. She knew she would attend another such evening if Ned required her to do so, but she felt sick at being a part of something that boded so ill for everyone.

Devlin stepped into the hall with her and gave her a quick peck on the cheek before leaving. As Serena turned to the stairs, she saw Ned staring down at her. Her heart quickened. He had waited for her! She hurried up the stairs, his eyes watching her every step. As she neared the top, he turned and walked into his bedchamber, shutting the door loudly behind him.

When Devlin returned to his apartments, Madeleine was sitting on the stairs, hugging her knees.

'I waited for you,' she said.

He gathered her into his arms with the overwhelming feeling that he had arrived home where he belonged.

She drew him into his room. 'Tell me of Almack's.'

He kicked off his shoes and unbuttoned his coat. She helped him remove it.

'I shall play valet again,' she said. 'But, please, tell me of Almack's. Was it beautiful? Tell me of its decorations.'

He tried to remember enough to answer her questions. 'It was plain. Indeed, I cannot recall that there were any decorations to speak of.'

Madeleine gave him a sceptical look as she untied his neckcloth. He must be joking with her. She recalled her sisters rhapsodising about the day they would attend Almack's. At the time, she thought it silly, but she'd always taken for granted that her future would include visits to 'the seventh heaven'.

'Do be serious, Devlin. I truly wish to know of it.'

He exercised his neck, free of its confining collar. 'I speak the truth. The assembly rooms were plain, nothing to signify. Seating around the edge. Plenty of space for dancing.'

She sighed, exasperated. 'Very well. Tell me of the dresses. What did the ladies wear? Were the dresses beautiful?'

He sat on the edge of his bed and removed his stockings. 'The dresses were of light colours, mostly. Lots of white.'

'Well, of course.'

She thought about the young ladies in dresses of white or pale pinks, yellows, and blues. Privileged, protected, caring only for the clothes they wore, the parties they were to attend, the prospective husbands they were to meet. Had he met a young lady there this night? Had he been attracted by her beauty and poise? Her unblemished reputation? It did not bear thinking of.

She hung his coat and picked up the scattering of clothes he had left on the floor. As she turned back to him, he was pulling his white linen shirt over his head, leaving his chest bare. She must become accustomed to the thrill of seeing him so, his muscles defined, the hair of his chest an inviting shadow.

She must also become accustomed to the idea that another woman would claim the privilege of running her hands up that expanse of male beauty. She brushed his jacket. 'Tell me of the music, then. Was it wonderful?'

He stood, barefoot, bare-chested, clad only in his knee breeches. 'The music? The orchestra played dance music. You know, country dances, waltzes and such.' He walked to her, placing his hand on her shoulder.

'Waltzes?' The scandalous dance in which ladies and gentlemen touched each other. Had he touched one of Almack's elegant ladies in a waltz? She began to regret her curiosity of this night. 'I suppose you danced the waltz?'

'Indeed,' he murmured, turning her around. She refused to look at him. 'It is now accepted at Almack's. Have you not had the pleasure of dancing the waltz?'

'My duties at Lord Farley's did not include waltzing.'

He lifted her chin so that she was forced to see his eyes in the candlelight. He placed her hand on his shoulder and took her other hand in his. 'I shall show you the steps.'

He counted out the steps. Back step, side step, together. Forward, side, together. His hand at her back guided her as he performed the steps slowly, gradually increasing the pace. Back, side, together. Forward, side, together.

Soon they were swirling around the room, and Madeleine was swept up in the dance and the pleasure of being in his arms. He hummed the music. Bump, bump, bump. Da, da, da. She laughed at how silly he sounded, and he continued louder, smiling at her.

As they twirled to the music he made, he drew her flush against his chest. With only her thin nightdress between them, she felt as well as heard his resonant voice. Her hand moved to his neck, her fingers into his hair. The music stopped when his mouth found hers and a new tune commenced, a new rhythm that carried them into his bed and relieved them of the remainder of their clothing.

This was a dance she still feared a little, but so much more did she crave it. His hands on her flesh. His tongue dancing with hers. The excitation when he entered her. The transport when her pleasure exploded.

The climax of the dance left her panting.

'That is not precisely as the waltz is done at Almack's,' he said.

She smiled. For the moment, she would pretend she was his exclusive partner in this waltz, and would content herself with that fact. 'It is a lovely dance,' she said.

Chapter Fifteen

As time progressed, Madeleine's days were spent in glorious domesticity. She could almost pretend she, Devlin and Linette were a family. She and Devlin shopped together, purchasing various sundries they'd previously done without, finding treats to bring home to Linette. They took Linette to the park. They sat in quietly in the parlour, Devlin playing with Linette and her wooden horse, Madeleine stitching laboriously. Soon, however, it became necessary for Devlin to make afternoon calls, shortening the illusion. Every evening was taken up with some splendid event. This night it was the Elbingtons' Ball, purported to be the event of the Season. Invitations were highly prized.

Madeleine helped Devlin dress as she'd done each night he left her in search of a woman to marry.

As he tried tying his neckcloth for the third time, he said, 'Maddy, we must talk of the future.'

She could not think of the future. Her mind was too filled with the present, with the idea that another woman would be in his arms tonight, dancing the waltz, perhaps planning a different future with him.

He went on, 'I think the country, don't you? A place for you to have a horse, and Linette a pony…'

'Whatever you decide, Devlin.'

What did it matter, after all, when another woman would spend both days and nights with him?

Madeleine smoothed the lapels of his coat and stood back to survey her handiwork. He looked dazzlingly handsome in his black coat, snowy white breeches and linens. How could any woman resist him? She kissed him goodbye and sent him off, pretending good humour, and returned to sew by candle-light, feeling empty inside.

When Devlin entered Lady Elbington's ball, the noise and crush was as unwelcome as the memories of battle. Indeed, settings like this one, with its noise, bustle, and discreet forms of indiscretion, were now the only places unwanted memories of battle threatened to intrude. Madeleine had chased them away from other parts of his life.

Hearing the faint echo of French cannonade in the rumbling of the voices, Devlin scanned the room. Miss Reynolds gave him a meaningful look from the far corner. He made his way to her side, where two gentlemen half in their cups paid court to her, undoubtedly drawn by her fair hair and skin, and the décolletage of her gauzy lime gown.

Amanda Reynolds and Devlin had developed an under-standing of a peculiar sort. Neither had any particular interest in the other, but each found the other to be of use. Miss Reynolds used Devlin when she needed to rid herself of the unwanted attentions of other men, or to make her chosen suitor jealous. Devlin used Miss Reynolds as protection from young ladies who might pin hopes on him. As long at his attention seemed at least partially engaged by the current Diamond, no matchmaking mama fancied her daughter his favourite.

Devlin bowed to her. 'Is this my dance, Miss Reynolds?'

'I do believe so, sir,' she replied. Some poor hapless soul had lost his moment with her. He suspected it was the young buck approaching whose eyes bulged with anger.

As they began the set, she thanked him. 'I do not know when I was in such need of rescue.'

Miss Reynolds delighted in the dance as she appeared to delight in every activity associated with courtship. When the set ended, Devlin caught the eye of the Earl of Greythorne, the gentleman Miss Reynolds hoped to bring up to scratch. Greythorne looked daggers at him.

'My rival has arrived,' he said.

Miss Reynolds grinned. 'Looking deliciously jealous. My thanks to you again.'

Devlin delivered Miss Reynolds to a group of her friends and made his way to Miss Duprey, feeling faintly guilty at the pleased expression on Miss Duprey's face as he approached. It would not be a disservice to her to engage her in a loveless marriage, would it?

He bowed to her. 'Good evening, Miss Duprey.'

She smiled shyly. 'Lord Devlin.'

He chatted with her in the inconsequential ways expected—of her health, her family's health, the weather. He engaged her for the supper dance, which happened to be a waltz. When her next partner came, he withdrew.

Devlin went in search of Serena, who he knew would be seated among the dowagers. Ned had taken to accompanying Serena and Devlin to the various entertainments. Very unusual of him, Devlin gathered from Serena. Ned spent little time in the card room, instead staying within sight of his wife, though dancing rarely with her. Devlin presumed the main purpose of Ned's presence was to keep watch over his younger brother, but it was not well done of Ned to so ignore his wife.

Devlin found Serena and sat beside her.

She cast him a look that barely disguised her concern. 'You dance often with Miss Reynolds.'

'We have become friends of a strange sort,' he replied. 'She relishes all this nonsense and I—' He was about to say that he detested it, but caught himself in time. 'Worry not, sister, there is nothing in it.'

While he tried to decide which of the young ladies present would be safe to dance with, Serena's gaze never left the couples performing the set. A wistful expression came across her face. Curse his brother for neglecting her.

'Are you engaged for the next dance, Serena? I would be honoured, if you are not.' The music had stopped. He stood and extended his hand to her.

'Devlin, you need not waste your time dancing with me,' Serena said.

'Indeed,' came a cold voice behind him, 'you ought to look to the unmarried ladies, not the married ones.' Ned moved beside Serena. The look he gave Devlin was stony at best. 'I will dance with my wife.'

'Ned.' Devlin forced a cheerful tone to his voice. 'What a surprise to see you on this side of the room. I all but forgot you were here.'

His brother glared.

'Serena, I leave you to your husband.' Devlin bowed and walked away.

The Marquess had lately become damnably ill-humoured. Steady Ned had become a man of erratic moods. No telling when he might erupt. Those days when Devlin could pour all his troubles into his brother's willing ear had vanished. Devlin could not even bear to ride to these evening events in Ned's carriage. Accompanying the silent Marquess and Marchioness was too unpleasant by half.

What had so changed this brother he idolised, Devlin could not understand.

He collected Miss Duprey for the supper dance. She kept her eyes demurely downcast except when he spoke to her. Her blue eyes were her best feature, Devlin thought. If he were hard pressed to describe her, he could say only that the rest of her was unremarkable. Conversation with her was easy enough, though no different than with the other young ladies he partnered. He listened with half an ear.

'Do you go to Vauxhall Gardens this Wednesday, Lord Devlin? My mother says we do not, but others have talked of it.'

Vauxhall. Good God, why had he not thought of it before? He could never take Madeleine to Covent Garden or to Almack's, but he could take her to Vauxhall! With the black cloth masks so common at Vauxhall Gardens, they could dance under the lights and watch the illuminations. They could stroll along the hedged paths or seek shelter in one of the grottoes. He quickened his step with happy anticipation.

'Do you go to Vauxhall, then?' she asked again.

He had almost forgotten her presence, even though he held her in the dance. 'I had not planned to go,' he said. But he began planning an excursion now.

He escorted Miss Duprey into the supper room and seated her at a table with some friends of her acquaintance. He offered to fill her plate, to which she pleasantly agreed.

Making his way through the crush around the sideboard, he heard a voice hail him.

'Steele?'

Devlin turned and saw a ghost, a most welcome ghost. He'd last seen Christian Ramsford struck down on the battlefield and had mourned his loss, but this was truly Ramsford, walking toward him.

'Ram,' he rasped, at first grasping the man's hand in greeting, then ignoring all propriety and embracing him in a hearty hug. 'Ram, I thought you dead.'

Ramsford gave an ironic smile, but his eyes glistened as Devlin supposed his own did. 'I thought you were long since put to bed with a shovel, as well. So, I suppose all those bottles of brandy consumed in your memory were for naught.'

'Damn, brandy's never a waste.' Devlin took a good look at his friend, outfitted in a superbly fitting coat of black superfine. Though the penniless son of a country vicar, Ramsford's size and presence always had commanded attention.

'What the devil are you doing here?' Devlin asked. A London ball was the last place he expected to find Christian Ramsford.

'Both my uncle and my cousin had the misfortune to drop dead.' Ramsford's voice was almost mournful. 'My father inherited.'

'Good God, Ram. You are heir to an earldom.' Devlin grinned at him.

His friend shrugged. 'I am escorting one of my sisters, and am also directed to consider the succession in my family line.'

'Come, I must select some food.' Devlin grabbed Ramsford's arm and pulled him into the throng around the food. Ram took a glass of champagne off a tray, downed it, and took another.

'You will sit at my table. I insist.'

Ramsford shrugged again, but followed him to the table where Miss Duprey sat. Devlin introduced him to the young people who had joined her, noticing the curious glances from the ladies present. Devlin was suddenly impatient to be rid of all of them for the sole company of his old friend.

Finally he was able to deliver Miss Duprey back to the ballroom. He drew Ramsford aside again. They stood near the open windows where the night breeze cooled the room and spoke of the war.

Amanda Reynolds, temporarily detached from Greythorne's grasp, boldly approached. She entwined her arm in Devlin's. 'You have all but deserted me this evening, sir.'

Devlin knew he was being used again. Miss Reynolds's true concern was the presence of a new gentleman, whose admiration she had not yet procured.

'Doing it up too brown, my lady,' Devlin said.

He introduced Amanda to Ram and realised the once-penniless vicar's son had the greater chance with her. He left them conversing in a strained manner until a red-faced Greythorne came to collect her. Before she was too many steps away, she turned, giving Ramsford a backward glance.

Devlin collected Miss Duprey for his second dance. Knowing that two dances was the limit propriety would allow, he then felt free to make his escape. After saying his goodbyes to the hostess and Serena, and ignoring his brother, he left the ball with Ramsford.

The two men found a comfortable tavern near St James's and spent several hours there toasting comrades they would never see again. The tavern, smelling of hops, gin and male sweat, was nothing like ones he and Ram frequented in Spain, but the camaraderie was identical. Devlin had missed it acutely.

When the night was well advanced, they finally emerged into the chill night. Devlin embraced his friend. The drink had turned him maudlin, but he was too foxed to feel embarrassed. He stumbled his way home, his baritone voice singing one of the raucous ditties still echoing from the tavern.

Near his residence, a man stepped in front of him. 'Good evening, Steele. I see you've had an entertaining evening.'

Devlin squinted, bringing the figure into focus under the lamplight. Farley.

'Bugger off.' Devlin shoved him aside, almost losing his balance. He was directly across the street from his apartments. It penetrated Devlin's foggy mind that Farley must know where he lived, that he was lurking in this neighbourhood for that very reason.

'Bugger off,' he said again, staggering as he started off across the street.

A whim had sent Lord Farley to spy on Steele this cool, mist-covered night, a whim and the frustration of an empty bed. The gaming hell's full coffers were not satisfaction enough.

Farley had known for weeks where Steele had taken Madeleine to live, had made it his business to know. Indeed, he knew all about Steele, his falling-out with his brother, his need for money, his search for a wife. The time was ripe to get Madeleine back.

Lord Farley gave one final glance toward the retreating figure of Devlin Steele and disappeared in the growing mist.

Chapter Sixteen

Madeleine was startled awake by a slamming door and pounding feet on the stairs. She'd dozed off while wrapped in a blanket on the windowseat of Devlin's room, where she worriedly waited for him. He'd never been so late before. He burst in the room, swaying as he swung around, looking for her.

She shot up in alarm, dropping the blanket. 'What is it, Devlin? What has happened?'

He clutched at her, pushing her nightdress half off her shoulder. His breath smelled foul with drink.

'Maddy.' His voice rose in urgency, but his words slurred. 'Promise me never to go outside unaccompanied.'

'I do not, unless for a little walk with Linette.' She pulled away from him. She had never seen him this way.

'No more. Promise me!' He shook her by the shoulders.

Why treat her in this manner? He was like a stranger. 'What has happened?'

He let go of her and rubbed his forehead. 'Nothing has happened. Nothing at all. But you will obey me in this. You will do as I say.'

Madeleine folded her arms across her chest, massaging sore shoulders. 'You are foxed.'

He glared at her. 'I am not foxed.' He took a step toward her, touching the wall for balance. 'Merely a bit disguised.'

She edged away from him. 'I have no wish to engage in a conversation with you when you are foxed.'

'Oh, stubble it, Maddy, and get into bed.'

She straightened. 'I will not.'

He held his hand against the wall and looked as if he would slip to the floor at any moment. 'I said get into bed. I cannot stand up much longer.'

Having enough of his behaviour, she marched past him, avoiding his attempt to grab at her. 'I will sleep in my own bed this night.' Reminding herself in time that slamming the door might wake Linette, she closed it quietly behind her.

Once in her own room, she leaned against the post of her bed, squeezing her eyes shut. She must remind herself that men disappoint. It had been foolish to believe Devlin an exception. She crawled into her lonely bed, its linens cool against her skin. His body would not warm her this night.

Devlin woke in his clothes, half sprawled across the bed, a whole arsenal of French cannon pounding in his head. Rain darkened the sky and he had no idea of the time of day. He sat up, and the room started to spin. As he waited for it to come to a stop, he tried to stop his thoughts from spinning, as well. What the devil had happened last night?

He remembered Ram. He remembered the two of them drinking toast after toast to dead comrades. He remembered shouting at Madeleine, God help him. He could not remember how he got home.

Devlin gingerly put his feet on the floor and took careful steps over to the wash basin. He splashed water on his face and rinsed out the foul taste in his mouth. He poured the pitcher of water over his pounding head. Still dripping, he glanced about the room.

He could not recall telling Madeleine about meeting Ram. He'd shouted at her, though. Why?

Devlin fumbled through his trunk for a worn pair of trousers and an old shirt. He flopped into a chair and tried to pull on his clothing. His head spun around like a child's toy top.

He sat bolt upright. Good God! He had got drunk and shouted at Madeleine. What else had he done?

As he took careful steps into the kitchen, he resolved to set about correcting his wrongs. Still struggling to recall what wrongs he needed to correct, he warmed himself in front of the fire. The kettle was hot and he brewed himself some tea, wondering where the others were.

Where Madeleine was.

Bart entered the room and shot Devlin a disapproving look.

Devlin waved his hand. 'I know. I know. I've been a wastrel. A miscreant. A scapegrace.'

Bart pursed his lips. 'Well, you've upset the lass.'

Devlin gaped at Bart. 'I did something to upset Sophie?'

'Not Sophie,' Bart huffed. 'Miss Madeleine.'

Devlin groaned. 'You do not know what I did to upset her, do you? I confess I remember little of it.'

Bart cut a piece of bread and handed it to Devlin, who accepted it warily, taking a cautious nibble. 'The lass did not tell me the whole, but I collect you were drunk as an emperor.'

Devlin chewed a piece of crust. 'Indeed.'

Bart opened his mouth. Devlin stopped him. 'Before you jump down my throat, I was with Ram.'

'Captain Ramsford?' Bart's expression changed to surprise. 'He is alive?'

'Alive and very well. I thought him dead, too. I saw him fall…that day.' He lifted his mug of tea and his hand shook.

'I'll be damned.'

'We left the ball together and found a friendly tavern.' He paused, taking a sip of tea, and closing his eyes. 'There were many toasts to be made.'

'By God, I'll drink to the fellow myself.' Bart opened a cabinet and removed a bottle. He poured a generous supply in a glass for himself and a dollop in Devlin's cup.

'To Captain Ramsford.' Bart raised his glass.

Devlin clinked his cup against Bart's glass.

Right at that moment, Madeleine walked into the room. She stared directly at the bottle on the table and then to the two men. Bart quickly drained the contents of his glass and hastily exited. Silently, Madeleine walked over to the kettle.

'There is tea brewed in the pot,' Devlin told her.

Without a word, Madeleine put a half-teaspoon of sugar and a mere drop of cream into her cup and poured the tea.

As she turned to leave, Devlin put a hand on her arm. 'Stay a moment, Maddy.'

She sat, her face expressionless, her posture rigid.

Devlin's stomach roiled and he took a bite of the bread, hoping to quiet it. He gave up the idea of telling her about Ram. It would sound like excuse-making. He needed some explanation, however, but what to say when the events were obscure to him? Worse, he had this awful feeling of foreboding.

'I remember little of last night, except that I behaved badly toward you.' He lifted her chin with his finger.

She swatted it away.

'I apologise, Maddy. I am sorry.'

Madeleine tried to avoid his intent expression. It conveyed a sincerity she could not quite believe. 'Apology comes easy when you do not know what it is for.'

He took her hand and stroked it, holding it in his grip when she would have pulled it away. 'I apologise for being drunk and for shouting at you. That much I do remember.'

She wished he would not touch her. His green eyes reflected the fire in the stove, his hair was tousled, and he had not yet donned his waistcoat and coat.

'Maddy,' he murmured, his voice low. His arm drew around her, pulling her close. 'Maddy.' The cotton of his shirt was cool against her skin, but a furnace seemed to burn inside her. His lips hovered over her ear, his warm breath tickling. 'What injuries did I inflict on you, my love? I wish to make amends.'

How was she supposed to tell him of his ridiculous dictate to be chaperoned, or his abominable order to get in bed, when his lips sent shivers directly to…to that part of her body that craved him? A true lady would not run her hands under his shirt. A true lady would not kiss him back. A true lady would not position herself upon his lap, straddling him, wanting him.

'Deddy!' Linette burst into the room.

Madeleine pushed away, but Devlin would not let her escape. Linette flung herself at Devlin and scrambled into what scant space was left on his lap.

'Deddy!' she shouted directly in his ear.

He let go of Madeleine and grabbed his head.

Madeleine chuckled. 'Linette, do not scream so. Deddy has the headache.'

'Poor Deddy,' Linette crooned, only a fraction lower. 'I will kiss it and make it aaallll better.'

Linette pulled down Devlin's head, squeezed it between her chubby little hands, and gave him a big smack of a kiss right on his crown.

'Dam— Dash it all.'

As he lifted his head and Linette beamed at her apothecary skills, Madeleine laughed.

He managed a wan smile. 'I think I shall be right and tight now, if I may only finish my tea.'

Linette stood on his lap to reach the mug. Madeleine tried not to laugh at his pained expression. Linette handed Devlin the mug. 'You slept all day,' she scolded, settling in his lap.

'I have no idea of the time.' He glanced at Madeleine.

'Near three o'clock,' she said.

'Da— Dash it. I have an engagement.'

Madeleine's smile faded. A peculiar feeling settled in her stomach. 'Do you need any assistance dressing?' Her words sounded stiff, even to her.

He gave her a pained expression. 'I can manage, I think.'

'I...I don't mind helping.'

'I want to help!' Linette jumped up and down in his lap.

'Linette!' He grabbed the child. 'Stop it!'

She stopped. Fat tears gathered in her wide blue eyes. Her lower lip trembled. Devlin, his head still pounding like a hammer to an anvil, felt like a cad.

He wiped a trickle of a tear from her cheek. 'Don't cry, Lady Lin. Jumping on me hurt me a little, you see.'

She sniffled.

He shot a look of appeal to Madeleine, who simply stared at him.

'No more crying now,' he said to Linette in a soft voice. He brushed the little girl's hair with his fingers.

Madeleine spun around and ran out of the room.

A few minutes later, Devlin hurried out of the house, barely pausing to close the door behind him. Soon after, Bart and Sophie took Linette to purchase beefsteak pies and sweetbreads for supper. Madeleine was left with nothing but her thoughts.

She went to the kitchen and filled a bucket from the pump. On her knees she attacked the floor, rubbing the hard bar of lye soap on the brush and scrubbing the wood, rinsing it with wet rags. She'd watched Bart do this job and it seemed not too difficult, but the lye soap stung and reddened her hands. She dipped them in the cool water. She considered what delicate white hands the lady Devlin called upon would have, and scrubbed harder.

She could barely help thinking about Devlin's afternoon calls. What clothes did the ladies wear? Were they all as elegant as the Marchioness? Did they smile prettily at him?

Had Devlin selected a lady to marry? He had not said so, but she sensed it was true. He had become quieter, no longer describing the entertainments he attended or the people he encountered.

What did *she* look like, this woman he must have selected? Was she beautiful? Intelligent? Accomplished?

Madeleine pressed the scrub brush down more firmly, the scraping sound drowning out her thoughts. Unbearable thoughts. She attacked the floor as if scrubbing dirt that had accumulated over eons. The apron covering her dress became damp from where she knelt, but at least she was being of some use. The pungent odour of the soap, the smell of the wet wood, the rhythm of scrubbing back and forth, even the sting of the harsh soap, distracted and somehow soothed.

Perhaps this was how people endured lives of drudgery. In any event, she vastly preferred numbing herself with hard labour than willing herself numb from the labour she had once been compelled to endure. Until Devlin rescued her and showed her joy.

Madeleine threw the scrub brush in the pail, splashing water on the floor. She would not think of Devlin. She would think of nothing at all.

A knock sounded at the door, firm and officious. Callers were rare at the house. In fact, the Marquess had been the only one. Madeleine hastily wiped her hands on her apron and rose. Cautiously, she peered from the parlour window and saw familiar matched bays harnessed to the elegant carriage bearing the Heronvale crest. He had come for Linette, after all.

Madeleine quickly stepped back from the window, her hand flying to her mouth and her heart pounding. Perhaps if she stood very still, he would think no one at home and would leave.

The knocker pounded again. She heard a voice. 'There seems to be no one at home, my lady.'

Through the slit in the curtains, Madeleine saw the Marchioness lean out of the carriage.

'I am sure someone is at home, Simms. I saw movement at the window. I shall knock myself.'

The footman descended the steps from the house and assisted the Marchioness out of the carriage. Beautifully dressed in a deep green walking dress, spencer and plumed hat, she seemed to float up to the door.

More knocking. 'Miss England, are you there? Please open the door.'

The Marchioness's behaviour was most improper. Ladies of rank did not knock on doors, nor did they visit this part of town. Only extreme foolishness or some urgent situation would explain it.

Blood drained from Madeleine's face. Devlin!

She ran to the door and flung it open, throat tight with anxiety. The Marchioness's hand was poised to knock again and the delicate blonde gasped with surprise. Madeleine could not speak.

'May…may I come in?' The lady's trembling smile did nothing to allay Madeleine's fears.

She stepped aside for the lady to enter. The Marchioness turned to the footman. 'Thank you, Simms. You may wait with the carriage.'

The footman bowed and, with one eyebrow arched, gave Madeleine an appraising look before retreating.

Madeleine closed the door and faced her visitor. 'Please tell me...has something happened? Is Devlin...?' She could not make herself coherent.

The Marchioness blinked her eyes in confusion. 'Devlin? I have not seen him.'

Madeleine's muscles, all taut for disastrous news, relaxed measurably. 'You have not come to tell me Devlin is hurt?'

The Marchioness blushed. 'No. Indeed not.' She cast down her eyes. 'The matter I have come upon is personal.'

Madeleine nearly laughed in relief. Devlin was not dead, or hurt, or married. She pressed her fingers to her temples, only then realising her hair hung in damp clumps around her face. She tried to smooth the tangled mess.

The Marchioness cleared her throat. 'May I speak to you for a moment?' She glanced toward the parlour.

Madeleine peered at her. 'I will not give up Linette. Devlin promised to make that clear to you.'

The lady blushed again. 'This is not about...I am so sorry... My husband meant no harm to you, I assure you.'

Madeleine regarded her with scepticism. 'He wished to take my child.'

The Marchioness's eyes pleaded. 'He did not realise. I do pray you will forgive him.'

'Forgive him?' Madeleine said, her voice rising. 'I doubt my forgiveness would be worth a farthing to him.'

The lady straightened and gave Madeleine a direct gaze. 'You sorely misjudge my husband, Miss England. He is the best of men. His interest in your child, misguided as it was,

was motivated solely by a desire to please me.' Her voice changed to one of conviction and authority. 'May we retire to the parlour, please?'

Madeleine nodded coolly, though somewhat abashed at her lapse in manners. She led the Marchioness into the small parlour, shabby looking compared to the one in Grosvenor Square.

'Some tea, my lady?' she asked with inbred hospitality.

'That is kind of you,' the Marchioness replied, a slight tremble to her words.

As Madeleine rushed to the kitchen, she glanced at herself in the hallway mirror. She was a fright, her apron wet and dirty where she had knelt. Her hair had escaped from its braid and was a tangle of wayward dark curls.

She set the kettle on the fire in the kitchen and pulled off her apron. The blue cotton day dress she wore would have been presentable had it not been soaked with water. Madeleine measured out the tea and poured the water into the pot. She attempted to rebraid her hair, wishing she had pins to bind it into some sort of submission. She found a few lemon biscuits to add to the fare and hurriedly assembled the tray.

She entered the parlour and placed the tray on the table next to the Marchioness. As Madeleine poured the tea, she noticed the lady twisting her fine lime kid gloves in her smooth, delicate, ivory hands. Madeleine handed her the cup and hid her own beet-red hands in the folds of her skirt.

'How may I be of service to you, ma'am?' Madeleine asked, determined to display good breeding, though not feeling gracious inside. Indeed, this interview was too puzzling by half.

The Marchioness's teacup rattled in its saucer. 'I do wish you would call me Serena.'

'I would not presume, madam.'

The Marchioness looked so disappointed, Madeleine thought the lady might cry. She felt a sudden sympathy.

'Perhaps you ought to tell why you have come,' she said in a soft, inviting tone.

The Marchioness burst into tears. 'I have nowhere else to turn. I do not know what to do.' She rummaged in her reticule and pulled out a white linen handkerchief, edged in elegant lace. She turned away and dabbed at her face.

Madeleine wrinkled her forehead in concern. 'Are you in trouble of some kind?'

The Marchioness shook her head, fair tendrils shaking.

'Is it your husband? Has he hurt you in some way?' Madeleine would not put it past that man to be cold and cruel to his wife, not after his treatment of Devlin and, above all, his eagerness to steal a child.

The Marchioness's head shot up. 'My husband is the best of men. There is no more honourable a man on this earth. He is nothing but good to me, always.' Her face crumbled again. 'It is I who am at fault. I am a poor wife. I cannot please him in the most basic of ways.' She dissolved into tears again.

Madeleine went to her and, crouching next to her chair, took her hand. 'Now, you mustn't cry. Whatever it is, I am sure Devlin can help put it to rights. He will be home shortly.'

The lady's eyes flashed pain. 'No, not Devlin. You.'

'I?'

'There is no one else I can ask. You are the only one I know who can help me.'

Madeleine stared at her in confusion. 'It is not my position to help a lady. I am the lowest of creatures, I assure you. What could I possibly do to help you?'

The Marchioness looked directly into Madeleine's eyes. 'You must teach me how to seduce my husband.'

Chapter Seventeen

Madeleine gaped in disbelief.

The Marchioness twisted her handkerchief. Her words came out in a rush. 'You see, I have been such a failure as a wife. I…I do not know how to give a man pleasure *that way* and my husband…he is very dear to me, you see. He is patient and makes no demands at all, but he cannot bear to bed me.'

Madeleine returned to her chair, collapsing into its cushion.

Tears poured down the Marchioness's cheeks. 'He knows I pine for children, and that is why he sought to adopt your daughter. For me! To make me happy. A wretch such as myself who cannot please him!'

Madeleine took a fortifying sip of tea.

The Marchioness sniffled, even that managing to sound ladylike. 'I thought perhaps if I had lessons in lovemaking, I could learn how to please him. I would be a willing pupil. So, you see, I thought of you.'

Madeleine's breath quickened. The Marchioness knew of her past? Perhaps the Marquess had discovered her identity. Had Devlin told him? Her cheeks burned in mortification. Surely neither of them would have spoken of it to this lady.

'Me? I know naught of love between a man and his wife.' Madeleine's voice was tight.

The Marchioness twisted her hands nervously. 'Not *marital* love, exactly. The other kind.'

Madeleine pretended calm as she took another sip of tea.

The lady continued. 'You see, it is clear Devlin is besotted with you. It fairly took my breath away, the manner in which he looked upon you that awful night. You are not married, so the attachment must be of another kind.' Her voice turned low and tentative. 'At least that is what I thought.'

Devlin besotted with her?

The Marchioness continued, 'Please help me, Miss England…Madeleine. Where else might I turn? I have not been exposed… That is, I have led so sheltered a life. I am not acquainted with anyone else who might…'

Madeleine understood. Only an improper female could speak of such matters. Ladies of the *ton* would not sip tea while chatting about the most effective way to arouse a man. Madeleine's stomach clenched with the memory of how she had learned such lessons. Farley had taken her step by step through what she must do to bring a man to pleasure. Over and over. Again and again. She had learned where to touch, what to say. Such lessons should never soil the ears of so delicate a lady.

She glanced at the Marchioness, who regarded her with a hopeful, pleading expression. Madeleine was unconvinced that the fault of the lovemaking rested upon this creature's shoulders. The Marquess showed no warmth.

She bit her lip. The Marquess had been kind and gentle to Linette, she remembered. Perhaps there was a bit of his brother in him.

She sighed. 'Very well, my lady. I shall try to help you.'

The lady's smile was beatific. 'Please call me Serena.'

Madeleine laughed in defeat. 'Serena, then.' If she were about to provide sexual lessons to a Marchioness, she might as well be thoroughly improper and use the lady's given name. 'Shall we go above stairs? I do not think I can discuss such matters in the parlour.'

Serena sprang to her feet.

Madeleine brought her into the bedroom she shared with Linette. Serena glanced around the room, her eyes resting on the child's bed. 'Is this where you and Devlin…?'

'My goodness, no!' Madeleine replied. 'This is the room I share with Linette…sometimes.' She added, 'Do you wish to see Devlin's room?'

'Yes.' Serena nodded firmly.

Madeleine groaned inwardly. How much more improper could they be? She opened the connecting door and they walked through.

Devlin's room looked as if a whirlwind had been trapped inside its walls. Madeleine had forgotten she had not set foot in his room since stalking out the previous night. She had not straightened the linens, nor picked up his clothes.

Serena's eyes grew wide with wonder. Her gaze fixated on the tangle of sheets and blankets on the bed.

'Let us return to the other room,' Madeleine said firmly, ushering her back through the door.

Serena spoke excitedly. 'When I was young, my bosom bows and I would sit upon my bed for a comfortable coze. Shall we do the same?' The fine lady planted herself cross-legged upon the bed. She pulled off her hat and spencer, placing them on the side table. Madeleine had no choice but to join her.

Madeleine faced Serena's bright, eager countenance. Serena looked as youthful as she must have been with those bosom bows.

Where to begin?

'Have you and the Marquess ever had…um…have you bedded?'

Serena leaned forward with enthusiasm. 'Oh, yes, indeed, but I fear I did something wrong, because it was so very *painful* the first time, and somewhat so every other time. My husband obliged by being very quick about it, so as to not distress me overmuch.'

So the Marchioness had not experienced the pleasure of lovemaking. Madeleine felt sorry for her. But was a lady supposed to experience the kind of frank pleasure she knew with Devlin?

Serena stammered. 'I…I am not sure I can explain all that happened. I was so nervous, you see.'

'That is of no consequence,' Madeleine said hurriedly. She had no desire to hear the details of the Marquess and Marchioness in bed. 'I must think a moment where to begin.'

She glanced at Serena, feeling the wiser, though the lady was at least ten years older. Madeleine had vastly more experience, but what did she truly know of love between a husband and wife? Farley had not taught her about that kind of love.

She closed her eyes and thought of Devlin. He had shown her all she would ever know of love. She set her chin firmly and began. 'I think you will find that lovemaking is very easy. Composed of easy parts.'

After all, it took a mere glance from Devlin to set Madeleine's senses aflame.

'First,' she said, 'you must look at your husband. Make sure he knows you are doing so. No glancing away, until you are certain he has felt your eyes upon him.'

'I shall look at my husband,' Serena repeated.

What else made the blood thunder through Madeleine's veins? When Devlin touched her.

'Next, you must find reasons to touch him,' she said in an

authoritative tone. 'Take imaginary fluff off his clothing. Brush his hand with yours. Arrange his hair with your fingers. Just touch him in ordinary ways.'

Serena's eyes glittered excitedly. 'What does that do?'

What it did for Madeleine. 'His body will come alive to you.'

Serena nodded. 'What else?'

'Well, you must contrive to get in bed with him.' Perhaps that was too obvious.

Serena's expression turned bleak. 'How can I do that?'

Goodness, Madeleine had forgotten that Devlin had resisted her initial attempts at seduction. Her cheeks grew hot as she recalled how she'd thrown herself at him. What had finally induced him to accept her?

His nightmare of Waterloo. 'You might pretend to have a bad dream. Would he come to you if you called out?'

Serena frowned. 'I doubt he would hear me.'

'Then you must go to his room and wake him. Seek his comfort. He would wish to comfort you, would he not?'

'Perhaps.' She sounded uncertain.

'Of course he would!' At least Madeleine hoped so. She had not been able resist Devlin's need for comfort. 'You must insist on not being alone. You must contrive to stay in his bed.'

Her pupil nodded resolutely. 'Then what?'

Then let nature dictate the next course, unless the Marquess and Marchioness had somehow thwarted nature. This was becoming absurd. 'You must cling to him.'

Tears formed in Serena's eyes. 'Will he allow me to?'

Madeleine took a deep breath. The Marchioness was truly an innocent. What man would refuse such a creature? Had any man ever refused to touch The Mysterious Miss M? Serena was so much more beautiful. 'You must ask him to hold you, then. He will not refuse, believe me.'

'What then?'

What happens after should need no lesson, if they both allowed what comes naturally to man and woman.

Madeleine's pupil needed very explicit instructions. 'If you feel the time is right, you remove your clothes, remove his clothes, and make love to him.'

'How?' She gave an anguished cry.

There was a limit to how much she would discuss. 'Serena, merely touch him all over. Anywhere. Kiss him. It will suffice, believe me.'

'What if it does not?' Serena's lip trembled.

'Then, what have you lost? You will have tried, after all. Would you wish to go on with the rest of your life, thinking you might have had happiness if you had only seized the chance?'

Unlike Madeleine, Serena had every reason to expect happiness, but Madeleine pushed that thought away.

Serena set her jaw firmly and sat up ramrod straight. The lady had made her decision. Madeleine smiled inwardly. Finally she felt useful.

Devlin had endured his promised calls to Miss Duprey and Miss Reynolds, mainly because he had hit upon the idea of bringing Ram with him. He still felt like weeping with gratitude to have found his friend left alive.

Ram's presence this day prevented Devlin from feeling too much obligation toward Miss Duprey, and, since Ram and Amanda Reynolds had taken such a dislike to each other, the sparks flying between the two of them diverted Devlin from his sour stomach and still-aching head.

He begged off Ram's invitation to pass more time in the tavern and made for home. As he neared his apartments, he tried to recall what had disturbed him so the previous night. Some ominous presence he could not grab hold of. He glanced toward his building. His brother's carriage was pulled up to the front.

Devlin broke into a run. What was Ned doing here? Why would his brother visit? To take Linette?

'What goes on here?' he snarled to the coachman.

The man looked puzzled. 'I've walked the horses, m'lord.'

Devlin jumped on to the side of the carriage and peered inside, ready to confront his brother.

The carriage was empty. 'Where are they?' he demanded.

The footman pointed to the house.

Devlin bounded into the house and found the parlour empty. The kitchen floor was dotted with puddles, a bucket and scrub brush lying in the middle of the room. Voices sounded above him.

Giggles?

He tore up the stairs. 'Ned! Ned! Where are you? By God, if I find you…'

He flung open the door to Linette's room.

Two female heads popped up in surprise.

'What the devil…?'

Madeleine and Serena sat on the bed, looking like two little girls caught in mischief.

'Hello, Devlin,' said Serena, who broke into giggles.

He scowled. 'Where the devil is Ned?'

'Ned?' Serena gave him a puzzled look. 'At White's, I should think.'

'Then where the devil is Linette?' Women. They made no sense.

'Linette went with Bart and Sophie to purchase some meat pies for supper. I suspect they may have also made a stop at the confectioners,' Madeleine said, barely concealing mirth.

Devlin put his hand up for her to stop talking. He rubbed his brow. 'Then Ned did not take Linette?'

'No, indeed!' a shocked Serena said. 'How absurd.'

'How could you think such a thing?' Madeleine scolded.

Serena bussed Madeleine's cheek. 'I think perhaps I should take my leave.'

Madeleine looked regretful. She reached for Serena's hat and helped Serena place it becomingly on her head. Then she assisted her into her spencer. The two smiled at each other.

'Would you mind telling me what the devil is going on?' Devlin said.

'Oh, Serena is leaving.' Madeleine smiled.

'I surmised that.' He touched his forehead. 'Why the devil is she here?'

Madeleine gave him an impatient glance. 'Devlin, I do wish you would not swear.'

'Damnation, tell me why my sister-in-law is visiting my... is visiting here.'

Serena swept over to him and gave his arm an affectionate squeeze. 'A mere afternoon call.'

He gave her a sceptical look. The two women walked down the stairs, arm in arm, chatting companionably. Madeleine rushed ahead to the parlour to gather Serena's gloves and reticule. Serena gave her a big hug, and Devlin thought he heard Madeleine whisper, 'Good luck.'

Why the devil was Maddy wishing Serena good luck?

Madeleine stood at the open door as the footman assisted Serena into the carriage. Serena waved out the window. Madeleine watched for several minutes after Serena had gone out of sight.

'She's left, Maddy.'

'I know,' Madeleine said in a dreamy tone. 'I was placing her in memory.'

The Marquess sipped his sherry and gazed absently out the window as he waited for his wife to appear for dinner. His heart was sick with grief, but he promised he would reveal nothing. He had seen a glimpse of the Heronvale carriage on St James's Street, near Devlin's residence. He had casually checked with Jem to see if Devlin had the use of it, but, as he feared, it had been Serena.

He gulped the remainder of his sherry. His wife having an affair with his brother? How much more painful could it be? Damn Devlin! Pretending to court one young lady while setting up housekeeping with another while dallying with his brother's wife. Ned squeezed the crystal wineglass, shattering it in his hand as Serena entered the room.

'Oh, my! What happened?' She ran over to him, behaving as if she cared that he bled.

'It is a trifle,' he said, wrapping his finger with his handkerchief. He twisted away, refusing to be duped by her solicitude.

She pulled the bell, and Barclay appeared. 'Some bandages, Barclay, if you please. And I'm afraid there is broken glass.'

'Immediately, my lady.'

Barclay returned almost at once with a basin of clean water and the bandages.

'Sit down, Ned,' Serena commanded, 'so I may tend to you.'

He opened his mouth to protest, but she took his arm and pushed him gently into a chair and knelt in front of him. Perhaps if he endured her ministrations he could dispense with them as soon as possible.

She held his hand over the basin and carefully removed his handkerchief. 'You have a piece of glass piercing your finger.' She placed her delicate finger and thumb around the piece of glass and pulled it out, dipping his finger into the soothing warm water. Patting his finger dry, she unrolled the bandage and wrapped it around the wound.

Ned could not bear another moment of this. In a voice tight with restrained emotion, he asked, 'Where were you before this?'

She glanced at him anxiously, biting her lip. He steeled himself for her lie.

'Ned, please do not be angry. I called upon Miss England.'

'What?'

'I know you will think it dreadfully improper, but I have worried about the girl since that night she ran out.' Though she was finished wrapping his finger, she held on to his hand, stroking it with torturous gentleness.

He pulled his hand away. 'Was my brother also there?'

'He arrived as I was leaving.' She stood up, but, before she moved away from him, did an unexpected thing. She stroked his cheek.

'Shall we go in to dinner so that the glass may be cleaned up?' She extended her hand to him, so he had to grasp it as he rose out of the chair. Then she took his arm and leaned against him as they walked to the dining room.

Dinner was an excruciatingly confusing affair. He halfway believed her story about visiting Devlin's mistress. It was the sort of kindness Serena might undertake, but he sensed she was not telling all. Throughout dinner, he felt her gaze upon him. Whenever he looked up, she gave him a smile, not at all like an unfaithful wife—or at least how he imagined an unfaithful wife would act. In addition, she looked extraordinarily beautiful. She wore a silk dress of the palest pink. A matching ribbon threaded through the loose curls of her shining hair. There was high colour in her cheeks and sparkle in her blue eyes.

'Where do you go this evening, Serena?'

She sighed. 'I have decided to stay home. I am sick to death of society.'

He raised a sceptical eyebrow. 'What of Devlin?'

She gave him a puzzled look. 'Devlin? Oh, can he not manage on his own now? He seems to get about well.'

Ned fixed his attention on his buttered lobster. When she spoke like this, he could almost believe her. After all, Devlin had his young lightskirt…and that beautiful child. He had no need for Serena.

What gnawed at Ned the most was that Serena ought to prefer his younger brother, with his easy, ne'er-do-well ways. Devlin could charm with a mere smile. Ned had always marvelled at that ability because he so thoroughly lacked it. What did he know of charm? Serena had married him because it was what her father wished. It had been a splendid match on both sides, true, but Ned had loved everything about her from first sight. It mattered not that his father had dictated the marriage.

He glanced up. Serena sat with her fork poised in her delicate hand, her eyes on him. After a long moment, she cast them down with a flutter of her long lashes. Ned grew warm.

'Do you retire early, then?' Ned asked, though it did not help his sudden flare of heat to remind himself of how Serena looked amidst white sheets.

Angelic.

'I am not tired,' she replied. 'Merely tired of the noise and crowds and gossip. Do you go out tonight, Ned?' She looked at him again, her gaze hopeful.

But for what? Did she hope for him to be gone? Or to stay? By damn, he'd not give her the satisfaction of wishing him away.

'I prefer a quiet evening. You know that, Serena.'

She tilted her head, pursing her perfect rosebud of a mouth. 'You have put yourself out in society very much, these past weeks.'

And how could he not? To avoid the parties and balls meant leaving Serena to Devlin.

Ned's jaw muscles clenched. 'To keep an eye on my brother.'

He took a long sip of wine. Her brow creased, looking disappointed.

She excused herself shortly thereafter, to leave him to his port. As she walked by him, her hand slid across the back of his chair, her fingertips lightly touching his back. The sensation remained long after she departed.

He went straight to his room after that, carrying a brandy decanter with him and freeing himself from his neckcloth as soon as he crossed the threshold. His valet appeared to assist him out of his coat and waistcoat. After his man hung up the clothing, Ned dismissed him.

He kicked off his shoes and sat in the worn leather chair that had been in this room for as long as he could remember. Stretching his legs, he poured himself a generous supply of brandy, but his hand hurt like the devil when he picked up the glass. No comfort in brandy if it brought pain. After draining the contents, he set down the glass and replaced the decanter's glass stopper. He hoped the brandy would help him sleep.

The drink fulfilled its promise, and dreams drifted though his slumber, disturbing dreams of Serena and Devlin and losing them both.

A soft voice called his name. 'Ned? Ned?'

He opened one eye and shot out of the chair. Serena stood in front of him, her pale hair and thin white nightdress glowing in the faint light from a branch of candles behind her.

'What has happened?' he cried, sure that only something dire would bring her into his room of her own accord.

Her hand swept through her long silken tresses. 'It was awful, Ned.'

'What?' He could not help it. He reached for her.

She seemed to crumble in his arms. 'The dream.' She shuddered. 'I could not find you anywhere. You were gone.'

Returning to the chair, he settled her on his lap. She cried softly against his shoulder.

'Shh, my love,' he murmured. 'I am here now.' He stroked her hair, inhaling the rose scent that always lingered there. She felt soft and warm, and his loins ached with a need he could scarce bear not filling. She'd best leave soon or he could not vouch for his control.

Her breathing finally relaxed. Not knowing if he wished her to stay or to go, Ned asked, 'Are you ready to go back to bed now, love?'

She grasped his shirt tightly. 'No, please. May I sleep with you? I cannot bear to be alone.'

When he placed her in his bed and stripped out of his clothes, he could have sworn that she smiled.

Chapter Eighteen

'Dearly beloved, we are gathered here…'

The sonorous voice of the rector echoed through the small church. Tears streamed down Madeleine's cheeks.

Sophie looked beautiful as she never had appeared to Madeleine before. She supposed beauty had led to Farley's interest in Sophie, but by the time Madeleine got to know her, fear had obscured the girl's looks. This day, standing next to her stalwart protector, Sophie looked radiant.

The dress Sophie had fashioned for herself was a vision of pale pink that swirled like a cloud whenever she moved. The colour put a bloom in her pale cheeks. Madeleine had woven a crown of tiny pink roses, the same colour as the dress, for Sophie to wear in her shining gold hair. Sophie gazed upon her loving groom with all the wonder and innocence of a virgin.

The clergyman droned, '…signifying unto us the mystical union that is betwixt Christ and his church…'

Madeleine was grateful beyond all measure that her friend had found the love of the good, solid Bart. She also envied Sophie painfully.

The humble furnishings of the church suited the parishioners—shopkeepers, merchants and other working people, useful people. It was not dissimilar to the church in her home parish where she used to receive angry glares from her governess for her fidgeting. As a child, she'd never been able to sit still for Sunday services. Now, what she would give for the peace of that country church. Perhaps if she had attended to her vicar's sermons, she might have avoided her sinful life.

Sophie coughed, bringing such a look of loving concern to Bart's face that Madeleine nearly started weeping again.

'Wilt thou have this woman to thy wedded wife, to live together after God's ordinance in the holy estate of matrimony? Wilt thou love her, comfort her, honour and keep her…'

Madeleine glanced at Devlin. Linette's tiny hand nestled in Devlin's strong one as they stood in front of the altar. He had never looked so handsome. He wore a simple morning coat of tobacco brown. Except for the superior cut, his clothes could not be distinguished from the style worn by Bart and other men walking about their business in this neighbourhood. He'd chosen attire that did not outshine the bride and groom.

Madeleine sighed. Truth was, Devlin looked exactly as she'd so often fantasised him, an ordinary man with whom she might share a cottage and a simple life. She shook her head. It was nonsense to hope. Soon she would never see him again.

Linette pulled away from Devlin's grasp and lifted both hands in the air. Automatically, Devlin reached down and picked her up. She leaned her head against his shoulder.

Madeleine's throat tightened. How would losing Devlin affect Linette? He had become so much a part of her world.

'…keep thee only to her, so long as you both shall live?' Bart responded in a strong, firm voice. 'I will.'

Madeleine imagined Devlin standing before an altar making these same vows. It would be a grander church, of course, St George's, perhaps. Would his bride, like Sophie, radiate innocence and suppressed passion? Would Devlin look upon her with the same astonished joy as that written all over Bart's face?

It did not bear thinking of.

Devlin turned toward Madeleine. His eyes, which he quickly averted, were filled with pain.

'I now pronounce you man and wife,' the rector concluded, raising his voice as if there were a church full of people to hear. 'You may kiss the bride.'

Sophie blinked rapidly and Bart's face turned beet red. He bent toward the tiny woman, his movement tentative, but he raised Sophie's chin with a gentle finger and placed his lips lightly on hers. They held the kiss for a long time until Madeleine thought she might break down in sobs from the pure beauty of the moment.

Bart and Sophie put their marks in the register, and the small party left the church to walk to a nearby inn. Devlin had arranged a private parlour for a proper wedding breakfast for the five of them. The room was comfortable, a place where Sophie and Bart could relax. Breakfast consisted of all manner of fare: chocolate, sliced ham, boiled eggs, pastries, sweetmeats and dishes of berries and cream. Devlin proved an excellent host, keeping up cheerful banter, so that Madeleine was able to laugh when she otherwise might have dissolved into tears. Even Sophie smiled, though Devlin's gentle teasing made her blush.

Devlin had secured a room for the night for the couple, stocked with wine and other delicacies. He had offered them a wedding trip, but Bart refused. Neither had family to visit, Bart explained, and unfamiliar places would only unsettle Sophie.

Madeleine hugged her little friend tightly when they said their goodbyes. Though it was for a mere night, the marriage meant that she and Sophie would never have quite the same relationship as before. Sophie clung to her for a moment, whispering in Madeleine's ear, 'Oh, thank you, Maddy. I am so very happy.'

Evening shadows darkened the bedroom while Devlin sat with Linette, trying to encourage her to sleep. Her eyes were red and puffy with fatigue from the excitement of the day, but stubbornly she refused to keep them shut.

After leaving Bart and Sophie to their wedded bliss, Devlin had been loath to return home. He had insisted upon taking Madeleine and Linette to the nearby shops where he showered trinkets on a reluctant Madeleine and an eager Linette.

Linette's bed was now littered with a family of handsome horseflesh. A mare, stallion and filly, finely painted with acute accuracy and beauty, were nestled next to the child, but were not helping sleep. Linette checked and rechecked to see if they were tucked in properly. Devlin made up stories about them, setting their antics in the rolling acres of Heronvale, where they galloped and frolicked and got into mischief.

Linette's eyes widened and twinkled, but did not close.

'I believe you need nice, dull nursery stories.'

Devlin glanced over to see Madeleine in the doorway. His heart leapt into his throat. No more than a silhouette in the dim light, the curved lines of her body made his pulse quicken.

'I can remember none of them. We need to purchase a book, I suppose,' he said, trying to ignore the alluring scent of lavender that always surrounded her.

'Perhaps if you sang to her.'

He gave her a soft laugh. 'If I sang to her, she might never sleep again.'

'Fustian. You have a fine voice.'

He reached out his hand. 'Come. You sing to her.'

Madeleine walked over to the bed, and he nestled her in front of him, wrapping his arms around her and resting his chin on her shoulder.

'My sweetling,' she said, fussing with Linette's blanket, 'you must try to sleep now. It is very late.'

Linette gave her a mutinous look.

'What if we sing to you together?' Devlin asked.

Linette nodded, eyes stubbornly open.

In a quiet baritone, he began, 'Hush a bye. Don't you cry. Daddy's gone for a soldier…' Madeleine joined in with her sweet clear voice, 'When you wake, you shall see all the pretty little horses…'

Neither of them could remember more of the song, so they repeated the lines over and over until Linette's eyes finally grew heavy. Devlin admired her will. The child clung to her happy day.

It had been a happy day indeed for Bart and Sophie, but for Devlin, one of excruciating agony. At the church, the vow Bart spoke to Sophie was the same one he would soon speak to a woman he did not love. He would never feel the unrestrained joy that shone on Bart and Sophie's faces when they were pronounced man and wife. By that time he would have packed Madeleine and Linette off to some comfortable cottage, never to see them again.

'…Daddy has gone for a soldier…' Madeleine sang. As Devlin accompanied her, the words echoed in his mind, *Daddy has gone…has gone…has gone.*

Linette's eyes remained closed, surrendering to the inevitable, as he would ultimately do.

Madeleine rose from the bed, a finger to her lips. He
followed her silently out the door, which she closed sound-
lessly.

'Finally.' She sighed. 'I thought she would never sleep.'

Devlin could not speak, his emotions too raw. The faint
pounding of French drums touched his ears.

Madeleine smiled at him. How did she remain so calm
when life was a shambles? 'You must be late dressing for the
evening. Shall I assist you?'

He stared blankly. 'I am not going out.'

Her shoulders relaxed slightly. Perhaps she was not so
calm after all.

'I would not leave you alone, Maddy.'

As soon as he'd said it, the irony of those words struck him
like the Frenchman's lance.

He stroked her hair away from her face and leaned down
to touch his lips to hers. Her arms wound around his neck and
he lifted her, kissing her as if she were the air he breathed.

How could he ever let her go?

In the days ahead, he vowed, he would savour each
moment with her. He would provide her with as many plea-
sures as he could contrive. Dancing at Vauxhall. Riding in
Hyde Park. Searching nearby shops for whatever she fancied.

This night he would love her with every muscle in his
body, every sinew, every nerve. He would give all of himself,
and glory in her response. He would show her that, although
they must part, his love would endure throughout eternity.

Devlin swung Madeleine into his arms and, like a groom
might carry his bride over the threshold, he carried her into
his bedchamber.

The next evening, the air was chilly as the boatman's oars
splashed rhythmically into the Thames. With shaking fingers,

Madeleine adjusted the black mask covering her face. Wearing a mask again reminded her of her nights with Farley, although this soft cloth rested almost like a caress against her skin. With a shiver, she wrapped her paisley shawl more tightly around her shoulders. When they reached the dock and Devlin assisted her out of the boat, the night air felt warmer.

She took Devlin's arm as they walked to the arched entrance of Vauxhall Gardens. He grinned at her, his matching mask making him resemble a devilish bandit. In his trousers and coat, he might have been any young man about town. He'd promised her anonymity, more important to her than a night of music and dancing, or a chance to again wear the golden evening dress he had purchased for her.

People from all walks of life crowded the entrance, many masked like she. Shop girls, she imagined, and clerks, maids and footmen, all mingling freely in their finery, differences of class obscured by the darkness. Was it the chance to pretend or the chance to hide that led others to conceal their identities? For Madeleine, the need to hide provided the chance to pretend. She vowed to pretend that life existed only within these intriguing walls, at least for the space of this one night.

Devlin paid the six-shilling fee, and they stepped through the entrance.

Madeleine gasped. She had stepped into the heavens. Glittering lights shone everywhere like stars come to dwell on earth. Not stars, really, but Chinese lanterns hung everywhere in the elm trees flanking the Grand Walk. The faint sound of music grew louder with each step they took.

'What shall we do first, my love?' asked Devlin, holding her tightly against his side. 'There is much to see.'

'I hardly know.' She glanced around her as they came to the Grand Cross Walk.

'Let us walk the paths, then, 'til you fancy to stop.'

Devlin took her for a stroll down the South Walk with its arches and painted ruins. He kept a wary eye on the young bloods waiting to pull an unsuspecting female into the darker byways. Plenty of men ogled her, and he was glad the glittering surroundings caused her not to notice.

The music was near as they wandered through the Grove, strains of Haydn contributing to the magic that was Vauxhall. As they walked past the supper boxes, Devlin noticed several familiar faces. This had been deemed the fashionable night for the *ton*, he supposed, but who decided one night over another was a mystery to him. Emily Duprey had told him she would not be in attendance. He was pleased. He wished to forget her existence for this one night and pretend there was no one but Madeleine.

Wearing the mask gave him a freedom he would not otherwise have enjoyed. With the mask, he could stroll through Vauxhall, brushing elbows with earls and dukes, Madeleine proudly on his arm, not hidden in the apartments near St James's. He was merely a man escorting his woman, not a gentleman with his mistress. In anonymity, he and Madeleine were like all the other strolling couples.

He smiled at Madeleine's delight, as they passed each new sight on the South Walk. She swore the painted ruins looked so real, she could walk into them. He wished they could walk into them and never return.

But the South Walk ended, returning them to the Grove. 'Time for us to dance, my love.'

He led her toward musicians playing in a balcony near the supper boxes. The conductor started a waltz just as they arrived, as if he were signalling their appearance. Devlin took Madeleine in his arms and, smiling down at her joyous countenance, whirled her to the strains of the music.

A short distance away in a supper box nearest the dancing, the Marchioness of Heronvale tugged at her Marquess's arm.

'Ned, did you see? I believe that is Devlin and Madeleine.'

He circled his arm around her waist. 'Madeleine, is it? Informal, are you not?' He nuzzled her neck, more interested in the scent of her hair and the softness of her skin than in two people dancing.

'Do behave, Ned,' she scolded, making no effort to move away. 'Look over there. It is Devlin, I am sure.'

He glanced where she had indicated. 'Wife, they are masked.'

'I am sure it is they.' She pulled him out of the box. 'Come, dance with me. We will get closer to them, and you will see. She wears the same dress as she wore to dinner.'

He needed no coaxing to hold her in his arms. These past nights together had been filled with a passion he had not dreamed existed for him. He knew not what had caused the transformation, nor did he care. Happiness was too tame a word for what he felt.

In his gratitude, he would do anything for her. Anything. Even dutifully dancing her near the couple who gazed at no one but each other.

Serena stood on tiptoe and whispered in his ear, 'See, it is they.'

Ned took the opportunity to hold her closer. He agreed it could be Devlin and his Miss England. He recognised the look in the man's eyes. It reflected what sang in his own heart. A pinprick of guilt pierced his happiness, for if that were his youngest brother, Ned's dictates forced the loss of that love. Now Ned understood how that would feel.

'Forget them, Serena,' He murmured gruffly. He clasped her against him in a manner that would get them banned from Almack's forever and would help him not think about the decisions he had forced on his brother.

Serena laughed, a sound more beautiful than the music. With a wicked gleam in her eye, she rubbed her hips against a part of him that now ravenously craved her.

Ned forgot about his brother and turned his thoughts to private recesses of the Gardens where two lovers might retreat. He swept Serena to the edge of the dancing area and led her by the hand to the narrow pathway of the Dark Walk.

Devlin barely heard when the music ended, barely registered the other dancers moving off the floor. Dancing with Madeleine had been magical. Stopping had been like coming out of a spell. She shook her head, as if sharing the same feeling.

He glanced around him. He was not two paces from Amanda Reynolds. Momentarily fearing she would recognise him, Devlin shifted away from her sight. He quickly realised it did not matter. Miss Reynolds would not trouble to notice someone dressed as gentry.

Madeleine uttered a weak cry and pulled at Devlin's arm, as if ready to bolt. She was also looking at Miss Reynolds and he had a moment's anxiety that Madeleine knew her, as well.

'What is it, Maddy?' he asked as she pulled at him.

'Oh, please, let us leave,' she cried, fear etched on her face. 'It is Greythorne.'

Devlin put his arm around her protectively and rushed her away from the dancing area. Finding a quiet spot near a fountain, he sat her on a bench. She trembled under his arm.

'What is it, Maddy? What frightened you.'

She gulped in air. 'Greythorne. I saw Greythorne.'

'You know him?'

She nodded, rocking back and forth.

A sick feeling came over him. 'From Farley's?'

She nodded again. 'Farley banned him from me.'

A man as depraved as Farley banned another from bedding her? 'Why?'

She shook her head, moving away from him.

He drew her closer, blood draining from his face. 'Tell me, Maddy.'

'No. I cannot.'

Devlin thought about Amanda. 'I need to know, Maddy. You must tell me.'

She looked at him worriedly. 'You will not confront him?'

His worry increased. 'Is it so bad?'

She nodded.

'Good God.' He rubbed his forehead. 'Very well, you have my word I will not confront him.'

She twisted her hands in her lap. 'I cannot speak this out loud.'

She knelt on the bench and whispered into his ear, in painful detail, the violence Greythorne had inflicted upon her to fulfil his perverted desires. He had read of such practices, having perused forbidden copies of de Sade's *Justine*. He had witnessed such cruelty during the war, but to have it inflicted upon Madeleine? Rage coursed through him. He clenched his fists, regretting giving his word. Greythorne would not live otherwise.

As if reading his mind, she warned, 'You promised, Devlin.'

He relaxed his hands and caressed her cheek with his finger. Folding her against his chest, he rocked her to and fro as he might have done to soothe Linette.

'Greythorne will never hurt you again,' he murmured. And the man would not hurt Amanda either. Devlin resolved to warn her before tomorrow's end.

'I know.' She cuddled against him. 'It was merely remembering.'

Well he knew about that. 'Let us not let this spoil our

evening. Come. We will avoid Greythorne and get refreshments. Our enjoyment need not end.'

He rose from the bench and tugged her to her feet. She came into his arms and he kissed her tenderly. She clung to him for a moment before taking his arm and strolling back to the revelry.

'I want to dance with you again,' Madeleine said, pulling him back to the place from where she had so recently fled.

They danced each waltz and strolled along the paths, enjoying each sight. They sat at one of the Garden's restaurants and ate paper-thin slices of ham, and the tiniest chickens Madeleine had ever seen, washing them down with arrack. When the bells rang, they watched Madame Saqui walk the tightrope.

When it was time for the fireworks, Madeleine hurried Devlin to the best vantage point and fairly jumped up and down. The display began, exceeding all her expectations. Rockets exploded in the air. Sparkles rained down as if all the stars in the sky suddenly fell. Catherine wheels hissed, shedding shards of lights as they spun. Words appeared as still more star showers brightened the sky. The air smelled of sulphur, and the acrid smoke blurred the scene, but still the fireworks boomed and burst in the air.

Devlin's hand dropped from Madeleine's arm. She turned to look at him, to share the excitement. His hands covered his ears. His eyes were clamped shut, a look of anguish on his face.

'Devlin, what is wrong?' She grabbed him as he started to sink to the ground.

He regained his footing with effort, but his whole body trembled. 'Have…to…leave.' The words barely escaped his lips.

She pulled him through the crowd, hurrying toward the gate. He allowed her to guide him, barely looking up, lost in a nightmare world she could only imagine.

'We are through the gate, Devlin,' she said as if speaking to a blind man. 'Let us go to the boats.'

When they were safely on the water and the sounds muffled by the cool air and the lapping of the oars, he relaxed a fraction. They pulled off their masks and he finally looked at her as if really seeing her.

'Devlin, please tell me. Are you ill?' She still held his arm tightly.

He gave her a wan smile. 'I am afraid the war came back to me.'

She stroked his cheek.

'The sound of the fireworks. It was like the cannon. And the smell...I...I thought I was there again.'

She hugged him fiercely. 'I am so sorry. I did not think. We stayed too long.'

He put his arm around her and she rested her head on his shoulder. 'You could not have known what I did not know myself, but it is all right now, my love.'

He held her close against the chill of the river air. 'I am sorry to have ruined our evening.'

She took his hand in hers. 'It shall always be a magic memory for me.'

As they neared the shore, Madeleine felt a shiver that had nothing to do with the night air. It was a premonition.

Her time with him was nearing its end.

Chapter Nineteen

The next day Devlin called upon Miss Amanda Reynolds as early as propriety would allow. He had borrowed Ned's curricle and meant to induce her to ride with him, the only way he could think to speak with her alone.

'A delicious idea,' she exclaimed. 'Greythorne usually appears at this time and he shall be told I am gadding about with you.' She clapped her hands merrily. 'Give me a moment to don suitable clothing.'

She left the parlour in a rush, obviously not noticing the serious look on his face.

Hyde Park was nearly empty this early hour. Amanda prattled on about Greythorne, the poor refreshments at Vauxhall, and the ball being held that evening. She enquired politely after his friend Ramsford, but in a way that quickly went to a change of subject.

Devlin scarcely heard her.

He drew the horses to a halt. 'Let us walk a little.' Handing the ribbons to Ned's groom, he lifted Amanda from the vehicle.

He seated her on a bench set a little away from the path.

'I must talk with you, Amanda.' They had become friends enough for given names, at least in private.

'So serious, Devlin,' she said with mock solemnity. 'Not some contretemps with the our dull little Miss Duprey, I trust?'

'No.' He took her hand. 'I am afraid it is a topic that is quite improper, but I must pursue it with you.'

An anxious twitch appeared at the corner of her mouth, but she continued to smile. 'Improper? La, you intrigue me, sir.'

Devlin took a deep breath and dove into the tale of Greythorne's predilections.

Her smile quickly fled. She blushed and turned pale by turns. She stared at him with wide eyes or glanced away in embarrassment. His own words sickened him and he could not still images of Greythorne inflicting these debaucheries on Madeleine.

Amanda Reynolds, cosseted darling of the *ton*, could not have imagined half of what he told her. He regretted having to impart these sordid vagaries of intimacy to her and tried to describe the whole to her without graphic explicitness. At the same time, the matter needed to be understood. Amanda must realise the kind of man she intended to marry.

When he finished, she shook her head. 'Such things are not possible! Why would you tell me this?'

He took her hand. 'Believe me, I did not wish to relate these matters to you, but when the knowledge of this came my way, I had to warn you.'

'How did you hear of this?' she stammered.

Devlin rubbed his brow. 'I cannot tell you. Suffice to say that I know of it from one who was his victim.'

She raised her brows.

'I will not say who it might be, so do not ask.'

She rose to her feet. 'I want to go home.'

'Of course.' He offered her his arm. She shrank from it.

They walked silently back to the curricle. He lifted her into the seat and climbed in himself, taking the ribbons while the groom hopped up on back.

When he pulled up to her town house, he said, 'I am truly sorry, Amanda. I had no wish to hurt you.'

She tried to smile at him, but her eyes were pinched with anxiety. 'I suppose I should thank you.'

He lifted her down to the pavement. 'You do believe my tale, don't you?'

'Oh, yes, I believe you.' She sighed. 'Why should you risk your reputation otherwise? I could ruin you for talking of such things to me.'

Devlin shrugged. 'I confess, I did not consider that.'

She did smile, then.

Devlin regarded her anxiously. 'Has he offered for you?'

She shook her head. 'Not yet.'

'Refuse him.' It was simply said.

Her smile fled. 'I will.'

Devlin watched her enter the town house. A horseman rode up beside him.

'Rather early for the Hyde Park set.'

It was Ram. Devlin still felt his heart swell at the sight of the friend he'd thought he lost.

He ignored Ram's comment. 'Good to see you, Ram. Calling upon the Diamond?'

Ramsford gave a snort. 'Don't be absurd. She would hardly find my presence creditable.'

Devlin tossed him a sceptical look. 'If you are not engaged, follow me to my brother's stable so I can rid myself of the curricle.' He had promised to call on Miss Duprey and would value Ram's company.

'I am not engaged. This gentleman's life is totally devoid of purposeful activity.'

They proceeded at a comfortable pace, Devlin feeling the company of his friend an effective antidote to dashing the dreams of the season's Diamond.

The visit with Miss Duprey was pleasant, but without a moment of interest. There was not one thing about her to dislike. Nothing to anger or irritate. Nothing to arouse any form of passion. For that he was grateful. He wanted passion from no woman except Madeleine.

Drums rumbled in his ears as he thought of giving up nights of loving her, days spent in her company. He almost felt as if the darkness would descend upon him, as it had at Waterloo, and he would again be alone with his pain with no one to see his suffering. No one would notice his life ebbing into oblivion.

He glanced at Ram seated across the room, conversing with a young lady also calling upon Miss Duprey. Perhaps some day he would tell his friend about Madeleine and Linette. Then at least one person would know that a piece of Devlin Steele lived and flourished somewhere in England.

'You are quiet today, my lord.' Miss Duprey's voice broke through the drum rolls. 'Are you unwell?'

Her discernment of his mood and her concern were to her credit. She might be bland, but at least she was not insensible.

'I apologise, Miss Duprey. I was merely woolgathering.'

She poured a cup of tea and handed it to him. 'If you are in need of a friendly ear, I am available.'

He gave her a wan smile. 'It is nothing, I assure you.' The drums grew louder. All the thoughts that swam through his head were none he could confide to her.

She cocked her head, a gesture that inexplicably appealed to him. It puzzled him how he'd singled her out for his damnable plan, but then a gesture, such as this, a fleeting look, a trill of her laughter, caught his notice and surprised him each time.

* * *

A quarter of an hour later, he and Ramsford departed the lady's parlour and walked to his brother's stable where Ram had left his mount.

'I should call upon the Marchioness, Ram. Are you game to keep me company?'

'It cannot be more of a deadly bore than the last place,' Ramsford said in a dry voice.

When they followed Barclay to the front parlour, the sounds of male and female laughter met their ears. Serena had other callers, no doubt. Perhaps she had given up on his brother and accepted the attentions of one of the many men who sought her.

As they stepped through the doorway, however, the only people present were the Marquess and Marchioness, standing quite close to each other, faces flushed.

Ned strode up, hand extended. 'Dev, good to see you.'

Devlin took his brother's hand, as surprised by the warm handshake as the friendly greeting. He introduced Ram, and presented him to Serena.

'I have seen our new Lord Ramsford many times. How lovely to meet you. You are most welcome as a friend of Devlin's.'

Ned sent Barclay to arrange refreshment and begged leave to speak to Devlin alone.

They entered the library, and Devlin could not help but remember the heat of temper that flared when he last set foot in the room.

'Forgive me for leaving your friend, but I wished to speak with you. Serena and I leave tomorrow for Heronvale. I…I have some business there and she accompanies me.' Ned's face flushed red.

Why should his brother bother to explain this? And why show embarrassment?

Ned gestured to one of the leather chairs in the room and Devlin sat. He poured them each a small glass of sherry.

'There is nothing amiss, I hope?' Devlin took the glass.

'No…no, nothing amiss. All is well.' Ned looked away, but Devlin thought he saw a grin on his brother's face.

'I doubt we will return before the end of the Season,' Ned continued, seating himself in the chair adjacent to Devlin's. 'I thought I should check your…your progress, so to speak.'

Ned's tone and demeanour might be convivial, but he remained thoroughly in control of Devlin's future.

'I have made no commitments as yet.' Devlin tried to sound matter-of-fact.

'The Season will be over in a matter of weeks.' Ned's voice turned tense.

Devlin released a fatalistic breath. 'I have made a selection.'

'And who is the lady?'

'Miss Emily Duprey.' It was as though a cage door closed upon him. Speaking of this out loud to his brother made it all too real. Too final.

'Indeed?' Ned sounded surprised. 'I had thought your interest lay with Miss Reynolds.'

Devlin met his brother's eye. 'My *interest* lies elsewhere.'

Ned had the grace to look faintly ashamed.

Devlin took another sip of the sherry. 'Miss Reynolds and I have an odd friendship. We harbour no other form of attachment.'

Ned fiddled with the stem of his glass. 'I know little of the Dupreys. Malvern, is that the property? A barony?'

'Yes.' Perfectly acceptable, thought Devlin. His brother ought to approve.

'Well…' Ned paused. A softness came into his voice. 'Have you settled Miss England and the child?'

Push the sword in deeper, brother, thought Devlin. 'Not as yet.'

Ned rose and walked to his desk and busied himself writing. He came back to Devlin and handed him a paper.

'This will allow you to draw money in my absence. You will need extra funds to procure a proper place for your…your charges. She must be well situated. Perhaps in Chelsea.'

Devlin accepted the draft and responded in a cool voice, 'I thought the country to be a better choice.'

Ned sat again and spoke as if they were settling some piece of property. 'Much better for them to be among an assortment of the middle classes. You do not wish for there to be questions about them. A "widow" and child will not draw attention in Chelsea.'

'No attention at all,' said Devlin mechanically, wishing to blurt out that Madeleine needed the countryside so she could ride. More so, he wished to tell his brother that sending away Madeleine and Linette was tantamount to destroying his own soul.

Devlin glanced at the bank draft. His eyes widened. Ned had written an uncommonly generous amount.

'We do not wish them to suffer,' Ned said softly.

Devlin eschewed a hack and slowly walked home. A persistent drizzle fell, turning the day uncommonly cold. The weather suited his mood.

When he opened the door to his apartments, Linette squealed, 'Deddy!' and bounded into his arms. His eyes moistened as he hugged her to him.

Madeleine appeared from the kitchen, wiping her hands on that abominable apron she wore.

'She has been asking for you all this day. I am nearly mad with it.' She smiled in amusement.

He drew her into the hug. Clasping them both to him, he thought he would be the one to go mad without them. When he loosened his grasp, Madeleine stared into his eyes. With a gentle finger, she wiped moisture from the corner of his eye.

'Come, let me take your hat and coat,' she said. 'You are damp and chilled.'

He put Linette down, but she continued to cling to his legs. 'Play horses with me.' She tugged at his trousers.

He patted the child's shiny curls. 'In a moment, Lady Lin.' Madeleine helped him out of his coat. 'Maddy, I would like to speak with you. Not this moment. When you are able.'

She smiled at him, but the emotion in her eyes was solemn. 'I am in the midst of learning how to cook dinner. Sophie and Bart are teaching me to make boiled beef and oat pudding. Does that not sound delicious?'

'Indeed,' he said, kissing her lightly on the cheek and allowing Linette to pull him into the parlour where her toy horses awaited.

There was not time enough to speak alone to Madeleine until well into the evening after Linette finally lapsed into slumber. Madeleine came into his bedchamber to set out his clothing.

'She is becoming more difficult to get to sleep.' Madeleine raised his evening coat, examining it carefully.

'We need to purchase a book of fairy stories,' he said.

'Indeed,' she agreed. 'Why, I can hardly remember when I last read a book. There is much I ought to read for myself. My mind is in sad need of improving.'

His spirits rose, but only a bit. It was something he could do for her. 'We must go to a bookshop. You may select whatever you wish for yourself and Linette.'

She blushed. 'Please do not countenance my hasty words. I do not expect you to—'

He raised a hand to silence her. 'We will go there tomorrow. I think if we go early you should feel comfortable.'

She was always more concerned about being seen with him than he was with her. For his sake, he supposed, although no one would look upon him with disfavour for being in the company of a beautiful unescorted female. They would merely assume he had an arrangement with her.

'I have brushed your evening clothes,' Madeleine said.

He was expected at the Catsworths' ball this evening, as were Miss Duprey, her brother and her ever-present mother. Amanda, Greythorne, and, thankfully, Ram also planned to attend. Devlin was especially concerned about Amanda Reynolds having to encounter Greythorne.

Devlin stripped down to his small clothes. 'Thank you, Maddy.' He fingered the cloth of his jacket. 'Well done.'

It was painfully ironic that Madeleine acted as his valet when he dressed for these evening entertainments.

She turned to get his clean shirt and he grabbed her arm. 'Sit with me a minute.'

Her eyes lingered on his bare chest, but she dutifully sat next to him on the bed. He should have planned for a neutral setting. The bed brought too many ideas to his head.

He leaned against the pillows and settled her in front of him, his arms around her, her soft hair tickling his chest.

'We must talk of where you will live,' he said.

She stiffened.

'There is little time left,' he continued.

'I told you that it is of no consequence to me where you place us.' Her voice seemed determinedly devoid of emotion.

It was detestable that she must be sent away where he would never be able to check on her, to make sure she was safe. He would never know how she fared. How his daughter fared.

He buried his face in her hair. 'Forgive me, Madeleine.' His body shook. 'I have made a mull of all of it and I cannot make repairs. Forgive me. I never meant to hurt you, to bring you to this end…'

She turned around, coming on to her knees in front of him. She took his face in both her hands. 'Oh, no, you mustn't say so!' She pressed his cheeks firmly. 'You saved us, Devlin. *Saved* us. What would my life be like—Linette's life—if you had not rescued us? Even Sophie. Would she have had any chance for the happiness she now possesses? You did this for us.'

She brushed his hair with her fingers and gazed tenderly at him. 'I shall be grateful to you my whole life. I shall never forget you. Never stop loving you.' Her hands flew to her mouth at these last words.

'Maddy,' Devlin managed, his arms going around her. To hear her say she loved him was unbearable, yet at the same time his heart soared with happiness. Madeleine loved him. She was not merely repaying him with her body. She loved him and, by God, he loved her in return. 'Maddy.'

He could not help himself, needing to show her his love. He rained her with kisses, freed her from her clothes and what few were left of his own. He poured himself into her, desperate to make the moment last, knowing it would be fleeting.

By the time he walked into the Catsworths' ball, almost too late to be fashionable, he moved in a haze of sexual satiation. His soul remained with Madeleine, but his body walked dreamlike through its paces. She loved him, and nothing else seemed the least important.

'Stee-eellle,' slurred a nasally voice. A tottering Robert Duprey grabbed his arm. 'M'sister's awaiting you. Bad form to neglect the chit. Ought to declare y'rself. Common knowledge, y'know.'

Devlin shrugged him off. 'You are presuming, sir. And you are drunk.'.

Devlin might next have sought out Miss Duprey, but her brother's insinuations, correct as they might be, angered him. He went in search of Amanda instead. It was never difficult to find her, since she shone more brightly than the other marriage-mart hopefuls. He spied her across the room. Greythorne was speaking animatedly to her, looking very cross. Devlin took a step toward her, but Ram appeared at her side. Ram clamped his fingers into Greythorne's arm and, a moment later, led Amanda into a waltz.

Devlin's throat tightened. He was turning maudlin at seeing his friend assume the role of protector over the fair Miss Reynolds. He glanced around the room and spied Miss Duprey and her mother. She did not see him.

Stepping back, Devlin turned on his heel and fled the ballroom, seeking the chill air of the evening...and home.

Farley hid in the shadows outside the Catsworth town house. Steele would be there. It was *the* event of the evening, after all. The ball would last into the wee hours, but he could stand the wait. He had decided to shadow Steele this night. If the opportunity presented itself, he'd plunge a knife in Steele's back. With Steele out of the way, Madeleine would have no choice but to return to him.

Carriages continued to arrive and a bustling of people crowded the pavement and the entrance. Farley hardly noticed the man walking in the other direction. It was not until the man disappeared around the corner that he realised the figure had resembled Steele.

Impossible. The ball had hardly started.

Farley would wait. Steele was bound to leave at his usual time and Farley then would be ready.

Chapter Twenty

'Oh, my!' Madeleine cried as she entered Lackington's bookshop on Finsbury Square. She had not imagined so many books to exist in the world.

'Devlin, this is impossible. I will not know how to look.'

He patted the hand holding his arm. 'We shall ask for assistance.'

They walked up to a large circular desk with four clerks behind. Two were idle at this early hour.

'May we assist, sir?' one asked.

Devlin asked the grey-coated clerk to escort them to books suitable for young children. They made a few selections, Aesop's Fables, one book both could recall from childhood, among them. Devlin then requested they be shown the equestrian section. He had in mind that what Linette would enjoy most of all would be a book with engravings of horses.

Unfortunately, such books also captivated Madeleine, and he, of course, could never be uninterested in such a subject. They pored over volumes containing a wealth of information on breeding, riding, equestrian care. They examined fine engravings of handsome horseflesh, arguing energetically over which volume would be most pleasing to Linette.

When their selections were made and they readied for their departure, Devlin glanced at the large store clock. It read half past one.

'We have been here almost three hours,' he told Madeleine as they stepped out the door.

She grabbed his arm and squeezed it in pleasure. 'I was not aware. Time passed so swiftly.'

The streets were bustling and Devlin looked about, realising the fashionable shoppers were out in abundant numbers, people he'd hoped to avoid, but only because they would distress Madeleine.

Her hand trembled as it clutched his arm. They stepped onto the pavement. Two ladies, one young, one middle-aged, approached.

Emily Duprey and her mother, Lady Duprey.

It was impossible to avoid them. Damn his carelessness. The most efficacious solution would be to pretend he did not see them. They, in turn, would ignore the beautiful creature on his arm, relegating her to a part of a gentleman's life that bore no speaking of.

Miss Duprey glanced up, a shocked look on her face. Devlin felt Madeleine hesitate.

Deuce. He had hoped to spare Madeleine this moment. Walking by would convey that Madeleine was his mistress. Miss Duprey was no naïve miss. At her age she was bound to be realistic about the dealings of men. She could weather the sight of him with a prime article on his arm, as could her mother. But could he bear Madeleine's humiliation?

He could not.

When they were abreast of the two women, he smiled and

gave them a small bow. 'Lady Duprey, Miss Duprey, good afternoon.'

The two ladies gaped. Lady Duprey appeared as if she would pop a blood vessel.

Devlin remained undaunted. 'May I make known to you Miss Madeleine England? She has accompanied me to this excellent bookshop.' He stepped aside to present Madeleine, who grasped his arm so tightly it hurt. 'Miss England, Lady Duprey and her daughter, Miss Duprey.'

Madeleine gave a stiff curtsy. 'How do you do,' she said, her voice barely audible

Lady Duprey hissed, muttering under her breath, 'This is the outside of enough.' She pulled at her daughter.

Miss Duprey paused and gave a shaky nod of her head. As her mother hurried her off, she turned and took one last brief glance at Madeleine, the shock still plain on her face.

After they disappeared through the doorway of the bookshop, Madeleine went limp beside him. He dropped the wrapped package of books as he caught her, easing her to sit on some nearby steps.

'Maddy,' he exclaimed, alarmed. Retrieving the books, he sat next to her. 'I am so sorry. Shall I get a hack?'

'Give me a moment, if you please.' She hugged her knees and rocked, hiding her face from him.

Passers-by began to take notice.

'I shall secure a hack.' Devlin hurried to the street and waved a hand to an approaching hackney coach. He almost carried Madeleine to the vehicle and bundled her inside.

'I am recovered now,' she said in a weak voice, her hand covering her eyes.

'Damn.' He rubbed her arms bracingly. 'There was no call for them to look at you such. They could not know...'

'It is of no consequence.' She continued to shield her eyes, and he feared she was crying.

'I am sorry for that, Maddy. You have probably deduced who they are.' He expelled a tense breath. 'Believe me, I would not for the world wished you to encounter the lady I…I mean, the one I…'

'Oh, no.' Madeleine felt her moan emerge from the depths of her heart. It was worse than she imagined. Much, much worse.

Devlin continued, 'Damn them. Their treatment was rag-mannered in the extreme. You appear perfectly respectable. You could have been my cousin or Ram's sister, for God's sake. They had no right to treat you so.'

She lowered her hand and gazed out the window of the hack. 'They had every right, Devlin.' She took a breath and faced him, looking directly into his eyes. 'They are my mother and sister. They thought themselves rid of me after I shamed them so.'

He stared at her, speechless.

The calm of fatalism descended upon her. 'Let us not go home just yet. Ask the driver to drop us in the park. I once promised to tell the whole of my story. You shall hear it now.'

He rapped for the coachman to stop.

They found a bench in the park. Devlin protested that she would be chilled, but Madeleine assured him the brisk air served her well. They sat in silence.

'It is unusually chilly for June.' He drummed his fingers on his knee.

She smiled at him, capturing his hand and squeezing it. Nearby, a bird flapped its wings, aiming for the sky. She fully expected any regard he had for her to also take flight.

'I grew up in Wiltshire,' she began, 'though I suppose your acquaintance with Emily has told you that. I was the youngest. There was my brother, my oldest sister Jessame, Emily, and me. I believe my mother was tired of children by the time of my birth. She bothered little with me. Our father had no interest in any of us, I do not think. In any event, I was a difficult child. Wilful. I never heeded governesses, or tutors or anyone. I was sent down from the few schools I attended. All I ever wished to do was ride my horse.'

He placed his hand over hers. 'You could be speaking of my childhood, you know. Except my father took an intense interest in every niggling aspect of my life.'

'But your life has been worthwhile. Mine has…' She cleared her throat, and took a deep breath. 'I was fifteen when Farley came to visit. He had some business with my father, I know not what, but my older sisters were allowed to take meals with him, while I was confined to the nursery. I cared not for stuffy dinners, but my sisters teased me about it ceaselessly. When Lord Farley saw me out riding one morning, I was ripe to have some revenge upon them.' She glanced at him, blinking rapidly. 'But I have told you this part.'

His gaze searched her face. She'd once spoken lightly of Farley's seduction. 'I suspect there was more to it than the trifling occurrence you made it out to be.'

'I suppose.' She crossed her arms over her chest. 'It was a fine jest on my sisters, you know. The man they spoke of incessantly was paying me attention. Imagine. *Me*. He spoke pretty words to me.' She hugged herself tightly. 'I had no idea the impression I made in my brother's old clothes. The shirt had become tight around my chest, and I could barely lace up the pants. I thought nothing of it. I simply loved to ride like a boy. In those days I'd wished I was a boy, for boys could do all sorts of exciting things, like race and be soldiers and such. I hated to sit still for sewing or pianoforte or French lessons.'

He regarded her, tenderness filling him. He wished he might have ridden over the countryside with that young girl.

She continued. 'Lord Farley told me later that my clothes would have aroused any man. I should have known that, but I never paid attention when the governess talked of such things.' She bit her lip. 'When Lord Farley kissed me, my only thought was that I had achieved something my sisters endlessly dreamed about. I could not wait to tell them.'

She stood up and paced. 'Lord Farley suggested we retire to the hunting box nearby. His kisses were not unpleasant, and I was eager to try anything, so I did.' She stared at him. 'He showed me more than kisses. I do not know how it progressed as it did, but I made no effort to stop him. My body responded to him, Devlin.' She stopped to see how her words affected him.

She sunk back next to him on the bench. 'I vowed never again to allow myself such feelings.' She stared straight ahead of her, as if the bushes and trees held her fascination. 'And I never did, until that night with you.'

He put his arm around her, laying her head on his shoulder.

It took several seconds for her to continue. 'He told me to come to his room that night. I did, of course. It was so exciting, you see. At the worst possible time...my father opened the door.'

Madeleine pulled away from him and buried her face in her hands. 'I knew I was doing wrong. I knew it was sinful. I deserved for my parents to send me away. It was only fitting.'

'The deuce it was,' he muttered. 'At your age, they ought to have had Farley drawn and quartered.'

'Oh, no. I enticed him, you see. Both he and my father said so. It was not his fault. A man cannot be expected to control those...those urges.' The expression on her face was resolute. She believed this nonsense.

Devlin grabbed her shoulders and made her look at him. Though his grip was firm, his voice was soft. 'Maddy, a gentleman must control such urges. Did I not do so when you first came to stay? It was not easy, believe me.'

She blinked and knit her brows together. 'But I seduced you, too. When…when I wanted to make love to you, you could not resist.'

He could not help but smile. 'Goose, you did not seduce me. There was no need to resist when we both were willing.'

She shook her head. 'You do not understand.'

'I understand Farley took advantage of an innocent girl.'

She shrugged. 'I suppose it makes no difference. When the deed was done, my fate was ordained.'

He stood and extended his hand to her. 'Come, let us walk.'

She rose and took his arm.

He kept her close beside him. After a while he said, 'I still cannot believe your parents allowed you to be carried off by Farley. Surely they must have known who he was.'

'Indeed, they did. My mother told me she always knew I was a shameful girl. She said I deserved to be with such a man. I was so foolish, I thought he would take me to Gretna Green. Only when we reached London did I realise what my mother meant.'

Devlin felt sick with rage. What kind of parent would send an innocent young daughter into the clutches of a man like Farley? It was unconscionable.

'In any event,' she went on, her voice curiously devoid of the hot emotions firing off in him, 'it was not long after that Lord Farley showed me my obituary in *The Times*.'

'Your obituary?'

'My parents fabricated my death. Farley told me there was a grave marked by a stone with my name upon it.'

'Damn them all.'

Devlin tried to convey some semblance of calm, but inside rage burned. Damn them all. They had taken a fresh, head-strong, spirited girl, robbed her of her life, and sent her into hell.

And he had left her there, all alone, when she had been only fifteen. He should have sent her to Serena or one of his sisters. Their kind hearts would have understood how to help her. Instead he had walked away, content to consign the pleasure of her company to fond memory.

Without speaking more of the matter, they walked through the park to their apartments. Madeleine busied herself with housework, while Devlin, still feeling the burden of abandoning Madeleine, turned the pages of the book for Linette, showing her the pictures of horses. His mind simmered. He did not make his afternoon call to Miss Duprey as had been expected. He did not attend Mrs Drummond-Burrell's musical evening that was touted the event of the season. Instead, he took a long walk in the drizzle and chill.

When he returned, Madeleine was in her own bed. He came to her side and her eyes fluttered open. In the light of the candle he carried, her eyes looked red and puffy. He blew out the candle, picked her up, and carried her to his bed.

His room was plunged in darkness. Wordlessly, they made love. The darkness and silence heightened the sense of melancholy in their lovemaking. Devlin felt rather than saw her and heard nothing but her breathing and the sounds of their bodies coming together. It was as if she had half-disappeared already and he was desperately clinging to what was left of her. When both were sated, he held her against him, his fingers combing her hair off her face, wet with tears. He still could not speak, but simply tightly held on to her until sleep finally came to him.

* * *

When morning came, Madeleine carefully manoeuvred herself out of the bed so as not to disturb Devlin. She found her nightdress in a heap on the floor and, as she donned it, gazed at the sleeping man. His handsome face was relaxed and peaceful, as it had not been since that fateful meeting with her mother and sister. At this moment he looked so much like Linette no one would doubt his paternity. She no longer doubted it, but accepted it as another of the painful paradoxes of her life. Like loving him and, therefore, having to lose him.

The foreboding sense that their idyllic interlude would soon speed to its end had lingered with her since the bookshop, and, thus, this day seemed grave indeed.

The feeling did not leave her when she busied herself preparing Linette's breakfast, accompanied by the child's irrepressible chatter. It was unusual for her to rise before Bart and Sophie, but perhaps the newly married couple were beginning their day in a happier mood than she.

Madeleine cooked coddled eggs and toast. When first Devlin brought them here, she could do nothing so useful; now she had learned so many skills. She could cook simple meals, scrub a floor, dust furniture and do simple sewing. She knew how to shop and how to bargain with shopkeepers. There was no doubting it. She was prepared to leave.

Bart came into the room, his face pinched with worry.

'What is it, Bart?'

'Sophie is feeling very poorly.' His voice was stressed.

'Shall I go to her?' Madeleine wiped her hands.

Bart nodded, giving her an agonised look.

Bart's room was spare but as orderly as Devlin's was disordered. Sophie lay on the bed, each breath coming with effort. Her face was nearly as pale as the linens she lay upon and dark circles showed under her eyes. She woke as Madeleine came to her side and gave a wan smile.

'We shall get the doctor for you, I think,' Madeleine said.

'Oh, no,' rasped Sophie, her voice thin and weak. 'There is no need. I shall be all right directly.'

'Indeed, you shall.' Madeleine patted her reassuringly. 'I will bring you some tea. Would you like that?'

Her waiflike friend nodded and wearily closed her eyes.

Madeleine returned to Bart in haste. 'Fetch the doctor. I cannot like the way she breathes.'

Bart immediately grabbed his coat and hat, hanging on a hook by the back door. 'I thought so, as well. I will get the man right now.' He let the door slam behind him as he rushed out.

Not long after, Devlin came into the kitchen.

'Deddy!' Linette squealed, scattering her wooden horses with a clatter as she bounded into his arms.

Her heart lurching as it always did at such tender scenes, Madeleine asked, 'May I prepare you some food, Devlin?'

He gave Linette a hug and a kiss and set her back on the floor. She happily returned to the corner where her horses lay. 'No, I must be off...a...a piece of business that must not be delayed.'

Madeleine faced him. She'd been about to tell him of Sophie, but changed her mind. No need to add to the stress evident in his countenance.

'Very well,' she said, trying to keep her voice even.

His mouth was set in a firm determined line. He held her gaze for a moment before he turned on his heel and left.

Madeleine squeezed her eyes shut and took long steadying breaths. Linette banged her horses on the wooden floor, saying, 'Gallump. Gallump,' as they galloped around her. Before Madeleine allowed herself further thoughts of Devlin, she hurried to check on Sophie.

* * *

His first piece of business complete, Devlin proceeded to Mayfair, knowing the hour was early for calls, but he had no wish to postpone this meeting. Best to dispense with it.

The Duprey butler ushered him into the parlour. Devlin paced the room where he'd spent several exceedingly boring afternoons.

The door opened and Emily Duprey crept in, glancing furtively behind her.

'Lord Devlin.' She cast him an anxious glance and shut the door.

'Miss Duprey, forgive the early hour. I wished to speak with your father.'

'As I understand. But if I could have a moment...' She regarded him with a worried expression.

He had no idea how to act with her. Since learning she was Madeleine's sister, dealing with her seemed an impossibility.

Suddenly he realised what had attracted him to her. The tilt of her head, the gesture of her hand, the shape of her brow and chin were Madeleine's. It was his attachment to Madeleine that led him to this woman, who at present was wringing her hands and regarding him anxiously.

He had wronged Emily Duprey. Led her to expect from him an offer now repugnant to him. According to her brother, the family considered it a settled matter, and it was for this sole reason he had returned to this house.

'Miss Duprey, I must beg your forgiveness, but after yesterday, you must realise that any further—'

'Never mind that, sir.' She cast him a pleading glance. 'My sister—'

Before she could continue, the butler arrived to escort him to Lord Duprey's study. He bowed to Miss Duprey, who wore a stricken expression on her face.

Lord Duprey, sitting behind a large desk, rose when Devlin entered the room. Lean and sallow-skinned, with a shock of white hair framing an aristocratic face, he approached Devlin. As he came close, Devlin recognised eyes of the same shade of blue as Madeleine's, except in this man bloodshot red surrounded the blue, and his lids were half closed in an expression of dissipation.

'Lord Devlin,' the man said formally, 'please sit down.' He gestured to a chair next to a table, where he poured them both generous glasses of sherry. Duprey, not waiting for his guest, took a long sip of the nut-brown liquid.

Devlin remained standing. 'I am very conscious of the early hour and have no wish to detain you beyond a moment.'

Duprey peered at him through the slits in his eyes. 'On the contrary. I am pleased that you have come. We have business to transact.'

'We have no business to transact. I came to make that clear to you.'

The older man walked back behind the desk and sat, taking another sip of his drink. 'You have singled out my daughter for your attentions in a way no one could dispute. It is time for you to honour this declaration you have implied so strongly.'

Devlin blanched. Surely this man had heard of the events of the previous day. 'I dispute your words, sir. I have shown no partiality, as anyone on the town knows. I have no intentions toward your daughter Emily, and I wish to make that clear.'

Lord Duprey's eyebrows lifted in a mocking expression. 'And I wish to make clear to you that you will honour your obligations to my daughter. You have been sniffing around her all Season, like some mongrel around a bitch. You will come up to scratch, or else.'

Devlin bristled under the crude threat, but he was determined not to lose his temper. He sent Duprey an equally mocking, but menacing look. 'Of which daughter do you speak?'

Duprey drained the contents of his glass and poured himself another from a decanter on the desk. 'So the chit told you, eh?' He laughed, a dry mirthless sound. 'Well, you will marry Emily Duprey and make this family an honourable connection to Heronvale's fortune. I care not a whit how much you bed that little whore.'

Devlin dove across the desk, grabbing Duprey by the knot in his neckcloth and scattering the desk's contents to the floor. The man's cheeks turned red as he sputtered for breath.

'You dare speak of her that way again and I will kill you.' Devlin released him and Duprey fell back into his chair.

When Duprey regained his breath, he smiled sardonically. 'I wonder what story she concocted for you, Steele. Probably some nonsense. I tell you, my luck was with me when she could not keep her skirts down for Farley— or, should I say, she could not keep her breeches up? Let me tell you, she was quite a sight in those clothes. Wished she wasn't my daughter once or twice.'

Devlin clenched his fists. Duprey again laughed, the racking sound repellent. 'Yes, indeed, her lustiness quite settled my debts. Got rid of the expense of another useless daughter, as well.'

'Do you mean you gave her to Farley in payment of gaming debts?'

Duprey drained another glass of sherry. 'Glad of it. Kept me from ruin.'

'Damn you, Duprey,' Devlin said through clenched teeth.

The smile remained frozen on the older man's face. 'Well, damn *you*, Steele, because you are going to marry Emily or suffer the scandal. Your brother dislikes scandal, I'll wager.'

'The scandal is on your head, Duprey, No one will receive

any member of your family after I tell them what you did to
Madeleine.'

'If they would believe you. My youngest daughter died,
you see. There is a grave to prove it.'

'An empty grave.'

'Oh, it is not empty. I purchased a suitable corpse as soon
as it became available.'

Bile rose in Devlin's throat.

Duprey raised the ante. 'So you would only expose the chit
to much sordid attention.'

Devlin gaped at the malevolent man seated so casually.
Surely he was bluffing, a gamester playing the cards the only
way possible when the deal was a poor one.

This wager, however, involved not cards, but the reputa-
tions of the people Devlin held most dear. What effect on
them if he played the game poorly?

Devlin spun on his heel and left the suffocating atmosphere of the Duprey town house. Inhaling fresh air into his
lungs. Devlin hurried to call upon his brother, only to
discover he and Serena had left early for Heronvale. He
begged paper and pen from Barclay and then rushed to his
brother's stable.

Jem was inside.

'Jem, thank God you are here. I need your help,' Devlin
said, not bothering with a greeting. 'Is there a mount to carry
me to Heronvale?'

'Yes, my lord,' Jem responded. 'His lordship took the
carriage with m'lady. How may I serve you?'

'Have someone get the horse ready immediately and you
deliver this letter to my apartments.'

The doctor gestured for Madeleine and Bart to follow him
out of the room where Sophie coughed softly as she lay abed.

The doctor spoke in hushed tones. 'She has a touch of consumption.'

Bart wrung his hands. 'Is there some palliative? A poultice?'

'I am afraid there is little I can do. Country air would be as good as any tonic I could concoct. Alas, this city…' The doctor shook his head. 'It is bad for the lungs.'

Bart gave Madeleine an agonised glance.

'Then she shall go to the country,' Madeleine said. 'Bart, you could take her, could you not?'

'It might be the very thing,' the doctor said.

Bart knitted his eyebrows. 'Perhaps I could take her to Heronvale. They would take us in. The Marquess said he was in my debt. I should ask Dev.'

Madeleine grabbed his arm. 'You must not wait, surely. He might be gone all day.'

'But what of you, Miss Maddy? I should not leave you.'

She smiled. 'You must. It is the only thing to do. I have become quite useful, you know. I am well able to care for things here. Do not give us a thought.'

Bart needed no more coaxing. As soon as the doctor took his leave, the worried new husband was off to hire a posting chaise for his ill wife. Madeleine set to the task of packing Sophie's belongings, refusing to listen to her friend's protests.

'Do not be nonsensical, Sophie,' Madeleine scolded. 'Devlin and I can manage very well.'

Sophie curled up on her cot, making herself even smaller. 'I cannot like being separated from you.'

Madeleine came to her side and put her arms around her. 'Please do not fret. Bart will care for you very well. He loves you, you know.'

Sophie's face took on a dreamy look. She nodded her head and lodged no further complaint.

* * *

Within two hours, Madeleine and Linette watched the chaise drive away, driven by four sturdy but otherwise unremarkable mis-matched horses. Linette, as always, was in raptures about the beasts, but whimpered to see the coach drive away. She hugged her mother's neck. Madeleine thought she might nap for a bit and took her upstairs.

She had no sooner put Linette down upon her small bed when she heard the knocker. Thinking perhaps Bart and Sophie had forgotten something, she rushed down the stairs and flung open the door.

Her sister Emily stood before her.

Chapter Twenty-One

Emily let out a gasp, her gloved hand flying up to cover her mouth. 'I had thought…I thought this Lord Devlin's residence.'

Madeleine eyed Emily warily. 'It is, but he is not here presently.' What could have induced her sister to come here? Surely their mother would not allow such an improper visit.

Emily twisted the cords of her reticule, looking even more discomposed. 'Oh, dear.' She glanced back at the street where a carriage drove out of sight. 'The hack has left.'

'Then you'd best come in.' Madeleine stepped aside, holding the door ajar so Emily could pass into the hallway. She continued to look anxious and confused.

Madeleine's heart beat with excitement. She had not spoken to a member of her family for almost four years.

Emily turned to her. 'I did not know you would be here. That is, I did not realise…' She gave a deep sigh. 'I do not understand any of this!'

Madeleine remembered her sister Emily, two years older, as far more knowledgeable and worldly than she. At this moment, however, she felt herself to be the wiser one. Among the jumble of feelings swirling around inside her was a strong desire to throw her arms around Emily in a sisterly embrace.

'Come into the parlour.' Madeleine led the way and closed the door behind them.

Emily spun around to her. 'Oh, Madeleine! I had no notion…' Tears welled in her eyes. 'I thought you were dead.'

Had news of Madeleine's fall from respectability been kept from Emily? Madeleine always assumed her sisters knew all about it and welcomed the ruse of her demise as her parents must have.

Emily continued, 'How came you to be with L…Lord Devlin? Oh, I do not understand any of it! And Mama would tell me nothing, and Papa said I was a fool and had better keep my mouth shut.'

'You did not know?' Madeleine still could not believe it. She took a tentative step toward her sister, who quickly closed the distance and gave her the embrace Madeleine had longed for.

'Madeleine, Madeleine.' Emily choked back sobs. 'I have felt so guilty. Jessame and I had teased you so, and then you disappeared. You were not found for ages. Papa said no one could see the…the body, because it had been outside so long… Although it could not have been, because you are here, so it must have all been a hoax.'

Madeleine patted her back. 'Now, do not cry, Emily. There is no need. Indeed, I am so sorry to have given you such a shock. Come, sit down and I will get us some tea.'

She persuaded Emily to sit on the settee until she brought the tea and, when they were seated together, gave her sister a somewhat amended version of the events that brought them both to the present moment. Among the details Madeleine neglected to mention were a precise description of the duties required of her by Farley, the exact nature of her relationship with Devlin, and, of course, the existence of Linette.

'So, you see, Lord Devlin has been so kind as to assist me, and when he comes into his fortune he will lend me the money to set up a...a dress shop.'

Perhaps this rose-colored version would help to preserve Devlin's opportunity to marry Emily, if that were still his intent. To think he might become a part of the family Madeleine had lost, however, was very difficult to contemplate.

She changed the subject. 'emily, why have you come here? You really should not have. This is a single gentleman's residence.'

'I know I should not have come, but I could not let Papa—' She grabbed Madeleine's arm. 'Papa means to force Lord Devlin to marry me. He threatens to send a notice to the *Gazette* that Lord Devlin has offered for me, but it is all untrue.'

'It is untrue?'

'Indeed.' Emily sighed heavily. 'I must stop him.'

Madeleine stared at her sister, fumbling at her words. 'But I thought...I thought Devlin did wish to marry you.'

'No, I do not think so.' Emily's brow furrowed. 'He courted the Season's Diamond as much as he did me, and I think she may have refused Greythorne for him...'

Madeleine's eyebrows lifted. Devlin courted a Diamond of the *ton*?

Emily continued. 'At least that is what they say. I am persuaded Lord Devlin never intended to marry me, no matter how much our brother Robert boasted of it all over town. Indeed, I tried to explain to Papa, but he would not listen.'

But Devlin said Emily had been his choice. Had that been untrue? Did he say that to cover up his wish to marry a Diamond?

'Why do you think Devlin would not marry you?'

Emily gave a little laugh. 'Oh, Madeleine, look at me. I am

no beauty. There is nothing to distinguish me from other ladies. Certainly nothing to compete with the pick of the Season.'

Her sister looked well enough, Madeleine thought. Indeed, Emily's face seemed comfortably dear. Madeleine had not realised how much she'd missed this sister she'd thought never cared a fig for her.

A door slammed and halting footsteps sounded on the stairs. 'Mama! Mama!'

Madeleine froze. Emily stared at her, eyebrows raised.

Linette ran in, coming to a stop when she noticed the strange lady seated next to her mother. Her thumb went into her mouth.

Resigned, Madeleine said. 'It is all right, Linette. Come give a curtsy to Miss Duprey.'

Linette, still sucking on her thumb, wobbled on one leg as she tried to accomplish her mother's request.

'Your child?' Emily asked, her eyes wide.

Madeleine nodded.

'Lord Farley's?' she asked.

Madeleine shook her head.

Emily stared at the little girl who climbed into her mother's lap and laid her head against her mother's breast, rubbing her eyes.

Emily's gaze met Madeleine's and held there for several moments. 'She is Lord Devlin's.'

Madeleine nodded. She did not expect Emily to understand how wonderful it was for her to have Linette, to believe that Devlin was indeed Linette's father and that a part of him would always be with her in Linette.

Emily walked to the window. 'Why should Lord Devlin pretend to be courting me or any other lady while living here with you and…and this child? What game has he been playing?'

A game to win money, money enough to support her and their daughter, a coil Madeleine had forced upon him.

She could not tell her sister this. The best she could do was preserve Devlin's chances to marry whomever he wished.

'I am not fit to be his wife, Emily. Not after Lord Farley. I assure you, I was no more than a momentary indiscretion on Devlin's part, but he would not abandon us.'

Emily rubbed her brow. 'It is of no consequence, I suppose. Tell Lord Devlin he may resist Father's trickery. I will not place any damage to my reputation at Lord Devlin's door. He has no obligation to me, and so I will say to anyone. I'll threaten to expose what Father has done to you. That will stop him.'

It would also expose her family to terrible scandal. 'I do not wish for our family to be hurt—'

'Father, hurt? He would never take such a chance. Leave it to me.' Emily briskly retrieved her reticule from the side table and headed toward the door. 'I must leave.'

'No, not so soon,' cried Madeleine, jumping to her feet with Linette still in her arms. Please, allow her a little bit of family for a few minutes more.

Emily turned back to her, the pinched expression on her face softening. Gently she touched Madeleine's cheek. 'I was always so jealous of you, Madeleine, more reason for me to feel guilt when I thought you dead.'

'Jealous of me?'

'You are quite a dazzling beauty.' Emily smiled at her with a wistful expression. 'That year before you disappeared, you had grown so pretty, you cast Jessame and me into the shade. We were green with envy.' She gave a little sigh and kissed Madeleine's cheek. 'I am glad you are alive. Please thank Lord Devlin for being so kind to me. I have had the loveliest time this Season.'

Madeleine could think of nothing to say to this. Emily

strode purposefully toward the door, pausing on the threshold. 'Madeleine?'

Madeleine rushed to her side. 'Yes?'

She gave a little laugh. 'I do not have the least notion how to get back home. Do you know where I can find a hack?'

Madeleine gave a tentative smile. 'Wait a moment. Linette and I will walk with you. There will be a hack near the shops.'

As they walked toward the shops, Madeleine begged for news about Jessame and Robert, thirstily drinking in each small tidbit of information Emily provided. Neither spoke of their parents. As they walked, a stylish phaeton came into view, the gentleman holding the ribbons doing an admirable job controlling a pair of spirited chestnuts.

'Oh, my goodness,' said Emily. 'It is Amanda Reynolds.'

The young lady seated next to the phaeton's driver was the loveliest creature Madeleine had ever seen, fair, delicate, with blonde curls peeping out of a modish bonnet. Her stylish fawn-coloured dress, topped by a matching spencer, adorned a perfect figure.

'Who is she?' she asked.

The two sisters paused to watch these passers-by.

'The Diamond I told you about,' Emily said. 'And I believe that is Devlin's friend with her. She does not like him above half. How shocking for them to be riding together with no more than a tiger for chaperon. What could it mean?'

Madeleine only half attended to these words. Her eyes were fixed on the Diamond, who looked beautiful even seated in silence next to the gentleman. Devlin's friend, another unknown piece of Devlin's life on the town.

Her knowledge of him was confined to their apartments and the few places he could take her. She could not have known he'd attracted this exquisite lady.

As the phaeton rolled past, the Diamond turned around and caught Madeleine's gaze.

Emily quickly covered her face with the brim of her bonnet. 'I must not let her see me.'

A hack pulled up at the end of the street, and Madeleine and Emily rushed over to it. After a swift hug, Madeleine bundled her sister into the vehicle and waved her goodbye, watching until the hack drove completely out of sight.

Lord Farley paced the pavement across the street from Devlin Steele's apartments, waiting. It had become his practice to spend some part of each day or night in this neighbourhood. He often caught a glimpse of Madeleine, but she was always accompanied by Steele, that brutish-looking man of his, or that insipid little maid.

He could hardly believe his good fortune when she bid goodbye to the female who walked out of the house with her. She was alone at last. The child did not matter. Farley crossed the street, timing it so that he placed himself between her and her door. She was as absorbed as ever in the child and did not attend to his approach.

He stepped directly in her path. She looked up and gave a strangled cry.

He smiled at her, his most winning smile, the one he'd used to attract her in the first place. 'Madeleine, my dear, it is my pleasure to see you.'

Her eyes darted to both sides and she protectively grasped her daughter's hand. 'Let me by, if you please.'

'I wish to speak to you.' He placed his hand on her shoulder. She wrenched away.

She picked up the child and tried to walk past him. 'I have no wish to speak to you.'

He blocked her way, putting his arm tightly around her

waist so that she could not easily squirm away. She struggled nevertheless. He held her more tightly against his side. With his mouth tantalisingly close to her ear, he said, 'I want you back, Madeleine.' He did not resist the opportunity, but let his tongue lap the delicate skin of her earlobe.

The sharp heel of her walking boot pounded into his foot. Pain shot through him and he dropped his hold on her. She hurried away, but not quickly enough.

He caught her arm and held it vise-like, his lips again near her ear. 'You will return to me, Madeleine, or one dark night that pretty soldier of yours will find a knife in his back.'

'No!' She struggled. The child began to cry.

Farley wrapped his fingers with Linette's curls. 'I wonder how easy it would be to snatch this child? The chimney sweeps would pay a pretty price for her, I own. Or perhaps a gentleman might fancy some sport with her?'

'Do not touch her!' shrieked Madeleine.

'I repeat, Madeleine. Return to me or I will carry out my threats. You will never know when I am about. I will get them, both of them, you may be sure.'

A man walked up to them with a swift step.

'Sir! Sir! Help me!'

The man faced Farley. 'Let the lady go.'

'This is not your affair,' Farley protested. 'It is only a trifling bit of spirit from my fancy piece here. Nothing to trouble you.'

'No, do not heed him,' Madeleine pleaded.

The man grabbed Farley by the back of his collar, pulling so forcefully, his breath was cut off.

'Unhand her,' the man growled.

Farley, gasping futilely for air, knew when the cards dealt could not be played. He acquiesced.

'Be gone.'

Farley brushed off his coat. Before he turned to leave, he bowed to Madeleine. 'Remember what I said, my dear. I will carry out my plans.'

Farley strolled off, taking care not to look nonplussed.

Madeleine clutched at Linette, whose little arms were tight around her neck and whose head was buried into her shoulder. 'I cannot thank you enough, sir. We are truly in your debt.'

The man bowed. 'Glad to be of service. May I escort you to your destination?'

Madeleine recognised the gentleman as the man who, moments before, had driven by with the Diamond. Devlin's friend.

'Thank you, but I am near my residence…' Madeleine glanced toward her door, just a few houses away.

The Diamond stood at the top of the steps at her door, watching her with interest. Madeleine could not avoid her, too afraid to go somewhere else until they drove off.

She allowed Devlin's friend to walk her to her door as Miss Reynolds watched. Madeleine halted. 'We are here. Thank you, sir.'

'Here?' he asked. 'These are Devlin Steele's apartments.'

As Miss Reynolds stood decorously, Madeleine said in a feeble voice, 'I…I am in his employ.'

'Indeed?' A smile, somewhat cynical, flashed across his face. Miss Reynolds looked shocked.

'Well,' said the gentleman agreeably. 'Let me make our introductions.' He gestured to the ethereal creature at his elbow. 'This is Miss Reynolds, and I am Captain Ramsford, a friend of Lord Devlin's.'

'Mama, I want Deddy!' whimpered Linette.

Ramsford's eyebrows shot up, and Miss Reynold's mouth fell open.

Blushing, Madeleine hurried to the door. 'I will see if Lord Devlin is at home.'

She rushed inside with Linette, caring not if they thought it rude to be kept waiting on the doorstep like tradesmen. Linette curled up on the stairs, still looking frightened. Madeleine called for Devlin, but there was no answer.

Before she stepped back outside she heard Lord Ramsford and Miss Reynolds through the crack in the door.

'Oh, my goodness,' Miss Reynolds cried.

'Compose yourself. You will see Devlin by and by.' He added in a mocking tone, 'In the meantime, you may depend on me.'

Noting Miss Reynolds used Devlin's given name, Madeleine stepped back outside. 'Lord Devlin is not at home.'

Ramsford peered at her quizzically. 'A pity.' He turned to Miss Reynolds. 'We have come on a fool's errand, as I predicted. Now, perhaps you will allow me to convey you home.'

Miss Reynolds gave him a scathing glance. Her forehead wrinkled, and she spoke to Madeleine. 'Who was that man who accosted you?'

Madeleine blinked. 'No one you should know, my lady.'

'Are you all right, Miss…?' Miss Reynolds lifted her eyebrows, obviously wanting Madeleine to reveal her name.

Madeleine lowered her eyes. 'I shall require no further assistance.' She ignored the other request. 'If you will forgive me, I must see to my daughter.'

Without a glance back, Madeleine rushed through the doorway, bolted the door, and went directly to Linette. 'Come, darling,' she said soothingly. 'The bad man will not scare us again.'

The afternoon crept by, spent soothing Linette, entertaining her and attempting to still her own agitation from the afternoon events. Madeleine longed for Devlin to return home. She had decided to warn him only about her father's trickery and Farley's threat. If he did not wish her to know of the Diamond, she would pretend ignorance. In any event, her future would be unchanged.

As time wore on, Madeleine grew more uneasy. When she peeked out the front windows, there always seemed to be some man loitering near the lamppost across the street. Not Farley, but familiar figures. His lackeys. He was having her watched.

Each minute Devlin did not return caused her increased agitation. She pictured him bleeding in some alleyway, a knife thrust into his back. And if that image were not disturbing enough, she envisioned him in the arms of the beautiful Diamond.

She jumped at a sharp knock on the door. With a pounding heart, she peered out the window. It was not Farley, nor one of his men, but a footman dressed in Heronvale livery. She opened the door. The footman handed her a note and left.

The note was addressed to her. With trembling fingers, she broke the seal and read: *My dearest Maddy. I am called away on urgent business. Everything will be settled upon my return. I will be gone only one night and will be home for dinner tomorrow. Explain to Bart. Kiss Linette for me. Yours, etc., D.S.*

She folded the paper again, her heart pounding in her chest. What urgent business was this? Did it involve the Diamond, perhaps? Well, at least Farley could not make good his threat. Devlin would not be killed in some alleyway this night.

Madeleine sat down again with her sewing, trying to calm herself. Linette played close by at her feet. Through the crack in the curtains, she watched two men conversing. They scrutinised the house. How long before they determined she and Linette were alone?

She pricked her finger with the needle and put her finger to her mouth to stop the bleeding.

She'd be damned if she would sit here and wait for Farley to come after her. Even if Farley captured her, he would still make good on his threats to Devlin and Linette. She knew Farley too well. Nothing would save the two people she loved as long as that man breathed life.

Madeleine's pricked finger remained poised in the air. Was that something she could do? She set her sewing on the side table and absorbed herself in thought. She could sneak back to Farley's establishment and wait for him. Surprise would be on her side. She could wait until he slept. Then she could kill him.

Almost without effort, the plan formed itself in her head. First, she would take Linette to the Marquess and Marchioness. They wanted to adopt her and would be very pleased to have her. Linette would receive every advantage under their care, and, if things went wrong, Farley would not dare to touch a child under the Marquess's protection.

But would Devlin be safe? The only way to be sure was to kill Farley. Devlin could then marry Miss Reynolds with no impediment. And have a happy life.

If she were caught, she would be hanged. If she escaped, she must disappear forever. If she failed...well, she must not fail.

Rushing over to the desk, she composed a farewell letter to Devlin. She had to write it several times before sealing the final effort. The bleakness of the task made her hand tremble. How to tell him to forget her? How to tell him how much she loved him? How to explain this was the only thing to be done?

At dusk, Madeleine, donned yet another costume. With her newly acquired sewing skills, she altered some old clothes of

Devlin's, stitching the trousers so that they fit her slim hips and came over her walking boots. She found an old cap of Bart's to cover her hair, and a caped coat. Shortened and its cuffs removed, the coat was large enough to hide Linette beneath and Devlin's sabre behind. Farley's lackeys would be watching the back door as well as the front, but the house shared an area with other residences, so a boy walking out the back would not arouse suspicion. She took the risk of leaving candles burning in the house to look as if they were at home.

She enlisted Linette's cooperation by promising her a visit to the Marquess, who would let her see his horses. She also promised that Linette would see Devlin soon, and that she would have a supreme adventure, but first she must be quiet and still, so the bad man would not discover them.

Linette played her role beautifully, as did Madeleine. A boy in a big coat sauntered down the street to no one's notice.

It was dark when Madeleine reached the Marquess's town house. She had no idea how to discover the servants' entrance, so she strode up to the front door. The huge brass knocker was removed. There was nothing to do but rap on the door with her knuckles.

The Heronvale butler opened the door and looked disapprovingly at her.

'Be gone, ruffian,' he ordered through a crack in the door.

'Please, sir, wait. It is Miss England. Do you remember me? I must see the Marquess. It will only take a moment.'

The elderly man's eyes grew huge as he gaped at her. 'The Marquess and Marchioness are not at home.'

The strap that she had devised to hold Linette dug into her neck, but she dared not reveal the child's presence. 'May I wait for them, please?'

The man regarded her with a concerned look. 'His

lordship and ladyship intend to spend an indefinite time at Heronvale.'

Heronvale?

Madeleine walked down the long steps to the street. This spoiled her plans to be rid of Farley and herself before Devlin returned. She must travel to Heronvale first.

She found her way to the Marquess's stable, where once she had come with Devlin for an early morning ride. She crept inside when the stable boy was not looking. It was not difficult to find a secluded corner in which to hide, nor to convince Linette to be very quiet so they could sleep next to the horses.

When the first rays of light shone through the stable windows, Madeleine rose and searched for the saddles. She was tightening the cinch when the stable door opened and the head groom walked in.

'See here!' he shouted, rushing over to her and grabbing her around the waist.

'Mama! Mama!' Linette shouted as she flung her arms around Madeleine's legs.

'What the devil…?' the groom exclaimed.

Madeleine recognised him as the man who had been with Devlin the night she had run away from the Marquess's town house.

'The Marchioness gave me permission. Do you recall me, sir? I am Lord Devlin's…friend.'

'Does he know you are here?' the man asked.

'No, Lord Devlin is away. That is why I must go to the Marquess. Lord Devlin told me I should.' Madeleine struggled for an explanation that would win his cooperation.

'Mama?' Linette gripped the cloth of Madeleine's trousers.

The groom straightened. 'Who is this?'

'My daughter.'

He regarded her, a thoughtful expression on his face. 'Why are you dressed like that?'

Madeleine thought wildly. 'I feared riding all that distance to Heronvale. It would not be safe as a woman. Please, let me borrow the horse. I promise to return it.'

He rubbed his chin. 'I do not think his lordship would like it if I let you ride off to Heronvale.'

'But you must!'

Already she was terribly delayed. It would have been so much better to have Linette safe and the deed accomplished by now. She needed to do this before Devlin returned. Before he stopped her.

The groom put his hands on his hips. 'I'll take you in the curricle. It will be faster and I think Lord Devlin would charge me to keep you safe.'

Madeleine thought she might kiss the man, so grateful was she. 'Thank you, sir.'

Farley fumed as his carriage sped along. The chit had hoodwinked him. It was late before his men realised that she had been alone in the house and, by the time he had given the order to break in, she and her child were gone.

It took more time to discover that Steele had hotfooted it to his brother's estate. Farley wagered that, somehow, Madeleine was headed there, as well. Farley and his men would reach the outskirts of Heronvale at dawn. He would send his men ahead to discover if she'd arrived there. If not, he would lie in wait for her.

She would not foil him again.

Chapter Twenty-Two

Devlin woke in his old room at Heronvale. For a moment he thought he was an invalid again and the past months merely one of his fevered dreams. A disquieting sense of unease lingered. It had nothing to do with the heated words he and his brother had exchanged. No, something more elusive.

He had confessed the whole to his brother, which had gone rather better than he could have expected, but they did not agree on the solution. Ned was in accord with Devlin about the impropriety of marriage to Emily Duprey, but did not agree that Devlin must marry Madeleine.

Ned's reasoning was sound, Devlin supposed. Ned had argued that Madeleine and the child deserved a peaceful life after all they had endured. As the wife of a Steele, she would be scrutinised. Would not some eager gossipmonger expose her past?

Who in society would trouble themselves with his business if he reactivated his commission in the army? Devlin had countered. Ned nearly turned apoplectic at that suggestion.

Devlin sat up in bed, stretching his limbs and trying to let the new day give perspective on the past one. In any event, Ned could not stop him from rejoining the army. Ned had, after all, given him the bank draft for Madeleine. It provided enough money to repurchase his commission. But how the deuce was he to silence Duprey?

At least Ned cared not a fig for the dust that would be kicked up if Duprey made good his threat, though Ned did not relish becoming the latest *on-dit* for the *ton*. Serena might suffer from it, he had said. Devlin had been surprised by the softness in his brother's expression when he spoke Serena's name. Come to think of it, Ned and Serena seemed unusually at ease with each other.

Devlin shrugged. Whatever the reason, he was glad of it.

He dressed quickly and headed for the stables. A hard ride would clear his mind and rid him of this sense of foreboding.

As he set the horse into a trot, he thought of Madeleine. What a race they could have if she were to ride the estate with him. They could explore all his childhood haunts, the special places he treasured from those simpler days.

The fields stretched ahead of him, some thick with crops, some fallow. He knew every inch of this land. Urging his horse into a gallop, he sped over them, jumping hedges, clearing fences, and letting the exhilaration replace all other thought.

Farley settled himself in the windowseat of the village's posting house. The ale was tolerable and the breakfast generous. More important, any traveller to Heronvale would by necessity pass directly in front of the window. His horse was kept ready, and he could depend on his own eyes if his lackeys failed to warn him if she came into view.

He regarded the innkeeper's daughter with an appraising

eye. She was comely enough, but too common for his tastes. He wondered how many men had their first tumble with a tavern wench. It would make a fetching costume for Madeleine to wear. He could just see the simple dress dipping low, revealing her full breasts as she bent to pour a drink. Farley took a deep swig of his ale. He'd be damned if he'd share her this time.

This time she would be all his, to do with as he wished.

Devlin's ride was ill fated, a bad omen to be sure. After his horse threw a shoe, he led her home on foot, taking up precious time he needed to conclude matters with his brother. The sun was high in the sky when he delivered the horse to the head groom.

'What's amiss, m'lord?' the old retainer asked, having spied him walking with the horse.

'Threw a shoe,' Devlin replied, handing over the reins.

As the man examined the hoof, Devlin made the mistake of mentioning Jem to him. This launched the proud father into a long discourse about his son and how the Marquess was right to value Jem so highly, him being very much like his father. Devlin attended to the conversation with disguised impatience. He had not eaten a bite that day and had much to do before he could return to Madeleine.

'And I was saying to your man yesterday, how I wish the young'uns could live here in the country where the air is not carrying some disease or another, but Jem would not hear of it, nor that wife of his…'

'Saying to my man?'

'Yes, m'lord. Mr Bart. And what a poor little thing that new wife of his is, so sick and all, but she'll be well enough staying with Nurse. Nurse still knows just what should be done, though I'd wager she is five and seventy, if she is a day.'

Devlin grabbed the groom's arm. 'They are here?'

The old man gave him a puzzled look. 'They arrived soon after you.'

Not waiting a moment for the groom. Devlin threw a saddle on one of the other mounts and raced for Nurse's cottage.

She was in her front yard, leaning on her stick, a basket over her arm. She dropped the basket and threw a hand across her chest when he thundered toward her.

'Goodness! Master Devlin, I declare. 'Tis so good to see you. I'm about to make a nice posset for that dear little one.'

'Where are they?' He swung his leg over to dismount before the horse had quite stopped.

'I have the dear girl all right and tight, Master Devlin, never you fear, but you must take a care you don't break your neck. I've told you many a time—'

He ran inside with her limping behind him.

Devlin found Bart seated by the bedside where a pale Sophie lay. Bart's face was pinched with worry.

'My God, what happened?'

Bart glanced up in surprise, 'Dev!'

Nurse poked Devlin on the shoulder with her bony finger. 'You'll not go racketing in this house, m'lord, and waking the girl. She needs her rest. If you want to be talking, get into the other room and keep your voices down.'

Devlin did as he was told, Bart rising to go with him. They went into the main room in the cottage.

'Is Madeleine with you?' Devlin asked anxiously.

'No, but she thought… What are you doing here?'

'Never mind that now. What of Sophie?'

Bart rubbed his face and flopped into a chair. 'She could hardly breathe. The doctor said the only hope was country air. Dev, I would not have come had I known you would be absent.'

'Now, no fussing,' said Nurse, walking in. 'I told you she'd be right and tight. Sleeping like a baby, she is.' She limped over to the fire and busied herself with the posset.

Devlin placed his hand on Bart's shoulder. 'You were right to bring Sophie here. I promise you Nurse will know just what to do for her. I trust Madeleine and Linette have done very well, so do not worry on that side. I had sent word to her that I would be away, but to be prudent I will return to London immediately.'

'We should not have left her,' Bart said.

'Nonsense,' countered Devlin. 'It was my error, leaving as I did with only a note. I must not tarry.'

As he galloped back to the house, that sense of dread returned. Madeleine was alone and she knew no one who could help her if anything went amiss. He must reach her without delay. Devlin ordered a fresh mount, and hurried to inform his brother.

Madeleine pretended to be calm as she sat beside the chattering Linette, who was in transports over riding behind two horses and spying so many more along the way. Jem patiently answered Linette's endless questions about the beasts, at the same time asking no questions of Madeleine. She was grateful to him for that.

They passed through a small village. 'Not long now,' he said.

Not long before she would hug Linette for the last time; kiss her little cheek for the last time. Madeleine might have managed it well enough if she could have handed Linette over to the Marquess in London, before she'd had all these hours to contemplate never seeing her little girl again. With each mile her soul ebbed away, bit by painful bit.

After this wrenching deed was accomplished, the rest of

it would seem easy. She would travel back to London, to the gaming hell where she would find Farley. She feared killing him, but only because she might be wicked enough to enjoy it. It should be a comfort to know that Devlin would have the life he deserved, with a beautiful wife who could be a credit to him instead of a mistress who placed his life in danger.

It was no comfort, however. Losing him would hurt as much as losing Linette.

Horses' hooves pounded behind them, and Jem steered the curricle to the side to give the riders room to pass. One rider came aside the curricle's team and grabbed the harness while others surrounded the vehicle, their horses whinnying and breathing hard.

'Get her!' someone shouted.

Madeleine immediately clutched Linette, holding the child tight while men grabbed at them both. The curricle came to an abrupt stop, Jem was on his feet, snapping at the men with his whip. Madeleine crouched on the seat, the shouts of the men harsh in her ears and the smell of horse sweat filling her nostrils. Jem's whip snapped and cracked above her head. A shot rang out, and Jem tumbled from the curricle.

Madeleine forced herself not to think of him. She tucked Linette beneath her feet and unsheathed Devlin's sabre, slashing it at her attackers as Devlin had demonstrated. She drove them back again. Through the din she could hear Jem moaning.

'Damn you, I said get the chit.' That was Farley's voice. He had come for her and to make good his threat toward Linette.

'Mama,' Linette cried, cowering at her feet.

'Cowards!' shouted Farley. 'Seize her now.'

The sabre sliced at the arm of one of the attackers. He fell back, cursing, blood spurting from his arm. Madeleine swung at another, but another man climbed on the curricle and grabbed her from behind. He squeezed her wrist until the sword clattered to the ground. Madeleine struggled against him. Farley rode near and plucked Linette from the vehicle.

'No!' Madeleine screamed.

She clawed at her captor's eyes and kicked him in the groin with all her might. With a cry of pain, he pushed her away. She lost her footing and fell hard on to the ground, the breath knocked out of her. With her cheek flat against the ground, she saw Jem writhing in pain, white-faced, blood staining his shoulder. The horses' stamping hooves sounded perilously close, the animals as panicked as she. The dirt they kicked up rained down on her. The horses bolted, sending Farley's man sprawling off the back in the wake of the curricle clattering down the road.

'Mama! Mama!' Linette's screams rose above the din.

Madeleine forced herself to rise. She groped for the sabre.

Farley dismounted, holding Linette as if she were a parcel of old rags. His men, one mounted, one not, circled around their comrades. The two on the ground were helped to their feet.

Ignoring that she was outnumbered, Madeleine took advantage of the distraction. She strode toward Farley, sabre in hand.

'Release my child.'

Farley laughed, the evil sound stilling Linette's cries. Gazing smugly at Madeleine, he held Linette in front of him, protecting his chest with her little body. 'Still wish to thrust your sword into me, my dear?'

'Let her go.' Her demand was useless, she knew. Two of his lackeys closed in on her again. She turned, slashing the sabre at them. Out of the corner of her eye a third man aimed a pistol at her.

'Do not damage her!' Farley ordered. 'Surround her. There are four of you and one of her.'

The men did as they were told. Madeleine spun around, turning to each of them as they jeered at her.

'Drop the sword, my dear,' Farley said, his voice sickly smooth. 'You and your child are mine now.'

Madeleine closed her eyes. Her heart despaired.

She heard a galloping horse and cries of surprise from Farley's men. Her eyes flew open, and she saw the horseman. Devlin.

He had no weapon save savage cries and murder in his eyes. He charged straight toward the men surrounding Madeleine, grabbing one of them as the man attempted to run. Devlin lifted him by the collar of his coat and tossed him down again. Madeleine raised the sabre, and Devlin grabbed it out of her hand. He became someone she had not imagined before, a demon on horseback, who easily scattered Farley's men. One reached a horse, mounted and beat a hasty retreat. The others ran for the woods.

With only a glance toward Madeleine, Devlin dismounted and approached Farley, sabre menacing. 'Unhand the child, Farley.'

Farley took a step back. Before Devlin could reach him, Farley drew a silver-bladed knife from his belt and held it against Linette's tiny throat. Its blade flashed in the afternoon sun.

'I would drop the sword if I were you, Steele.' Farley's upper lip curled.

Devlin lowered his sword very slightly.

'I mean it,' growled Farley. He pressed the blade against the child's neck, drawing a trickle of blood. She shrieked.

'No,' pleaded Madeleine.

Devlin watched the blood drip over Farley's fingers to stain the front of Linette's dress. The child, her face chalky white, was rigid, terror bulging her eyes. His vision blurred, and, distinctly as if it were happening to him again, he felt each stab of the French cuirassier.

He shook his head clear, ignoring his old demons and the panic that accompanied them. 'Let the child go, Farley.' Devlin's voice was steady.

'I'll give you the brat.' Farley sneered. 'But I keep the mother.'

'No deals,' said Devlin, advancing.

'She's mine.' Farley's voice went up a pitch and he placed the point of the knife below Linette's chin. 'You stole her from me and now I want her back.'

Devlin halted. There was no way to disarm Farley or strike him before he cut deep into Linette's throat.

Panic rose again and again he pushed it away. Battle was much like a game, he reminded himself, a series of points and counterpoints. As in the card came they'd played not more than three months ago, Devlin must wait until Farley made a mistake.

'I did not steal her.' Devlin kept his voice deceptively calm. 'You offered her, remember? You lost at your own game.'

'Your play was dishonest!' Farley waved the knife.

'It was not, as you well know. You gambled and lost,' he continued reasonably.

'Now you lose!' Farley gave a mirthless laugh. He swung the knife dramatically back to Linette's throat. Devlin's grip hardened on the hilt of the sword.

Suddenly, Farley's gaze left Devlin's face and focused behind him, his jaw dropping open. Devlin turned.

Madeleine had mounted one of the horses. The agitated beast bucked and twisted and kicked. It huffed and blew, its eyes wild. Devlin fell back, away from its kicks. Farley gaped, eyes frozen on the out-of-control animal.

How was Madeleine able to remain in the saddle? Devlin had visions of her falling off and being trampled to death by the horse's hooves. Somehow she hung on. The horse leapt and vaulted ever closer to Farley, who gave a terrified cry. He dropped Linette to the ground, and covered his face against the lethal hooves of the approaching horse.

Devlin grabbed Linette, covering her with his body. Let the hooves kick at him. He would use his body to protect his child.

'Drop the knife, Farley.' Madeleine shouted from the rearing horse. Devlin glanced up.

The horse came under perfect control, advancing slowly toward Farley. White-faced, Farley sank to his knees.

Devlin stood, holding Linette, who had her small arms tightly wrapped around his neck.

'Is she all right?' Madeleine asked, her voice trembling as she backed up the horse.

'I think so,' Devlin replied. He gave her a half-grin. 'Excellent horsemanship.'

She shrugged.

With an enraged cry, Farley charged toward Devlin and Linette, his knife raised.

Madeleine kicked at the horse. The animal shot forward, rearing and whinnying. Its hooves came down on Farley, knocking him to the ground. Madeleine pulled the animal away and forced it back under control. Farley moaned and rolled over. The knife protruded from his chest. Blood soaked his clothing and pooled next to his now-still body.

Chapter Twenty-Three

Madeleine stared out the window. The setting sun cast a reddish glow over the impressive Heronvale park and the rolling countryside. A fire crackled in the ornate marble fireplace at the end of the room, but the cup of tea on the table beside her grew cold. She tucked her feet underneath her on the settee and tried to banish the image of Farley's death from her mind.

The door opened.

'There you are.' Devlin walked into the room.

She looked up at him for a moment and back to the window.

He sat beside her and put his hand gently under her chin, turning her face to him. 'Are you all right?'

Concern shone in his eyes. She could not bear it. She nodded.

He smiled at her, drinking her in with his gaze. 'I see Serena found a dress for you.'

'She has been kind.'

The Marchioness had taken Madeleine and Linette under her wing as soon as they reached Heronvale. They were cosseted and pampered, cleaned up, and dressed in clothes that were hurriedly found in attic trunks.

He put his arm around her and tucked her next to him. She rested her head on his shoulder. It was enticingly comfortable.

'Where is Linette?' he asked.

'I believe the Marquess and Marchioness took her to the stables.'

'Ah, that should please her.' He kissed the top of her head. 'Did you visit Sophie?'

'Yes.'

Sophie had burst into tears when she'd seen her. Madeleine held her and rocked her as if she had been Linette.

'Did you…settle things?' Madeleine asked.

There had been much commotion when they arrived at Heronvale. Devlin had carried the injured Jem on his horse. They had left Farley's body where it lay.

He snuggled her closer to him. 'All is set right, Maddy. Ned spoke to the magistrate, and no further enquiry will be required.'

She closed her eyes. 'I thought I would enjoy killing him.'

He stroked her hair. 'Death is not something to enjoy, but you did not kill him, my love. His own treachery did that.'

He should not call her his love, she thought. Did he now feel even more obligated to her? He should not.

She turned her gaze to the scene from the window. 'Heronvale is very beautiful,' she said.

'I am pleased you like it.'

His arm felt so strong around her and his body warmed hers. She wished she could remain in his warmth and strength forever, but it was time to settle the matters between them, as well.

'Perhaps Linette would be happy here.'

'Linette?'

Madeleine pulled away from him. He regarded her with a puzzled expression.

'I have decided that I should…should agree for Linette to be adopted by the Marquess.'

Devlin's brows lifted. 'Are you mad?'

'It would be best for her, do you not think?' She forced herself to speak casually.

'No, I do not think.' He scowled. 'Perhaps you had better tell me where this addled-brained idea came from.'

She rose from the settee and folded her arms across her chest. 'Well, they can offer her so much more than I. I am persuaded her life would have more advantages.' She walked toward the window. 'She would still see you from time to time, as well.'

He stood as well, matching her tone, but with an edge of sarcasm. 'And where will you be while Linette has this idyll?'

'Oh, I shall do well, I think. You needn't concern yourself.'

He gripped her by the shoulders. 'Tell me what this is about.'

She avoided his eyes. 'My sister Emily visited me—'

He interrupted her. 'And she said I was to marry her. Well, I am not.'

Madeleine tried to pull away from his grasp, but he would not release her. She tried to boldly meet his eye. 'She told me you did not court her, but another lady. The Diamond of the *ton*.'

He blinked in surprise. 'Amanda Reynolds? Not exactly so.'

'I met Miss Reynolds, Devlin,' Madeleine said, her voice soft. 'She would make you a lovely wife.'

'You met Amanda Reynolds as well?' His hand flew up in surprise. 'I was only absent a few hours.'

She continued earnestly. 'She is beautiful, Devlin. The catch of the Season, Emily said. And I thought she had such kind eyes…'

'Damn her eyes!' he barked. 'What do her eyes matter to

me?' He grabbed her shoulders again. 'I am not going to marry Amanda Reynolds.'

She pulled back.

'Do you know why I came here, Maddy?' He spoke softly. She shook her head.

'It was to inform my brother that I would marry you.'

Her gaze shot up.

'You, Maddy. Not your sister. Not Amanda Reynolds. You. It is you I love.'

She stared at him, her eyes wide and wary.

He gazed at her with tenderness. 'I came to inform my brother that I would marry you. I did not ask his approval. I checked with my old regiment. If I rejoin the cavalry, I may be able to support you and Linette, if you can bear following the drum. Others have done it, Maddy. Perhaps we can, too.'

'Follow the drum,' she repeated.

'We may be sent to Canada, at best, although it might be Africa or India or some other ungodly place, but we would be together.'

'You cannot mean to rejoin the army. Not after Waterloo.'

He set his jaw firmly. 'I can master Waterloo.'

She reached up and stroked his cheek with the back of her soft hand. 'But what of your inheritance? Your estate?'

'What good is money to me, my love, if you and Linette are not with me?'

'Oh, Devlin,' she whispered, 'have we not always known we could not be together?'

'We must be together, Maddy.'

Laughter sounded in the hallway. Ned and Serena walked in the room, Ned carrying Linette on his shoulders. He leaned over and flipped her over, causing a squeal of delight.

'Mama!' Linette ran over to Madeleine and jumped into her arms. 'I saw a pony and Markiss let me ride her!'

'That is wonderful, sweetling.' Madeleine hugged her daughter for a moment before the child squirmed out of her arms, reaching for Devlin. He squatted down to her level, giving her his total attention, though she told him exactly what she'd told her mother.

Madeleine stared at them, trying to memorise the moment. It was so beautiful, it hurt.

The Marquess regarded her, his expression of concern much like his brother's. 'How do you go on, Miss England?'

She shot him a suspicious glance. 'I suspect you know that is not my name.'

He smiled at her. 'Madeleine, then, if I may?'

His wife took his arm, approval shining in her eyes.

'As you wish, my lord,' Madeleine murmured.

Devlin stood, facing his brother. 'I have asked Madeleine to marry me, Ned.'

'How lovely,' exclaimed Serena.

The Marquess, however, knit his brows.

'I have not accepted, my lord,' Madeleine was quick to add.

'Oh, dear,' said Serena.

Devlin put his arm around Madeleine.

The Marquess pursed his lips. 'It is not a wise course.'

'Oh, nonsense!' Serena broke in. 'It is plain as a pikestaff they are in love with each other.'

'Darling,' Ned said, his voice softening as he turned to his wife, 'there is more to marriage than love.'

'A contract? A business matter? A merging of two fortunes?' Devlin spoke with heat. 'That may have suited you, Ned, but not me. I am a younger son. I will not even reside in England. What can it signify who I marry?'

Ned's cheek twitched. 'This plan of yours to rejoin the army is unconscionable.'

'If it is the only way I may be with Maddy, it is worth it,' Devlin said.

'You will be with no one if you lie dead on some battlefield,' his brother shot back.

Devlin's teeth clenched. 'I love Maddy and I will do anything to stay with her. Loving her is the only thing that matters.'

'You have to stay alive, don't you?'

'Oh, please stop.' Madeleine cried. 'Stop arguing on my account.'

'Oh, pish. Of course love matters,' exclaimed Serena, her eyes flashing at her husband. 'If you love Devlin, Ned, you ought to simply give him his estate and have done with it.' She placed her hands on her hips. 'More to marriage than love... Nonsense. Ned, you told me you loved me from our first meeting, as I have loved you. It has made all the difference.' She spun around to Madeleine. 'Tell me, Madeleine. Do you love Devlin?'

Madeleine gazed at Devlin. 'I love Devlin more than life itself, but he deserves a better wife than I can be.'

Devlin gave her a returning look of adoration.

Serena smiled at them. She turned to her husband. 'See?'

Ned shook his head. 'What I see is trouble ahead for them.'

'Did you know that Madeleine taught me how to love you, Ned?' Serena persisted. 'I went to Devlin's apartments and begged her to teach me what to do.'

Ned's jaw dropped.

'So, you can place our happiness at her door.' She placed her hand on her stomach. 'We would not have this baby if not for Madeleine.'

Both Madeleine and Devlin gaped in surprise.

A slow smile lit Ned's countenance. He moved toward his wife and took her in his arms, lifting her, and twirling her around. While Madeleine and Devlin watched in astonishment, Ned placed his lips on Serena's and held them there, deepening the kiss until it was clear they had forgotten there were witnesses in the room.

'Mama,' Linette piped up, 'Markiss kiss.'

Serena and Ned broke apart, red-faced.

'Um,' Ned mumbled. 'If you will pardon us…'

As Serena's laughter trilled, Ned took her arm, but paused, turning back to Devlin. 'We'll settle the estate papers and the bank draft later.' He escorted his wife out of the room.

Devlin stared at the door. He turned to Madeleine, amazement on his face. 'You are responsible for that?'

Madeleine felt her face grow hot. 'I told her only what you have taught me about love.'

He walked over to her and gently lifted her chin with his finger. 'I have not yet begun to teach you about love. Marry me. Come live with me at Edgeworth. We shall breed a stable of horses.'

'I cannot.' Her voiced cracked. 'My past.'

His arms encircled her. 'No one will know of your past. Your family will be ruined if they speak of it, and Farley is no longer a threat. No one else knows of you.'

'People will wonder.'

'Then we will give them a fiction to believe.' He held her close against him, her head resting on his chest. 'Perhaps you could become the daughter of a merchant or some such. We could say we secretly married years ago when I was on leave from Spain. Linette would be legitimate, then. How would that suit you?'

She relaxed against the steadiness of his heartbeat. 'Oh, I suppose. It is merely another mask, is it not? But not a shameful one.'

'I will give you the life you deserve.' Devlin took a deep

breath and squeezed her tighter. Lifting her face to his, he placed his lips tenderly against hers.

'Deddy kiss!' Linette squealed, running over to them.

Laughing, Devlin and Madeleine lifted her up between them and kissed again.

Epilogue

The two magnificent horses raced over the countryside, neck and neck, clearing every fence and hedge. Their hooves beat the earth like thunder, until at the stone marker on the rise, their riders drew them to a halt.

'I won,' Devlin said. 'Arrived before you this time.'

'Oh, no, indeed,' said his wife. Her apparel gave her the appearance of a slim lad, but the cascade of mahogany-coloured hair down her back belied that impression. 'I won.'

From this high vantage point, Devlin surveyed the fields of his estate, thick and fragrant with hops. He gave silent thanks to his brother. For the first time in Ned's life, he had acted in a way their father would have disapproved. He had given Devlin Edgeworth, and his fortune, as well.

In the centre of this picturesque scene was the house, not as grand as nearby Heronvale, but more precious to Devlin because he shared it with his wife. In the distance Devlin watched their daughter, mounted on a white pony, jumping the low bars set up by Jem, as their best breeding mares grazed nearby. Unseen but also busy at work were his steward, Bart, who managed to recall every niggling task necessary to run the estate, and Sophie who, under much protest, had created Madeleine's unusual riding outfit.

'It is beautiful here,' sighed Madeleine. 'I never hoped for so much happiness.'

He grinned at her. 'Do not be so happy. I won this race, you know.'

She pursed her lips. 'Only because I have been a little tired of late.'

'Tired?' He gazed at her, worry furrowing his brow. 'Maddy, are you unwell? Perhaps you should not be riding today.'

'Not unwell precisely,' she said, turning her steed to make a more sedate way down the hill.

He rode beside her.

She sighed. 'I could not resist one more run. I shall not be free to do so again for some time.'

'What the deuce are you talking about?'

She grinned at him, a mischievous twinkle in her eye. 'I am due to give Linette a brother or sister next summer.'

He pulled his horse to a halt. 'What?'

Madeleine rode back to him. 'I am increasing, husband.'

'Good God! And you are racketing all over the countryside, hell for leather? I ought to throttle you!'

'Not throttle,' she said, coming along beside him, the two horses head-to-tail to each other. The sultry look on her face heated his loins. She smiled and leaned toward him. 'Kiss.'

Devlin Steele did as his wife bid him.

* * * * *

Celebrating Our Authors

MORE ABOUT THE BOOKS

MORE ABOUT THE AUTHOR

WE RECOMMEND

Celebrating Our Authors

DIANE GASTON ON
The Vanishing Viscountess and
The Mysterious Miss M

I feel so very fortunate to be able to spend my days in Regency England. I sometimes think I am really there, hearing the sounds and smelling the scents, feeling the cobbles of the streets beneath my feet. Then I open my eyes and realise I'm still here in Virginia, nearly in view of Washington, DC. When I wrote *The Mysterious Miss M* I had never been to England, but even then I felt the place was imprinted on my soul. This illusion is so much stronger now that I have had two lovely trips to the UK. Now I can *really* feel my characters walking through Mayfair, passing Lock and Co., hatters on St James's Street, striding into White's. I can even envision my hero and heroine in the Pump Room in Bath or sitting down for dinner in the grand dining room in the Royal Pavilion in Brighton or ascending a marble staircase in an elegant country house like Chatsworth.

'...I can really feel my characters walking through Mayfair...'

So why is it that Tanner, who first appeared in *Innocence and Impropriety*, insisted upon setting his story in locations where I did not feel so at home? *The Vanishing Viscountess* begins with a shipwreck, because I wanted a very exciting opening for the book. This meant I had to figure out where a packet ship from Ireland could be wrecked, and what the coastline would appear like. That was just the beginning. I also had to figure out where Tanner and Marlena would go after the shipwreck and how they would travel to their ultimate destination: Edinburgh.

Celebrating Our Authors

Although I had seen parts of the Lake District and the outskirts of Edinburgh, it had been through the window of a tour bus in the spring. I needed to know how it looked off the road in autumn. So I spent a lot of time touring the countryside on the internet. I found a wealth of images. Photographs of the towns and countryside through which my characters needed to ride. Examples for the crumbling castle in which Tanner and Marlena take shelter (Morton Castle) and for Marlena's family estate (Knowsley Hall). I used mapquest. com and Google Earth to help plot out this journey, based on the coaching routes of the time period. This virtual journey just made me want to return and travel the distance myself!

In addition to the geography, I also needed to learn a lot about titles, legal issues, and horses. Writing *The Vanishing Viscountess* turned out to be a wonderful adventure, but not one I could have accomplished on my own. My very special thanks to friends who helped me: Nancy Mayer, Anke Fontaine, Alyssa Fernandez, Delle Jacobs, Emily Hendrickson, Gaelen Foley, and Jo Beverley. I'm certain you will recognise some of these names. These are all knowledgeable ladies who love writing Regency romance — as I do!

Celebrating Our Authors

FURTHER RECOMMENDED READING

If you would like to find out more about this fascinating period in history, Diane Gaston recommends the following books.

Our Tempestuous Day: A History of Regency England by Carolly Erickson – a wonderful, comprehensive history of the important people, events and social issues of the era.

Jane Austen: In Style by Susan Watkins and Hugh Palmer – more about the clothes, houses, and entertainments of the Regency.

Beau Brummell by Ian Kelly – a stunning and comprehensive and ultimately tragic portrait of the man and the era he influenced. I wound up caring about this fascinating man.

Waterloo: A Near Run Thing by David Howarth – the story of the battle is told from reminiscences of the soldiers who experienced it and this approach makes it come alive and read like a novel, complete with a moving love story.

Galloping at Everything: The British Cavalry in the Peninsular War and at Waterloo, 1808-15 by Ian Fletcher – detailed and readable account of the experiences of the cavalry regiments.

Mrs Hurst Dancing and Other Scenes from Regency Life 1812-23 by Diana Sperling – lovely watercolours of Regency life done by a young woman of the time. A truly personal, unique and whimsical view of the Regency.

5

Please note these are Diane Gaston's recommendations. Inclusion on this list does not indicate recommendation by the publisher, or any representation as to the content of these sources. Nor does it indicate that any of these entities have endorsed her books or use of their listings here.

Celebrating Our Authors

Celebrating Our Authors

AUTHOR BIOGRAPHY

When Diane Gaston was a little girl she learned all the words to popular love songs. When she played, her dolls acted out tragic love affairs with the current TV or movie heart-throb. She thought everyone in the world made up romantic stories in their heads to get to sleep at night.

The third daughter of a colonel in the US army, Diane moved often as a child, as far away as Japan one year. But mostly she lived in the Washington, DC, area, where she now resides. The life of an 'army brat' bred strong values of duty and honour and discipline, although it also meant many moves, many new houses, but also new friends. Until new friends could be made, reading books passed the time.

It was always the romance in books that Diane liked best. She read Nancy Drew more to see what Nancy and Ned were up to than caring how the mystery was solved. She will never forgive Louisa May Alcott for not letting Jo wind up with Laurie in *Little Women*. She much preferred the happy ending of *Jane Eyre* to the tragic one in *Wuthering Heights*.

When Diane attended Ohio University she chose to study English literature. There she again read Jane Austen's *Pride and Prejudice*, and first read DH Lawrence's *Lady Chatterley's Lover*, bringing her closer to the romance fiction she soon learned to love. Susan Howatch's *Cashelmara* and *Penmarric* were early favourites, but when Diane discovered Georgette Heyer and then a whole genre of Regency romance, she felt as if she'd found the world where she truly belonged.

Diane's real-life career, however, consisted of helping others craft their own happy endings. She'd earned master's degrees in both psychology and social work and became a county mental health therapist. She also married and raised a daughter and son, now grown up.

At the county mental health centre where Diane worked, she and her colleagues would sometimes fantasise about what job they dreamed of having. Diane always said hers would be writing romance novels. When her life settled down enough, that's exactly what Diane set out to do. It took years, but finally her dream came true with a phone call from Mills & Boon. Shortly afterwards, Diane put her mental health career behind her and became a full-time writer of Regency romance. Her books have gone on to win prestigious romance awards such as the National Readers' Choice Awards, the Orange Rose, and, the biggest award of all, a Romance Writers of America RITA®.

'... It was always the romance in books that Diane liked best...'

Before ever selling a book, though, Diane reaped a world of friendships through her romance writing, a wonderful bonus to living her dream. When not writing, Diane enjoys e-mailing with her friends and travelling to England for research. But no more moving. She's lived in the same house for over twenty years now, shared with her husband and three very ordinary house cats.

Diane loves to hear from readers and friends. E-mail her at diane@dianegaston. com or write to her at PO Box 523131, Springfield, VA 22152, USA. Visit her on the web at www.dianegaston.com

DIANE GASTON ON WRITING

What do you love most about being a writer?

Being a writer is a dream come true for me. I get to spend my days in Regency England and I get to recreate that magical, wonderful, exhilarating feeling of falling in love. Over and over. I love creating stories, thinking up characters, bringing them to life, and figuring out what will happen to them. I love bringing my characters to the happy ending.

Where do you go for inspiration?

I have amassed a huge collection of research books: books on the history of the Regency era, on the furniture, the houses, the fashions, the important figures of the period, books on the Napoleonic War. I am lucky enough to have a set of Annual Registers of the Regency period. These were printed each year about the previous year and documented the proceedings of Parliament, the births, deaths, and marriages, world events, poetry. The most useful section in the Registers, however, is the selected news events, month by month. Merely reading some of these events brings up story ideas. The idea for starting *The Vanishing Viscountess* with a shipwreck came from reading accounts of shipwrecks in the Annual Registers. Sadly, in those accounts I've yet to read one where the women and children survive.

'... I fall in love with my heroes in each book...'

Where do your characters come from and do they ever surprise you as you write?

Sometimes I imagine that my characters

Celebrating Our Authors

really lived in the Regency period and that their stories are merely being revealed to me. Usually, they start with a small idea. Maddie from *The Mysterious Miss M* started from my idea that I wanted to write a love scene in the very first chapter. I needed a heroine who might make love to the hero on first meeting and I needed to make both her and the hero sympathetic. I'd also read a lot about how the daughters of the well-to-do were often blamed and banished if they'd been seduced or victimised. Soon the idea of Maddie began to form. Once I get a general idea of the person like that, their past lives almost emerge in my mind full-blown, as Maddie's did. I think my years as a mental health therapist have given me a sixth sense about the backgrounds of my characters. They do surprise me, though. When I first created Tanner, he was merely supposed to be a spoiled wealthy man who paid other people to solve his problems. I didn't realise at first that he really performed important tasks, even if he didn't give himself credit for them.

Do you have a favourite character that you've created and what is it that you like about that character?

My favourite characters are always the ones in the book I'm currently writing and they generally are my heroes. I fall in love with my heroes in each book – I just don't tell my husband! Tanner was an exception, though. Much as I loved Flynn from *Innocence and Impropriety*, it was always Tanner who secretly had my heart. I loved his contrasts – fabulously wealthy but totally lacking in conceit; being such an important man but thinking himself useless. I loved his sense of humour and fun.

Celebrating Our Authors

When did you start writing?

Unlike most of my writing friends, I never really aspired to be a writer. I did think writing romance novels would be a dream job, but I thought only 'special' people could do it. When my children were old enough not to need me every minute and I'd accomplished all I wanted in my work, I started reading again and relearned how much I loved romance novels. Coincidentally, a friend of mine returned to university to earn a degree in creative writing, and she gave me the courage to try writing, too. That was about twelve years ago. It took me about eight years of writing before I was published, but I've loved every minute of the journey.

What one piece of advice would you give to a writer wanting to start a career?

Finish the book. Avoid the temptation to make that first chapter perfect. Move on and finish the book. You will learn so much about writing, about constructing a plot, about tying up threads of the story if you write it to the end.

What are you currently working on?

I'm working on Adrian Pomroy's story. Adrian made brief appearances as Tanner's friend in *Innocence and Impropriety* and *The Vanishing Viscountess*. He will be back as Viscount Cavanley and will assist a heroine who suffers the Regency equivalent of a paparazzi onslaught. When the lady becomes pregnant, the newspapers and caricaturists go wild trying to discover the paternity, but the lady will never tell — not even Adrian, who is the unborn baby's father.

I plan to explore the effect of a media frenzy on a person's life and on a couple trying to build a relationship. Coleridge called the Regency 'the age of personality' and public curiosity about personalities such as Beau Brummell, Lord Byron, Wellington, Emma Hamilton, and Harriette Wilson was great. Instead of YouTube, there were caricatures on display in shop windows and for sale. Newspapers were filled with gossip, even though the names of the celebrities were given in initials. I suspect to the targets of the gossip, it felt much the same in the Regency as it does now.

Celebrating Our Authors

A DAY IN THE LIFE

My husband and I could not have more
opposite biological clocks. He's an early riser
and I'm a night owl, so when he kisses me
goodbye in the morning, I'm half asleep. I
usually rise by seven-thirty am, though, and,
glamorous life that I have, my very first task
of the day is cleaning out the kitty litter.
Once the kitties are happy, I sit down to
check e-mail for a little while. I try to start
writing by nine. Sometimes, though, I look
up and it's almost eleven o'clock. I usually
take a break at noon and visit Curves, my
local all-women's exercise salon. If it were
not for Curves I'd get no exercise at all.
Sometimes after Curves and lunch, I have a
hard time settling back down to write.

I usually write on a laptop, most often on
the couch in my den next to a glass door
that looks out onto the woods behind the
house. Sometimes at dusk I see deer walk
through the woods. Inside, I usually have a
cat or two to keep me company. If I'm lucky
one will sit right next to me and warm me.
Sometimes I write on my bed with my
research books strewn around me. Rarely am
I able to write without needing to stop and
research something, either on the internet or
by pulling books off the shelves in my 'book'
room upstairs. I can't call the room an office,
because I never work in there; it just houses
my books and my other assorted writing
clutter. Some days the writing goes so well
I start at nine and forget Curves and write
until late in the afternoon and it seems like
no time has gone by at all.

Typically, though, I usually run out of steam
at about four pm and turn back to e-mail,

'...Sometimes
I write on
my bed with
my research
books strewn
around me...'

or work on my blogs, or do other writing-related things. My husband is home by five or five-thirty and we tend to keep 'country hours' for dinner, eating by six pm at the very latest. I am so-not-a-cook; therefore dinners are simple fare, usually ready in half an hour or less. After dinner my husband and I usually watch television, with cats present, of course. My husband is a master at using the TV's remote and he has the control at this time of night. Because he retires early, in his early to bed, early to rise fashion, I wait to watch the programmes he'd hate. I'm usually checking my e-mail, chatting online or doing other writing tasks at the same time.

I'm on the computer so much that I feel lost if I go a day without it; it is my main way of keeping up with my friends. Whenever I get the chance, I love to go out to lunch with friends and, once in a while, I spend the whole day with writing friends, talking about writing. That is the best sort of day.

When I drag myself up to bed, it is almost always after midnight and my husband is fast asleep. I read until I fall asleep, always with cats for company.

DIANE GASTON'S FUTURE PROJECTS

After I finish Adrian's story, I would like to start a new set of connected books all taking place in the Regency and including that 'Regency Underworld' tone of unusual characters and situations that show the darker side of Regency life. I'm thinking of starting with three soldiers who all share some sort of traumatic experience in Spain that affects their future lives. That is all I have at the moment, though. That little glimmer of a story idea. That is how *The Mysterious Miss M* began, come to think about it. And *The Vanishing Viscountess*. And all the books in between. Whatever the future project turns out to be, I will aspire to write an emotional story with compelling, complex characters, and a tale readers will enjoy.

If you enjoyed *The Vanishing Viscountess*, we know you'll love these great reads.

A Compromised Lady by Elizabeth Rolls

Something had wrought a change in Thea Winslow. As a girl she had been bubbling over with mischief. As a woman she seemed half lost in shadow. But Richard Blakehurst couldn't miss the flash of connection between them when his hand touched hers. It was as if he had awakened something deep inside her.

Seeing Richard again brought back the taunting memory of their dance at her coming-out ball. She *must* tame her wayward thoughts because Thea doubted even her considerable fortune could buy Richard's good opinion of her if ever he learnt the truth…

On sale from 1st February 2008!

The Dangerous Mr Ryder by Louise Allen
(first in *Those Scandalous Ravenhursts*)

It is whispered about the *Ton* that one Mr R – long known for his ability to escape the honest bonds of matrimony in favour of a *dis*honest day's work – has finally met his match!

He knows that escorting the haughty Grand Duchess of Maubourg to England will not be an easy task. But Jack Ryder, spy and adventurer, believes he is more than capable of managing Her Serene Highness.

He's not prepared for her beauty, her youth, or the way that her sensual warmth shines through her cold façade. And what started as just another mission is rapidly becoming something far more personal…

On sale from 7th March!

MILLS & BOON
Historical

On sale 1st February 2008

Regency

A COMPROMISED LADY
by Elizabeth Rolls

Something had wrought a change in Thea Winslow. As a girl she
had been bubbling over with mischief. As a woman she seemed
half lost in shadow. But Richard Blakehurst couldn't miss the
flash of connection between them when his hand touched hers.
It was as if he had awakened something deep inside her.

Regency

PICKPOCKET COUNTESS
by Bronwyn Scott

To bed a thief!

It's Brandon Wycroft's duty as the Earl of Stockport to catch
the 'Cat', a notorious thief who is stealing from local rich
homes to feed the poor. Discovering the Cat is a woman, his
plan of action changes – to a game of seduction!

Mysterious and tempting, she teases him and, as the net closes
around the Cat, Brandon realises he wants to protect as well as
bed her. But the only way to catch her is to spring the parson's
mousetrap – and make her his countess!

On sale 1st February 2008

THE UNWILLING BRIDE
by Margaret Moore

Promised to Merrick of Tregellas when she was but
a child, Lady Constance was unwilling to wed a man she
remembered only as a spoiled boy. Convinced he had
grown into an arrogant knight, she sought to make
herself so unappealing that Merrick would refuse to
honour their betrothal.

Yet no sooner had this enigmatic, darkly handsome
man ridden through the castle gates than she
realised he was nothing like the boy she recalled.
And very much a man she could love...

Celebrate 100 years of pure reading pleasure with Mills & Boon®

To mark our centenary, each month we're publishing a special 100th Birthday Edition. These celebratory editions are packed with extra features and include a FREE bonus story.

Now that's worth celebrating!

4th January 2008

The Vanishing Viscountess by Diane Gaston
With FREE story The Mysterious Miss M
This award-winning tale of the Regency Underworld launched Diane Gaston's writing career.

1st February 2008

Cattle Rancher, Secret Son by Margaret Way
With FREE story His Heiress Wife
Margaret Way excels at rugged Outback heroes...

15th February 2008

Raintree: Inferno by Linda Howard
With FREE story Loving Evangeline
A double dose of Linda Howard's heady mix of passion and adventure.

Don't miss out! From February you'll have the chance to enter our fabulous monthly prize draw. See special 100th Birthday Editions for details.

www.millsandboon.co.uk

2 FREE

BOOKS AND A SURPRISE GIFT!

We would like to take this opportunity to thank you for reading this Mills & Boon® book by offering you the chance to take TWO more specially selected titles from the Historical series absolutely FREE! We're also making this offer to introduce you to the benefits of the Mills & Boon® Reader Service™—

- ★ FREE home delivery
- ★ FREE gifts and competitions
- ★ FREE monthly Newsletter
- ★ Exclusive Reader Service offers
- ★ Books available before they're in the shops

Accepting these FREE books and gift places you under no obligation to buy, you may cancel at any time, even after receiving your free shipment. Simply complete your details below and return the entire page to the address below. You don't even need a stamp!

YES! Please send me 2 free Historical books and a surprise gift. I understand that unless you hear from me, I will receive 4 superb new titles every month for just £3.69 each, postage and packing free. I am under no obligation to purchase any books and may cancel my subscription at any time. The free books and gift will be mine to keep in any case.

H8ZED

Ms/Mrs/Miss/Mr ....Initials ....
BLOCK CAPITALS PLEASE

Surname ....

Address ....

....

....Postcode..........................

Send this whole page to:
UK: FREEPOST CN81, Croydon, CR9 3WZ